For Sylvie and Vic Lobina
with love

Wartime
at
Liberty's

Fiona Ford

arrow books

1 3 5 7 9 10 8 6 4 2

Arrow Books
20 Vauxhall Bridge Road
London SW1V 2SA

Arrow Books is part of the Penguin Random House group
of companies whose addresses can be found at
global.penguinrandomhouse.com

Penguin
Random House
UK

First published in Great Britain by Arrow Books in 2020

www.penguin.co.uk

A CIP catalogue record for this book is available from
the British Library

ISBN 9781787464247

Typeset in 10.75/13.5 pt Palatino
by Integra Software Services Pvt. Ltd, Pondicherry

Printed and bound in Great Britain by Clays Ltd, Elcograf S.p.A.

Acknowledgements

There are so many people who have helped bring this book to life and first up in what I shall try to make a short list is my wonderful agent Kate Burke at Blake Friedmann. Kate is always on hand for brilliant advice and lots of coffee and I'm forever grateful to her for putting up with me. Next up must surely be my phenomenal editor Emily Griffin who has a brilliant habit of making everything I write just so much better. Emily, I don't know how you do it but I'm very grateful that you do – thank you.

I would also like to thank the rest of the team at Arrow who work so hard on the covers, the marketing, the general admin and really the whole kit and caboodle. You're a brilliantly talented team and I'm forever grateful to you for making the Liberty Girls series what it is today.

Thanks too to my brilliant author pals: Kate Thompson, Dani Atkins, Sasha Wagstaff, Jean Fullerton, Faith Bleasdale, Rosie Hendry and last, but definitely not least, Elaine Everest. Your support, help and general fabulousness make this job so very much easier and I'm delighted on a daily basis to have you in my life.

My fantastic family and friends – thank you for answering my pointless and daft questions. You are all far too patient with me and I hope you know how much I appreciate you all.

To the wonderful Beverley Ann Hopper and Sandra Blower. You two have championed this series from the beginning and without your support and the rest of the fabulous Book Lovers Group you run so tirelessly, I can't imagine I would have half the readers that I do. Thank you so much for loving my Liberty Girls as much as I do.

Finally I should like to thank you, lovely reader, for picking up the book and joining me on this very special journey. I love hearing from you and if you have any comments or wartime memories to share, or if you just want to chat all things Liberty's, then please drop me a note via my Facebook page at: facebook.com/fionafordauthor.

Prologue

August 1942

The sight of him standing at the top of Hampstead Heath took her breath away. He had always been her past, her present and her promise of tomorrow. But now, as Florence Canning watched her husband Neil's blue-green eyes glower with anger, she wasn't sure she recognised the man standing before her.

'You have given up singing like I asked you to, haven't you, Flo?' he said, his voice so quiet that Flo struggled to hear him.

'Yes, of course I have,' she responded. 'You know that.'

'So why don't I believe you?' he said. 'Flo, let me ask you one last time: are you still singing?'

Flo gulped as she gazed into his face. Catching the clench of his jaw and the tightness in his neck, she knew that it was time to tell him the truth. She might have had her reasons for lying to him, and for continuing to sing when he had expressly told her not to, but she couldn't carry it off any longer.

'Yes, I am still singing,' she admitted.

Neil's cheeks pinked with fury. 'So why lie to me?'

Flo felt a grim sense of dread. She wondered that herself now. Why hadn't she written to him and come clean? Why hadn't she put her foot down and told him that music ran through her blood? It always had and it always would. She and her Aunt Aggie, who had brought her up as if she were her own mother, had always sung everywhere together. Regardless of whether she was singing at school, at church or with her aunt at home, Flo felt a joy like no other when she lost herself in the music. She used to love accompanying her aunt when she went to perform as after-dinner entertainment, and seeing the change that came over Aggie when she sang. When she died a couple of months earlier, Flo had found relief from her overwhelming sadness by taking over Aggie's old singing evening at the local pub.

'I couldn't give it up, Neil,' she said with searing honesty, 'it made me feel connected to Aggie. She was never happier than when she was singing for an appreciative audience and that's how I feel too. It's been hard for me since she died. You're gone and now so is she. There's an ache in my heart that can only be healed when I sing ...'

Her voice trailed off as Neil shook his head in sadness. He looked past her shoulder and out on to the heath beyond. Flo followed his gaze, trying to understand what he was thinking. He looked as if he had listened to her, taken her words seriously, but she wasn't sure.

'I appreciate I might have been a bit heavy-handed when I wrote telling you not to sing,' he said eventually, his gaze coming back to meet hers. 'But, Flo, what really upsets me is that you lied to me.'

Flo felt her cheeks flush with shame. The one thing she had always known about Neil was that he hated dishonesty. His own mother's lies had torn Neil's family apart when he was young.

Neil's voice was now so low that Flo struggled to hear him. 'After my mother took up with that singer, the lies that spouted from her mouth and the excuses she made while they carried on ... They made my father's life a misery before they eventually ran off. I can't stand any kind

2

of betrayal, and here you are – my own wife – lying to me and I feel sick.'

Flo nodded, the tears falling down her cheeks now. 'I'm sorry. I don't know what else to say. I suppose I just couldn't find the courage to tell you I didn't want to stop. I was scared of what you would say. I didn't mean to let you down.'

'But you did, and I don't know if I can forgive you,' Neil replied, his voice breaking with emotion.

Cold fear flooded Flo's heart. 'You can't mean that. I made a mistake.'

'Yes, you did, and at the moment I'm so angry with you I can barely look at you. I'm going back to the ship early.'

'Neil, please—' Flo begged only for Neil to cut her off.

'I can't, Flo.'

With that he dropped a kiss on to her forehead and walked away.

As she watched his retreating back disappear over the brow of the hill, Flo felt engulfed in panic. What had she done?

Chapter One

Two months later

As the final notes of 'I'll Be Seeing You' came to a close, a polite round of applause rang throughout the little front room in Islington. Wiping away her tears, Florence Canning lifted her chin and clapped the loudest, aware that as chief mourner, it was up to her to show her gratitude for the wake thrown in her husband Neil's honour.

Singing might have been the last thing she felt like doing, but Florence, or Flo as she was better known, was well aware that sing-songs were the norm in the street and always had been. Whether it was a wedding, christening, or in this case a funeral, song had always marked an occasion. Usually Flo was only too happy to join in or, if her Auntie Aggie was singing, she would accompany her on the piano. Flo had grown up around music and Aggie used to joke that Flo had burst into song long before she could walk. She certainly had the looks for it. With her twinkling green eyes, peaches and cream complexion and tall, slim frame, Flo knew how to make the best of herself, especially when it came to putting on a performance.

But not any more. As far as Flo was concerned there would be no more singing, not today, not tomorrow, in fact never again. She had made a silent vow that she would never so much as hum, and despite the fact she could tell her father-in-law, John, had finished and was now encouraging her to get up and give them a song, Flo kept her eyes fixed on the floor. She didn't care how much people tried to cajole her: singing was not for her, not any more.

Instead, Flo shook her head and moved out into the cramped hallway. She sank on to the bottom step of the staircase, the wood creaking beneath her weight as she did so. The familiar noise made her smile. Funny how in one moment you can feel as if your world has shifted, while in another it can seem as though everything is exactly the same. This bottom step had creaked in just the same way when her Uncle Ray was alive and had been the signature noise to so many memories, including the first time she had kissed Neil goodbye after he joined the Navy. He had stood on the very same step, the wood groaning in as much inward protest as Flo, as he promised to return home safe and sound once the war was over.

She pushed the memory from mind and leaned her head against the bannister. The sad fact was Neil had been unable to keep that promise. He had been killed serving on the HMS *Veteran* last month. The destroyer had been hit by two German torpedoes south of Iceland in a devastating attack and there had been no survivors.

Today, as she had said goodbye to her husband at his funeral, the realisation that she would never see him again had hit her squarely in the stomach. Unbidden tears began to well again. Flo bit furiously on the insides of her cheeks to try and stop the sobs. She would save them for later, when she was alone. Aggie had taught her that.

'Nobody wants to see your tears, sweetheart,' she had always said. 'Save them for behind closed doors.' And that was precisely what she would do when everyone had gone home. She would weep and weep until there were no more tears left to be shed. In the space of twelve months she had married the love of her life, said goodbye to the aunt who had been like a mother to her and now she had buried her husband.

As the sound of singing started up again, Flo looked around the humble home that her aunt had left to her in her will. She had lived in this two-up, two-down in the heart of North London since she was five years old and had never wanted to be anywhere else.

The autumn sunshine cast a rich glow across the parquet floor as it poured in through the glass front door, and wearily Flo got to her feet. This house felt like someone else's house now. In fact her entire life felt as if it belonged to someone else. The things she had once loved, the trips to the pictures, her friends and even her job at Liberty's had all lost their sparkle. Without Neil, Flo wasn't sure who she was any more or what she was supposed to do with her life.

The one thing she knew she was supposed to do was make sure today's guests were well fed and looked after. She might have no enthusiasm for it, but she owed her husband that much at least. Placing her hand on the doorknob to go back into the parlour, she caught sight of Dorothy Hanson, Mary Holmes-Fotherington, Alice Milwood, Rose Harper and Jean Rushmore. Her friends and fellow Liberty girls were all gathered in the kitchen, talking in hushed whispers.

'I'm worried about her,' she heard Mary say. 'She's barely eaten a bally thing since the news about Neil broke.'

'She's lost her husband,' Alice fumed. 'Of course she's not herself. Be patient, Mary.'

'It's not about being patient, it's about concern, Alice,' Mary whispered loudly. 'She's here in this house all alone ...'

'She's not alone, she's got me and Bess lodging with her,' Jean piped up indignantly. 'We're keeping an eye on her.'

'With the greatest of respect, Jean, you and your sister don't know Flo like we do,' said Alice. 'I know you're doing your best, but, well, it's possible we might be able to do more.'

'But that has to come from Flo herself,' Dot put in firmly. 'She's a grown woman, Alice. If she wants help she has to come to us; we can't nanny her. Trust me: I've lost a husband; that's the last thing she needs.'

Flo could stand it no longer and walked towards her friends, chin lifted and her mind made up. 'Finally one of you has got something to say I can agree with. Dot's right, I am a grown woman, why are you talking about me like this?'

'We're just worried,' Rose insisted, her round tortoise-shell spectacles slipping down her nose. 'We only want to help. You've shut yourself away when you should be leaning on us.'

'And you haven't been back to work since Neil died last month,' Mary said gently, her raven bobbed hair gleaming. 'Don't you think it would be good for you to return to Liberty's?'

Flo said nothing. She had no interest in returning to work, which in truth surprised her as much as it did the girls. She had always thought of Liberty's as her second home. Like Alice, she had started there as a Saturday girl before swiftly moving up the ranks to become fabric manager. She had even briefly been promoted to deputy store manager earlier in the year, after her predecessor, Mabel Matravers, had been sent to prison for making illegal hooch. However, Flo had found the role too isolating, preferring life on the shop floor amongst the customers and fabric she had come to adore.

But since the terrible day when a buff-coloured telegram marked 'Priority' had arrived at Liberty's, Flo no longer viewed the store as her second home, instead she saw it as a place of misery. All she could remember was how she had rushed down to the stock room, and read the words *regret to inform you your husband Ordinary Seaman Neil Alan Canning was killed immediately.* She had been so shocked that she had been sick all over a roll of one of the most expensive silks.

That night after she had received the news Flo had thought she would die from grief. She had felt a sharper, deeper pain than any she had experienced before. For hours, Flo had lain in their marital bed, eiderdown wrapped around her, with Neil's pillow clutched to her chest. She wept for the boy she had played with as a child, the man he had become and for the future they had been robbed of.

Her manager Mr Button had told Flo she could take off as much time as she needed while she grieved and organised the funeral. It had been an offer she had been happy to take, much to the surprise of her friends, who had been convinced that working at the store would be her salvation. But Flo had lost her appetite for the work she had once loved. The store was tainted now; she wasn't sure she could ever face that department again.

'We've been doing a bit of thinking, darlin',' Dot said, gingerly rubbing Flo's back as if she were no more than a baby. 'We wondered if you might like to come and stay with me for a bit.'

Flo looked at her blankly. 'But I have a house. I live here.'

'We know that,' Alice replied, rolling her blue eyes impatiently, 'but you would have a bit more support at our place.'

'We thought there might be a few less memories there,' Dot offered. 'When my George died all those years ago, my sister bundled me up and made me stay with her for a few weeks. At the time I thought she was being an interfering old bag, but now I know it was the best thing for me.'

'So you're making me stay with you?' Flo asked, raising an eyebrow.

'No—' Mary said, only for Dot to interrupt.

'Yes, darlin', we're making you stay with us. I've plenty of room, especially now George's sister's girl no longer needs a room off me.'

'Violet?' Mary mused, at the mention of Dot's niece. 'I thought she was going to stay with you because she had a new job at Marks and Spencer.'

'She was. But she's been put in a branch up west and found lodgings with a girl her own age. Which is why,' Dot continued, turning back to Flo, 'I've got room for you. And yes, we're also making you go back to work. It's been almost three weeks; it's time. Life goes on and you must too.'

Flo said nothing as the sound of laughter drifted through the kitchen from the parlour. The girls were right; life carried on and she had to get back to her job, and by the looks of things stay with her friends for a bit. Just because Neil had gone didn't mean the world had stopped, no matter how much she wanted it to. She stared angrily out of the kitchen window, her gaze falling on to the courtyard garden filled with growing vegetables. Even the blazing hot sun on this unusually warm October day was a reminder she had very little control over what happened in life. If there were any justice it would be raining. Big fat cold raindrops with miserable, dark grey skies.

But life wasn't just. If it were then Neil would never have died. And if he did have to die, then his final letter to her wouldn't have been full of so many cruel words. And now Flo wouldn't feel as though she was the very worst wife in the world who would never know happiness again.

Chapter Two

Just as Flo had hoped, the sun was replaced with miserable skies and rain as thick as stair-rods the following morning. As she stepped off the Tube at Oxford Circus, she felt the rain slide down her neck and winced as the cold droplets found their way down her back. Picking up her step, she made her way towards Liberty's, unable to ignore the devastation of war that surrounded her. Even though bombs scarcely fell any longer, you didn't have to walk far in London to see the destruction.

Around her lay shelled shops and homes, with ghosts of their former lives on display for all to see. Cracked mirrors hung on walls, neglected washing on lines and faded, torn wallpaper were all stark reminders of lives stamped out mid-flow.

Checking the little silver watch Neil had given her six years ago on her twenty-first birthday, Flo saw she had plenty of time before she was due on the shop floor. Today was Friday and was always one of the busiest days of the shopping week. She hadn't been sure that today would be the best day to return to work, but Dot had told her that yesterday they had taken delivery of some new utility print fabric, and that now would be the perfect time: dealing with the new stock would take her mind off things. Flo was too tired to argue. After all, Dot seemed to have it all planned out. Once she had said goodbye to the last of her guests Dot had presented her with a suitcase full of her belongings and, together with Alice and her ten-month-old son Arthur, they had marched promptly to the bus stop to travel to Dot's little Bell Street terrace in the Elephant and Castle.

They had arrived about an hour and a half later and Dot had shown her the box room Mary used to sleep in; then she told her there would be a cold supper of potted meat sandwiches if she was hungry. But Flo wasn't, and the moment Dot showed her to her room, she had promptly fallen asleep and not woken until it was time to get up that morning.

She had hoped that a good night's sleep might help make her feel better, but she awoke feeling wretched, the memory of Neil's final words to her engraved on her mind. Yet instead of dwelling on them, Flo got ready for work and prepared to get in early. Perhaps the best way through this mess was to try and act as though she cared about her job, and that included getting to work early to examine the new fabric. Usually fabrics were broken into sections, such as silks, Tana Lawn and Sungleam, but since utility fabric had come into force earlier that year it had become the only material customers were interested in, and with such scarce supplies of the rest, everything else had taken a back seat.

Flo had been sixteen when she had been taken on to work in the stores run by the Liberty's stalwart Percy Wilmington. Now, eleven years later, she was manager of the department and along the way Liberty's had been loyal to Flo. They had trained her, promoted her and even gifted her and Neil a gorgeous china dinner service when they wed.

Rounding the corner of Carnaby Street, the iconic building came into view and Flo couldn't help but smile as she saw it. The store might not have the queue of Daimlers with chauffeurs opening doors for women draped in fur any more, but it remained every bit as elegant.

Making her way to the back entrance, she pushed open the heavy wooden door and ran up the stone staircase towards the ladies' staffroom. The staff quarters were nowhere near as grand as the front of the house, but it made no difference to Flo. She had always loved every part of the store, front or back – in fact Neil used to joke that she would live in Liberty's if she could. But that was then, and this was now. Liberty's was just something she had to endure; there was no pleasure to be found in any area of her life any longer.

Hanging up her coat she checked her appearance in the mirror that hung just beside the door and smoothed an imaginary crease out of the green A-line skirt she had teamed with a paisley print blouse. Satisfied, she opened the door and hurried downstairs, stepping on to the shop floor, where the smell took her breath away. In her three-week absence she had forgotten how the heady combination of furniture polish and wood oil always made her feel at home. Perhaps Dot had known a little of what she was doing after all.

Breathing in great lungfuls of the familiar scent, she made her way across the atrium towards her department and paused as she drank in the sight that never failed to impress her. Made from two wooden warships, the shop was four storeys high and grouped around three court-yards, which Flo thought, as if realising it for the first time, gave the appearance of medieval inns rather than a shop.

Elsewhere, stained glass, carved balustrades and the six shields depicting the families of Shakespeare and Sir Thomas More surrounded her. Liberty's would always be here, she thought, and the idea gave her a drop of comfort as she turned her gaze towards her own department. Her eyes came to rest on a man standing authoritatively by the rolls of the new utility fabric she had been hoping

13

to inspect. He was a stocky man with deep-set brown eyes and an intense brooding look. Flo wondered what the new deputy store manager, Henry Masters, was doing here.

She knew only scant facts about Mr Masters, as he had joined Liberty's just a couple of months earlier. He was originally from Yorkshire, in his late thirties and had been brought in by Mr Button, who had worked with him at Bourne and Hollingsworth. They had served together in the army, where Mr Masters had been injured, which was why he hadn't been called up to serve during the current war. As she watched him lean on his stick, his lame right leg no doubt giving him trouble, Flo saw him run his fingers across each fabric and then pause before holding it up to the light. In that moment she felt uneasy at the level of interest he was taking in her department. She thought back to the speech she had heard Mr Masters make when he joined the store, remembering how he had said he wanted to spend time in each department. Was that what he was doing now?

'Mr Masters, we don't usually see the deputy poring over the fabrics,' she said, walking across the floor, unable to stand the suspense any longer.

The deputy looked up and greeted Flo with a small smile. 'Morning, Mrs Canning,' he began in his gruff northern tones. 'I heard you were coming back today. It's nice to see you. How are you feeling?'

Flo felt herself bristling at his kindness. She couldn't stand anyone being nice to her, not when she didn't deserve it. 'I'm fine, thank you, sir. I'm sorry I was away for so long.'

The deputy store manager waved her concerns away. 'As long as you're ready to come back,' he replied. 'You should take as much time as you need.'

'Thank you, sir, but I'm fine. You look like you're keeping yourself busy.'

'I thought it was about time I started looking at the fabrics in the department. As you've just had a delivery I thought it was a good opportunity. You don't mind, do you?'

'Of course not,' she said smoothly, 'but if you had let me know I would have been more than happy to talk you through everything myself; that way you could have got up to speed more quickly.'

Henry looked up and raised an eyebrow. 'That was a very polite way of telling me I shouldn't poke my nose in where it doesn't belong, Mrs Canning.'

Flo felt her cheeks flame. 'Oh no, Mr Masters, sir, I didn't mean it like that—'

'I'm teasing.' Henry chuckled. 'Besides, you'd be well within your rights. I am poking my nose in. When I used to run fabrics for Bourne and Hollingsworth one of my favourite jobs was checking over the new stock. It was thoughtless of me to have jumped in, especially when Mr Button alerted me to the fact that you were returning to work today. I'm sorry.'

'Not at all,' Flo said smoothly. 'I didn't realise you had experience of working in fabrics.'

'Many years ago,' Henry replied, stepping out of Flo's way. 'There aren't too many departments I've not worked in, Mrs Canning, and I do like to maintain a hands-on approach.'

Flo nodded. 'I can see why Mr Button wanted you to work with him.'

'Edwin has taught me a lot,' Henry replied, his eyes crinkling with fondness. 'Which reminds me, he won't be in today – or tomorrow in fact; he's got a lot of meetings.'

Flo's face fell. 'We usually have a meeting about the new range of prints. Is everything all right?'

Henry nodded, his intense, brooding look returning to his face. 'Mr Button has asked me to take over his workload for the next few days instead so we can still have a meeting and discuss any plans you might have.'

'Oh.' Flo felt wrong-footed. She always enjoyed the private chats she and Mr Button had about the department. Not only was her boss always full of good ideas but she had a tendency to think of him as the father she never had, especially as Mr Button had given her away at her wedding.

'Is that a problem, Mrs Canning?' Henry probed.

'Not at all,' Flo said brightly, composing herself. 'I'll be there at three.'

Henry frowned. 'Let's make it four, shall we? I want to run through the department's takings again before we meet.'

'All right.' Flo nodded. With that Henry walked away and Flo couldn't shake the feeling that although life went on, change was in the air.

Chapter Three

Flo was surprised to find she felt slightly nervous as she made her way up the long wooden staircase and then back into the staff area. As she walked through the labyrinth of corridors towards Henry Masters' office she tried to calm her pounding heart. All day long she had been fretting over what he could possibly want to change in fabrics and as she neared his door she was alarmed to see Marjorie Allan from the ready-to-wear department dabbing her eyes as she hurried past Flo.

Wiping her sweaty palms discreetly on her skirt, Flo took a deep breath and rapped on the deputy store manager's door.

'Come in,' a voice bellowed.

As Flo pushed open the door to what used to be her office her eyes roamed the room, greedily drinking in every detail. The office looked vastly different from when she had occupied it herself. The desk had been pushed over to the window so it was easier to look out across the rooftops and on to the city beyond, while the pair of hard wooden chairs Flo had always neatly stacked in the corner to create more space were now perched on the other side of the desk. Gesturing for her to take a seat in one of those chairs, Henry cleared his throat and did at least appear to look welcoming.

'Thank you for coming, Mrs Canning,' he began warmly.

'You're quite welcome, Mr Masters,' Flo replied. 'It's always a pleasure to discuss the department and any changes we can make to improve life for our customers and our staff.'

Henry cleared his throat and ran a hand through his thick brown hair. Catching his eye, Flo was alarmed to see he looked as nervous as she felt. His whole demeanour had changed since the morning. He reminded her of a lost little boy, and in that moment she wanted nothing more than to lean across the table and give him a reassuring squeeze on the shoulder that everything would be all right.

Clearing his throat once more, Henry steepled his hands together and sat up ramrod straight in his chair.

'This won't be easy for me to say, Mrs Canning, but I've been going through the books and the fabric department is not performing as well as it should.'

Flo arched an eyebrow. 'Mr Masters, sir, I don't wish to sound flippant but with the war I don't think anyone's sales have been on the up, yet we have seen an upsurge in our takings since the last quarter. The board and the family are so thrilled that they are treating us to a departmental dinner on Saturday night.'

Henry held up a hand to silence her. 'I appreciate that, Mrs Canning. The family and the board all understand that everyone is pulling together and your latest efforts have not gone unnoticed. Yet the store as a whole is not in the shape it needs to be and that's why we must make changes across every department.'

'What sort of changes?' Flo asked hotly. She was of course well aware that fabrics wasn't the department it used to be but who could honestly say business was thriving when the country had been besieged by war for three years now? All the shops as well as Liberty's were focusing on survival, and Flo thought that she and her team were doing a good enough job at that, especially recently.

However, one look at the new deputy's face told her that was far from the case.

'I know it's difficult,' he began earnestly, 'and you and all the staff here are working incredibly hard under tough circumstances, but the truth is we need to push harder. You must understand that better than anyone, Flo – you after all have sat in this chair.'

The use of her first name surprised Flo, and she smiled in understanding. Yes, she knew full well the pressure from the family and the board, not to mention juggling the demands of the staff. It was more than a full-time job. There were days she had taken her work home with her as she tried to make sense of sales charts and keep on top of the paperwork, causing her Aunt Aggie to roll her eyes and tell her to get out and enjoy life while she was still young.

'What is it you want to change?' she asked softly.

'We need to look at the stock we're selling more closely,' Henry explained, his voice calmer now. 'Customers might like to look at as much as we can offer them but let's be honest: the scrap of silk we have left is never likely to be sold and it's taking up valuable shop space. Far better to go through the books each week and see exactly what's sold and place anything that's unpopular in the stockroom. I know Liberty's is based on beauty, Flo, but war's not beautiful and we need to be more practical.'

'I can't say I disagree,' Flo said sadly. 'It's something that had crossed my mind, but I didn't dare suggest it to anyone for fear of uproar from customers and staff.'

Henry laughed. 'Well, you can put the blame squarely on my shoulders.'

'Is that all you wanted to discuss?' Flo asked hopefully.

'I'm afraid there's more. I want to put an end to staff taking Saturdays off. I know employees have always been able to have one in four weekends off but it's our busiest shopping day and I want all hands to the pumps so we can take as much money as possible.'

'That won't go down well with the girls,' Flo said.

Henry said nothing. Instead he drummed his stout fingers across the desk as he appeared to be trying to work out what he wanted to say next.

'Go on,' Flo coaxed, unable to bear the suspense any longer.

'I'm afraid, too, that I'll need you to let one of your girls go.'

Flo stared at the deputy manager in disbelief. 'I'm sorry?'

'I need you to let one of your employees go, Mrs Canning,' Henry repeated. 'I'm asking almost all the other departments to do the same.'

'But why?' Flo asked. 'Everyone in fabrics is rushed off their feet as it is. We won't manage if we have to lose a member of staff.'

'I appreciate that, Flo, truly I do,' Henry said. 'But the board is looking to make cutbacks, everything is so expensive and with turnover nowhere near what it was, we need to look at rationing where we can.'

Alarm flooded through Flo as she digested this news. She only had Dot, Alice, Mary and Jean as it was. The idea of losing any of them was unthinkable.

'Surely there must be another way,' Flo protested. 'What about if we lower the commission or give everyone a pay cut?'

Henry leaned forward in his chair and shook his head. 'We can't ask people to work for less than they do already; the prestige of working for Liberty's is one thing but it's well known our rate of pay isn't as high as other stores. That prestige will only go so far if we start asking people to accept less in pay or commission.'

'What does Mr Button say?' Flo asked. 'I can't believe he would think this was a good idea.'

'If Mr Button were here he would say exactly the same thing,' Henry said in a firm voice. 'In fact this was his idea; I just happened to agree with it.'

'Well, where is he?' Flo said. 'I'd quite like to hear this from the horse's mouth, if it's all the same to you.'

For a moment Henry looked as if he were about to lash out at Flo, but instead he sighed and gazed out across the rooftops. Flo watched him, suddenly worried she had gone too far.

'He's going to be away from the store a lot,' Henry said eventually. 'He's been asked by the Board of Trade to become a consultant on all things utility as they look to expand the model.'

'Oh,' Flo replied, feeling wrong-footed. One of the main reasons she had been drawn to returning was the comforting presence of her store manager. 'So you're in charge then?'

Henry returned his gaze to Flo and looked at her as if daring her to challenge him. 'Is that a problem?'

Flo shook her head. 'I suppose not.'

'Good, so can you let me know who you wish to let go as soon as possible. I'll need to make the changes as quickly as I can for maximum efficiency.'

'So who do you suggest I get rid of?' Flo asked. 'They are all wonderful workers.'

Henry shrugged. 'That's a matter for you to decide. I'm sorry but you will know who the department can best manage without.'

'Surely there must be some other way?' Flo tried again. 'Isn't there another department they could join?'

'I'm sorry.' His voice was softer now, and Flo could tell he was upset about this too. 'I wish there was. The board

21

and I have been through the figures and are all agreed that this is the only way to ensure the survival of Liberty's.'

Recognising that there was nothing more to say, Flo got to her feet and walked out of the office without a backwards glance. Not for the first time that morning she found herself wishing she had never come back to Liberty's; everything around her was changing and Flo hated it.

Chapter Four

It had taken Flo a good few seconds to remember that she wasn't going back to her home in Islington that night and was instead, albeit temporarily, returning to Bell Street.

Since Henry had dropped his bombshell earlier that day, she could think about little else. Flo was faced with an impossible choice and she was no closer to making it. As she veered between the pros and cons of firing each girl, Flo felt wretched.

She couldn't fire Alice. Not only was the girl her deputy department manager but had a son she was raising all alone since her husband, Luke, had left her for a French Resistance fighter earlier that year. Since then Alice had found new love with handsome GI Jack Capewell, but Flo knew her friend's first priority was her son, Arthur, and putting clothes on his back and food in his belly. What sort of a boss – or friend come to that – would Flo be if she sacked her?

Then there was Mary. She had only been with the department a year after being dishonourably discharged from the women's army, but had fast become a close friend and firm favourite with the customers. With her wealthy upbringing and double-barrelled name, Mary had barely known one end of a needle from the other when she arrived in the fabric department and Flo hadn't been sure she was right for the job as sales assistant. However, she had quickly proved her worth, and when the truth behind her discharge was revealed Flo was proud of the way every one of the Liberty girls raced to her side and rallied round. Now she was not only a vital part of the department but she also carer to Rose and her father Malcolm, with Rose partially blind and Malcolm's injuries from the last war. The two of them hated to admit it but they relied on Mary and the rent money she brought in.

Dot was a possibility, Flo mused. But Dot was also courting store manager Edwin Button. The two had been childhood sweethearts and had reunited a year or so ago after becoming reacquainted through the store. Mr Button might be one of the fairest men she had ever known, but even he might be against her sacking his sweetheart.

Lastly of course there was Jean. She was the newest girl to join the group and together with her sister Bess, who worked in a munitions factory over in Hayes, had moved into Flo's house after Aggie's death. Bess usually stayed in alternative lodgings nearer the factory during the week, but at the weekend returned to London and shared Flo's old room with Jean. Flo had taken Aggie's room, which was smaller but looked out onto the allotments at the back. The girls were like chalk and cheese; Bess was overbearing and loud while Jean was timid and polite. Bess was small and round with a flat nose and eyes as brown as berries. Jean was tall, thin and striking with her cat-like green eyes and wide open smile. The only thing that made them look like sisters was the jet-black hair that fell to the small of their backs. Yet despite the girls' differences, in the three months they had been living together the arrangement was working out well.

Flo chewed her lip. On the face of it, Jean was the right one to give the push to: last in, first out. But on the other hand, she was such a sweetheart, Flo wasn't sure she could do it to her.

Now, as she stepped off the Tube at the Elephant and Castle and made her way through the dark streets towards Bell Street, Flo resolved to push it all from her mind. She needed a night away from it and the idea of spending a quiet evening with Alice, Dot and Arthur was just what the doctor ordered.

Flo had barely rapped on the heavy wooden door before it swung open. There on the doorstep, grinning for all she was worth, was Dot.

'Well, come on in then, don't stand there letting all the light out on to the street. We'll get fined,' she said, practically pulling Flo inside.

'I'm just coming,' Flo mumbled as Dot shut the door gently behind her.

'Arthur's asleep upstairs,' Dot said.

'What is all this?' Flo asked. 'You don't usually roll out the red carpet when I visit.'

'I want you to feel at home,' Dot said, her grey eyes flashing with impatience. 'That's why I thought we'd have a little get-together this evening. I've invited everyone over for something to eat.'

Flo groaned inwardly as she walked down the dark narrow hallway towards the brightly lit kitchen. The last thing she needed was a set of visitors, and today was no exception. She had only just seen everyone at the funeral yesterday. Surely Dot could see that?

But then she remembered the excitement on the older woman's face as she had swung open the door, and knew that this was Dot's way of showing her affection. Flo shouldn't be so ungrateful.

Walking into the kitchen, she saw all her friends gathered around the large scrubbed wooden table beneath the window.

'Surprise!' Mary's green eyes were filled with warmth as she held a teapot aloft. 'You timed that well.'

'And I made mock duck,' Alice added proudly, gesturing to the large plate of food on the table.

'Here, you must be exhausted,' Jean said from her position next to Rose as she pulled out a chair for Flo to sit on.

'Thanks,' Flo replied, sinking her weight on to the chair.

She looked around the beaming faces. There was Rose, sitting opposite, her long auburn hair hanging like a shimmering curtain around her shoulders. And there was Bess, Jean's sister, sitting quietly in between Mary and Mr Button. She smiled gratefully at the older girl. The two barely knew each other, but it was nice of her to take the time to come all this way after her busy week in Hayes.

'How was your first day back, dear?' Mr Button asked, his copper eyes crinkling with kindness. 'I imagine it was something of a shock.'

Flo arched an eyebrow. 'There were definitely a few challenges I couldn't have predicted.'

Mr Button smiled. 'As is so often the way.'

'You're a dark horse though. Why didn't you tell us about the Board of Trade position?' she replied.

At the mention of those illustrious three words, the girls babbled excitedly amongst themselves. 'I only found out about it last week,' Mr Button said above the noise. 'And I promised I wouldn't tell a soul.'

'He told nobody but me, and as you know I am the soul of discretion,' Dot said solemnly.

As she handed out the plates to everyone, Flo stifled a giggle. Dot was discreet when she wanted to be; otherwise she had a tendency to tell anyone and everyone anything she pleased.

'So when do you start, Mr B.?' Mary called across the table.

'Already have,' Mr Button smiled. 'Last Monday.'

'And what can you tell us?' Rose asked.

'Absolutely nothing.' Mr Button chuckled. 'Sworn to secrecy. I can tell you I'll be working in consultation with a few others, and lending my expertise to various projects regarding the utility idea.'

'Sounds exciting,' said Alice.

'It is.' Mr Button beamed. 'As is Flo's return to work today.'

At that, Flo smiled and helped herself to some of the mock duck Alice had prepared.

There was silence for a few mouthfuls as everyone tucked into the food, and Flo was grateful. She needed a chance to gather her thoughts together and food was the perfect excuse.

'So, Bess, will we be seeing you at the departmental dinner tomorrow evening?' Mr Button enquired. 'You would be welcome to join Jean as her guest.'

Bess frowned. 'You sure I'm allowed to come to this dinner?'

Flo nodded. 'We're all allowed to bring a guest. Alice will be bringing her friend Jack—'

'Ooh, that handsome GI you've been knocking about with,' Bess interrupted, her eyes alive with mischief.

'His name is Jack,' Alice said sullenly.

'And I will be bringing Rose as my guest,' Flo said as she narrowed her eyes at Bess, making it clear she wasn't going to stand for any smutty remarks.

Bess shrugged, the gesture clearly lost on her, before wrapping a loving arm around her sister. ''Course I'll be there. You can count me in for a free meal any day of the week.'

Flo gritted her teeth. There were times she found Bess's blatant honesty a little too much to bear.

'And I've got something I want to talk about as well,' Rose put in. 'Mr Button and I have been meeting over the last few weeks.'

'Careful now!' Bess sniggered. 'People will talk.'

'And we have been talking about the idea of a Liberty's fundraising evening,' Rose went on proudly. 'You know, raising money for the war effort. The staff at Smart and Williams raised enough for a Spitfire last year.'

A fresh wave of excitement rippled across the room.

'When were you thinking of, darlin'?' Dot asked.

'December. Around then anyway, when everyone's in a good mood.'

'And what sort of show did you have in mind?' Alice asked.

'We were thinking about a variety show, lots of different acts from all the departments.'

'Ooh, what a wonderful idea.' Mary grinned. 'I can do my impressions.'

Flo hid a smirk as she caught the expressions of horror on the girls' faces. Mary's impressions were at best hit and miss.

'Actually, we were rather hoping you might be our star turn, Flo,' Rose put in.

'Me?' Flo frowned. 'What could I possibly do?'

'Sing!' Mr Button beamed. 'You've a beautiful voice, Flo. We would be honoured if you would sing for us.'

At the mere suggestion Flo felt a wave of horror crash over her.

'I'm sorry, but no,' she said firmly, indicating the subject was closed.

Ignoring the looks of surprise on her friends' faces, Flo returned to her plate of mock duck. The idea of singing again, of doing something so rich in pleasure, was unthinkable. She would go through life doing what was strictly necessary – pleasure wasn't something she deserved after what she had done.

Chapter Five

As usual the store was filled with shoppers that Saturday. Flo thought the girls looked like a fully choreographed dance troupe as she watched Mary step into line behind Alice to serve a regular.

The hierarchical system of each sales assistant serving on the basis of seniority was a long-established tradition at Liberty's and one Flo enjoyed preserving when so much was changing. Gone were the liveried commissionaires who would hold the doors open for customers and gone were the beautifully decadent tearooms in the crypt. Instead the brown and white tiled basement was now home to the ARP canteen that fed hungry wardens and fire-watchers after long cold nights spent guarding the roof of Liberty's.

'Mrs Canning, what are you doing about this queue?' a voice hissed in her ear, breaking her train of thought. 'It's almost out of the door.'

Whipping her head round Flo was alarmed to come face-to-face with Henry, standing with his arms folded. Flo was surprised to find she felt a pulse of alarm.

'It's all under control. The girls know precisely what they're doing,' she said evenly, doing her best to keep her nerves hidden.

'And where's Miss Rushmore?' he barked, lifting his wrist to check his watch. 'It's half past two. She can't be at lunch.'

'No, she's on a half-day. It was arranged earlier in the week before I had a chance to let the girls know that there is to be no more time off on Saturdays,' Flo said hurriedly.

'And where is Mrs Hanson?' he asked coolly.

'She only works part-time; as you know she job-shares with Mrs Milwood.'

There was a pause then as Flo watched Henry survey the shop floor with a practiced eye. Flo shifted uncomfortably. She knew that the department looked busy, but that was the way it was sometimes. Everything was under control – the girls were old hands.

Proving her point, as Mary said goodbye to her customer, she moved seamlessly on to the next lady, who was busy stroking a micro-floral-printed Tana Lawn. Within seconds Mary had greeted the customer, made her smile, offered to measure up and was leading her to the long wooden cutting table.

'As you can see we have a well-organised system,' Flo said, unable to keep a hint of smugness from her voice.

'It might be well organised, Mrs Canning, but you've still got customers waiting,' Henry replied, gesturing towards a group of women waiting by the department's entrance. 'This is not the standard Liberty's expects.'

Flo felt a flash of fury. 'So what do you think will happen when we lose a valued staff member? I know you want to make cutbacks but this is a very real example of what the department will look like on a Saturday afternoon when we lose a girl.'

If Henry looked surprised at Flo's outburst he didn't show it. 'Mrs Canning, I was merely—'

But Flo had heard enough. 'I'm sorry, Mr Masters, but since our meeting all I've thought about is who I have to sack, and now you're down here telling me that my department is failing. Much as I would love to stand here and debate this issue with you, I must get back to work.'

Without so much as a backward glance, Flo approached the group of women who were clustered around the utility prints and smoothly enquired as to how she could help.

For the next couple of hours, Flo threw herself into her work and did her best to forget all about Henry and the terrible predicament she found herself in. Instead she served, answered questions, dealt with paperwork, cuddled a regular customer's baby and offered valuable sewing tips to a group of women who had popped into Liberty's by chance. They were so enchanted by the fabrics on offer they wanted to try making their own clothing for the first time.

Despite the altercation with her superior that afternoon Flo found she enjoyed herself, loving nothing more than getting involved with the cut and thrust of the store. Dot had been right: it was what she had been missing. Yet she couldn't help fretting over the exchange with Henry. Insolence was not tolerated at Liberty's and Flo knew that she shouldn't have spoken to her superior in the way that she had, no matter how much she thought it deserved.

At around four o'clock, there was a lull in trade, and Flo decided now was as good a time as any to go upstairs and apologise.

'Just popping up to the office. Can you run the floor for a few moments?' she asked Alice.

Alice put down the packet of needles she was sorting and gave Flo a quizzical look. 'Yes, of course. Everything all right? Only I couldn't help overhearing you tearing strips off Mr Masters.'

Flo's cheeks flushed with embarrassment. 'Oh my days! I was hoping nobody heard.'

'It's all right,' Alice soothed, taking Flo's arm and steering her over to the stained-glass window to talk. 'None of the other girls heard a thing; it was just me. But, Flo, you never talk to anyone like that, especially not someone in charge. What's happened?'

More than anything Flo longed to confide in someone, but she also knew that she had been sworn to secrecy. 'Let's just say that Mr Masters wants to make some changes, and I lost control, letting him know that I'm not very happy about them.'

'Like?' Alice demanded.

There was a pause as Flo gathered her thoughts. She didn't want to lie to Alice but nor could she tell her every-thing. She didn't want to burden Alice with the worry of whom she would let go from the department. 'Like he doesn't want me going around giving anyone time off on Saturdays any more,' Flo said with a sigh. 'He was upset Jean wasn't here this afternoon, that's all.'

Alice raised an eyebrow. 'And that was what you tore strips off him about?'

'Well, I think he was letting me know that we were busy and I should have followed his instructions.'

Alice nodded and Flo couldn't miss the movement in her left cheek that told her that her deputy manager was angry. 'Why didn't you tell me about this new Saturday arrangement, Flo? I'm supposed to be your second in command.'

'I'm sorry. Mr Masters asked me not to say anything to anyone until the other departments had been given the same orders.'

'Even so, you should have spoken to me. I could have helped you. Not only that, but I need time to be with Arthur on Saturdays.'

'This is why I didn't want to say anything until things are sorted out,' Flo wailed, the collar of her dress feeling suddenly tight. 'But I am sorry I didn't discuss things with you first, that was wrong of me.'

The grey light that poured in through the window gave Alice's face a slightly haunted quality. With a start, Flo realised this would hit her oldest friend hard. She had been through so much in the last few months, with the loss of her sister, Joy, her husband deserting her and his country and of course her new relationship with Jack, though blissful, was also a source of worry. She was still a married woman and despite the end of her marriage being far from her fault, complete strangers weren't shy about passing judgement.

'I'll make sure everything's all right for you, Alice – you know that, don't you?' she found herself saying urgently.

Alice gave her a genuine smile, her blue eyes filled with a sudden warmth. 'Flo, don't make promises you can't keep. I don't want that and I would never hold you to them. You're under a lot of pressure by the sounds of things. I won't say a word to the other girls but you'd better find Mr Masters now and try to apologise.'

'Thanks.' Flo broke into a grateful smile.

'But before you go anywhere, I want you to know you can always talk to me, about anything. It won't go anywhere, I promise.'

'I know,' Flo said.

Alice gripped her wrist, her blue eyes shining with sincerity. '*Do* you know, Flo? Because it feels as if you don't. There's so much you're keeping from me. Not just what's going on at the store, but you. Why don't you want to sing any more? It was what got you through Aggie's death – why have you given up on it now?'

Flo felt a sudden compulsion rise up. More than anything she wanted to tell someone, anyone about Neil's final letter, but as she looked at Alice's worn and tired complexion, Flo knew she couldn't add to her old friend's burden. She had made her bed; she was going to have to lie in it.

Chapter Six

Later that evening Flo found herself in a Chinese restaurant in the heart of the West End nestled between Henry and Mr Button. The restaurant was full of customers enjoying their Saturday night, and the scent of fried onions and spices filled the air.

Glancing around, she could see that everyone was in a good mood, which only made her feel worse about the fact she really didn't want to be there. She was exhausted after her first full Saturday back at the store, and all she wanted to do was go back to Bell Street and collapse on her bed.

Yet her friends' outfits alone told her that wasn't an option, given they had all arrived dressed in their finery. Flo began to wish she had made more of an effort, instead of leaving on the black woollen midi dress she had worn all day.

Flo had been too busy in the end to talk to Henry and apologise for that afternoon's outburst, and the conversation so far between the two of them had been stilted at best. She was desperate to bring the subject up and make her apologies but each time she tried one of the girls would ask her something and Henry would talk to someone else.

Now Flo turned her attentions to Mr Button. He was doing his best to be as charming and friendly as ever, but it was clear from his lined face and bags under his copper-coloured eyes that his new role was taking a toll.

Instead she let her eyes roam across the table, taking in the sight of her friends and colleagues all enjoying themselves. How on earth was she supposed to sack any one of these girls?

She opened and closed her mouth, desperate for something to say, and thankfully was saved by the arrival of their food. As the waitress placed a plate of fried rice and chicken in front of Flo, she inhaled the rich scent of exotic spices. She hadn't realised how hungry she was; perhaps this meal wouldn't be so bad after all.

Picking up her fork, she suddenly felt something sharp against her ribs and realised Dot had leaned across poor Jack to catch her attention, her chest hovering dangerously close to his chicken noodle dish.

'How about you give us one of your songs after all this, Flo love? Put us all in a celebratory mood.'

Flo looked at her in surprise. 'I don't think so, Dot.'

'Oh, don't be such a spoilsport,' Mary scolded. 'A song from you would finish the evening off in style.'

'I said no.'

'But you could think about it,' Rose said in a small voice.

Irritation flared and Flo put down her cutlery and glared at the group. 'I've already told you all I don't want to sing, and I wish you would leave it alone.'

There was a brief silence then before Jack stepped in. 'I always wanted to know, Flo, how you first got into singing. I mean, I know your aunt sang, but did you ever sing with her or when you were young?'

Flo looked up from her plate and smiled at him in surprise. 'I always used to sing as a kid. When Aggie first took me in after my mother ran off – Dad dumped me with her and Uncle Ray – if things were tight she would do a turn at the local pub and sometimes she'd be asked to go and sing at one of those posh houses.'

'What you mean – after dinner in some big old mansion?' Alice asked.

Flo nodded as Mary leaned forward to speak. 'It happens all the time. Mummy thought nothing of getting our charlady's sister to sing after one of her legendary supper parties. She sang like an absolute nightingale – should have been in the Albert Hall.'

'There you are, Mrs Canning,' Henry said warmly, spearing a piece of ginger root into his mouth, 'you're clearly wasted at Liberty's. You should be in the Albert Hall.'

Flo turned to the deputy manager in surprise. Catching his eye, she saw he had the faintest of smiles across his face and felt herself relax. She was about to say something when Dot beat her to it.

'Don't you go giving her ideas,' the matriarch warned. 'She's too good for us as it is.'

'Precisely,' Alice exclaimed. 'We'd be lost without her. Still, Flo, if times ever get tough you could take a leaf out of your aunt's book.'

'What – sing at posh houses for a few bob?' Flo scoffed, turning away from Henry and glancing back at her friend. 'I know Aggie was good at it, but I don't think it's for me.'

'Made her happy though, darlin',' Dot chimed sadly. 'She used to love hobnobbing with those posh types. She told me how she would take you when you were a little 'un and wouldn't sleep; the sound of her singing would send you right off.'

'You might want to try that with Arthur one night.' Alice laughed. 'Doris down the road has got him tonight and I just hope he's not going to send her around the bend.'

'Is he still keeping you awake all night?' Mary asked.

'He's teething again,' Alice replied by way of explanation.

Mary grimaced. 'I suppose I'll have to cope with that when David and I adopt baby Emma.'

Flo shot her a sympathetic smile. Mary and her fiancé David, who was an army doctor, were planning to adopt his sister Mabel Matravers' baby as soon as they were married. The former deputy manager was likely to spend several years in prison for masterminding the illegal hooch ring she had set up with her husband Alf.

'Poor little fella's really going through the mill,' Jack added. 'I remember my Jack Junior going through just the same thing. It'll pass; we'll get through it, honey.'

As Flo watched Jack place his right hand over Alice's left one and give it a squeeze, she found the tender action surprised her. A pang of longing for her husband hit her in the stomach, so sharply she felt as if she had been speared with one of the restaurant's chopsticks. Would this longing for the man she had adored ever end?

'I'm just getting some air,' she said quickly. 'I'll be back in a minute.'

Flo didn't wait for a reply; instead she left the table and fled down the stairs and out into the dark street beyond. The grief of a future without her husband and aunt by her side, supporting her, loving her, hit her so hard she felt as if she had been physically struck. As she lifted her chin towards the dark skies and seeing nothing but emptiness, Flo heard the sound of footsteps echoing behind her.

'Bit cold for standing out here all night,' Bess called.

Flo gave a half-smile. 'I just needed a break.'

There was silence for a moment.

'Thanks for letting me come tonight,' Bess said eventually. 'We don't get nothing like this up the factory.'

'You're welcome.' Flo was surprised. Bess wasn't usually known for pleasantries and it made a nice change. 'Do you like working at the munitions factory then?'

'It's all right. The girls are easy enough to rub along with and the work's simple.'

'Don't you worry about it being ...'

'Dangerous?' Bess finished. 'Not really. I mean, it's risky, but the way I see it is that it's not as risky as, say, what our boys are doing abroad fighting for our freedom.'

Flo said nothing; her mind was full of Neil. He had lost his life fighting for their freedom. What had she done for him? Lied to him so much he had been disgusted by her.

'Penny for 'em,' Bess said, cutting through her thoughts.

Flo came to and shook her head. 'Sorry, miles away. I was just thinking about what Dot said. You know, about my aunt singing in the posh houses.'

'You didn't know about that then?'

'No, I knew.' Flo nodded. 'I used to go with her as a little girl. Aggie would come alive as she sang. She was like a star the moment she opened her mouth.'

'Sounds as though you have some very fond memories,' Bess said, her tone gentler now.

'I do. She used to say I was her good-luck charm, that she always sang better when she knew I was there.'

'What a lovely memory,' Bess replied. 'What about your mum?'

'No idea. She left me with Aunt Aggie when I was a nipper. Aggie was never too clear about why, but I always thought my dad had something to do with it. I imagined that she ran away from him and started a new life.'

'Well, if that's true aren't you angry she didn't take you with her?'

Pursing her rosebud lips Flo thought for a moment; then she shook her head. 'I never saw it like that. She did what she had to. My old man was a wrong 'un and Aunt Aggie was as good a mum to me as I could have hoped for.'

'What about your uncle?'

'He was a kind man.' Flo smiled fondly as memories of Uncle Ray flooded her mind. Flo missed him; he had died when she was only eight.

'Families, eh?' Bess sighed. 'Not all they're cracked up to be, are they?'

'In my experience you make your own family in this life,' Flo said wisely.

Bess regarded her carefully. 'So, has your family got something to do with the reason you're not singing?'

Flo stared at Bess, aware her heart was racing. She had half expected Alice, Mary or even Dot to ask her outright but Bess was almost a stranger. She had no business or right to pry into her private life. Flo opened her mouth, about to unleash her fury, when something stopped her. The look in Bess's eye told her she wasn't trying to provoke her, she simply looked concerned.

'It's not something I like to talk about.'

'I gathered that,' Bess replied, her gaze fixed firmly on Flo. 'But it might help if you do. And although you barely know me, trust me, I won't judge.'

Shakily, Flo let out a long breath. To her surprise she found she did want to tell someone; the burden of it all was pressing heavily on her chest and lungs. So much so that at times she struggled to breathe. The thought of what she had done winded her as surely as if she had been punched.

'I lied to my husband about my singing,' she admitted. 'I told him I'd stop, and I didn't.'

'Why?' Bess asked.

'Because he said it wasn't proper for a wife to be doing such a thing.'

Bess smirked. 'Knew it all, did he, your Neil? Tell you what to eat of a morning and what colour knickers to put on 'n' all?'

Blooms of colour appeared in Flo's cheeks. 'Don't you judge me, or my family, you don't know the half. I thought you said you *wouldn't* judge?'

'Sorry,' Bess said, holding her hands up in defence. 'That was wrong of me, I didn't mean it, Flo. Please tell me.'

Flo ran her tongue over her teeth. 'Neil wrote to me after Aggie died and told me he didn't want me to sing in the pub any more. I was angry but told him I'd think about it. After all, I loved singing; it made me feel better about life. So when you moved in, I wrote to him and told him I'd stopped and that I'd opened a guest house instead to make ends meet.'

'Blimey! That was a whopper,' Bess gasped.

Flo couldn't help smile at the girl's honesty. 'Yes, it was. And a whopper that caught me out when Neil paid me a surprise visit in August.'

Bess's hands flew to her mouth. 'You mean when Jean and I went away to Bangor to see our friends? You told us Neil had returned home, but you never said it had gone badly.'

'I didn't want to tell anyone,' Flo admitted. 'A part of me hoped I could salvage things. I never imagined it would be too late and he would die hating me.'

Bess reached out an arm and placed it on Flo's shoulder. 'I'm sure he didn't hate you. But look, I'm sorry. You don't have to tell me any more if you don't want.'

Flo said nothing and together the girls went back inside the restaurant. About to follow Bess up the stairs, she pushed her hands into her pockets and her fingertips brushed against the envelope she always carried with her. It was like a perverse talisman, she realised, something she hated to have with her, but something she could never stand to be without. Pulling the envelope out, she ran her finger over the address, enjoying the feel of the pen indentations across the paper. It was time to release the burden she had been carrying around for so long.

'Here,' she said, thrusting the paper into Bess's hands.

Bess frowned. 'What's this?'

'These are Neil's final words to me,' Flo said. 'This was the letter he wrote to me when he got back on board his ship.

16th September 1942

My dearest Flo,

I'm sorry it has taken me so long to reply to you. I could fib and tell you that we've been busy, but the truth is I haven't stopped thinking about you since the moment I left you on the heath. I was so angry with you for lying to me that I just couldn't see past that. I wanted to get away, to think about things and that's all I've been doing since we set sail.

You have always known how I feel about lies. My mother lied to my father for years, leading us and him a merry dance while she carried on her affair with that singer. She broke his heart and mine when she eventually left us for that man. I saw how lies broke up my family; you saw it too, Flo. I suppose that's why I can't understand why you would lie to me.

I do know I perhaps shouldn't have told you not to do something. You were right, of course: I didn't want you singing because of my mother. I suppose I thought you might meet some tall, dark and handsome fella and go running off into the night with him. I couldn't admit it to you that day but I can now. Even though that's the real reason, I don't think you should ever have gone behind my back like you did.

I keep going over it. It was such a huge lie and it's shaken me. I want to forgive you, I want us to move past this, but at the moment I don't think I can.

That's why I think it's best if we keep our distance for a while, and take some time to think about things.

Your husband,
Neil

Chapter Seven

The following morning was Sunday and Flo woke feeling bone tired. She shifted about in the hard single bed and did her best to shake herself awake. It had turned out to be a very late night. After the meal, Dot had insisted everyone return to the little Bell Street terrace for a sing-song. Flo hadn't sung but she had played the piano.

Once everyone had grown tired of singing, Bess had given her a friendly nudge, and Flo had taken a deep breath and shared the letter with her friends. Unsurprisingly they had all been incredulous, but Flo was too tired to talk it all through then and there. Instead she had promised that they would discuss it the following morning.

Slipping her feet into her threadbare slippers, Flo reached for her dressing gown and padded down the stairs. As she walked into the kitchen, eager to find tea and toast, she saw to her surprise all her friends had beaten her to it and were gathered around the table. Their faces were filled with compassion and for a moment she wondered what they had been discussing. But then it hit her that the truth was out in the open now. Everyone knew her husband had detested her when he died, and there was nothing she could ever do to put that right.

'I suppose I don't need to ask what you're all talking about,' she said, helping herself to a cup of tea from the pot that stood at the centre of the table and taking a seat next to Mary.

'We're only trying to help you, Flo love,' Alice said in a soothing tone as she bounced Arthur on her knee. 'We're not talking out of turn.

'We're here for you,' Mary said kindly, giving her arm a gentle squeeze.

'I feel awful about it. I shouldn't have lied,' Flo said with a sigh, running her hand across her face. 'I keep going over it and thinking about what would have happened if I'd just admitted that I loved singing and I didn't want to give it up.'

Mary pushed the remnants of her cold tea away. 'Because you didn't want to have to deal with the consequences of what he would say. He didn't hate you, he was just angry; you've got to stop thinking that way.'

'Do you really think so? Flo asked doubtfully.

'Yes,' Alice said firmly. 'Neil adored you, you know that.'

'Things are often said in marriage that people don't mean,' Dot said, rolling her eyes skywards. 'Heaven only knows me and my George shared a few cross words and said a fair few things we shouldn't have. When he died, Flo love, I went over every little word that he said, looking for deeper meanings in everything.'

There was a brief pause then as the girls searched for the right thing to say. Flo felt almost sorry for them. She knew there was nothing that could make it better.

'You can't hold on to this, Flo,' Alice said, breaking the silence. 'Do you remember when Joy died? I said some terrible things to her before she was killed but I realised I had to look at our relationship as a whole, not just a little part of it.'

'But Joy did sleep with your Luke,' Rose pointed out not unreasonably.'

'Precisely,' Flo added. 'What you said wasn't unreasonable. What I did was unforgivable.'

'In that moment perhaps,' Rose reasoned. 'But haven't we all behaved badly? My Tommy's due home for forty-eight hours' leave at Christmas. I'm worried sick about all the things I said in my letters when I went blind and I'm terrified he's going to look at me and think I'm not the girl he married. But it's marriage, Flo, good, bad and ugly.'

Bess reached across the table for the pot to top up the girls' cups with tea. 'You were just very unlucky, Flo. Neil never hated you. Look at what he said – he said he wanted to find a way back to you, to just give him some time. Those aren't the words of a man who really hated his wife, not deep down.'

'Do you think?' Flo asked again.

'Of course,' Jean insisted.

'You can't let this be the reason you never sing again,' Mary added. 'You're too talented to let that go. '

Flo looked down at her hands, unable to face her friends. 'I can't. Singing now just reminds me of how I lied to Neil, when I knew that it was the one thing he wouldn't tolerate. Just the thought of singing makes me feel as if I've let him down. I can't do it again. I won't.'

'You can't stop doing something just because your husband didn't approve,' Alice insisted. 'Luke didn't like me doing so many extra things after work, did he, when he turned up this year? But he had his own set of secrets he was keeping from me.'

'What's your point, Alice? I don't see how this situation with Neil is the same.'

'I'm not saying it is,' Alice replied patiently. 'What I am saying is that our menfolk often have their own problems they try to make ours. You've said Neil didn't want you singing because it reminded him of what happened with his mother. Well, you weren't his mother—'

'No, you were his wife, and as such he should have treated you with a bit more care.' Dot thundered, cutting across Alice. 'I know he's dead and all that, Flo, and no you shouldn't have lied like you did, but bloody hell, we all make mistakes, your Neil included, so forgive yourself.'

'What I'm trying to say,' Alice continued, shooting Dot a warning glance, 'is that sometimes working out what's best for you isn't necessarily what's best for your husband.'

'And that means they have to lump it,' Dot put in. 'Isn't that right, Bess? I'm sure you've told a fella or two where to go in your time.'

Jean raised an eyebrow as Bess leaned back in her chair, eyes filled with amusement. 'I don't know what you think I am, Dot, but I can tell you that yes, I've told a fella or two what I think of them now and again. It's the only way with 'em. Ladies are much easier. You can't talk to a fella; they don't understand.'

'Quite,' Jean added. 'But I do think the world's changing. I mean, look at us all now doing the jobs of fellas. We've every right to be listened to; they should know that.'

'Good Lord.' Mary laughed. 'It's like the Liberty's branch of marriage guidance in here this morning.'

'Speaking of which, how are you getting on with your marriage plans?' Dot asked, changing the subject. 'Do I need to put a date in my diary yet or are you and David still mucking about?'

Mary rolled her eyes and Flo felt glad for a moment that the attention was off her. Things had started to feel a bit uncomfortable and much as she appreciated her friends' support she was glad of a break.

'Yes, we have set a date. Invitations will follow shortly.'

'Well, when is it?' Alice demanded, a lock of blonde hair falling from the turban on her head. 'I hope it's not next week; you need to give us time to start altering frocks and whatnot.'

'We've decided on January.' Mary beamed.

Flo clapped her hands together in delight. 'Ooh, a winter wedding.'

'Well, about flipping time.' Dot smiled. 'We shall all be there cheering you on in the front row, won't we, girls?'

Alice giggled. 'It's not a night at the Palladium, Dot. But you're quite right, we will be there cheering you with bells on, Mary. The question is, will we all be able to get the time off work?'

As all faces swivelled towards Flo, she rolled her eyes. 'I'm sure something can be arranged.'

Dot slammed her hands on the table and got to her feet. 'Well, I'm pleased we've sorted that out. And, Flo,' she said, fixing her gaze on the fabric manager, 'stop torturing yourself like this. You made a mistake, but that mistake doesn't mean you and Neil never loved each other and it doesn't mean you have to give up on your dreams.'

Chapter Eight

Several days later, Flo was back on the shop floor elbow-deep in paperwork. She didn't want to sing again, the talk with her friends hadn't changed that, but she did know she needed a distraction from the endless grief and so she resolved to throw herself into her work.

After all, there was still so much to think about, not least whom she was going to let go from the department. She shivered at the thought. Whilst Flo had been put in the unfortunate position of sacking someone before, she had never had to do so for no good reason. Now, as she saw Jean walk across the department floor, her heart sank. She knew what she had to do and there was no point putting it off any longer.

The fairest and perhaps only way to let someone go was to get rid of the newest employee. Last in, first out. Only now as saw Jean hurry towards her, dressed simply in a knitted twinset and A-line skirt, hair skilfully curled into a victory roll, Flo felt as if she had an aviary of birds flying about in her stomach. Was she really going to do this?

Clearing her throat, she smiled nervously at Jean. 'Have you got a moment? I need to talk to you about something.'

Jean smiled back. 'Yes of course.'

'Let's go down to the stockroom,' Flo offered, deliberately ignoring the inquisitive glances of Alice and Mary.

As she made her way down the stairs to the stockroom, Flo squared her shoulders and willed herself to be brave. Jean was a young, capable woman and she would understand.

Gesturing for Jean to sit on a box opposite her, Flo smiled again and did her best to put herself and Jean at ease.

'As you may know, Jean, with the war on now, Liberty's, in fact all stores, are not doing as well as they were.'

'I know,' Jean sighed. 'But what can we do? Should we try a special promotion or something? The new prints have been doing well; is there something we can do to push those a bit more?'

Flo shook her head. 'The family and the board don't want us to think about promotions, they want us to cut our staff numbers.'

'Cut our staff numbers?' Jean echoed, her eyes filled with confusion.

'That's right,' Flo continued, her voice shaking. 'Every department has been asked to lose at least one member of staff to try and save the store money.'

'Oh no, Flo, that's terrible,' Jean cried. 'Do you know who you'll get rid of from fabrics?'

At the look of earnestness on Jean's face it was all Flo could do to stop herself weeping at the situation she found herself in. 'Yes, Jean, I do know, and I'm sorry to say that the decision has been made to let you go.'

Jean's mouth fell open in shock. 'Me? But what have I done?'

'Nothing,' Flo blurted. 'Absolutely nothing at all. You're a wonderful member of staff and I hate to lose you. I'll give you a glowing reference for your next job. But someone had to leave, and I couldn't decide who, so it seemed the only fair way to do it was to let the person go who had joined us most recently.'

Jean nodded miserably, taking in the news.

'We, all of us, I mean, are devastated by this,' Flo babbled. 'I want you to know I'll do all I can to help you find something else, and of course you and Bess won't be homeless, you can stay at my house, regardless of how long it takes for you to get work elsewhere.'

Jean lifted her head sharply from the floor causing a lock of hair to fall forward from her victory roll. 'Thank you, but that won't be necessary. Me and Bess have always paid our own way and we won't stop now. You'll get your rent on time as you always do, and don't worry about helping me get something else either, I'll take care of myself.'

'Jean please,' Flo begged as Jean turned to walk away.

But Jean shook her off as she hurried up the stairs. 'I'll go and get my things, Mrs Canning. Don't worry, I'll be gone in minutes.'

As Flo took in the sight of Jean's retreating figure she hated herself. Why did she feel as if she was getting everything so wrong at the moment?

The rest of the day passed slowly. Flo broke the news to Henry quietly and matter-of-factly. He merely nodded his head and slipped an envelope across the table to Flo with Jean's final wages and a bit extra for the inconvenience.

With closing time fast approaching, Flo found herself breathing a sigh of relief. It had been a terrible day and one she longed to see the back of. She had told the rest of the girls, quickly and efficiently, and to their credit they must have sensed she didn't want to talk about it, as they had merely nodded and said how sorry they all were.

It had been a blessing, yet when she saw Bess dressed in her brown overalls and khaki woollen overcoat stomping across the floor towards her, a part of her wasn't surprised.

Reaching the till that Flo was standing behind, Flo could see Bess's eyes were narrowed with anger and her whole face was flushed red.

'How could you?' she growled. 'How could you sack Jean?'

'It wasn't like that,' Flo began. 'I didn't have a choice.'

'You didn't have a choice about sacking someone, or you didn't have a choice about sacking Jean? There's a big difference there,' Bess thundered.

'I had to pick someone,' Flo explained, doing her best to try and stay calm. 'I didn't want to sack anyone, and so I thought the fairest way was to pick the girl who had joined us last.'

Bess raised an eyebrow. 'The fairest thing? Surely the fairest thing would be to choose someone who was bad at their job and that certainly wouldn't be Jean. She's been with you through thick and thin; when you had that trouble earlier in the year with that old manager – Mrs Claremont – she was loyal as hell to the fabric department, and when you were getting stitched up by her as well it was Jean that found the evidence you needed to get you off the hook. She's that upset by the way she's been treated she's traipsed all the way over to the factory in Hayes to cry on my shoulder. Now I'm here to tell you what I think of your behaviour.'

Flo stared helplessly at Bess; she couldn't disagree. 'I hate this as much as you do. Jean was a wonderful part of the fabric department, a truly valued member of staff; my hands were tied.'

'Were they?' Bess protested. 'I mean, you could have sacked yourself.'

'The idea did cross my mind,' Flo admitted.

'But then you thought Jean was a better bet.'

Glancing over Bess's shoulder, Flo saw an approaching customer back away.

'Look, I'm sorry,' Flo began, lowering her voice. 'I know this isn't easy but I will help Jean look for something else.

And of course I don't expect full rent from either of you while she doesn't have a job.'

'Oh, that's big of you,' Bess snapped. 'But we don't need your charity.'

'I'm not trying to offer you charity, Bess,' Flo said wearily. 'I'm trying to do what's right.'

Bess leaned forward; she was so close Flo could feel the warmth of her breath against her skin. 'That girl means the world to me, you understand? The world. There is nothing I wouldn't do for her, and while I'd very much like to tell you where to shove your offer of help, neither one of us can afford to and Jean knows that as well as I do, so I'll say thank you, yes please and flamin' well find her something where she ain't gonna get sacked in the next five minutes.'

Flo was slightly shocked at the way Bess didn't mince her words, but if truth were told she thought she had it coming.

'Well, I'm pleased to hear that,' she said evenly. 'I'll start putting the word out immediately. Try not to worry.'

But Bess had already turned on her heel and stalked back across the floor leaving Flo all alone.

Chapter Nine

A feeling of dread enveloped Flo as she got up the next morning and thought about the day ahead at Liberty's. The last thing she felt like doing was going into work. Her gaze strayed to the photo of Neil she kept beside her bed. Running a finger across his face, Flo felt the tears well. She longed to talk to him more than anything in the world. He always knew just the right thing to say to make her feel better and as she stared into his blue-green eyes, she felt her loss as keenly as if Neil had just died. He had been her best friend as well as her husband and not for the first time she wondered just how she was supposed to live without him.

Hearing movement downstairs, she quickly roused herself and got ready. Surprisingly, she arrived at Liberty's early and shucked off her coat and bag, storing them in her small locker. Checking her appearance in the mirror that hung in the ladies' staffroom, it was no surprise to discover that after a night of no sleep, the bags under her eyes hung as heavy as lead, and her eyes looked like pins in one of Liberty's pin cushions.

Emerging from the staffroom Flo made her way down the stairs, only to see Henry up ahead of her.

'Hello, sir,' she called politely.

Henry turned around and raised an eyebrow at Flo. 'You don't look like a woman ready to take on the world.'

Flo smiled weakly. 'The only thing I feel ready to take on is a cup of tea.'

'It's horrible sacking someone who doesn't deserve it. I'm sorry.'

Flo shrugged. 'I suppose it couldn't be helped. I could have done without Bess turning up here late last night shouting the odds, though I can't say I blame her.'

'Well, I can, this wasn't your choice,' Henry said with a frown. 'Bess should understand that.'

'People protect those they love, don't they?'

'I suppose so.' Henry sighed. 'But listen, Flo, if you need any help you know where I am.'

Before she had time to reply, he had gone back up the stairs, and she made her way to fabrics. As usual she had a lot of paperwork to catch up on, and before she knew it, a whole hour had passed and it was time for the shop to open.

Stuffing the paperwork under the till as Dreary Deirdre completed the last of her morning checks, Flo stood ready to welcome customers when the department phone rang – it was the superintendent's office.

'Just to let you know that Mary Holmes-Fotherington won't be in today,' came a plummy voice down the line. 'She is most unwell with stomach influenza and sends her apologies.'

'Right, of course,' Flo replied. 'Thank you for letting me know.'

Replacing the receiver, Flo let out a large sigh. Her heart went out to her friend – Mary was never sick – but equally she knew she would now be short-staffed until the early afternoon when Alice was due in. However were they going to manage?

Her eyes landed on the rolls of utility fabric that had been so popular recently. Customers hadn't stopped coming in and buying reams of the material ready for the winter season. Today was Saturday, one of the busiest shopping days of the week; there was no way she was going to manage alone until Alice arrived.

As the first few customers snaked their way through the store, Flo drummed her fingers against the lined wooden desk and thought quickly. She couldn't ask anyone in neighbouring gifts or jewellery to help out; they were as short-staffed as she was since the cuts. Only yesterday the queues in gifts had been coming out of the door as they tried to keep up with demand on skeleton staff.

The anger Flo felt at having to let go a valued staff member rose as her thoughts landed on Henry Masters. This was all his fault, she thought uncharitably; he could fix it. With that in mind, an idea bloomed and Flo lifted the telephone receiver to speak directly to his office.

He answered on the first ring, and Flo made her request. There was a brief pause, and then a small chuckle as Henry told her he would be down to the shop floor immediately.

Almost as good as his word he arrived fifteen minutes later, just as Flo was saying goodbye to a regular customer. 'I thought you said you were rushed off your feet?' Henry said, looking doubtfully around the almost empty shop floor.

Flo lifted her wrist to check her watch. 'We will be. This is the quiet before the storm, Mr Masters. In around twenty minutes we shall have the pre-elevenses shoppers, keen to browse and perhaps keen to spend.'

'You do know your department, don't you?'

'I make it my business to know everything about it,' she replied, her tone grave. 'It's not just a department; it's a way of life for us girls. We live and breathe the fabrics here.'

Henry had the good grace to look bashful. 'I apologise. Now, how can I help?'

Flo felt a sudden flash of inspiration. 'I'll need you to get back to your roots, Mr Masters,' she said finally, her eyes focusing on a customer heading towards them. 'You told me how you used to be a sales assistant in fabrics many years ago; I need you to be a sales assistant again.'

If Henry was surprised at the instruction he didn't show it. Instead he walked across the floor, approached the customer who was now looking at the rolls of popular print and made a point of asking what she was hoping to make.

As the morning wore on, Flo was right about the surge of customers all looking to find the perfect print for the perfect pattern they had their eye on. For the next two hours Flo and Henry worked side by side, offering advice, suggesting appropriate accessories, and cutting fabric precisely in a way that meant very little waste. As Henry cut a weighted woollen fabric for his customer, she watched impressed as his scissors sliced through the fabric as if it were butter and then he accurately measured and priced, all with a smile on his face. Deep down Flo knew that it wasn't his choice to sack Jean and that he was just acting on instructions from higher up. Perhaps it was time to forgive and forget.

'Now do come again, Mrs Withers,' said Henry as he rang through her sale and simultaneously handed her the copy of her sales order. 'You will look marvellous in that palm-leaf print, the belle of the ball.'

The elderly Mrs Withers let out a laugh so high-pitched it rang in Flo's ears. 'Now, now, Mr Henry, I'm old enough to be your mother.'

A look of horror passed across his face. 'Not at all, Mrs Withers, not at all, my sister perhaps, but certainly not my mother, I won't have it.'

Another tinkling laugh left Mrs Withers' mouth and Flo found herself wincing at Henry's obvious but clearly calculated approach to customers.

'Oh Mr Henry, I shall come and see you again.' The older woman giggled in a girlish fashion. 'You are a tonic.'

'We shall look forward to it, Mrs Withers.' Henry beamed as he bade her goodbye.

Once Mrs Withers was safely out of earshot, Flo sidled up alongside Henry. 'You've done that before.'

'Once or twice,' Henry admitted.

'The ladies seem to like you,' Flo said airily as she ran her fingers through the sales forms. There were more than usual for the time of year; her boss had done well.

Henry laughed, running a hand through his salt and pepper hair. 'I don't know about that, but what I will say is I had forgotten how tiring it is on the shop floor.'

'Can be,' Flo agreed. 'But surely you dealt with worse than this at Bourne and Hollingsworth?'

'I didn't spend as much time as I should have done on the shop floor,' Henry admitted. 'I was so busy being a manager I let the sales assistants handle most of the work. I'm surprised you're here so often to be honest.'

Flo shrugged. 'I like it. When I was doing your job, albeit briefly, I hated being stuck in the office all the time. I like talking to people.'

'I can see that.' Henry nodded. 'I suppose I appreciate a bit of peace now and then; my little brother Stan can be a very noisy young man.'

Flo looked up at him in surprise. 'I didn't know you had a brother.'

Henry smiled. 'Oh yes, a half-brother – young Stan is ten. He's been living with me since he was seven.'

'Are you close?' Flo asked.

'We are.' Henry nodded. 'I've been looking after him since our mother died, and I suppose being so much older than the boy I see myself as brother and father to him. We've been through some difficult times but Stan keeps me on my toes. He's an intelligent lad – dunno where he gets it from.'

'You're not doing so badly,' Flo replied, her tone gentle now. 'You're doing a brave thing; not many men would raise a child on their own.'

Henry frowned at the compliment. 'You do what you have to, but hell'd freeze over first before I put that lad in a home. Everything I do, I do for that boy.'

'Where's his father?' Flo asked.

'He died at the start of the war. Bomb dropped on him in Aberdeen where he was working in the dockyards.'

'I'm sorry,' Flo said. 'He's a lucky boy to have you as his big brother.'

'I don't know about that,' he said. 'But it's like you said earlier, Flo, we'll do anything for the ones we love.'

Chapter Ten

October's warm weather had turned into a grey and cold November, bringing with it a surge in customers interested in the range of woollen fabrics Liberty's had on offer. Henry assumed it was all down to the fact that the weather had turned, but Flo liked to think she knew the customers a little better and that trade had been up over the first half of the month because morale amongst the public was high.

News had broken that the German army in North Africa were retreating in Egypt at the hands of General Bernard Montgomery. The papers were full of reports of German soldiers fleeing from El Alamein after being relentlessly attacked by Allied land and air forces night and day who, in the process, captured more than nine thousand prisoners of war, including the German army General Ritter von Thoma. It was welcome news all round, and a part of Flo enjoyed eavesdropping on customers' conversations where they talked about the wonderful job Churchill was doing and the possibility of the war ending.

And so when Rose had telephoned down to the department just before lunchtime and said Henry wanted to go over the weekly takings with her, Flo found her mood was buoyant at the prospect.

Making her way up to the office, she knocked loudly on the door and heard a sharp 'Come in'.

Stepping inside she was surprised to see her superior sitting on his chair with one leg perched high on his desk.

Flo couldn't help raise an eyebrow – where on earth did he think he was?

'Please excuse me, Mrs Canning,' he said in gruff tones. 'I don't usually sit about like this but my leg's giving me real gyp today.'

Flo felt a flash of concern. 'I'm sorry.'

Henry waved her apology away. 'Nought for you to be sorry for. But I wonder if you wouldn't mind doing me a small favour.'

'Go on,' she said cautiously.

'I wonder if you would mind going to Sandhurst Road School to collect my little brother Stan.'

'Now?' Flo asked aghast.

Henry nodded. 'He's had a nasty fall in the playground and the school wants to send him home. I would go myself but my leg's frozen and I know when it's like this I just have to sit it out.'

Opening her mouth to speak Flo found she was speechless. She had been asked to do many things that weren't in her job description during her time at Liberty's but picking up a child from school was a first.

'Why me? I've got a department to run. Surely you could get one of the girls to do it?'

Henry looked sheepish. 'I appreciate I'm asking a lot here. I don't usually ask for anything where Stan's concerned; we've been through a lot, me and him, and we're a team. But, well, although we don't know each other very well, you strike me as the best woman for the job so to speak, and there's nobody else I can ask.'

Flo laughed. 'Charming!'

Henry looked contrite. 'Sorry, I didn't mean it like that.'

Flo smiled. 'I know you didn't, but, sir, I don't know anything about children.'

The deputy store manager laughed. 'I didn't myself when I took him on but I soon discovered he doesn't bite. Please,' he said, his expression softening. 'I trust you.'

'You're not really leaving me a lot of choice, are you?' She sighed. 'Fine, I'll go.'

After Flo had issued her instructions for the afternoon to Alice and Mary, she made her way to the school.

South East London wasn't an area she knew well at all. After boarding the bus and buying a ticket from the smartly dressed clippie, Flo settled into a seat and stared out of the grimy window. The scenery that passed before her became more unfamiliar with every mile they travelled. She couldn't help marvel at how different the south of the city looked to the north. London was so large that to Flo it felt as if the city was a collection of small villages, each with its own individual traits and characteristics.

Catford, with its red-brick terraces, had an identity that was all its own. Like everywhere it had suffered at the hand of Hitler and with every corner the bus turned you could see fresh devastation. But it was the sight of so many children playing a complicated-looking version of hopscotch amongst the dust and debris of bombed-out housing that really caught Flo's attention. She had lost count of how many times she had seen children playing amongst the wreckage and she had become used to it, but in this moment it struck her how sad that was.

As the bus turned into the road nearest the school, Flo shook her head and pulled the cord to get off. Thanking the driver, she stepped on to the street and walked towards the small school, an autumn chill catching at her throat. Tightening the scarf around her neck, Flo paused for a moment as she took in the sight of the school. Like any other it had entrances marked 'Boys' and 'Girls', and a small concourse at the front where the children played at break times. Narrowing her eyes she tried to spot a main door, but not finding another obvious entrance decided to hedge her bets and walk through the door marked 'Girls'.

Inside the smell of polished wood flooring and disinfectant took her right back to her own school days. Suddenly a memory of how she and Neil had played together in a school just like this one jolted her back to the past and she was struck with a feeling of longing for the man and boy that had been her one constant throughout her life.

'Can I help you?' A brisk voice brought her swiftly out of her daydream.

Whirling around Flo came face-to-face with a stiff-backed unsmiling woman with a thick head of grey hair.

'Yes, hello, I'm Mrs Flo Canning. I'm here to collect Stanley Masters,' she said politely.

The woman frowned. 'I haven't been informed that a child is due to leave school early. I am his teacher and nothing escapes my attention.'

Flo frowned in her turn. 'Stanley's brother and guardian, Henry Masters, received a telephone call earlier from someone at the school. Apparently Stanley has hurt his knee rather badly. Mr Masters has been detained at work and he sent me.'

The teacher, who still hadn't introduced herself, Flo noted with some frustration, was about to speak when the sound of someone clattering down the corridor caught their attention. It was a woman in a white overall.

'Mrs Hallam, what are you doing running about like that?' the teacher exclaimed. 'We are here to set an example to the children.'

'Sorry, ma'am,' the woman said as she came to a stop. 'Miss Buckland, Stanley's teacher, asked me to tell you that she sent for his guardian after an accident in the playground but we were that busy in the canteen I didn't get a chance.'

The teacher raised an eyebrow. 'We'll discuss this later, Mrs Hallam,' she said in a tone that brooked no argument. 'But in the meantime perhaps you could show Mrs Canning to the sick bay so no more of her time or mine is wasted.'

'Of course, ma'am,' Mrs Hallam replied in an even tone as the teacher stalked off down the corridor.

As the woman turned to face Flo, Flo briefly assessed her. Mrs Hallam looked to be about fifty. Short, with a creamy complexion and rich brown hair now flecked with grey, she had an air about her that made Flo feel relaxed.

'Blimey, I don't miss school,' Flo said with a small shudder once the teacher was out of earshot.

Mrs Hallam giggled, her warm grin lighting up her face. 'Don't mind her. She can't cope with the job really, so that's why she snarls so much. The kids run rings around her, which is why she doesn't know the half of what goes on. Come on, let's go and get Stanley.'

'Is he all right?' Flo enquired as she followed the woman down the corridor. 'I don't know him, you see. His brother asked me to do him a favour and we've never actually met.'

There was a pause then as Mrs Hallam stopped suddenly in the corridor and gave Flo a good look up and down. Flo felt a surge of worry that Mrs Hallam would suddenly refuse to give Stan over to her. What would Henry say if she arrived back at work empty-handed?

Mrs Hallam smiled again; then she carried on walking up the corridor. 'He's all right. Looks worse than it is but we haven't got enough staff to take care of him so that's why Miss Buckland – his teacher – thought it best to get him home.'

Flo nodded in understanding. Staff shortages were something she knew all about.

'So have you worked here long?' Flo asked as they rounded a corner and walked down yet another long corridor.

'About a year. I love working with children. Here we are then,' Mrs Hallam said brightly as they stopped suddenly outside a white wooden door marked 'Sanatorium'.

Mrs Hallam pushed it open, and Flo followed her inside to see a forlorn small boy with a thick clump of red hair lying on a hard-looking bed with a big bandage wrapped around his right knee. He looked up at them both uncertainly, his eyes the spitting image of his older brother's.

'Stan love.' Mrs Hallam smiled gently. 'This is Mrs Canning. She's here to take you back home.'

The little boy looked from Flo to Mrs Hallam before he eventually spoke. 'Do you mean proper home or Henry's home?' he asked in a thick Yorkshire accent.

Flo frowned. She wasn't sure what Stan meant by proper home. 'Well, we're going to meet your brother at Liberty's, then I imagine he'll take you back to his house from there.'

At that Stan rolled his eyes. 'Henry's always at that shop. Do I really have to go there?'

'It's a lovely shop,' Flo protested. 'Have you ever been?'

'Once,' Stan grumbled. 'It was boring.'

Flo nodded as if thinking quietly to herself. 'Hmmm, shops can be boring. I mean, even when they're built of warships they can be very boring.'

Stan's eyes lit up. 'Liberty's is made of a warship?'

Flo nodded, her eyes dancing with enthusiasm. 'Oh yes, but I thought you knew that already.'

'No!' Stan had shuffled to the edge of the bed now. 'What else has it got then, Mrs?'

'Lots of things,' Flo grinned. 'It's got secret passageways and all sorts of treasures.'

'Treasures?'

'That's right, things like a model of the *Mayflower* and carved animals in the staircase, and the tearoom in the basement looks like a dungeon!'

Stan's jaw dropped open in amazement and Flo bent down so she was at his eye level. 'So, I know the shop's boring, but your brother would be ever so grateful if you'd come with me.'

'Can we go now?' he begged.

'You can go now,' Mrs Hallam chuckled, winking at Flo. 'Have you got everything?'

Stan nodded and gingerly stepped down from the bed to walk towards Flo. Instinctively she held out her hand to help steady him and was surprised when he gripped it for dear life.

'Can you manage?' she found herself asking the boy.

Stan nodded as together they made their way towards the door.

'We'll see you tomorrow then, hopefully, Stan.' Mrs Hallam opened the door. 'You'll be right as ninepence in the morning.'

At the expression, Flo felt a tingle along her spine. She knew it was a common enough phrase but the way the dinner lady said it took her back in time to her childhood. It was an expression Aggie had always used.

'Well then, I'll love you and leave you,' Mrs Hallam said. 'Those dinner plates won't clean themselves. Stan knows the way out, don't you?'

Without waiting for an answer, Mrs Hallam turned and began walking briskly back along the corridor, her heels clacking along the wooden flooring. As Flo watched her figure dart around the corner she couldn't shake the feeling she had seen Mrs Hallam before, but for the life of her she didn't know where.

Chapter Eleven

It was almost closing by the time Flo finally got back to the fabric department. It had taken her far longer than she had anticipated to get back from Catford, and she hadn't counted on how difficult and painful it would be for Stan to walk anywhere. She had ended up carrying him from Oxford Circus, leaving her absolutely exhausted by the time she returned to the shop floor.

'You are alive then.' Dot chuckled as Flo walked into the department; Dreary Deirdre was just starting to perform the store's usual nightly checks.

'Just.' She smiled, rolling her eyes. 'How have things been here?'

'The same as usual,' Mary replied. 'Nothing too taxing.'

Walking around to the back of the cash register Flo started leafing through the day's takings, when she felt a wave of tiredness crash over her. It was no good, she was done in physically and mentally and there was about as much point in looking at those books now as there was wishing Neil would walk through the doors.

Shoving the books underneath the till, she lifted her chin and suddenly became aware of three sets of eyes staring at her in concern.

'Fancy a drink after work, darlin'?' Dot asked in her sing-song voice. 'You look like you could do with it.'

Flo winced at the idea. 'All I really want is my bed, Dot.'

'Oh come on, misery guts,' Alice cried. 'A port and lemon'll do you the world of good.'

'And you've earned it going all the way to Catford like that,' Mary put in.

Mulling the idea over, Flo thought for a moment. A drink with her pals could be just what she needed. What would she be going home for? To stare at Dot's four walls and grieve over her losses?

'All right then,' she sighed, 'but I wouldn't mind changing. I feel ever so grimy.'

'I'm sure we can find a spare frock for you somewhere,' Dot reasoned, looking at the girls for confirmation.

Mary sniggered. 'Just make sure you don't borrow anything of Dot's; you'd fit two of you in one of her frocks.'

At the cheeky remark Dot's nostrils flared. 'And it's a good job she won't be borrowing anything off you, because if your dresses are anything like as big as your gob she'll get lost in one.'

With that the girls fell about laughing and Flo felt a surge of warmth flood through her. Yes, a drink could be just what the doctor ordered.

Half an hour later Flo found herself sitting in the smoky saloon of the French Pub, greedily sipping a milk stout in one of the spare dresses Alice kept in the Liberty staffroom. Glancing around at the tired old wooden beams, she asked Alice, 'Is Jack coming tonight?' over the din of the group and the chatter of other men and women who had all finished work for the day.

At the mention of the handsome GI, Dot's face lit up.

'Yes, but that don't mean he's got chocolates or stockings for you,' Alice pointed out with a smile.

A look of innocence passed across Dot's face. 'Can't a person just enjoy the company of a young American gentleman without expecting anything?'

'A person can, but you can't, no.' Mary's eyes twinkled with mirth.

Right on cue, Jack appeared at the doorway and gave them all a wave, before gesturing that he was going to the bar.

'Don't go asking him about stockings the moment he sits down either,' Alice hissed in Dot's direction.

'As if I would! Might ask him about chocolate though,' she said in a stage whisper.

At the cheek, Flo shook her head at her old friend. 'You're a tonic, Dorothy Hanson.'

'It's been said before.' Dot smiled, patting Flo's hand, before turning to Rose. 'How are you getting on with those fundraising plans of yours?'

Rose groaned. 'All right but there's so much to prepare I could really do with a hand. And it doesn't help that Mr Button is away all the time. There's so much I need to ask him about the night, but he says to ask Mr Masters about it, only Mr Masters isn't that interested. I don't suppose you'd reconsider doing a turn for us, would you, Flo? I'm desperate for a good singer.'

Flo shook her head. 'I won't sing. But I'll talk to Mr Masters for you. He owes me a favour after today.'

'Yes, that was a flamin' cheek getting you to go all that way for his brother like that. Hardly Liberty business is it,' Dot complained as Jack returned with a tray full of milk stout. He chuckled.

'Uh-oh, who's upset you now, Dot?'

Flo smiled by way of greeting at him, but couldn't miss the way Dot's eyes lit up at the box of chocolates he had in his hand.

'Nobody you need worry about,' Dot reassured him, standing up to kiss Jack's cheek and take the box of chocolates at the same time.

Rose turned to Jack. 'Busy day?'

'I've been in Surrey all day. I'm there three times a week training our guys.'

Dot frowned. 'You must be knackered with all that travelling about.'

Confusion passed across Jack's features. 'Knackered? Sorry, what does that mean?'

'Tired,' Alice explained. 'Just don't let her give you a lesson in cockney rhyming slang.'

Dot winked. 'I know all the swear words! Now then, as Jack's here, how about we call time on shop talk.'

'Well, what should we talk about then?' Rose frowned. 'There's so much happening in the store at the moment.'

'Honey, from what I can gather there's always something happening at Liberty's,' Jack teased.

'We could talk about Mary's wedding,' Flo suggested.

At the change in subject the girls' eyes lit up.

'Do you know where you're going to hold it?' Alice asked.

'We thought the little church around the corner from Bell Street. It's not very big but should be enough for us.'

'Oh, where we had Arthur christened,' Alice said in surprise.

'The very same. I thought it was such a lovely church.'

'It is,' Rose agreed. 'It's where me and Tommy got married.'

'And me and George, Gawd rest him.' Dot sighed, her face clouding over for a brief second. 'It's a happy place, Mary, and it'll do you proud.'

Mary nodded happily. 'You will all be there, won't you?'

'As if you even have to ask!' Flo exclaimed.

'I know it sounds silly,' Mary said softly as she played with the stem of her glass. 'It's just that with no family, I don't want to look a twit.'

Flo offered Mary a sympathetic smile. She knew how difficult it was to get married with no relations to support you.

'You leave it to us,' Dot said firmly.

71

'That's what I hoped,' Mary replied. 'And I was also hoping Mr Button would walk me down the aisle. Do you think he would, Dot?'

'If he can find the time, darlin',' Dot muttered darkly, knocking back the rest of her drink in one.

Flo blanched in surprise at the sudden change in mood. 'What's up with you?'

Dot pushed her glass away and folded her arms. 'Ignore me. It's just Edwin's never bloody well about.'

'Well, he is busy with the Board of Trade,' Rose pointed out carefully.

'We're all busy,' Dot fumed. 'But we still manage to find time for one another. I've got my sister coming over next week and I thought it would be nice for the two of them to get reacquainted after all these years, but can Edwin find the time, can he hell.'

'But it's not as if he's swanning about,' Flo protested. 'He's working.'

'Yes, with Betty bloody Fawcett, who's also offered her services to the Board of Trade,' Dot muttered. 'He's always with her.'

Mary looked at Dot in astonishment. 'You can't surely be jealous of Betty Fawcett. She's been shopping at Liberty's for years.'

'Precisely,' Alice said crisply. 'Besides, she's drop dead gorgeous and a film star in her twenties. Mr Button's ancient, he's—'

'I dare you to finish that sentence, lady,' Dot snapped, cutting Alice off mid-flow. 'Look, I know you think I'm being daft,' she said, her tone gentler now, 'but Edwin's always with her, and when he's not with her and he's with me he's always talking about what she said or what Evie Allingham said.'

'Who's Evie Allingham?' Mary asked.

Dot's lip curled with disdain. 'She used to be some big-wig up at fabrics in Botheringtons.'

'Oh yes,' Alice replied. 'The department store over Tottenham Court Road way; they do a very nice line in budget material.'

'Precisely.' Dot sniffed. 'Why the Board of Trade wants to encourage people from lesser department stores beats me. They should have come to Liberty's for the best girls.'

As the girls sniggered at Dot's snobbery Flo felt the tension in her shoulders unwind. She might have her problems but, in that moment, she was grateful for the companionship of these women around her.

'We might be the best girls, but we're not without our problems,' Rose said, a hint of sadness to her voice.

'What's the matter?' Flo asked gently. 'You haven't had more bad news about your sight?'

Rose shook her head. 'Tommy's coming back next month and I'm worried that it's a bad idea.'

'Goodness me. What on earth's got into you?' Mary cried. 'You should be looking forward to seeing him, not worrying about it.'

'You don't understand,' Rose said, pouting slightly. 'This will be the first time he's seen me since the incident. He might not like the fact I can barely see.'

'What rot,' Mary fired indignantly.

'She's right,' Alice agreed. 'How many times has Tommy written to you now and told you that he loves you, that he doesn't mind about your eyesight? He wants to be there for you.'

'I know that's what he says,' Rose wailed, 'but that's in a letter, not real life.'

Dot let out a long sigh. 'You know we were just talking about how lovely it was that Mary is getting married in the same church as you and me wed in, Rose darlin'?'

'What's that got to do with anything?' she asked, puzzled.

'Well, do you remember what you said in that church?'

'Erm, well, we said our vows,' Rose replied, still looking unsure.

Dot slapped her hand down hard on the table, causing Flo's milk stout to slop over the sides of her glass. 'Exactly. And in those vows you both promised you would love each other in sickness and in health. Now, unless you two were pratting about up the altar when you said those things it won't make a bit of difference whether you've lost most of your sight or developed another head. Your Tommy loves you no matter what and it's high time you started believing that.'

There was a pause then before Rose let out a small smile. 'All right.'

Dot rolled her eyes at the gesture before addressing the girls. 'Does anyone have any real problems? Because it strikes me that most of us are worrying over flamin' nothing.'

'Nothing, apart from Jack's sister sticking her oar in.' Alice sighed.

'Come on now, honey, you know Gracie doesn't mean anything by it.' Jack said consolingly.

Flo frowned and ignored Jack. 'What's Gracie got to do with anything?'

Alice sighed. 'She's written to Jack and told him that I, as a married woman with a child will bring nothing but trouble to his door and he should get shot of me sharpish.'

'What a lot of nonsense. As if you brought any of this on yourself,' Flo said. 'What does Jack think?'

'That Gracie doesn't know anything about Alice.' Jack smiled, ignoring the fact that the girls were talking about

74

him rather than to him. 'And that she's thousands of miles away on a farm in Montana and doesn't have the first idea about what's happening in England.'

'Well, you're right,' Flo agreed. 'She doesn't know you, Alice. Look, this was never going to be easy for either of you. But what Gracie thinks doesn't matter – what matters is what Jack thinks.'

Jack reached over and wrapped an arm around Alice's shoulders. 'And I happen to think you're okay.'

Alice laughed as Dot rolled her eyes. 'Anyone got anything else?'

Flo thought for a moment. 'Just make sure this wedding of yours isn't on a Saturday, Mary,' she muttered darkly. 'I don't want to give Mr Masters cause to sack anyone else from the department.'

'All these sackings sound bloody silly to me,' Dot spat. 'How about some of them fat cats on the board take a pay cut? That'd save the company a few quid.'

Flo smirked. 'I don't think even that would pay for all the wages that have to be cut. We have to face it, girls, times are changing and we have to make the most of things.'

'Too true,' Mary agreed, sipping her drink. 'Take this new adoption act that's coming into effect next year, for example. David and I are having to jump through all manner of hoops to adopt little Emma even though David is Mabel's sister. It's not enough to be related to a child you want to look after any more.'

'What do you mean?' Flo asked.

'Well, we've got to be approved by the council now. In the past, any willing adult could take a child on; now if you've been in trouble with the law or aren't of good moral character there's a chance you won't be approved,' Mary explained.

'In my day we had none of this carry-on,' Dot said sagely. 'We looked after a kiddie and that was that.'

'Well, times have changed,' Flo said, not unreasonably. 'This new act that's coming in is going to mean kids are better looked after.'

'Load of old nonsense and red tape if you ask me,' Dot continued as if Flo hadn't spoken. 'Sounds like summat that flaming Public Morality Council has got involved in.'

'Public what?' Rose quizzed.

'You must have heard of it,' Flo put in. 'Full of old gasbags poking their nose into other people's business. All concerned about the morals and state of our private lives.'

Rose shook her head. 'It's passed me by, that one.'

'One of the customers was telling me about it a while ago,' Flo continued. 'Her friend's husbands was a member and it had caused quite a stir.'

'Full of very religious types, isn't it?' Mary asked.

'Apparently so,' Flo said.

'Well, what's the point of them then? They don't really want to interfere in our lives to make sure we're all upholding our morals, do they?' Rose asked doubtfully.

Flo smiled and shook her head. 'No, they're more concerned with prostitution and homosexuality. They monitor what's going on and report anything untoward to the police.'

'Like spies,' Jack put in.

'Exactly like spies!' Dot said. 'If you ask me they've got nothing better to do with their sad little lives. They're a disgrace in my book. What with this bunch of do-gooders, not to mention interference in the wellbeing of kiddies, the government should be getting their priorities right and bleedin' well sorting this war out. Churchill ought to be bringing our boys home.'

Flo took a large gulp of her drink. She had to admit that she didn't disagree, but one look at Mary's anxious face told her this was not what she needed to hear.

'I'm sure it will all go smoothly and it's just a formality, Mary,' Flo offered. 'The council will approve you and David with no problem at all. Especially once they see your wedding plans are all sorted out.'

Mary smiled gratefully at her friend. 'I hope so. Emma would be the making of our family.'

'To family,' Dot said suddenly, holding her half-empty glass aloft.

As the girls clinked glasses together, Flo felt a sudden sense of grief wash over her as she realised her family was all gone.

Chapter Twelve

Jean's absence was never felt more keenly as the continued autumn rain and cool winds brought hordes of shoppers into Liberty's. With customers looking for fabric to make coats, winter skirts and the new slacks women were wearing up and down the high street, Flo had a job to keep every customer happy as they waited far longer than usual to be served.

Once again, Flo had needed to enlist the help of Henry to get through the queues, and once again, he had impressed her with his knowledge of the stock and the way he handled the customers.

But after the fourth day in a row Flo had called on his services, she had to admit he looked as if he had reached breaking point.

'I'm wearing you out, aren't I?' she said during an unexpected lull in trade.

Henry smiled. 'Not at all. I'm just a bit tired. I've got a lot of work to do, reports and such like for the board, and of course Stan is still off school.'

Flo raised an eyebrow. 'Stan still isn't well?'

'No, he's on the mend, and Celia has been very good to us.'

'Celia?' Flo probed.

'Yes. Mrs Hallam from the school. We go way back.' Henry smiled. 'She was friends with my mother back in Yorkshire and she helps me out with Stan when she can.'

'That's nice,' Flo exclaimed. 'And what a coincidence that you both ended up here in London.'

'Not really,' Henry admitted. 'She's from London originally. After I left the army, I worked in a factory with Mum and Celia for a while then in 1935 Mr Button offered me a job at Bourne and Hollingsworth. When I took Stan in four years later Celia told me she felt ready to move to London too so we found her a job at the school. She's known Stan all his life, and since our mother died it's been nice for him to have a woman about.'

Flo understood exactly what Henry meant. Aggie had been wonderful throughout the years. But even so there had been times she had desperately wanted her own mother.

Henry smiled fondly at Flo. 'Flo, I know that these staff cuts were not the best thing for your department, or any other come to that.'

Flo pursed her lips at the statement, resisting the urge to reveal her true feelings. 'We all have to make sacrifices.'

'I should have pushed back against the board more,' Henry continued. 'I made a mistake and I'm sorry. I should have fought harder for you, for this department, and instead I let them railroad me. I was too concerned with making a good impression in a new job.'

'Don't be silly,' Flo said in a firm tone. 'I've done your job and I know the pressure you're under. The board wouldn't have given you a choice.'

'Even so,' Henry replied with a grimace, 'I went back to the board last night after yet another busy day and told them we had to reinstate Jean, that the department needs her.

'Do you mean that?' Flo asked, looking at him in astonishment.

'I do,' Henry replied gravely. 'I should never have made you sack someone. I'm sorry.'

Something like happiness flooded through Flo for the first time in months as she contemplated the idea of giving

Jean back a job that should never have been taken from her in the first place.

'You're absolutely sure about this? The board aren't going to change their minds?'

'No,' Henry promised, his eyes twinkling with kindness. 'Once they found out that the deputy manager was working overtime, they realised it wasn't appropriate. I made them see what they should have seen all along. Why don't you pop over to visit Jean tonight after work and we'll get her back here as quickly as possible? We want it to seem as though she never left.'

Together with Alice, Flo made her way to Islington to see Jean. However, her response was not what Flo had expected. Jean had barely looked Flo in the eye as she'd shown her and Alice inside, and when Flo had told her what she considered to be happy news, Jean hadn't looked as thrilled as she had hoped. In fact she seemed reticent and even worried about the prospect of a return.

'Are we all coming back?' Jean asked, her face full of doubt as she sat at the kitchen table opposite Flo and Alice.

'Not everyone, no,' Flo admitted. 'But after spending some time in the fabric department himself, Mr Masters has seen that we simply cannot manage without you, Jean.'

'Not all departments are as unique as ours,' Alice added. 'We're fortunate in some ways that Mr Masters can see that.'

'I see.' Jean nodded. 'It just don't seem right somehow. That I get my job back and all those other girls don't.'

Alice smiled at her. 'I know that, love, but you have to think of yourself. You want to come back to Liberty's, don't you?'

'I do,' Jean agreed, nodding so fiercely that a lock of hair fell from the loose chignon at the nape of her neck, 'but it don't feel right to be going back to work when the others can't.'

A cloud passed across Flo's face. She knew Jean was correct, but what else could she do? She couldn't fight everyone's battles.

'There are many things in this world that aren't right, Jean. We both know that. I wish I could give everyone else their jobs back, but I can't, I can only give you yours – so what do you say? Will you return?'

Jean said nothing and instead looked towards the window as if she could see beyond the blackout curtain.

'What do you think Bess would say if she was here?' Alice asked.

Jean turned back to the girls and smiled at the mention of her sister. 'She already told me that if anyone offered me my job back then I should take it sharpish. She reminded me that we need the money and, given I could be called up any day, she said I should make the most of this and the WVS work I do as well.'

'Sounds like good advice,' Alice replied. 'So what do you think? You know how much we want you back.'

'We do,' Flo echoed. 'And I hope you know how sorry I am I picked you. It wasn't a reflection of you or your hard work or how much I value you. Please come back to us, Jean.'

Jean looked first from Alice to Flo and then back out towards the window. It was all Flo could do not to beg her for an answer but instead she turned to look at the kitchen. It seemed Jean had been letting the place go in Flo's absence. The once gleaming butler sink overflowed with dirty cups and a stack of mismatched tea towels lay haphazardly on the wooden work surface, which was covered in tea stains.

'Please, Jean,' Flo urged again.

Jean gave the girls a small smile. 'All right. I'll come back.'

Flo clapped her hands together in delight. 'That's wonderful. We've all missed you so much. Things haven't been the same without you.'

'There are a few conditions, however,' Jean said. 'I want a pay increase.'

'You want a what?' Alice echoed in disbelief.

'A pay increase,' Jean said, her gaze unwavering. 'To make up for getting sacked. If I'm as important as you say then it shouldn't be a problem.'

Flo stifled a smile. She had to admire Jean's cheek and if she was honest she couldn't blame her. The girl had been treated shabbily and Henry had said she could if necessary give Jean an extra shilling a week to encourage her to return.

'All right,' Flo said gravely. 'An extra thruppence a week.'

Jean arched an eyebrow. 'A shilling.'

'A tanner,' Flo counter-offered. 'And I won't go any higher so don't try and make me.'

There was another brief pause as Jean considered the offer. Flo glanced at Alice; she was shaking her head at the girl's nerve. The extra money would bring her almost in line with what Mary was earning.

'All right,' Jean said eventually.

'Good.' Flo beamed. 'Now, let's celebrate. Alice, can you stay for a bit?'

'Yes, Dot's got Arthur and she told me to take my time.'

'Lovely. I'll buy you each a drink at the Lamb and Flag.'

'You can't say fairer than that, Jean.' Alice smiled. 'Come on, get your coat.'

With that Jean leapt to her feet and made her way into the hallway to collect her bag and coat with Flo and Alice following behind. As Flo slid her feet into her well-worn court shoes, there was a sharp knock at the door.

Opening it, Flo came face-to-face with a tall blonde woman about the same age as her and dressed in the same factory uniform as Bess.

'Can I help you?' Flo asked, noting the sombre look on the girl's face.

'I'm looking for Jean Rushmore. Is she here?'

'Yes, I'm here,' Jean said, pushing her way past Flo to address the girl. 'Are you from Bess's work?'

The girl nodded. 'I'm Catherine. The boss sent me to talk to you. Jean, I'm sorry to have to tell you this but Bess was injured this afternoon.'

Flo saw the colour drain from Jean's face as she opened her mouth to speak.

'What's happened?' she demanded.

The girl shook her head. 'I'm not properly sure. I was on my tea break when it happened. Something to do with a shell casing not being sealed properly and an explosion.'

Jean's hands flew to her mouth. 'No, not my Bess. Not my darling girl. Is she all right?'

'I hope so – I think so,' Catherine replied, looking for all the world as if the accident had affected her too. 'The doctors are looking after her now. Would you like to see her?'

Wordlessly Jean nodded, and flew out of the door.

Alice and Flo exchanged knowing looks. Jean hadn't asked, but there was no doubt about it. They would go with her and give her the support she would no doubt need. Jean was a Liberty girl, always was and always would be.

Chapter Thirteen

Less than two hours later Flo, Alice and Jean were sitting in the stark white hospital corridor of Hayes Cottage Hospital, with doctors and nurses rushing past them, talking in hushed tones and calling out terms not one of the girls understood.

'I just don't understand how it can have happened,' Jean cried for the fourth time since they arrived. 'How could she have been injured so badly?'

'Steady now, Jean,' Alice soothed. 'We don't know how bad things are yet.'

'Precisely,' Flo agreed. 'The people at the factory will have given her excellent first aid.'

'You've got to have hope,' Alice added gently. 'Without hope you've got nothing.'

With that Flo met Alice's gaze and exchanged a knowing look. They had both faced loss and despair over the past twelve months. If anyone knew about hope helping you through your bleakest moments they did.

'Well, we know that she's lost her hand for a start,' Jean wailed as if she hadn't heard the girls. 'We know that she's been burnt.'

'But we don't know how badly yet,' Alice countered. 'You've got to be strong for her now, Jean. Trust me, if there's one thing I know it's that however bad things are your sister won't cope if you're standing about weeping at her bedside.'

Just then they heard the sound of footsteps coming towards them. Immediately the girls got to their feet as a weary-looking nurse approached them. Flo saw her uniform was a pale primrose colour, which meant she was a junior nurse. A flash of hope flooded through Flo; surely things couldn't be that bad if a junior nurse was coming to talk to them?

'Miss Rushmore, my name is Nurse Stevens and I've been helping your sister Bess Green.' She ran her finger along a sheet of white paper. 'Are you her next of kin?'

Jean nodded again.

Nurse Stevens frowned. 'She has no husband?'

'No, he died before the war,' Jean mumbled, her gaze cast downwards.

Flo blanched in surprise. She had no idea Bess had been married; the girls had never said and as far as she was aware Bess always used the same surname as Jean.

'I see.' Nurse Stevens frowned again before glancing back up at Jean and addressing the girls. 'Well, as you know your sister was involved in an accident at the factory.'

'Do you know what happened?' Flo asked.

'It seems Mrs Green was working with the shells. She took the casing, filled it with powder, then when she put the detonator on top she tapped it too hard and it exploded. It's all too common; sadly some girls are killed when they're involved in similar accidents,' Nurse Stevens said, her face grave.

'Just how badly injured is she?' Jean asked.

'Well, Mrs Green has lost her right hand and suffered superficial burns to her face, neck and hands, but that seems to be all,' Nurse Stevens explained. 'She has been comparatively lucky.'

85

'Lucky?' Jean echoed in disbelief. 'Bess has lost her hand, how on earth could she be considered lucky?'

The nurse's eyes levelled with Jean's. 'Many girls like your sister who work in those factories come in here with worse injuries than that,' she said coolly. 'Your sister will learn to live without her hand and her burns will heal in time. It could have been far, far worse.'

As Nurse Stevens finished talking, Flo squeezed Jean's hand. 'She's right, Jean. Now the rest is up to you. I know it's a shock, but Bess needs your help.'

Jean nodded. 'I will always be there for Bess. I love her more than anyone else in the world.'

At that the nurse's gaze softened and she gave Jean a small smile. 'And I know she will be grateful to have you. Now, what we will do is keep Mrs Green in the hospital for a while for observation then we shall transfer her to a convalescent home not far from here.'

'Will Jean be able to visit?' Alice asked in a practical tone.

'Of course,' Nurse Stevens replied. 'We encourage family members and friends to come during visiting hours; it helps our patients see there is light at the end of the tunnel.'

'See, Jean,' Flo said encouragingly, 'it's going to be all right.'

Jean said nothing and as Flo looked at her friend she could see that she hadn't heard a thing she had said. Instead, she was no doubt focused on Bess and what the future would look like. Flo understood. She had been just the same when Neil died, unable to hold on to a single thought as so many fears, worries and memories passed through her mind.

'I would suggest that whilst she will be grateful to have you around, Jean, Mrs Green would also like the support of your mother, and I think she could be a great help to you too. Could you contact her and let her know what's happened?' Nurse Stevens said, her voice more gentle now.

Jean nodded. 'I'll tell her, but I don't reckon she'll be able to come. She lives on the Isle of Wight; it'll be hard for her to make the journey.'

The nurse nodded. 'All right, well, perhaps in time.'

'Can I see her now?' Jean asked. 'She'll want me to be with her.'

Nurse Stevens nodded. 'Of course. But I must warn you that your sister is barely conscious because of all the medication we've given her and she's covered in bandages. It's nothing to worry about, but I want you to know that the sight of her will be quite shocking at first so you should be prepared.'

Jean nodded and stepped forward before turning back to glance at Flo, gesturing for her to come along. Spotting the exchange Nurse Stevens shook her head.

'I'm sorry,' she said, 'the rest of you will have to wait a few more days. Family only for now.'

With that Nurse Stevens turned on her heel and led Jean down the corridor towards one of the wards.

As Flo sat back down on the hard wooden chair, she glanced at Alice and could see her face was contorted with worry.

'You all right?' Flo asked.

'I was going to ask you the same question,' Alice replied. 'How are you feeling?'

As Alice gestured around her at the hospital ward, Flo nodded; she knew what her friend meant. 'You mean am I all right with being around such a tragedy after Neil's death?'

Alice winced at the bluntness of Flo's statement. 'I didn't mean it quite like that.'

'Truly, Alice, I'm fine,' Flo lied, her mind full of Neil.

'So what's on your mind?'

'To be honest I'm wondering why Jean told the nurse her mother lived on the Isle of Wight.'

'Did she?'

'Yes, and I could have sworn blind she told me they had lived in Cornwall.'

'Well, I'm sure you've just got hold of the wrong end of the stick, Flo,' Alice reasoned. 'I mean, Jean's not going to lie about where she's from.'

Flo shrugged. 'Then there was the fact Bess is called Mrs Green. Did you know she had been married before?'

Frowning at the question, Alice shook her head. 'I didn't, but then I don't know Bess well enough to know about her personal life.'

'Well, I ought to know, they lodge with me,' Flo exclaimed.

Alice sighed. 'Just because we're friends doesn't give us all the right to know each other's secrets.'

'I know.' Flo shifted in her seat. 'I just get the sense something's not quite right. And if Jean or Bess are in trouble, well, we owe it to them to help in any way that we can.'

Chapter Fourteen

Over the days that followed, Flo barely saw Jean. Understandably she had devoted herself to her sister, taking most of her belongings from Flo's home and moving them temporarily to Bess's lodgings in Hayes.

Naturally, Jean's return to Liberty's was put on hold, as Henry, Mr Button and the board all agreed Jean should have as much time as she needed before returning to work.

In fact it was something Mr Button had been stoic about as he called Flo up to his office the following day.

'You must insist that Jean doesn't return until she's ready,' he said to Flo, his fingers steepled together as he contemplated the situation. 'The board all agree this is a delicate matter and we want to help any way we can. Jean will have to become her sister's carer once Bess is discharged, at least for a time until Bess gets used to things. Consequently, we need to give her as much time as possible to sort this situation out. It's a shame as she has only just been reinstated.'

Flo nodded. 'Of course, we're all desperately sad for them both.'

'Have the hospital given any indication of when Bess will be discharged into the convalescent home?'

'I don't think so,' Flo said, 'but Jean will hardly want to leave her even when she is moved.'

'Understandable,' Mr Button agreed. 'They are close, aren't they?'

'They are.' Flo nodded. 'It's made it that much harder for Jean that she blames herself.'

Mr Button frowned as the strong November wind caused the sash windows to rattle. 'Why on earth is that?'

'Because they needed the money when they moved to London. That was why Bess volunteered to be a canary girl. At twenty-eight shillings a week the pay was far better than any other work she could have got.' Flo sighed. 'Jean feels that if she too had gone for something that paid more highly rather than working in a job she adored, Bess might not have had to work in a dangerous munitions factory.'

'That's a lot of ifs, buts and maybes,' Mr Button said with a raised eyebrow. 'But it's natural to feel guilty when our loved ones are put in danger.'

At the remark Flo said nothing. She was all too aware of the guilt she felt on a daily basis over the way she had deceived her husband. She was doing her best to be strong, but often she would find herself staring aimlessly at order books, wondering how on earth so much tragedy could hit her small but perfectly formed family. It seemed to Flo that there was very little fairness left in the world.

'Can you manage without Jean or would you like an extra set of hands?' Mr Button asked, interrupting Flo's thoughts.

Flo jumped in surprise at the offer of extra help. 'What about all the cuts you've had to make lately? Do you have the budget for more help?'

Mr Button's eyes twinkled with mischief. 'Not really, but we can't afford to leave fabrics short-staffed. How would you feel if I lent you Mr Masters occasionally?'

At the thought of Mr Masters based in fabrics more frequently Flo smiled. Sales would definitely be on the up whenever he was on the floor.

'I think Mr Masters would be a great help,' she said. 'But I'm not sure he would be enough, sir, and nor am I really sure he has the time, what with his extra duties.'

Giving a slight nod of his head, Mr Button leaned back in his chair and thought for a moment. 'What about if I asked Evie Allingham to help out on the floor?'

'Evie Allingham?' Flo echoed in disbelief. 'But doesn't she work at Botheringtons?'

'Not for some time, though she still has a brother on the board there,' Mr Button replied. 'I believe they are estranged. Regardless of all that she's extremely knowledge-able about fabrics, which is why she has been consulting for the Board of Trade alongside me. Mrs Allingham is also a highly talented seamstress and has always held Liberty's in very high esteem. After all,' he said, letting out a tinkling laugh, 'Botheringtons is hardly Liberty's, is it? I think she would be a real asset to the shop floor.'

Flo thought for a minute. There was no doubt that they would need an extra pair of hands but how would Dot react to Evie working at the store?

'Have you spoken to Dot?' she asked before she could change her mind.

Mr Button frowned. 'What on earth does it have to do with Dorothy? But no, for what it's worth I haven't men-tioned it to her. Should I?'

'No, not at all, sir,' Flo said quickly. 'I think it's a mar-vellous idea and I'm sure Dot will too. Thank you, sir, we shall look forward to welcoming Mrs Allingham to the department.'

'Over my dead body,' Dot said, kicking a box of buttons in the stockroom with such force the box tipped over, spilling its contents across the floor. 'How can Edwin even think of getting that woman to work here?'

'I don't think it's going to be that bad, Dot,' Flo said consolingly as she stooped to pick up the flood of buttons. 'It's only temporary.'

'There's nothing temporary about that floozy's intentions. She's after my Edwin,' Dot hissed. 'And I tell you this as well: if she thinks she can come in here and get her feet under the table without a fight she's got another think coming.'

'Dot, I really think you're getting this out of proportion,' Flo said. 'She's only joining us temporarily, and part-time at that. Mr Masters is going to help us out too.'

At the mention of Henry Dot raised an eyebrow. 'I heard he was a big hit with the ladies last time he was on the floor.'

'He was certainly good with the customers, if that's what you mean.'

'And you 'n' all.' Dot said in a knowing tone. 'Seems as if our deputy manager's taken a shine to you.'

Flo blushed. 'Don't be silly, Dot. I appreciate his knowledge about fabrics, that's all. He knows what he's on about, as does Evie Allingham. She's not interested in Mr Button; you've got to stop this, you'll send yourself mad.'

Picking up the upended box, Dot promptly sat down; then she rubbed her eyes with the heels of her hands. 'Oh, ignore me, Flo, I'm sure you're right. I'm being a silly old sod, but it was sweet of you, darlin', to tell me before breaking it to the others.'

Sitting beside the older woman on the box, Flo said, 'All this jealousy isn't like you. Why are you so bothered now?'

Dot looked at Flo. 'I don't know what's got into me, love. I suppose it's because I've finally realised just how much I've loved having Edwin back in my life. I fought against my feelings for so long – I felt I was letting George down by finding love again. It was daft of me to get so upset, as if my George, the most loving, loyal, funny and wonderful man in the world, would ever think I was betraying him. I know now he would have wanted me to get on with life.'

Flo nodded. The idea of ever loving another man seemed unthinkable. Although Dot had been alone for almost three decades – was that something she was willing to face?

'I suppose now I've realised how much I love the bones of Edwin, I'm terrified someone's going to take him away,' Dot continued. 'I've only just got used to having someone special in my life again; I don't want to lose him.'

Immediately Flo clamped an arm around Dot and pulled the matriarch in towards her. 'You're not going to lose him. It's you he loves; I can see it in his eyes. And to be honest, it doesn't matter a jot if Evie Allingham has set her sights on Mr Button because he's not going anywhere.'

Dot lifted her head from Flo's shoulder and smiled. 'When did you get so wise?'

'I learned it all from you,' Flo replied coyly.

'Then take this from someone who knows,' Dot said sagely. 'It's early days and I know the idea of being with someone else couldn't be further from your mind now, but don't close yourself off from living your life. You're still here, and you deserve to find happiness, with whoever, doing whatever. Do you hear me? Don't run from it, Flo darlin'.'

Flo shuffled uncomfortably in her chair. 'I'm not running, Dot, I just couldn't imagine ever being with anyone else. I will only ever want Neil.'

'I know that,' Dot said quietly. 'I'm not saying that you should even think about finding someone else. What I am saying is don't stop living. It took me a long time to understand it myself, but your Neil's gone now ...'

A stabbing pain pushed its way through to Flo's heart and she felt the loss as sharply as she had when she'd first discovered that Neil had died. 'I just keep going over and over it,' she whispered. 'I keep thinking that if I had been honest with him, if I had just told him the truth about me singing and why it was important to me, then perhaps he wouldn't have died and we might have been able to sort things out.'

'Don't be so silly,' Dot cried, her mouth falling open in alarm. 'You can't think like that. Nothing you did or didn't do affected what happened to that blessed boat, and I can tell you this for sure: your Neil didn't hate you, he could never have. He loved you, Flo. He always loved you, no matter what he said.'

'But that letter ...' Flo's voice trailed off miserably as she remembered the pain of those words.

'That letter was him spouting off like all men do,' Dot insisted. 'You mustn't take that to heart, love. How many times have we all said things and regretted them? I bet you told Neil on more than one occasion what a soft sod he was, but I bet he didn't go around thinking you hated him.'

Flo shook her head as she wiped the tears from her eyes.

'Then that's what you have to think about, that and the fact he wanted you to be happy.' Dot said patiently. 'So if you find happiness then don't turn your back on it just because you think you're doing a disservice to Neil. Your heart's big enough to love all sorts of things and people in all sorts of ways.'

'Like yours, you mean?' Flo sniffed.

'Just like mine, darlin',' Dot replied, holding Flo's hand and giving it a squeeze.

'And does that heart stretch to loving Evie Allingham?' Flo asked cheekily.

There was a pause then before Dot spoke. 'I'm human, Flo love, not a bloody saint. I refer you to my earlier comment – over my dead body.'

Chapter Fifteen

As it turned out, Evie Allingham was delighted to be asked to join Liberty's and she started on the floor the following Thursday. Flo knew that Mr Button had asked the new fabric recruit to work just a couple of afternoons a week. Consequently, it came as something of a surprise when she found a petite woman with dark hair piled high on her head, in a fabulously elaborate style, rifling through the rolls of utility print early that morning.

'Can I help you?' Flo asked sharply.

Spinning round, the woman, who Flo could see was easily in her early fifties, gave her a winning smile. 'You must be Mrs Canning, the fabric manager. I'm Evie Allingham.'

'Pleased to meet you,' Flo said, extending a hand towards the woman as she breathed in great clouds of Bourjois's popular perfume, Evening in Paris. 'I've heard a lot about you.'

'And I you,' Mrs Allingham replied. 'Mr Button can't sing your praises enough.'

'That's very kind. And he tells me great things about you, of course.'

'Oh, all nonsense.' Mrs Allingham chuckled, waving Flo's compliments away. 'I'm a glorified seamstress is all.'

'I'm sure you're a lot more than that.' Flo was warming to the woman. 'As I understand it you virtually ran the fabric department at Botheringtons – not to mention the store! – and that was well before we women were having to step up and take on these roles.'

'Stuff and nonsense,' Mrs Allingham insisted. 'We had a much smaller operation, though we did of course always want to have Liberty's customers.'

Flo laughed at the woman's honesty. 'Our customers are fantastic and very loyal. We like to say that once a customer crosses the threshold of Liberty's they never want to leave.'

'That's certainly true,' Mrs Allingham said, running her hands longingly over the rolls of new utility print. 'I could never understand how Liberty's did it, the fabric at Botheringtons was always good, but never quite this good.'

'Well, you've crossed over to the other side now,' Flo said cheekily, 'and it's a pleasure to have you here. Though I must confess I wasn't expecting you until this afternoon.'

Mrs Allingham looked shame-faced. 'I wasn't supposed to be here but darling Edwin let me sneak in a little earlier after I told him how desperate I was to lay my hands on Liberty fabric.'

Flo would have preferred it if Mr Button had spoken to her first about letting in a new staff member unsupervised. She didn't want to make a fuss but there was something about it that didn't seem right. However, before she had a chance to comment further on the matter the sound of footsteps behind her caught her attention. Turning around she saw Alice, Rose and Mary walking across the floor towards the department.

'Right on time, girls,' she said with a smile. 'This is Mrs Allingham. She's here to help us out a couple of afternoons a week.'

'Four afternoons, dear,' Mrs Allingham put in. 'And please, I know all you girls call each other by your first names so do address me as Evie. I so want to fit in with you all.'

Alice extended her hand. 'I'm Alice Milwood and it's very nice to meet you, Evie. If you need any help with anything be sure to let us know.'

'I'm Rose Harper,' the younger girl said, stepping forward and extending her hand in the direction of Evie. 'I work upstairs and just popped down here for some paperwork and this is Mary Holmes-Fotherington.'

'Lovely to meet you.' Mary smiled. 'Do let us know if there is anything at all any of us can do to help you.'

Evie clapped her hands together excitedly. 'And it's wonderful to meet all three of you. I must say I am so thrilled to be working with you.'

'And we are as well,' Flo said evenly as she made her way towards the desk to go through the sales figures for the previous day. 'Now, may I suggest you spend the morning in the stockroom familiarising yourself with the stock we have – and the guard books of course.'

'Oh, there's no need for any of that,' Evie cried. 'I've been working in fabrics longer than you've been alive. The Lord has sent me to help you, my dear, so just hand me my sales book and I'll get going.'

Flo frowned. She wasn't sure what God had to do with this particular moment, but Liberty's had procedures. 'We do have a strict hierarchy in service, Evie, I'm sure you understand that.'

Evie shrugged. 'Who are we to get bogged down in such matters? Edwin asked me to help out and I'm good with customers.'

'And keen on taking our commission,' Mary muttered, just out of Evie's earshot.

Flo glared at Mary, before turning to Evie. 'I really do think that on this occasion it would be better for everyone if you would do as I ask, Evie. Call it humouring me if you prefer.'

A cloud passed across Evie's features for a second before she gave a small nod of her head. 'Very well then, but, Flo dear, a word of advice: seniority isn't always how long you've spent at a place, but more the wealth of knowledge you've built up. That was the way of it at Botheringtons anyway and it served us rather well.'

Flo felt a small burst of rage pass through her. Evie might seem nice enough but she surely couldn't expect to come in here and dish out orders. Smiling sweetly, though she felt anything but, Flo rested her gaze on the department's newest recruit. 'And while I appreciate that, Evie, and of course have nothing but respect for you coming to work here and all the experience you have gained, I'm afraid I must remind you that at Liberty's we do things a little differently and it's perhaps just one of the many reasons our customers return to us time and time again. That's the Liberty way and it's served *us* rather well over the years.'

As she finished speaking Flo was sure she saw sparks fly from the corners of Evie's thin-lipped mouth and braced herself for retaliation. Yet the woman recovered quickly and instead gave Flo a small smile. 'You're quite right, Flo. Do call me when you need me.'

With that Evie turned around and made her way to the stockroom. Once she was out of sight Flo let go of the breath she hadn't realised she had been holding.

'Blimey, she's a handful, ain't she?' Alice marvelled.

'Reminded me of my old French teacher at school,' Mary added, tugging her black woollen dress straight. 'Frightening beast she was. I thought you and her were going to slug it out amongst the rayon, Flo!'

Flo rolled her eyes. 'Don't be ridiculous, Mary. Though I'll admit she's mildly terrifying.'

'Mildly?' Rose echoed. 'We don't want another Mrs Matravers.'

At the mention of their old deputy store manager the girls fell quiet.

'Anyway,' Flo said, turning brightly to Rose, eager to change the subject. 'You wanted some paperwork from me?'

To Flo's surprise Rose shook her head. 'No, I wanted to talk to you. The fundraising evening is coming up soon and we need to start rehearsing. Can you make Sunday night for a first rehearsal in the sewing room?'

Flo looked doubtful. 'I told you, Rose, I'm not singing.'

'I know that,' Rose said, her tone gentler now. 'But you can play the piano beautifully and I'm short a pianist after Mr Hannington from carpets let me down. Surely you wouldn't mind doing that?'

At the request, Flo cocked her head and regarded her friend. Even though she did a good job of disguising the fact she struggled to see, the white stick she carried and the way her eyes roamed were giveaways. Rose had been through so much, yet despite a setback earlier that year had returned stronger than ever. Here she was doing her best to muck in and make an effort, putting all her troubles behind her. Shouldn't Flo be big enough to do the same?

'Yes, come on, Flo,' Alice chimed in. 'You can't put it off forever. Besides, it will do you good to at least be around music again. I bet you've not been near a piano since ...'

Alice's voice trailed off and Flo felt a pang of grief rise within her. It had been several weeks since Neil's funeral and though she liked to think she was coping there were still times when the pain would strike her suddenly and severely. She felt the beginnings of that pain edge their way through her body and it was all she could do not to cry out with the agony of it all.

Catching Alice's gaze, Flo began to shake her head, only for Mary to reach for her arm. 'We all know something of grief here, Flo,' she began in a low voice. 'Each of us has lost something precious and each of us has coped with more than our fair share of dark days. Yet you have your very own magic remedy built right inside you. Not only does that beautiful voice of yours give great joy to others but you also have the power within you to slip somewhere else while you're singing. To lose yourself and your pain for just a few moments while you're doing it. I think I speak for all of us when I say that we wish we had a gift like that. If you don't want to sing out of guilt because you think you're doing something Neil would have hated then that's up to you, but at least play the piano. You deserve a break from the torture.'

As Mary brought her speech to a close, Flo stood and thought for a moment. Her friend was right. Music did bring great comfort, it always had, and now just when she needed this salve more than ever she was denying herself it.

'All right,' she said shakily. 'I'll do it. Rose, what time is rehearsal?'

Chapter Sixteen

Sunday morning dawned bright and clear and for the first time in weeks Flo found herself less burdened by grief than usual. She wasn't sure if it was because she had finally had a good night's sleep, or because she was thinking about playing the piano. But whatever it was, Flo was grateful for it all the same.

Getting off the bus in Hayes, Flo stifled a yawn. She and the rest of the Liberty girls, together with baby Arthur, had got up early to visit Bess in hospital, where by all accounts she was doing well. Flo was pleased to hear it, yet despite feeling rested, the earliness of the hour along with the fact they had endured a slow Sunday bus service had left her feeling weary.

As she and the girls got off the bus, which dropped them a few yards from the hospital, Flo realised that what she actually felt was fear. She wasn't sure if she could cope with the doom and gloom that a visit to Bess's bedside would no doubt bring. Yet Flo also knew that she had to put her own feelings aside. This wasn't about her. This was about Bess and Jean and being there for them in the way the Liberty girls had always been there for her in her hour of need.

Together the girls walked across the road and into the main entrance of the cottage hospital. The smell was the first thing Flo noticed. A heady concoction of carbolic soap that assaulted her nostrils. Struggling for breath, Flo spotted Jean sitting by the door on a hard wooden chair. Gesturing to the others, Flo rushed over to greet her.

'How are you, Jean love?'

Jean smiled as she got to her feet to greet the girls. 'All right. The doctors are with Bess now. She's really looking forward to your visit.'

"Course.' Dot beamed, laying a comforting hand on Jean's forearm.

Taking time to drink in the younger girl's appearance, Flo was relieved to see a brief smile flash across her features. Jean looked pale and drawn, and Flo could see she was putting a brave face on things. She was glad that she and the girls had made the long journey; it would be worth it to try and rally Jean.

'That's what we're here for,' Alice put in. 'You're not alone, Jean, and neither is Bess.'

'How is she?' Flo blurted.

'As you'd expect.' Jean sighed. 'Bess is angry. She always gets angry when things don't go her way and, well, this is something that she says she'll never get used to.'

'She will,' Flo said in what she hoped was a reassuring tone. 'You can get used to anything with enough time. Look at Rose.'

Jean nodded as Rose gave the girl an encouraging smile. 'You make it look so easy. '

Rose laughed. 'Easy was the last thing it was. But some very good friends helped me realise that life went on. Your Bess will get there.'

Turning to Flo, Jean looked hopefully up at her. 'And you, you've been so brave since you lost Neil. I don't know how you do it.'

'I don't know about that. I just keep going through the motions and putting one foot in front of the other, hoping one day it will work out all right,' Flo said, not wanting to reveal the truth that she also often wondered how she was dragging herself through each day.

'Perhaps Bess might listen to you both then,' Jean said, a hint of eagerness to her voice.

'I take it she won't listen to you, darlin'?' Dot asked bluntly.

Jean shook her head, misery etched across her face. 'She won't eat, drink or sleep, let alone talk to me, and I'm worried about her.'

With that Jean gestured for them all to follow her down the corridor and Flo realised she was taking them to Bess's room. Jean pushed open the door and the girls followed her inside.

'Look who I found.' Jean smiled as she steered Flo to the foot of the bed.

The sight of Bess took Flo's breath away. She looked like a lost child swaddled in blankets, and her arm wrapped in white bandages, and she was still yellow from the munitions she worked with. Only the crown of her head showed her true hair colour. Yet despite Jean's protestations she did appear to be making good progress. The burns on Bess's face had started to heal and there was a little colour in her cheeks.

But she also looked as though she had lost weight. The once well-built girl now looked birdlike.

'She's been asleep all morning,' Jean murmured, perching on the bed next to her sister.

'Poor mite,' Alice soothed. 'She needs her rest.'

'Not going to help her hand grow back though, is it?' Rose crudely pointed out.

Mary's eyes widened. 'You can't say things like that.'

'Why not?' Rose shrugged, gripping her cane. 'It's the truth, and if there's one thing I would have appreciated, it was someone telling me the truth when I was in hospital.'

'She's right,' a voice croaked.

Glancing down at the bed, Flo saw that Bess was now awake and looking stonily at the girls.

'How are you, Bess?' Flo asked.

'Oh, you know,' she replied, doing her best to shuffle herself upright. 'As well as can be expected – that's the phrase, isn't it?'

Dot nodded. 'And what do they expect, darlin'?'

Bess smiled at the bluntness of the question. 'Finally a bit of straight talking. I could do with that instead of Jean here trying to drown me in a bath of positivity.'

'It's important,' Jean replied. 'You have to keep your hopes up.'

'About what?' Bess protested. 'As Rose has just rightly pointed out it's not like I'm going to grow my bloody hand back, is it? What's positive about that?'

'Bugger all,' Rose agreed. 'And you've every right to feel fed up. I always felt as if I had to be brave when I first went blind, but I wish I'd roared and wailed a bit like I wanted to. It's hard, love. Even though you know there's a war on, that there's someone else worse off than yourself, that you're supposed to be grateful for the fact you're still alive, it doesn't change the fact you feel downright rotten. The sooner you realise you're allowed to feel like that, the sooner you'll get on with the business of healing and getting used to your new life, because there is a life still waiting for you, Bess, trust me.'

There was a pause then as the girls looked at Rose in surprise. She hardly said two words to a goose and yet suddenly she had made a speech so full of insight it would rival those of Winston Churchill.

'Thanks for that,' Bess muttered. 'You want to start giving the Woman in White a run for her money when she waves the ships off with words of wisdom like that. The men on board'll bloody well top 'emselves.'

Rose looked suddenly shame-faced. 'Sorry.'

'Nothing to be sorry for,' Bess said, her tone softer now. 'You're right, and I know you understand just how I feel.'

'I am trying,' Jean said, dropping a kiss on the young woman's head.

Bess squeezed Jean's arm gratefully with her one good hand. 'I know, and I'm grateful you've never left my side.'

'Has your mother been?' Mary asked.

Rose opened her mouth to speak only for Bess to start talking over her.

'She's too busy but she's sent a telegram.'

'So how long you in here for then?' Dot asked, ignoring hospital regulations and perching next to Jean on the end of the bed.

Bess shrugged. 'A few more days. Then they want me to go to a convalescent home and recuperate for a while.'

'That's a good idea,' Dot agreed. 'It'll help get you used to things before you're back at Flo's. I take it that's what you're still intending?'

Bess and Jean looked at each other and smiled. 'If Flo doesn't mind?'

'I'd be delighted. We'll get everything sorted out for you.'

'Thanks,' Jean beamed. 'We weren't sure. I mean we may not be able to pay as much without Bess's wage and my Liberty's savings.'

'Don't worry about that one bit,' Flo urged. 'It will just be nice to have you both back home where you belong.'

The girls grinned at one another and Flo's smile widened as she saw Jean plant another kiss on Bess's forehead. Perhaps things would work out all right in time.

'So what's new at Liberty's?' Jean asked.

'Well, we've got you a replacement,' Dot said. 'And a right cow she is too.'

'A temporary replacement,' Flo said, shooting Dot a warning look. 'And she's not a cow, and she doesn't have designs on Mr Button.'

At that Dot snorted. 'Mr Masters is helping out as well. Very popular he is with the ladies.'

'Dot!' Flo admonished. 'Will you leave Mr Masters alone?'

'Only saying,' Dot protested, a small smile playing on her lips. 'Anyway, apart from that the fundraising rehearsals start tonight.'

'Oh, excellent.' Jean smiled. 'Are you doing something, Flo?'

'I am. I'm playing the piano, which is more than the rest of you.'

'We're doing costumes, lady,' Alice exclaimed as Arthur yawned and wriggled in her arms.

Mary laughed. 'Yes, don't blame us for the fact you've got a talent we don't have.'

Flo rolled her eyes at their teasing. 'I'm only doing my bit.'

'And I think it's brilliant,' Rose ventured, 'which is why I've decided to resurrect first-aid nights for the public again.'

'Bravo!' Mary applauded. 'About time. Those events were very popular.'

'I know,' Rose agreed. 'I'm feeling so much better about everything now than I was when I started them and I want to move forward. That's why I was hoping, Bess, that when you're well enough, you'd come and talk to us about your experiences.'

'Mine?' Bess looked at Rose in disbelief.

'Well, there was first aid on the spot, wasn't there, when you had your accident?' Alice said, getting to the point.

Bess nodded. 'There was. And doctors told me that without it, my burns would have been far, far worse.'

'So will you?' Rose begged.

'All right,' Bess sighed. 'I mean it's not like I can say no, is it, Rose? You'll only start shouting again.'

With that the girls broke off into laughter, and Flo couldn't help noticing how Jean had never stopped holding her sister's good hand. With a pang she thought how much easier life would be just now if she had someone to hold her hand through her pain.

Chapter Seventeen

There was no other way of describing it, but Flo felt decidedly out of sorts as she made her way back from the hospital to Liberty's. With Rose at her side chattering endlessly about how well Bess had looked and how marvellous it would be when she was recovered enough to join them for first-aid training, Flo found herself nodding and replying in all the right places but her heart wasn't in it.

Instead, all she could think as the bus crawled closer to central London was just how nervous she felt at the thought of playing the piano. She had hummed to herself in the bath since Neil's death, sad lonely melodies filled with pain and anguish, but she hadn't been near a musical instrument. And although she knew that she wasn't breaking her vow of never singing again, playing the piano felt dangerously close.

Despite the warmth of the bus, she shivered at the thought of it, struck by a sudden panic that she would be unable to perform. What if she'd forgotten how to play?

By the time she and Rose reached Liberty's, Flo had worked herself up into such a state that she all but flung herself into the pleating room as if she were about to face the executioner. She just wanted it over with.

'Blimey, someone's keen,' Henry said playfully as Flo burst through the doors and rushed over to the old upright piano in the corner.

'She's been like this all the way back from Hayes,' Rose said, out of breath as she struggled to keep pace with her friend.

Flo lifted the lid of the piano and, pressing gently on middle C, she hummed lightly, relieved to find it was in tune.

'I haven't been like anything, Rose,' she said, turning to face her friend. 'I just want to get on, that's all.'

Rose said nothing, merely shaking her head and scurrying away. Returning her focus to the piano, Flo sat on the stool, her fingers hovering over the keys. As she stared at the notes before her, she realised she was nervous. Taking a deep breath, willing herself to get on with it, Flo pressed lightly on the keys, the first few notes of 'Moonlight Sonata' coming to her instantly. And the music immediately took her to another world; it was as though she could feel herself floating up, out of her body and away to a far-off land where all her heartache disappeared.

As the piece came to an end, she opened her eyes and was surprised to find Henry staring at her, his round eyes filled with surprise.

'You're very good.'

'Thank you,' she replied.

'I mean, did you play all that from memory, no sheet music at all?' he asked, propping himself up on the edge of the piano on one elbow.

Flo nodded. 'I used to play piano as a kid for my Aunt Aggie when she was practising her singing, and for myself, for fun.'

'But I thought you sang?' Henry frowned. 'Didn't you do a turn at a pub?'

'Not any more,' Flo replied, turning her gaze back to the keys, indicating the matter was closed.

'Everything all right?'

'Fine,' Flo replied monosyllabically.

'Well, if that's you when you're fine, I should hate to see you when there's summat really wrong,' he quipped in a broad Yorkshire brogue.

Flo paused for a moment and smiled as she looked back up at him. 'Sorry,' she sighed, running her hands across her face. 'It's been a long day.'

'You went to see Bess, Rose tells me,' Henry said.

'Yes. She's doing well.'

'And how are *you* doing, Flo?' he asked in a quiet voice.

Opening her mouth, Flo was about to reply and say all was fine, when she stopped herself and gazed into Mr Masters' eyes. Something told her that he wanted to know how she really was, and she was sick and tired of pretending.

'Not very well,' she admitted. 'I don't want to play the piano.'

Henry nodded, his face full of understanding. 'Any particular reason? Sick of Vera Lynn perhaps?'

At the unexpected comment, Flo roared with laughter. How could anyone be sick of Vera Lynn?

'No.' She smiled, realising this was the first time she had laughed properly in days. 'Nothing like that. It's just today's been a bit of a difficult day, that's all.'

'Well, you looked like you were enjoying it a minute ago. You looked like you were somewhere else completely.'

Flo said nothing. The truth of the statement only caused her to feel even more guilty at having a few moments away from her anguish.

'Was visiting Bess more difficult than you thought it would be?'

Flo nodded, her hands folded in her lap. 'Yes. It made me think of Neil. I kept wondering if he suffered in his final moments or if he went quickly. Did he think of me as he died, did he still hate me for what I'd done?'

Henry wrinkled his nose. 'Why on earth would your husband have hated you?'

Flo looked at Henry's face. He looked genuinely interested to know, and before Flo could stop herself, the entire story of how she had lied about the singing she had adored and Neil forbidding it came tumbling out. By the time she had finished she hardly knew what to think about herself. She was a terrible person, no matter what the girls had said. She deserved to go through life feeling regret for what she had done. She had let her husband down, and she would have to find a way of living with the guilt.

'I should have been more sensitive,' Flo finished. 'He hated the singing because of his mother. She ran off with a singer. It caused such misery in the family, and I think my singing in the pub reminded him of that terrible time.'

'He should have been more sensitive to the fact that singing made you feel better when you were reeling from the loss of your aunt,' the deputy store manager ventured.

Flo looked up at him in surprise. The pleating room was noisy now as it filled up with performers ready to practise.

'I'd never thought of it like that.'

'There are two sides to every story, Flo,' Henry said. 'But you mustn't worry over whether or not you were a good wife. We've all done things we wish we hadn't and they don't make us who we are.'

As Henry broke off, Flo could see his chin was lowered and his brow furrowed with anger.

'You look like a man who knows something about that.'

Henry's expression softened. 'We've all made mistakes but I do know your decision to keep singing doesn't define you or your marriage. It was just a part of it. You and Neil still loved one another and he wouldn't have written to you so passionately if that weren't true.'

Flo paused for a moment. What if her boss was right? What if this would have been something they would have got over in time?

'You know, Flo,' Henry said, his tone measured as he interrupted her thoughts, 'we all make mistakes with family; it doesn't mean you don't love them any less.'

'It sounds like you know something about that,' she repeated softly.

Henry paled. 'I understand guilt only too well, and just how hard it is to live with. Since I was fifteen I have blamed myself for my father's death.'

Flo looked at him in surprise. 'How could you be responsible for your father's death?'

Briefly closing his eyes, Henry took in a deep breath. 'Over twenty years ago I worked in the mines with my dad. It was a filthy, dangerous place but I was fifteen and what my dad said went. I didn't argue, I respected him, but that didn't mean I always did what he said. One day, I'd had enough and one of my pals suggested bunking off; we wanted to go to the pictures instead. I told Dad I felt too ill to work. Usually he'd never have stood for it – men went down them pits with all sorts wrong with them but they were tough – only Dad knew I wasn't really cut out for life down the mines, no matter how much he wanted me to follow in his footsteps. So instead of tearing strips off me he sighed and said he'd cover my shift. Mum was out all day working herself as a charlady so I knew once Dad had gone that I could go out.'

'So what happened?' Flo coaxed.

'What happened next is that there was an accident down the mine. The shaft broke and killed three men. One of them was my father.'

'I'm so sorry,' Flo breathed.

'It's me that should be sorry, and I am – every single day of my life. If I hadn't lied about being ill like that then Dad would never have gone into work because of me. It's all my fault and I've spent my life ever since that day trying to atone for what happened.'

Instinctively, Flo stood up and reached her hand out to comfort him. 'This isn't your fault. It was just a horrible accident.'

'I know that's true, Flo, but that doesn't stop me blaming myself, or constantly asking what if.' He looked at Flo and rested his hand on hers. The feel of his skin against hers gave Flo comfort and instinctively she felt a bond being formed between the two of them, a connection that only those who felt guilty over the loss of a loved one could understand.

'And I bet you play that game in your head regularly enough too.'

Flo felt her cheeks flush with the knowing in Henry's eyes. It was if he were staring into her soul.

'Yes,' she said. 'I've lost count of the times I've said "what if" in the last month. But you must see that you were in no way to blame for your father's death.'

Henry shrugged, his eyes never leaving Flo's. 'Maybe, maybe not, but what I do know is I've learned to live with this pain and you will too.'

Chapter Eighteen

It meant a lot to Flo to know that Henry understood what she was going through. Their heart-to-heart had helped clear her mind, and had given Flo fresh perspective on Neil and her marriage. She knew she would never forget her husband and that there would be days that the grief would find her. But perhaps there was a way she could carve out a different life for herself.

The following week, after a morning meeting with the other heads of department, Flo saw Dot, Alice and Mary in animated discussion looking like a group of customers who had just found a bargain in the Liberty New Year sale. As for Evie, Flo noticed she was on her own by the window running through what looked like paperwork. Flo did a double-take – the paperwork was her responsibility. Whatever was Evie doing with it? There was no time to find out as Dot beckoned her over.

'You can't have been on the shop floor for more than five minutes, whatever's happened now?' Flo remarked, eyebrow raised.

'She's been here half an hour,' Dot fumed. 'She and Edwin were going through some of the worsted wool fabrics.'

'Worsted wool?' Flo frowned. 'Why?'

'She wouldn't tell us,' Mary hissed, her cheeks flushed with indignation. 'Said it was Board of Trade business.'

'I'll give her Board of Trade business,' Alice snapped. 'Who the flamin' hell does she think she is?'

Flo pinched the bridge of her nose and breathed deeply. She should have known the relative peace and calm of the last few days wouldn't last.

'Let me talk to her,' she said.

'I'll come with you,' Dot said forcefully.

Flo rounded on her. 'No you won't, I am department head. Besides, we don't want a repeat performance of last week when you two nearly went at it like a pair of alley cats. Leave it to me.'

Without waiting for a reply, Flo made her way over to Evie and found that she was actually knee deep in pattern books.

'Morning, Evie,' she called brightly. 'What have you got there?'

Evie's head snapped up and she smiled warmly at Flo. 'Mrs Canning, good morning. I was hoping I would find you. What do you think of this?'

The cool late November sunshine streaming through the windows made it difficult for Flo to see what Evie was handing her. Tilting her head she could make out that Evie was showing her a pattern for a man's utility suit.

'Very nice. But why are you looking at men's suits?' Flo managed, handing the paper back to Evie.

Evie's cheeks flushed with excitement as she checked behind her shoulders to see if anyone might be listening. Catching Dot, Alice and Mary's faces watching agog, Flo felt Evie's hand pull her towards the window away from the girls.

'It's a surprise,' she said in a hushed tone.

Inwardly Flo rolled her eyes. She was fed up with Evie's theatrics. 'All right,' she said, turning away from her. 'If you can't tell me I quite understand, just put the pattern back in the files when you've finished.'

Evie's jaw dropped open in surprise, which gave Flo a small amount of satisfaction: she clearly hadn't given the response Evie wanted.

'No, I can tell you, Flo,' she said earnestly. 'It's just not for everyone's ears.'

'Go on then,' Flo said in a bored tone.

'Well, it's all rather hush hush, but Edwin and I heard last night that the one and only Max Monroe has offered to perform at our fundraising night.'

'What? *The* Max Monroe – the singer who performs with ENSA?' Flo gasped, too stunned to be angry with Evie any longer. 'When? How?'

'Yes, the world-famous singer who entertains the troops as part of The Entertainments National Service Association,' Evie said brusquely. 'It's no secret that Mr Monroe adores Liberty's. Anyway, Mrs Hamble from jewellery told me that when he was in last week – purchasing a beautiful ring, I believe – he was chatting to one of the girls about the fundraiser. Next thing you know he's asking to speak to Edwin, and offering his services as a headline act.'

Stunned, Flo couldn't believe what she was hearing – she had grown up listening to Max Monroe. Aggie had adored his records and together they had danced to them in the kitchen, singing along. Those had been some of the happiest times of her life, and now to think that she was going to get a chance to meet the man behind the music! She couldn't believe it and wished with all her heart that Aggie were alive to see this moment. She would have been over the moon; with a smile Flo imagined her dancing in the aisles of the Palladium as Max performed his famous hit 'Lullaby of the Night'.

'Really? But why would he want to sing for our gala night?' Flo asked.

'Because he will be at home on leave and thinks it will be a wonderful fundraiser.' Evie sighed. 'Really, Flo, I thought you would be delighted rather than be asking me all these questions.'

'It's wonderful,' Flo admitted. 'I'm just a little surprised. That doesn't tell me why you're looking at pattern books, however.'

'We're going to make him a suit out of Liberty print for his performance!' Evie gushed. 'What better advertisement for Liberty's and show of support for Mr Monroe?'

Flo had to admit it was an inspired idea. But why hadn't Mr Button consulted her? Not only was she in charge of the fabric department but she was also on the fundraising gala committee.

'We thought Dorothy and Alice might like to run it up,' Evie said loudly, 'they're such talented seamstresses.'

'With an awful lot on their plate,' Flo pointed out.

Just then Dot, who had clearly had enough of standing back waiting to find out what was going on, joined them, hands on hips, looking for all the world as if she meant business. 'Did I hear my and Alice's names being taken in vain?'

'We were just saying what talented seamstresses you are. Edwin and I—'

'What the hell's Edwin got to do with me being good at sewing?' Dot snapped. 'And I should say it's Mr Button to you, you're not at the Board of Trade now, we're on the shop floor, lady.'

Flo tried not to laugh. Evie had such an air of arrogance about her.

'There's no need to talk to me like that, Dorothy, I was trying to pay you a compliment.'

'Like hell you were,' Dot muttered under her breath, before she caught the warning glance Flo gave her. 'What has me and Alice being good at sewing got to do with anything anyway?'

'We were just saying that Max Monroe is going to perform at the fundraiser,' Flo put in quickly before Evie could upset Dot any further. 'Mr Button thought we could make him a utility suit out of Liberty fabric as a thank you ...'

'And an advertisement,' Evie put in sagely.

Dot nodded, her mouth pressed into a firm line as she looked between Flo and Evie. 'And you want us to knock up this suit, do you? Out of the goodness of our hearts, even though Max Monroe can clearly afford to have his own suits made?'

'Well, really.' Evie tutted. 'I would have thought you would have wanted to help the war effort. Edwin's always saying how enthusiastic you are to help, but your attitude leaves a lot to be desired. I shall have to tell Edwin he's got the wrong woman.'

'Oh, you'd like that, wouldn't you?' Dot spat, drawing herself up to her full height. 'I've seen the way you look at him, darlin'. Where's your respect? You're all but flinging yourself at him night and day.'

'How dare you!' Evie thundered. 'I'm a respectable widow with all my morals very firmly intact, thank you. I've met women like you before, nothing but troublemakers. And if Edwin did have designs on me, who could blame him?'

Dot threw her head back and cackled with laughter. 'Oh darlin', the only designs he's got on you are ones for your funeral corsage. You're that old, it's a wonder you're still standing!'

'Why, you—' Evie began, taking a step towards Dot only for Flo to step between them.

'Ladies, please,' she hissed. 'That is quite enough. If the two of you want to brawl like a pair of alley cats then take it outside and do it in the street where you belong. But I will not have this on the shop floor. You should both know better.'

'She started it,' Dot snarled, nostrils flaring.

'I don't care who started it,' Flo said, her eyes flashing with anger. 'You'll stop it immediately before the store opens. Any more of this carry-on and you'll both be out of a job.'

With that the warring women turned away from one another.

'Sorry, Flo,' Dot said.

'Yes, sorry, Flo,' Evie whispered.

'I should think so,' Flo growled. 'Max Monroe is due to be the entertainment, not you two. Now, Evie, down to the stockroom to sort out the right fabric for the suit. Dot, I want you over at the Counting House looking through our invoices for the month so the paperwork's ready for filing.'

At the instructions both women's faces fell, but there was something in Flo's steely gaze that told them not to argue. As they shuffled off to their respective posts Flo let out a shaky breath. That feeling of lightness had been wonderful while it lasted.

Chapter Nineteen

Flo was glad when lunchtime arrived and she could take a well-earned break. Despite her warnings the petty arguing between Evie and Dot had barely stopped all morning and she had felt as though most of her time had been spent keeping an eye on the two women, rather than concentrating on the fabrics in her charge.

Flo felt the crisp breeze ruffling her hair as she walked through the streets of Soho. She hoped the fresh air might clear her head. Slumping on a bench in Golden Square she watched passers-by scurry past, all in a rush to get somewhere. Flo had half an hour left of her lunch break and was determined to make the most of it, rather than hurrying back.

She had once loved everything about her job at Liberty's but she realised she was fast falling out of love with the store. It pained her to admit it, but it was the truth. Her role felt more like a job than a labour of love, with problem after problem to resolve. The constant arguing between Evie and Dot didn't help and she wasn't relishing the idea of returning for the afternoon.

Leaning back against the bench, a woman rushing through the square caught her eye. As she neared Flo could see it was Jean, walking in the direction of the store.

'Jean!' Flo stood up and waved to attract her attention. 'Are you all right?'

As the young woman approached, Flo could see her face was flushed red with excitement.

'I was just on my way to see you. I wanted to let you know the latest.'

'Go on,' Flo coaxed.

'Bess is being discharged from hospital; she's going into a convalescent home.'

A burst of excitement coursed through Flo's body. It was about time there was some good news.

'That's wonderful. When? Where?'

'She's being discharged the day after tomorrow and is moving to the home just up the road from your house in Islington so I'll be able to move back in with you if you'll have me.'

'Well of course!' Flo beamed. 'It will be wonderful to have you home.'

'It also means I can come back to Liberty's part-time now too.'

'That'll be a relief.' Flo sighed, thinking of Dot and Evie at one another's throats. Perhaps there was a way she could ensure they were never on the same shift if Jean was returning part-time. 'I'm thrilled for you both. Is Bess happy?'

Jean sat next to Flo, her woollen coat pulled up high around her neck to keep out the chill.

'Depends what you call happy,' Jean admitted. 'She's worried about money now she knows she can't go back to the munitions factory, and she's grieving for the loss of her hand.'

'I do understand but people cope with worse,' Flo said matter-of-factly. 'I know that might sound harsh, Jean, but Bess was lucky compared to a lot of people. Her skin's on the way to healing nicely now, and she will get used to life without her hand. Bess is resilient.'

'I know,' Jean sighed, 'it's just she's so capable and she's always been the one to take care of me. Now it's me looking after her, it feels wrong somehow. Bess really needs my help and I don't know if I'm strong enough to give it to her.'

Flo rested a hand on Jean's forearm. 'You're stronger than you think. Look at how you found the courage to stand up to Mrs Claremont, and look at how you've been by Bess's side since her accident. You've given up your job, your home, and you leapt to her aid. That's strength, Jean. She's your sister and you're showing her pure love.'

There was a pause then as an embarrassed flush crept up Jean's neck at Flo's words.

'I'd do anything for her.'

'And that's all she needs to hear,' Flo soothed. 'Trust me, just knowing you're there for her is all Bess wants.'

Jean's news gave Flo a much-needed boost after a difficult morning, and even though the grey November clouds had given way to rain, Flo was feeling a little more like her old self.

Making her way back to the shop floor after lunch, Flo was in such a hurry to check Evie and Dot hadn't murdered one another by the rayons that she almost collided into Henry on the stairs.

'Careful,' he admonished as Flo knocked him with her elbow.

'Sorry,' she said, feeling breathless. 'I didn't see you.'

'Clearly.' He smiled, rubbing his elbow. 'In a rush?'

'Just eager to get on with work,' Flo replied.

'Well, if you have five minutes could you come up to my office?' Henry asked.

Flo frowned. 'Sounds ominous.'

'It's not.' Henry laughed. 'Won't take long.'

Realising she had very little choice, Flo followed her boss back up the stairs and together they made their way through the labyrinth of corridors that led to Henry's office.

'Sit down,' he said, clearing away a pile of guard books that covered the chair opposite.

Flo did as instructed and sat with her hands folded in her lap as Henry took a seat behind his desk.

'I've been doing some thinking,' he went on.

'Oh yes?'

'About you. Well, about your musical talents really,' he continued.

Holding her hands up to stop him right there, Flo shook her head. 'Mr Masters, really, that's very kind of you but you don't have to worry about anything like that.'

'I'm not worrying,' he replied. 'But I've been thinking how music has obviously helped you feel better during some very difficult moments in life. If you don't mind me saying so, I do think it's a shame you don't want to sing any more but I understand. However, playing the piano is clearly good for you. I watched you last Sunday and you were a natural; the music transported you to another world.'

Flo looked at him in surprise. That had been the last thing she had expected him to say.

'Well, thank you,' she said eventually. 'And it's true I enjoy it, but I'm not going to be singing at the fundraiser if that's what you're getting at. Rose has already given me a hard time over it.'

Sensing her discomfort, Henry waved his hands in despair. 'Oh Flo, sorry, I'm making a real hash of this, aren't I? Let me start again. Stan's school are desperate for someone to play piano for their music lessons. They are horribly short-staffed and I wondered if you wouldn't mind helping them out? As you know the board is keen for employees to lend a hand in the community and this fits the bill perfectly. It would be one or two lunchtimes a week.'

As Henry brought his speech to a close, Flo looked into his eyes and could see how much this meant to him. She realised that she was not only flattered to be asked, but that this could also be a very good thing for her too. Henry was right; she missed being involved in music. At the rehearsal she had enjoyed losing herself in the melodies she played, and it had been enough of a salve to provide temporary relief from her pain. It seemed like the perfect opportunity – but there was also her job to consider. She wasn't just a sales girl; she was department manager.

'I just saw Jean outside,' she said carefully. 'She says Bess will be discharged into a convalescent home nearby the day after tomorrow and she thinks she might be able to return part-time.'

Henry's face lit up at the news. 'Well, that's wonderful. And of course it means we would be able to spare you to take time off and help out at the school. And before you ask, I've spoken to Mr Button and he too thinks it's an excellent idea.'

A smile crept across Flo's lips. 'All right then.'

Henry slapped his hand on the desk in excitement and got to his feet. 'Excellent. Can you start tomorrow? One o'clock sharp? After the children's lunch?'

'All right,' Flo nodded.

'And you'll be reporting to Mrs Hallam. She doubles as the singing teacher. Should have been on the stage, in my opinion, but she'll show you the ropes.'

Infused by Mr Masters' excitement, Flo got to her feet with a huge grin on her face. 'Thank you, I appreciate this.'

As she walked out of the door and down to the fabric department, Flo felt her spirits lift. She hadn't realised she had been looking for another challenge to throw herself into, but now it was here, she felt it could be just what she needed.

Chapter Twenty

It was a very gusty and cold Tuesday lunchtime that saw Flo make her school debut as pianist. Pushing open the wooden double doors that formed the main entrance to the school, she was surprised to find she felt oddly nervous. She had been plagued with doubt on the bus all the way to Catford, wondering what she would do if she didn't know the songs. What if the children laughed and pointed at her?

Walking down the corridor towards the hall Flo mentally kicked herself. She would send herself around the bend if she carried on like this. Where was her gumption? She turned the corner and saw Mrs Hallam up ahead, who waved and smiled, and Flo found herself relaxing. There was something instantly comforting about the older woman.

'Flo, love, it's good to see you,' she said, immediately linking her arm through Flo's.

'And you, Mrs Hallam.' Flo smiled. 'Thanks for inviting me.'

'My pleasure, and please call me Celia when we're not in front of the kids,' she replied over the din of the dinner bell. 'Though it's me that should be thanking you, especially because there's every chance you might change your mind when you hear the little darlings sing.'

Flo made a face. 'Are they that bad?'

'Depends if you like the sound of a bag of cats being half strangled to death.' Celia chuckled. 'No, I'm being unkind.

That's not fair on cats. To be honest, Flo, some of them are all right, but we've got through that many piano players in the last few months that our lessons have been sporadic at best.'

'Well, I'm here to remedy that,' Flo said politely.

Celia raised an eyebrow as she led Flo into a large hall. 'Piano's over there, love – all tuned up she is, if you want to go and familiarise yourself. I'll fetch the hordes.'

With that Celia left and Flo sat down on the hard wooden stool. She lifted the lid of the battered wooden upright and traced her fingers across the keys before leaping into 'Three Blind Mice', the song she always liked to warm up with. The moment she struck that first key, she felt as if she had come home, and she lost herself in the music just as she had at the fundraiser rehearsal. The sound of the simple melody lifted her heart and for a moment there was no loss of Aggie and Neil to grieve over, no Liberty's, no Bess, Jean or any of the other girls to think about, there was just the music.

All too soon the sound of excited chatter lifted her from her own world and brought her back to reality as a group of about twenty children filed into the room. Reluctantly Flo stopped playing and smiled at the children as Celia arranged them in a small group to the side of her.

'Now, I've got a wonderful surprise for you,' Celia exclaimed. 'Mrs Canning has agreed to come and play piano for us two days a week. I would like you to give Mrs Canning a very warm Sandhurst Road welcome by putting your hands together.'

The children applauded so noisily, the sound of clapping echoed around the room. Flo beamed and bowed her head at their smiling faces. Spotting Stan in the front, clapping harder than any of them, she gave him a little wave, which made him smile even harder.

'Thank you, children!' Celia, beaming, interrupted the applause. 'Now, today I thought we would start with "The Holly and the Ivy" for the end-of-term assembly. Are you ready?'

The children nodded and Celia turned and raised her eyebrows at Flo. Hurriedly she rifled through the battered sheet music that stood on the music rest. It was a folk song she knew well, and as soon as her fingers struck the keys she was able to switch off and let her hands do the work. Turning her gaze towards Celia and the children she was surprised to find they were quite good. Henry had been right about Celia too: she had an exceptional voice. Flo wondered if she had received training – she certainly seemed to know what she was doing and, best of all, she was inspiring the children to perform as well as they could.

Watching Celia now, who was smiling at the kids with encouragement, Flo was struck with that same feeling she had experienced the last time she had met her. She couldn't work out if it was Celia's smile, her mannerisms, or if she just had one of those faces that seemed familiar.

By the time her hour was up, Flo was surprised to find how much she had enjoyed herself. Stan had stood up and given her a clap and then the rest of the children had followed suit. Flushed with pleasure she waved them goodbye and told them all how much she was looking forward to seeing them in a couple of days.

'That went well,' Celia said as the last of the children filed through the doors.

Flo shut the lid of the piano. 'It did, didn't it?'

'You're a natural, love, you should be on the stage, but I heard that you're not singing any more,' Celia said with a sympathetic smile. 'Henry told me all about it. He seemed quite worried about you.'

'He's a lovely chap.'

'That he is. We've been through a lot together and have been friends a long time,' Celia said with a hint of wistfulness. 'His mother would be so proud of him, taking on that little brother of his too. He's a good man.'

Flo nodded; she was beginning to realise just how lucky she was to have someone like Henry Masters in her corner. He had been a friend when she needed one the most, not only offering a shoulder to cry on, but also giving her practical help and support.

'Henry tells me you were a friend of his mother's,' Flo said.

Celia nodded. 'That's right. I met her when I first moved up north. I didn't know anyone when I arrived and we met at the steelworks. I'd got a job there in the canteen; Ida, Henry's mother, was my boss. She was a right laugh, soon took me under her wing. Oh, the times we had.'

Flo smiled as Celia's eyes took on a faraway expression. Flo could practically see the cogs of her memory turning as though she were back there.

'Did you used to sing there too?' she found herself asking. 'You're a bit of a natural yourself.'

Celia laughed, embarrassed by the compliment. 'Me and my sister used to sing all the time when we was nippers. Then when we were older we'd sing in the pubs, gathering everyone together. They were some of the best times of my life. But when I met Ida, well, she was a wonder herself. There wasn't a song she couldn't sing; we used to entertain the masses on Friday lunchtimes after teatime. Brought the house down, we did ...'

As Celia trailed off, Flo couldn't miss the look of wistfulness in her eyes. 'What about now?' Flo asked. 'I mean I know Ida's not with us anymore, but do you still sing in the pubs?'

Celia shook her head. 'Not any more, love. Besides, it's a young woman's game and I'm too old and too knackered now to do much more than sing for the kids.'

'You're not old!' Flo admonished. Celia had barely more than a few laughter lines around her eyes; Flo placed her a couple of years older than Aggie.

'I still love it though,' Celia continued as if Flo hadn't spoken. 'Takes me away somewhere else when I sing, just like it does for you.'

'Sorry?'

'I saw that look in your eyes, Flo.' Celia smiled. 'You weren't with me in a dusty school hall, you were far away, no doubt living the life of your dreams. Powerful thing, isn't it, following your passions?'

'It's the music,' Flo mumbled, embarrassed to have been caught out like that.

'Get away,' Celia grinned. 'Music's in your blood, girl, just like it is in mine.'

Flo thought for a moment. It was in her blood, but look at how much trouble it had caused. Sometimes following your passions wasn't the right thing to do at all.

'Anyway,' Flo said, scooping up her bag and coat. 'I'd better get back to Liberty's; the customers will be wondering where I've got to.'

Celia nodded as she walked her to the door. 'Thanks for coming today, Flo, I really enjoyed it and I know the children did too. I hope to see you again on Thursday?'

As Flo looked into the Celia's blue eyes, she felt something stir. There was no doubt about it: she felt a connection to this woman, and instinctively felt safe. 'You will. I'm looking forward to it already.'

Walking out into the fresh air, Flo felt a little of the grief she had been carrying for so long now start to shift.

Chapter Twenty-One

Flo enjoyed her second music session at the school as much as the first – they were the highlight of her week. She loved nothing more than getting lost in the music, watching the children's delighted faces as they connected with the songs.

Henry had given her a very welcome gift and she was desperate to thank him. That was why, this Sunday morning, she was taking Henry and Stan to Hampstead Heath, with the promise of a cup of tea and sticky bun in the tearooms, before they joined the girls at the convalescent home to visit Bess over in Edmonton.

It had been Henry who had suggested the outing to visit Bess and he had also insisted that he call her Henry when they were away from the store. Both actions had surprised Flo, and the fact he wanted to extend the hand of friendship to Bess was not something she had expected. She wasted no time telling him this as they devoured cups of tea and freshly baked scones, which tasted to Flo like a little piece of heaven.

'Extending the hand of friendship is something I've always done,' Henry admitted. 'When Dad died, we had so many visitors to the house that it proved a great distraction and also made me realise how loved he was in the community.'

'It must have been a great support to your mum too,' Flo mused, watching Stan take a huge bite out of his second scone.

Henry nodded. 'It was the only thing that pulled her out of those dark, dark times. It was awful, and she rallied, but it was hard for her being so much younger than Dad.'

'How do you mean?' Flo asked, above the din and clatter of cups against saucers.

'She was thirty-three when he died, Dad was forty-eight, so there was a big age gap. She was too young to give up on life.'

'Did she remarry?' Flo asked.

'Eventually,' Henry said. 'But the trouble was that the man she met wasn't a patch on my dad.'

'Was he Stan's father?' she said, chancing a look at the youngster, who was too busy shovelling in the remnants of his scone to pay attention to the grown-ups talking.

Henry nodded. 'We never really got on. He did treat my mum all right, though, and that's all I could have really asked for.'

'Your poor mum,' she managed, 'to have lost two husbands.'

'She broke down after her second husband died,' Henry said, looking across at Stan and ruffling his hair. 'And this one's been a godsend. Everything I do is because of him, and I want him to have a good life.'

'Well, he certainly seems happy enough.' Flo beamed. 'You love singing at school don't you, Stan?'

Stan nodded, crumbs flying from his mouth as he gave Flo a grin that lit up his entire face. 'I like "Everything Stops For Tea" best.'

Flo and Henry laughed at the pride on Stan's face. He was so easy to be around, Flo thought, and she could understand easily why Henry had taken him under his wing. He would be a wonderful little boy to have as a son. For a moment it hit her how much Neil would have adored a son like Stan. She and Neil had planned to have children, and she felt winded at the pain of how her hopes and dreams had been so tragically snatched away. She rubbed her chest to try and get some air into her lungs.

Henry leaned across the table and squeezed her shoulder. 'Flo, are you all right?'

Looking down at his large hand she relaxed and nodded.

'How about we get some fresh air then?' he said gently, before turning to Stan: 'Fancy a run around?'

Flo had anticipated the journey to the convalescent home taking a lot longer than it actually did. With it being a rainy December Sunday Flo had counted on a lengthy service with many changes and lots of time between them. However, they had struck gold with only one bus change that arrived within five minutes.

They arrived earlier than the rest of the girls, which gave them a chance to take in their surroundings. It had stopped raining now and the late afternoon sun bathed the large stone house with a golden glow. Set in well-tended grounds, the convalescent home looked like a stately mansion, with its gleaming white pillars, double front door and sweeping gravel driveway.

'Not bad is it?' Henry said admiringly.

'Are we at another park?' Stan asked, his voice filled with hope.

Flo laughed, and found herself taking the little boy's hand. 'No, we're going to visit a friend of ours who's poorly.'

Stan's eyes widened. 'How poorly? Will she die?'

'She's all right, Stan,' his brother reassured him. 'Nobody's going to die.'

'I certainly hope not,' came a familiar voice. 'At least not today anyway.'

132

Spinning around, Flo saw Bess walking up the path behind her.

'Bess! What are you doing out of bed?' she asked, rushing forward to kiss her cheek.

'It's not a hospital, Flo,' Bess admonished good-naturedly. 'We're encouraged to get out for some fresh air and now the rain has gone it's time to make the most of it.'

'Good idea.' Henry smiled. 'This is my brother, Stan.

'Nice to meet you,' Bess said with a glint in her eye. 'You tell that brother of yours not to sack my sister again.'

'All right,' Stan said. 'Henry' – he turned to face his older brother – 'don't sack this lady's sister again.'

Flo was doubled over with mirth as Henry nodded and promised that he wouldn't.

'We missed Jean on the shop floor,' Flo said after she had recovered from her fit of the giggles.

'She's a hard worker,' Bess agreed, sitting on a wooden bench by the door. 'It's good for her to be around me less. She's been a tower of strength, but I worry it's too much.'

'She's not been herself, that's true,' Flo said, taking a seat next to Bess. 'But she's strong.'

'She's had to be,' Bess muttered, before turning to the little boy. 'So how old are you, Stan?'

'I'm ten years old,' he said with pride. 'I like football and mud.'

Bess giggled. 'They're two of my favourite things too.'

Stan stared at her in surprise. 'But you're a girl! Girls don't play football, and they don't play in mud.'

'Well, this one does.' Bess smiled. 'Or at least she did.'

As Bess cast her eyes downwards, Flo followed her gaze. Her right arm was in a sling, the missing hand still bandaged up. Flo ran her eyes across the rest of Bess, and was pleased to see she looked as if she was on the mend. Her burns were healing well and she had some of her colour back in her face. She had lost the yellow skin tone too after being away from the munitions factory for a few weeks. Looking at her hairline, Flo could see that Bess's hair was beginning to grow back. Like everything in life the scars were beginning to heal, but Flo also knew that not every injury was visible.

'How are you doing really, Bess?' Flo asked in a low voice.

Bess turned her face up towards Flo and smiled. 'I'm all right. I'm beginning to come to terms with what happened and I'm ready to go home.'

'Have they said when that might be?' Flo asked.

'No idea,' Bess sighed. 'But I won't make a fuss, though I do want to start living a normal life as much as I can.'

'Quite right.' Henry nodded approvingly. 'Rose mentioned that she wanted you to take part in her first-aid nights at the store. She's starting them up again next week.'

Bess's face brightened at the prospect. 'Well, count me in, I'd love to help.'

'Already?' Flo asked visibly shocked. 'Don't you think it's too soon?'

'Not for me.' Bess shook her head in defiance. 'I've spent most of my life fighting to survive. Now things are different; at least I can encourage other people. There are times when I'm still hit by the weight of what happened. I look down at my right hand and I feel shocked to see nothing but a stump. But I know that so many other people have faced worse traumas than I have. Look at Rose, she's lost much of her sight and is still doing her bit for the war effort. She is an inspiration to me, and it's only right I pay her back in some way.'

'Well, if you're sure then the event starts at six next Wednesday,' Henry offered.

'I'll be there,' Bess promised.

Flo looked at Bess's face. She could see she meant it too. There was something about her determination that inspired Flo. If Bess could get on with making the most of her life after a setback, perhaps Flo could too.

Chapter Twenty-Two

Up until eleven that morning Flo had been enjoying a run-of-the-mill Tuesday at work. She had answered a lady's queries about what was likely to be in the legendary Liberty's New Year sale, she had dealt with a customer who wanted to buy some new utility print, and also sorted through the long-neglected button drawer.

She was just considering whether or not she had time for tea before the lunchtime rush when the sound of a confident stride echoing across the shop floor made her look up and give a start of surprise.

Larger than life, with a smile that engulfed his entire face and a set of dazzling white teeth that perfectly offset a thick head of black hair that was unbelievably rich and deep in colour: the man in front of Flo was instantly recognisable.

'Max Monroe,' the man said, extending his hand towards hers. 'I'm delighted to meet you.'

'And I you, sir,' Flo replied cautiously. 'Florence Canning, fabric department manager.'

Usually they were briefed about any important customers coming into the store but nobody had said a word to her about Max Monroe putting in an appearance.

Just then the sound of another set of heels skittered across the floor. 'Max darling, I'm so sorry I wasn't here to greet you.' Evie's voice boomed loud and clear as she sidled up to him. 'Mrs Canning, this is Max Monroe.'

'Yes, we've just done the introductions,' Flo said, aware her tone was a little clipped. 'Tell me what brings you to the fabric department today, sir?'

'Darling Max is here to pick out a fabric for the suit we're making him,' Evie gushed, linking her arm through his to try and drag him away to the rolls of print.

Hearing the sounds of Dot saying goodbye to her customer, Flo turned to the Liberty's matriarch. 'Mrs Hanson, allow me to introduce you to Max Monroe.'

'Hello, sir. Pleasure to meet you. Is there something we can help you with today or are you happy browsing?'

'Mr Monroe is a star,' Evie hissed. 'He is not just browsing. Dot, go and fetch him a cup of tea,' she ordered before turning back to Max, who had remained silent as he watched the exchange agog. Now, however, he put his hands up to protest.

'Really, there's no need.'

But Evie smiled reassuringly. 'Dot doesn't mind, do you?'

'I ain't fetching nobody nothing,' Dot said in a firm tone. 'I am more than happy to help Mr Monroe with his purchase but I ain't anybody's whipping boy! If the man wants a cuppa, I suggest you fetch it yourself, Evie Allingham.'

Flo giggled inwardly as she watched Evie turn puce. Turning to their unexpected guest, she gave him a sweet smile that didn't quite reach her eyes. 'Actually, sir, I am sorry but nobody will be able to fetch you a cup of tea as we don't allow beverages on the shop floor. I'm sure you understand?

Max Monroe nodded and smiled at Flo. 'Ladies, it's not a problem at all. Why don't we just pick out some delicious fabric, Mrs Hanson. I would love to hear your recommendations. You look like a lady who knows her way around a suit.'

'She does when there's a fella in it,' Evie muttered under her breath, just loud enough for Flo and Dot to hear.

Flo winced as she watched Dot draw herself up to her full height and shoot Evie a menacing stare. This wasn't going to be pretty.

'Mr Monroe, it would be my pleasure to show you some of the fabrics I think would work. Would you follow me please?' Dot said in a calm voice that surprised Flo.

As she led Mr Monroe out towards the fabrics, Flo turned on Evie and whispered, 'In the stockroom. Now!'

Leading Evie down to a quiet corner of the room, she rounded on the new employee. 'I've had just about enough of your petty jibes, Mrs Allingham,' she hissed.

Evie seemed dumbfounded as she opened and closed her mouth. 'How dare you talk to me like that? I'm a consultant on the Board of Trade. You should show me some respect.'

'And you should show your colleagues some respect,' Flo snapped. 'You didn't make a fool of Dot with that cheap insult of yours, but you did make a fool of yourself.'

'That woman has been mean to me ever since I got here,' Evie protested.

'You've done nothing but wind her up,' Flo retorted. 'And do you realise you sound like a child? Now stay down here for a while and sort the remnants pile. I don't want to have this conversation with you again.'

With that she turned on her heel and left Evie simmering in the stockroom. Walking up the stairs towards the shop floor, Flo did her best to calm down; it would not be good at all to greet customers fuming. Taking a deep breath to steady herself, she walked out on to the floor and saw to her delight that Dot was talking animatedly to Max Monroe.

'I hope you're taking advantage of all of Mrs Hanson's expertise?' Flo smiled as she watched Dot take out a roll of worsted wool. 'If anyone knows about fabrics it's this woman.'

Max frowned. 'But I thought you were in charge.'

'I am.' Flo nodded. 'But Dot has a wealth of experience.'

'And not all of it in fabrics either,' Dot replied tartly. 'Not that anyone takes any notice of me.'

Laughing, Max ran his hand along the fabric as instructed by Dot. 'I can't believe that's true for a second.'

'No, it's not.' Flo chuckled. 'We would be lost without her.'

'You'd survive.' Dot winked at Max. 'Now, sir, how about this one? It would be good for performing, wouldn't it, Flo?'

Flo ran her hand across the material. It was one of her favourite heavier fabrics, which moved with the wearer. 'I agree. It's perfect for a performance. I had a dress made up in it last year that I liked to use when I sang.'

'You sing?' Max's eyes lit up.

Flo looked abashed. 'Not any more. I used to … I play the piano now.'

'Don't you pay any attention to her,' Dot said with an eye roll. 'She's a natural. All talent she is, Mr Monroe. You've never heard anything like it, yet she won't sing no more.'

'Why?' Max asked, getting right to the point.

Flo found herself faltering; it was such a personal thing to explain, but much to her surprise Max seemed to understand.

'You don't have to tell me; the ingredients that make up our talents are deeply personal. I've had times in my career when I couldn't sing,' he replied in his lilting, slightly American accent, that Flo guessed came from spending so much time working in the States.

'Really?' Flo gaped at him in surprise.

'Really,' Max affirmed. 'You'll come back to it when you're ready.'

Flo nodded, amazed someone understand so readily.

'In the meantime, you said you played piano?' He scratched his chin thoughtfully. 'I like to take a chance on new performers and my regular pianist can't get the time away from ENSA. How would you feel about accompanying me for my performance? Might get you in the mood to sing?'

Flo opened her mouth to speak, only for Dot to beat her to it. 'Are you sure, Mr Monroe? I mean, you ain't heard her. She's good enough for our girls, but you must have a professional on stand-by. She could make those ivories sound like an out-of-tune parrot for all you know.'

Max laughed once more, revealing all his gleaming white teeth as he did so. 'I'm willing to take the chance if you are,' he said, turning to Flo. 'If Mrs Hanson speaks this candidly in front of you I have a good feeling. What do you say?'

'I should be honoured.'

'Then that's settled' – Max beamed – 'as is the material for my outfit. Are you going to run it up for me, Mrs Hanson? If your sewing skills are as sharp as your tongue, I'll be in safe hands.'

At the quip, Dot giggled. 'Yes, Mr Monroe, I can run up your suit. Now if you'd just like to accompany me to the pattern-cutting table, I can measure you up and we can go from there.'

'Excellent, thank you, Mrs Hanson. And, Mrs Canning, I shall look forward to your accompaniment at rehearsal on Thursday.'

With that he turned on his heel, leaving Flo shaking her head in surprise. What a treat to be playing the piano for

Max Monroe. Aggie would have been over the moon and it struck Flo with astounding clarity just how cruel life could be that she wouldn't be here to see it.

She wondered what Evie would say as she was the one who had brought Max in. But Flo quickly realised she didn't care what Evie thought. In fact she didn't care what anyone thought. It was time to take a leaf out of Bess's book and start living her life while she still had the chance. You never knew what was around the corner.

Chapter Twenty-Three

That Wednesday Flo returned to her new role at the school with more than a spring in her step. Learning that she would be playing for Max Monroe had left her feeling elated and more than confident in her own skills as she walked into the large school hall.

Lifting the piano lid Flo ran her fingers across the keys and found she couldn't stop smiling.

'Well, you look like the cat that got the cream,' Celia marvelled as she walked into the hall. 'What's happened to you?'

'Nothing … Well, something.' She explained to Celia that her piano skills were now in demand. Jaw dropping in shock, Celia tried to talk, but failed, standing there looking like a goldfish for what felt like hours but was in fact only a few seconds. 'You're playing for Max Monroe?'

'The very same.' Flo grinned.

'Oh my days!'

'Well, why don't you come?' Flo said suddenly. 'Bring your husband.'

Now it was Celia's turn to make a face. 'My husband's long gone. Just me now.'

'Oh, I'm sorry,' Flo said sincerely.

'No need to be,' Celia said brightly. 'But my sister would be screaming in her grave if she knew I was working with someone who was playing the piano for Max Monroe of all people. She loved him, she did … Flo love, are you all right?' Celia asked, squeezing Flo's arm gently.

Flo, who had become lost in reminiscence, came to. 'Sorry,' she said, blinking the unexpected tears from her eyes. 'I was just thinking about my aunt.'

'Oh love, I am sorry,' Celia apologised. 'I shouldn't have been so silly. And your husband died not so long ago as well, didn't he?'

'Yes,' Flo said, feeling a lump catch at the back of her throat. 'I'm so sorry, Celia, I don't know what's got into me.'

Taking her arm, Celia led Flo to a chair and instructed her to sit down.

'It's grief, Flo,' Celia said, her voice barely more than a whisper. 'It's a funny thing. Hits you when you least expect it. I've loved and lost in my time and there were days I thought I would never get over it. One day I'd be fine, then the next it was as though someone had hit me square across the back of my head. I've never felt a pain like it.'

Flo nodded. 'It's as though I have become a duller version of myself,' she said, grateful now for this chance to be honest. 'Before, I used to feel so happy that even when war broke out, even when Neil joined the Navy, I could see the pleasure in life. Now I sometimes I wish I could get run over or even bombed, just so something would take me out of my misery.'

There was a silence then and for a second Flo wondered if she had gone too far. But when she saw there were tears in Celia's eyes, she could tell her new friend understood entirely.

'I felt like that when I said goodbye to my husband. He was a waste of space, but he was my waste of space. When he was gone, it was as though my world went with him. Then when my sister died I was so angry and I wondered how I could stand to be in a world filled with so much pain.'

Flo nodded. 'I keep trying to be brave, really I do.

At that Flo felt Celia wrap her warm hand over her cold one. 'Sweetheart, I understand, and I'll tell you this: you never have to put a brave face on anything when I'm around.'

Despite Flo's tears, it had in fact turned out to be a lovely lesson. The children had pulled Flo from her dark mood; they had adored singing the Max Monroe songs that Celia had insisted they try, and although Flo had been worried about deviating from the official hymn book she was expected to play, Celia had assured her all would be well and she would take the blame if there was any trouble. As Flo made her way back to work, she couldn't take the smile off her face.

She pushed open the old staffroom doors at Liberty's and took off her hat and coat. Keen not to become doom-laden once more, she made her way to Rose's office. There was only an hour left of store trading and instead of going back to the shop floor she had offered to help her friend set up for the first-aid night. As she neared Rose's office Flo was surprised to hear the sound of laughter. Pushing open the door, she saw Bess and Rose sitting opposite each other giggling over a mound of first-aid supplies.

'What's all this?' Flo gasped in surprise.

At the sound of Flo's voice the girls grinned. 'We're putting the world to rights,' Rose said. 'Bess has been reminding me what life was like when I was in hospital and recuperating.'

'Oh no,' Flo groaned, perching on the edge of Rose's desk. 'Is the convalescent home that bad?'

Bess shook her head. 'It's not bad, I mean I'm free to come and go as I like now and I'll be able to stay with Jean in a few weeks for a couple of days at a time to help me get used to normal life. It's just not what I'm used to. Me and Rose here were swapping war stories.'

Flo nodded in understanding, very much aware that this seemed like a private conversation she had intruded upon, and she got to her feet, intending to go. 'You must let me know if there's anything I can do, Bess, won't you?'

'You're doing more than enough,' Bess said reassuringly. 'You just keep taking care of my Jean. I worry about her.'

Flo sighed. 'And she worries about you.'

'There's no need for her to worry about me,' Bess replied tightly. 'I'm the one that looks out for her; she knows that. Now shall we get down to the crypt and start sorting everything out?'

'Good idea.' Rose smiled, getting to her feet.

As Bess followed, Flo took a minute to assess her. She looked as if she was doing much better than she had been. Her face had filled out a bit more now, and the long dark hair she had always worn long down her back had been cut into a short bob around her ears, highlighting her angular cheekbones. Although she still had her right arm in a sling, Flo was delighted to see that the old fire was in her heart. Bess was a survivor, of that she was certain.

Chapter Twenty-Four

Downstairs in the crypt, Flo was thrilled to find Rose running her first-aid night with ruthless efficiency. She was barking orders at Bess and the volunteers from the Red Cross with the confidence of a woman who had been doing this for years. Once the chairs had been put in place, Rose had stood there with one hand clamped around her white stick and the other resting on her hip, her eyes screwed up so hard they formed two slits in her face. It was the only sign that something was wrong and, for a moment, Flo thought her heart might break.

'Everything's perfect, Rose,' Flo whispered in her ear.

'Are you sure?'

'More than sure.' Flo nodded. 'It's nice to see you like this – back in charge again, I mean.'

Rose blinked slowly, the unexpected compliment clearly catching her by surprise. 'I am trying. And I'm trying to be encouraging for Bess too, and all for the other people who are coming here tonight who will have been affected by the blasts.'

'You're doing so well. The chairs are laid out in perfect rows, the first-aid leaflets are at the back next to the tea urn and the Red Cross props are on the stage all ready for our volunteers to use,' Flo reassured her friend.

'Thanks, Flo,' Rose said, nodding approvingly.

'You're welcome. Looks like this might be the making of Bess,' Flo said, watching Jean's sister directing some of the staff that had come down to see if they could help.

'It's what I needed when I was first injured and struggling to come to terms with my new life,' Rose admitted. 'I just wish I'd stuck to it instead of falling in with a bad crowd.'

Flo nudged her playfully. It was sometimes easy to forget that Rose had followed a minor criminal path with Alice's sister a few months ago as she struggled to come to terms with the loss of much of her sight.

'That's all water under the bridge now,' Flo said quietly. 'You must forget it. You're doing brilliantly tonight.'

Rose flushed with pride at the compliment. 'I just hope we get a few people in now.'

Hearing the sound of people already filing through the doors and taking a seat, Flo chuckled. 'I don't think you'll be disappointed.'

In fact it seemed that the world and his wife were on their way to support the first-aid night as row after row of chairs were filled with members of the general public and Liberty's staff alike.

Spotting Mary, Dot, Jean and Alice, complete with Arthur in her arms, Flo waved excitedly and beckoned them to join her and Rose.

'Look at all this,' Alice gasped in wonder as Arthur gurgled with delight.

'I think he approves,' Flo said, kissing the little boy tenderly.

'What's not to approve?' Mary agreed. 'You've done a fine job, Rose.'

'Is Bess all right?' Jean asked anxiously.

'She's fine,' Rose replied. 'You mustn't worry so much about her. I know it's only natural but you've got to let her find her own way. Don't coddle her all the time.'

'I'm not coddling her,' Jean protested. 'I'm protecting her. She needs my help.'

'Help, yes,' Rose admonished, 'but she doesn't need smothering.'

Dot leaned forward and held Rose's hand. 'Nobody's smothering nobody. This is all new territory for Jean. We know better now how to handle things, but don't start lecturing people, Rose. Jean is bound to be concerned. Bess is her sister, and you have to remember that.'

At Dot's advice, a look of contrition passed across Rose's face. 'Sorry, I didn't mean to go on.'

'You didn't.' Jean chuckled. 'Well, not much anyway. Now, haven't you got bandages and safety pins to go and sort through?'

Rose laughed. 'I get the hint, I'll see you girls later.'

As Rose slowly walked away clutching her stick, Flo saw Jean cast her eye about looking anxiously for Bess.

'She's over there,' Flo said, pointing towards the back of the room, where Bess, much to her surprise, was deep in conversation with Evie.

'I'll just go and rescue her,' Jean said hurriedly. 'No doubt Evie will be chewing her ear off about something.'

'Good idea.' Dot sniffed. 'Poor Bess is no doubt being lectured about something or other.'

But Dot's words were lost on Jean as she scuttled across the floor.

'Whatever can Evie want with Bess?' Alice asked.

'Who knows, who cares?' Mary snapped, arms folded. 'What Evie wants is anyone's guess.'

'Who's nicked the sugar out of your tea?' Dot exclaimed. 'You've been in a bad mood all day.'

Mary managed a smile. 'Sorry, girls. It's just I've got my first interview with the adoption people in a couple of days. I'm nervous, and I wish David were here with me.'

'Well, it can't be helped,' Flo soothed. 'You'll make a great impression; there's nothing to worry about.'

'It's just a formality, isn't it?' Alice said, switching Arthur from one arm to the other as he began to cry.

'I don't know,' Mary replied, reaching out a finger to stroke Arthur's cheek. 'Mrs Matravers might raise a last-minute objection. She could be out of prison in two years if she behaves herself and she would no doubt want to have custody of her daughter.'

Dot snorted. 'When has that woman ever behaved herself? No court in the land would let that woman near a child, not even her own. No, Mary darlin', Alice is right, this is just a formality: you and David will make perfect parents.'

'But the law is so much stricter now,' Mary whined as if Dot hadn't spoken. 'This new adoption act they're bringing in next year means it's going to be much more difficult.'

'Not for you, Mary, surely,' Flo said. 'You and David would be model parents, anyone can see that.'

'David might be, but I'm not,' Mary said, looking furtively around her and then lowering her voice: 'What if they find out about what happened in Ceylon? What if they find out about why I was discharged from the army?'

There was silence then as the girls considered what Mary had gone through last year. To have lost a baby was one thing, but to have conceived a child through a brutal and violent attack was something else.

'You put that straight out of your head, darlin',' Dot said, breaking the silence and wrapping an arm around Mary. 'You've suffered more than enough for what went on and you don't deserve to suffer no more. You've nothing to be ashamed of and when you go into that room tomorrow and meet with all them bigwigs, I want you to hold your head up high and remember you are more than good enough to take on baby Emma. Don't you let anyone say otherwise.'

'Thanks, Dot,' Mary said, leaning forward to kiss her cheek. 'I don't know how you always manage to say just the right thing, but you do.'

'And sometimes the wrong one,' Alice laughed, shooting her landlady a cheeky smile.

'You girls give over,' Dot admonished. 'I just say what needs to be said, that's all.'

'Speaking of which, you very much kept your mouth shut when Evie was being so rude to you in front of Max Monroe yesterday,' Flo exclaimed over the chatter of the people in the rows in front of them.

Dot took Arthur from Alice's arms and held him close to her chest. 'The thing I've discovered in this life is that if you give people enough rope they'll hang themselves. There was no need for me to show Evie up; she did a good enough job of that herself.'

Alice snorted. 'Yes, word went round the entire store how you made her sort through the remnants pile, Flo.'

Flo shrugged. 'What was I supposed to do with her? She had been unspeakably rude. How she's on the Board of Trade I don't know.'

'Neither do I,' Dot sighed. 'People are funny folk, that much I do know.'

With that Flo's gaze drifted towards Evie at the back of the room. She was still locked in conversation with Bess and Jean and it looked as if it was getting quite heated. Bess's cheeks were flushed with colour and her eyes were narrowed in anger, while Jean's head and shoulders were slumped, her whole body radiating despair. As for Evie, she was wearing that smug expression which so frequently graced her face.

Looking at the trio, Flo felt a stab of worry. Just what was going on between them all? She could understand why Evie would need to talk to Jean: there were after all plenty of Liberty and department matters that always needed discussing. But what did Bess have to do with it? As department manager, it was down to Flo to get to the bottom of whatever was going on.

Steeling herself for Evie's sharp tongue, she gave the girls a brief smile before she threaded her way through the crowds towards the warring women. Yet she had only taken a few steps when the sound of Rose clapping her hands together caught everyone's attention. Realising the first-aid night was just about to start, Flo returned to her seat. Finding out whatever was going on would have to wait until later.

Chapter Twenty-Five

Flo arrived at work the next day feeling exhausted. The night had been a brilliant success for Rose, but Flo had hardly slept for worrying over the exchange she had witnessed between Evie, Jean and Bess. Flo couldn't understand it and had worried that it would ruin the first of Rose's first-aid nights, even though she had gone to so much trouble to organise everything.

Yet to her credit, Bess hadn't let her anger show when she had been invited up by Rose on to the little makeshift podium to talk about her accident. In fact she had looked positively fired up with pride as she talked about how lucky she was to have Jean by her side, insisting that the best thing anyone could do in the face of an emergency was offer love and support to their nearest and dearest. It had been an unusual yet rousing speech that had captured the hearts of everyone there and Jean had been reduced to tears.

Afterwards, Flo had hoped to have a word with the girls to make sure Evie hadn't been bothering them but they had disappeared so quickly she hadn't had a chance. Consequently Flo had put the heated exchange out of her mind. Or at least she had tried to. At 5 a.m. that morning, she had finally given up on sleep and decided to get up and make a head start on the day. She was due at the school again later, but first wanted to ensure the department she was trying her best to love again was in no way neglected.

Now, in the quiet of fabrics, Flo focused on tidying, sweeping and organising, finding the melodic plod of the task at hand soothing. In fact she was so focused on her work she didn't hear Mr Button come up behind her, his arms full of paperwork.

'Flo,' he said, clearing his throat.

Jumping out of her skin, she whirled around to face him, her heart pounding. 'Mr Button, sir! I didn't see you there.'

'I just wanted to check you were all right. I see so little of my department managers these days that I couldn't resist coming to say hello.'

Flo smiled with affection at the store manager she was so fond of. 'And it's very nice to see you, sir. You look busy.' She gestured to the pile of paperwork in his hand.

Mr Button sighed. 'Yes, these are the minutes of the Board of Trade meeting last night. I wondered if you wouldn't mind giving them to Mrs Allingham when she arrives as she couldn't make the meeting?'

Flo put down her sweeping brush and took the files from her boss's hands. 'There's a lot here.' She marvelled at the weight of them.

Mr Button rolled his eyes heavenwards. 'Yes, they keep us fairly busy, but I can't complain – it's nice to feel useful.'

'I imagine Mrs Allingham feels just the same,' Flo said carefully.

'I imagine she does. Since giving up her position on the Botheringtons' board some time ago I think she wanted something to fill her time.'

'Why did she give it up?'

'Something to do with her brother, I think. He's still there of course, but they've been estranged for years. The two fell out over their mother's will many years ago. She had left everything to Mrs Allingham, as her own husband had died in the last war.'

'Upsetting her brother in the process.' Flo nodded in understanding.

'Precisely, my dear. The sad fact of course is that Evie lost all the money,' Mr Button continued. 'She was taken advantage of by some cad or other who presented her with a business opportunity that didn't exist. As a result Mrs Allingham turned to religion. She believes the Church is the salvation for all, and is almost fanatical about getting everyone to denounce anything she perceives to be immoral.'

'That sounds a little harsh,' Flo exclaimed. 'Though I must say she has had a few choice words to say about some of our more bohemian customers.'

Mr Button frowned. 'Has she? I must have a word. I told her when she joined us that she needed to keep comments like that to herself.'

'Oh no,' Flo cried, not wanting to cause any more trouble in the department. 'She never says anything in earshot; it was just a surprise to hear someone say those things. Still, at least it makes a bit more sense now why she is the way she is.'

'Is everything all right, Flo?' Mr Button asked gently. 'You've had an awful lot to contend with of late; I wonder if perhaps you need some time off?'

Flo shuddered at the thought: time off idling away at home dwelling on her misfortunes was the last thing that she needed.

'I'm fine, thank you, sir.'

'Are you sure?' Mr Button tried again. 'You can talk to me.'

'I know, sir.' Flo nodded. 'But I'm fine. Anyway, tell me how you are. It feels as if it's been ages since I saw you.'

'I'm fine too, Flo. Nothing a few days off with Dorothy wouldn't cure anyway.'

'I think she'd like that herself,' Flo said. 'She misses you.'

'I miss her. I don't see her anywhere near as much as I want to.'

'She's noticed,' Flo replied drily. 'And it's not lost on Mrs Allingham.'

'Making trouble, is she?' Mr Button said, getting to the point.

'A bit,' Flo admitted this time. 'Nothing Dot can't handle.'

At that Mr Button gave a knowing laugh. 'I'll bet. Perhaps it was a mistake inviting Mrs Allingham to work here. I thought she would be good for the department, especially when Jean was away.'

'No, her expertise is very useful.' Flo admitted. 'I just wonder if she has ideas above her station, shall we say, and of course it doesn't help that she and Dot are constantly at loggerheads.'

Mr Button laughed, 'You have a way with words, Flo, and I understand what you're getting at. This department has been through enough in recent months. Let me talk to Henry and see if we can't make things a bit easier for everyone. I may not get to spend as much time as I would like in Liberty's but I can make sure that every staff member here is as happy as they can be.'

With that Mr Button gave Flo an encouraging smile and Flo felt sure that some of her problems at least were on their way to being resolved.

Despite Mr Button's promise, Flo was still worried about what her lodgers had been up to with Evie. Settling herself at the school piano at lunchtime she wondered if there was a way to find out what had been going on between them all without upsetting anyone.

'Penny for them?' Celia grinned, approaching the piano, her hands full of sheet music, before the kids arrived.

'You don't want to know.' Flo sighed as she glanced over with interest at what was in Celia's arms. 'What have you got there?'

'More Max Monroe melodies,' she gushed. 'The kids loved singing something a bit different and I thought it would be excellent practice for you too.'

Flo took the music Celia proffered her and laughed. 'That's very kind of you but this is about the children not me.'

'Nonsense! They love it,' Celia said, pushing her concerns away. 'Besides, I love it too – takes me back to my youth. And you clearly adore it. You're a very gifted pianist.'

Flo shrugged. 'I do love it, but I love singing more.'

'And you'll come back to it in time,' Celia promised. 'In the meantime it looks to me as if you've the weight of the world on your shoulders.'

'That obvious?'

'A bit. Want to talk about it?'

'I really don't,' Flo replied honestly.

'Well, in that case what about a drink one night?' Celia suggested.

At the idea Flo lit up. 'Why don't you come along and meet the rest of the girls from Liberty's? They've all heard so much about you.'

Now it was Celia's turn to look surprised. 'What a lovely idea. You sure the girls won't mind?'

'Not a bit,' Flo promised. 'Pop over after the shop closes this evening. It's rehearsal night so we can all go across to the pub for a well-earned drink before the rehearsal and you can meet Max Monroe.'

Celia gasped. 'Oh my days! Are you sure?'

'More than sure!'

Celia giggled excitedly. 'I can't wait.'

At that point the children filed into the hall and with a start Flo realised that she couldn't wait either.

Chapter Twenty-Six

That evening, after an afternoon full of rain and cloud, Flo found herself in a warm and cosy pub waiting for the gala night rehearsal to start. As Flo glanced around her at the clientele she noticed that most people appeared to be in a reflective mood. Flo could only assume it was because the papers had been filled with news of the British ocean liner, SS *Ceramic*. It had been torpedoed and then sunk by the Germans near the Azores. Flo had found herself gripped by the reports, especially after discovering there was one survivor who had been taken as a prisoner of war. Flo couldn't help thinking about the men who had perished, the women they had left behind and the wife of the surviving man, who now faced a long, difficult road ahead in a German prisoner-of-war camp.

The news had been a stark reminder of the loss of her husband and she had felt sick with heartache, preferring to hide herself away and get on with her work rather than to socialise. She had hoped that after her chat with Celia she would become more capable of managing her grief. She wondered when the pain would ever end.

By the time she was due to meet everyone in the pub she felt a little better. As well as the girls and Celia, Henry had asked to join them, and Dot had issued him with a warning the moment he'd set foot in the pub.

'You'll have to behave yourself,' she'd warned as he took a seat. 'No boss talk. You're not the boss out of hours.'

Henry laughed. 'Fair enough. Now what can I get you all to drink?'

'Port and lemon,' Dot piped up quickly. 'And if you're buying you can be an honorary Liberty girl more often.'

As the girls gave their orders, Flo sank her head back against the hard wooden plinth of the pew she sat on and felt her shoulders begin to soften.

'So tell me again what the council said?' Alice asked Mary as Henry set a glass down in front of her.

Flo glanced across at her friend and noticed her face was flushed red and her eyes crinkled with excitement. Mary had worn that look for most of the afternoon, after returning from her council meeting about adopting baby Emma.

'They said I was approved. That we both were.' Mary beamed. 'They will need to do a few last-minute checks but otherwise when David and I marry next month baby Emma will be legally ours.'

'And Mrs Matravers is happy with the arrangement?' Dot asked. 'Not that it should be any of her business.'

'David has written to her and she agrees it's the best thing. It's a relief to know we have her support otherwise it could have been very difficult.'

'Well, I think we should raise a glass to you,' Jean said, holding her milk stout aloft. 'It's nice to have a celebration.'

'To celebrations,' the girls chimed in.

'What else are we celebrating then?' Dot asked, her face blank.

The girls laughed.

'Well, there's Bess getting out of hospital and doing so well,' offered Jean.

'And there's the fact I've taken matters into my own hands with Jack's sister and written to her,' Alice said – her voice full of pride, Flo noticed. 'I decided to reason with her.'

'Blimey! Flo marvelled. 'Whatever did you say?'

'I told her that I adored her brother, and I would never hurt him, that I understood the way she felt, that I would be protective of my sibling too if it were me, but that she really didn't have to worry.'

'Good on you, darlin',' Dot said, lifting her drink to her lips. 'What does Jack think?'

At that Alice's face fell. 'I didn't actually tell him.'

The girls burst out laughing but Flo couldn't miss the look of despair across her friend's face.

'You didn't tell him?' Flo echoed. 'He's going to have kittens when he finds out.'

'No he won't,' Alice protested. 'He'll be pleased I took the pressure off his shoulders.'

'If you say so.' Dot sniffed. 'Though if you ask me, what we're really toasting, Alice, is your last days on earth – or at least they will be when Jack finds out what you've done.'

At that the girls chuckled once more while Alice just shook her head in mock disbelief. Taking another sip of her drink, Flo saw the door open and watched Celia burst in looking around her uncertainly. Flo got to her feet and waved her hand to beckon her over.

'You found us all right!' Flo exclaimed, inviting Celia to take a seat next to her.

'No trouble at all,' she replied, nodding quiet hellos to the rest of the girls as they introduced themselves.

'We're just in the middle of celebrating,' Mary said, her eyes shining with happiness, 'so you've come at a good time.'

'Well, I'm delighted,' Celia smiled as Henry returned from the bar with a port and lemon for her. 'The kids have been rotten sods all afternoon, so it's nice to hear some good news after the time I've had.'

Celia's honesty caused the table to fall about with laughter. Flo took a moment to survey her new friend properly. Her navy skirt was covered in dust and the laughter lines around her eyes seemed to have increased just in the last few hours.

'You must have your work cut out up at that school,' said Dot.

'Some days,' Celia admitted, taking a long sip of her drink.

'Well, it's very nice to meet you,' Dot went on. 'Flo talks about you all the time.'

Celia beamed at Flo. 'And it's lovely to meet you all. I've heard lots about you from Henry, and Flo too of course, so I feel as if I know you all already.'

'We're thrilled you've helped Flo realise her passion,' Mary ventured.

'Even if she still won't sing at the fundraiser,' Rose muttered under her breath.

Giving Rose a sharp nudge in the ribs, Dot turned to Celia and smiled pleasantly. 'So did you never marry then, Celia?'

'I was married once. Not any more, however. It's a long story.'

'It always is, darlin',' Dot replied with a hint of knowing. 'So you're on your own then?'

Celia nodded and Dot sighed in understanding. 'Sorry to hear that. My George has been gone over twenty-five years and every day without him feels like a burden.'

'But you've found Mr Button again now,' Flo put in.

'Pah! Not if Evie Allingham has anything to do with it.' Dot's voice was full of scorn.

'You can't believe he's interested in her!' Alice replied.

'No – and you should know by now he's not remotely interested in anyone but you,' Rose offered.

'Plus Evie Allingham is incredibly religious,' Flo added. 'Mr Button was telling me all about how she was brought up that way and now she has become almost fanatical about morals after some rogue ripped her off causing her to lose all her money.'

'I didn't know that!' Dot exclaimed.

'Neither did any of us,' Mary said. 'But it explains why she's so judgemental with some of the customers.'

'And Mr Button won't like *that*,' Alice ventured. 'Plus if she really is as religious as he says, she won't be interested in taking someone else's man.'

'Perhaps she is just winding me up then,' Dot mused, draining her port.

'I should say so,' Celia agreed. 'Sounds like you've fallen on your feet, Dorothy. I should forget all about this Evie character. She may have designs on your Edwin, but he won't have designs on her.'

'Quite right,' Henry said knowledgeably, earning himself a glance of surprise from the rest of the table.

'Isn't it time we were heading back to the pleating room for rehearsal now?' Flo said, looking at her watch. 'Max is due any moment and we won't want to let him down.'

Celia clapped her hands together in delight. 'I can't believe I'm going to meet Max Monroe!'

'He's a diamond,' Dot said. 'You're in for a treat, Celia darlin'.'

With that the girls filed out into the night and walked back across to Liberty's. As they led Celia through the store, Flo delighted in the oohs and aahs her new friend uttered. She remembered only too well how astounded she had been when she had first walked into the store and seen the magic of Liberty's and all its secrets unveiled for the first time.

Following Celia's delighted gaze, Flo saw that she was looking at the wood-panelled room on the ground floor, which was locked with an iron gate.

'This is the fine jewellery room. It's where we keep all our very precious pieces,' Flo whispered. 'We show important customers like Queen Mary our rare and precious items in there, away from prying eyes.'

'You mean the Queen herself has been in that room?' she gasped.

'Let me tell you that there's even a special sofa in there, just for the Queen herself,' Flo replied, giggling as Celia's mouth fell open in shock.

Linking her arm through her new friend's Flo dragged her away so they could catch up with the others. Reaching the pleating room she pushed open the door and was surprised to see Max Monroe had already arrived and was chatting away to Mr Button.

'What are you two up to, gossiping away like a couple of old women?' Dot chuckled, being her usual forward self.

'We were just discussing former glories, if you must know.' Mr Button grinned. 'Max here was telling me all about his time in the army.'

'Now of course I sing for ENSA,' Max chimed in.

''Course you do,' Alice exclaimed. 'You're everyone's favourite.'

'You're too kind, my dear.' Max chuckled. 'It's a way to serve my country. Heaven knows I'm too old now to fight for it.'

'And I'm too injured,' Henry said bitterly.

Flo looked at him in surprise. She'd had no idea he felt that way, assuming he had been content with the service he had given his country and his role looking after Stan.

She was just about to open her mouth to comment when Max Monroe beat her to it. 'You look like a man who's done the best he can. Do you sing, sir?'

Henry's morose expression from moments earlier fell away as he smiled in reply. 'Only in the bath.'

'Well, if we ever need anyone for a bathtime fundraiser, I'll be sure to engage your services.'

With that everyone laughed politely and introductions were made. As Flo turned to introduce Celia and told Max she was a singer, Flo watched the woman tremble.

'Pleasure to meet you,' she stammered.

'And you,' said Max. 'Now, if you're a singer, how about you join me for a song?'

At the request, Celia's eyes widened in amazement and Flo thought she might pass out on the spot. In that moment a memory of Aggie came to mind, and Flo couldn't help wondering if she might have behaved in the same way – she had been such a huge fan.

'Are you sure, Mr Monroe?' Celia asked, finding her voice eventually. 'I mean, I just sing with school kids.'

'I'm more than sure,' Max replied, flashing her a devastating smile.

Turning to Flo, who had seated herself at the tiny piano, which had been hauled into the corner of the room, he nodded and instinctively she began to play ' My Kind of Romance'.

As usual Flo lost herself in the music, and found that she was enjoying watching Max and Celia perform together. Celia really was a natural, whether she was singing with a roomful of schoolchildren or with an international star. She had a presence like no other and as she hit the high notes, Flo felt a stirring within her. She hadn't felt this way since she used to watch Aggie sing, so confident, so capable that she caused a stir wherever she went. Flo closed her eyes and enjoyed the rich sound of Celia's voice. For a second it felt as though her aunt was still alive.

Chapter Twenty-Seven

The next week at work, Flo felt happier than she had in months. As she took her turn to serve her favourite customer, Mrs Rodgers, she felt a spring in her step.

With no customers on the shop floor, Alice and Dot sorting out the patterns and thread reels, and Rose running through the inventory, Flo decided to take advantage of the lull and go through the department accounts. Since Max Monroe had been seen coming into the store word had got round and there had been an upsurge in trade with many female customers wanting the chance to meet Max as he arrived for a suit fitting. Dot and Alice had toiled for hours on end after work on the suit, with baby Arthur often in his pram snoring away beside them. After the rehearsal last night they had finally presented the suit to him, and had been delighted to find that he was thrilled and very grateful for the work the girls had put in.

Now, as Flo reached for the paperwork underneath the till, she began to make her way through the figures. It was a laborious task, but Flo found that it was nice to concentrate her mind on something other than all the doom and gloom that had worked its way into her life of late.

Running her finger down the row of figures, she was pleased to see that the department takings were up from the last quarter, a fact that would please Mr Button and the board. Yet turning the page, she frowned as she saw the princely sum of one hundred pounds had been taken from their earnings and approved by the Counting House.

This made no sense at all. Money was meant to come into the department not go out, unless it was for simple petty cash items like stamps and stationery. Why would the Counting House have agreed to pay out that amount of money? Turning back to the figures, she saw the initials scrawled next to it – EA – and felt a flash of anger. So this was something Evie had been involved with? What was she up to? She should know full well that anything unusual like that had to be run past Flo first.

Slamming the book shut, Flo shoved it under the drawer and was just about to make her way up to see Mr Button and demand some answers when the sight of Mary leaning against the wooden doorway took her breath away. She wasn't due to work until this afternoon, having taken the morning off to see the council for one last visit before the wedding and then the adoption was finalised.

She looked lost, scared and as if she had been crying. Flo rushed to her side. 'Mary love, what's happened?'

'It's David, and Mrs Matravers,' she said haltingly.

'What do you mean?' Flo demanded. 'Sorry, love, but you're scaring me. Whatever is the matter?'

'David's had his leave cancelled,' Mary said tearfully. 'We won't be getting married in January now. And Mrs Matravers has said that with the war so full of uncertainty it's better for Emma to remain in the custody of the state. She thinks Emma should stay in the orphanage and then, when she's released from prison, she can come and take her home and raise her as should have been the way all along.'

Flo felt a surge of anger. The deputy store manager had caused more than enough damage already. 'Steady on,

166

'love, what have the authorities actually said?' she asked, leading Mary to the chair behind the till.

'They said that they would meet Mrs Matravers and try to reason with her. She's not due to be released from prison for at least another two years as the judge wanted to make an example of her, and that's a long time for a baby to remain in care when there is a family ready and waiting to take her,' Mary explained, her voice catching with emotion.

'Oh Mary love, what a disappointment. And all this has come about because David had to cancel his leave?'

Mary nodded, before reaching into her handbag for a handkerchief. 'David's furious. He sent me a telegram this morning and says he will try and talk to her but I don't think it will do any good. Oh Flo, I can't quite believe all this is happening. I'm not getting married, and I'm not going to be a mother to Emma.'

At that Mary broke into a fresh round of tears, causing Dot and Alice to come running.

As they approached, Flo scanned the floor to check for customers and, seeing the floor was still empty, quickly filled the other women in on what had happened.

'That cheeky cow,' Dot fumed. 'I'll crown her for this.'

'Dot, language,' Flo growled, though privately she agreed with her.

'But your wedding is just postponed, isn't it?' Alice said, squeezing Mary's hand in support. 'You will wed at some point?'

Mary nodded and sniffed. 'Yes, the next time David's on leave. We'll get a special licence if we don't have enough notice. Oh, I'm sorry for weeping like this, girls, it's all just been such a disappointment.'

'Of course it has,' Rose soothed, as she had joined them by now. 'But you'll get to be mother to baby Emma, of that I'm sure.'

'That woman wants stringing up for all the damage she's caused,' Dot seethed.

'I must say I'm stunned at her callousness,' Rose put in, 'but we all know she hasn't got a heart.'

'But what should we do?' Mary sniffed. 'I've been building up a real bond with Emma lately, I've visited her at the orphanage every week and I feel she knows me now. I'm letting her down.'

'You're doing nothing of the sort,' Rose protested hotly.

'Have you thought about going to see Mrs Matravers?' Dot suggested. 'Might do you the power of good if you had a heart-to-heart.'

Mary shook her head. 'I'm not sure I'd trust myself to say the right thing.'

'A letter then,' Alice said.

Dot snorted. 'Because that's worked so well for you. You heard from Gracie yet?'

At the question Alice's face fell. 'I'm sure it's just a matter of time.'

'And does Jack know you've written to her yet?' Flo asked.

Alice shook her head, earning herself an eye-roll from Dot.

Looking around at her friends Flo felt a sudden surge of irritation. They were bright, capable women yet they were all making themselves powerless in the face of life-changing events.

'I've had enough of all this,' she thundered, causing the girls to look up in alarm. 'Alice, it's time you told Jack what's going on. Your marriage floundered because of lies and secrecy; the last thing you want is that to happen with Jack. Mary, you can't take this lying down. I don't think you should write a letter to Mrs Matravers or speak to her but I do think you should ask Mr Button to make your case. She respected his opinion, she may listen to him now.'

'I can't do that,' Mary spluttered.

'You can and you will,' she said firmly. 'And Dot, you need to start really believing that Mr Button loves you. He's not interested in Evie and never will be, so forget it. You're lucky to have a relationship like you do. I had one like that once and now it's gone there isn't a day that goes by when I don't wish my Neil was still here. Don't jeopardise it by being daft. And, Rose,' Flo said pausing for breath, 'you need to stop pushing me about singing.'

'I'm not,' Rose protested.

'You are, darlin',' Dot put in helpfully.

Flo's expression softened. 'I know you mean well but I'm happy as I am playing piano and you should be happy that's enough for me.'

'But *are* you happy, Flo?' Mary countered.

Flo looked up at the dark wooden ceiling and thought for a moment. She wasn't happy as such, but there were moments where life didn't seem quite as terrible as it had when Neil had first died.

'I think I am,' she said slowly, 'and that's thanks to you girls. You've all been so kind to me these past few months and that's why I want you all to be happy too. You've got to take charge of your own lives.'

As Flo finished the girls looked at her in awe.

'All right,' Mary sighed, 'I'll talk to Mr Button.'

'And I'll talk to Jack,' Alice agreed.

'And I'll give you a break about singing,' Rose said softly. 'I didn't realise – I just wanted you to be happy, but if you are then I'll keep quiet.'

'Thank you,' Flo breathed, turning to Dot. 'And are you going to stop giving Evie a hard time?'

'Not on your life!' Dot chuckled. 'I wouldn't trust that woman as far as I can spit, though for your sake I'll make sure there are no scenes on the shop floor.'

Flo laughed; she expected nothing less from her friend, but she did expect more from herself. She wanted her friends to have a happy ever after. Was it possible she could ever find hers?

Chapter Twenty-Eight

It was the end of the week. Christmas was fast approaching and the night of the fundraiser had finally arrived. The day had been a busy one on the shop floor and, despite the lack of goods to sell, the store had been inundated with shoppers eager to make the most of their ration book coupons and buy what they could.

Flo was pleased she had something to take her mind off Christmas Day itself. It would be her first without both Aggie and Neil, and the thought of it left her reeling. She was trying her best to put on a brave face, but in truth she would be glad when the wretched day was over.

Just like last year, Liberty's had been gifted a tree by Princess Valentina, who was a regular customer and friend of the store. Evie, along with Flo and Dot, had decorated the tree that morning with twinkling glass baubles they had reused from last year. Although it didn't have the usual glamour that Liberty's and their customers commanded, it was still a spectacle and Flo had been delighted with the finished result. Concentrating on the decorations had also taken her mind off the concert that evening, but now, stepping into the grand foyer of the Palladium, Flo felt the nerves take hold.

Determined to collect herself, she stood in the centre of the rich red carpet and took a deep breath. Instead of focusing on her nerves she concentrated on the scene around her, a trick her aunt had taught her when she first started singing in public. Dressed in her best floor-length plum velvet dress, which her aunt had made for her years ago when she'd started performing, Flo glanced around, drinking it all in. Her eyes roamed over the carved wooden beams and the sweeping staircase that led to the dress circle and circle above, complete with gold rails, and she couldn't help feeling overwhelmed by the grandeur of the place. Real stars had performed here, and now she would be joining them.

'Taking it all in?' a voice called behind her.

Whirling around she came face-to-face with Henry, dressed in a black jacket and dark trousers, his white shirt freshly starched. She smiled at the sight of him. 'I'm glad you're here.'

'Why? You're not nervous, are you?' Celia asked, appearing alongside him next to Stan, resplendent, Flo thought, in a navy wool utility dress.

Flo grimaced. 'A bit.'

'You'll love it when you get up there,' Henry promised. 'And you look wonderful.'

'He's right,' Celia agreed. 'You're a natural, love. Enjoy this moment; you've more than earned it.'

'Are you doing "Baa Baa Black Sheep"?' Stan asked suddenly, causing the three adults to burst out laughing.

Flo shook her head as she watched the little boy fiddle with the braces that were holding up his short trousers. 'Sadly, Stan, I'm not. But I will be playing "Sunshine on Sestan Bay".'

Stan brightened at the news. 'We can all sing that one, can't we, Henry?'

'Erm, well ...' Henry paused, only for Celia to take over and give Flo a wink.

'We can certainly all mouth the words with Mr Monroe when he sings it, can't we?'

'I suppose,' Stan replied, somewhat mollified.

At that Flo checked her watch and felt a surge of dread in the pit of her stomach. 'I'd better go.'

'Break a leg.' Henry chuckled. 'Although on second thoughts, don't! I can't cope with any more staff out.'

'Shouldn't have sacked so many then, should you?' Flo teased.

Spinning around, Flo found a stagehand who showed her to her dressing room. The walk through a corridor crammed with props and rails of glamorous costumes, past shelves full of pots of half-used make-up with brushes on the side, reminded Flo a little of Liberty's and she felt her nerves subside just a little.

As the stagehand showed her to the door, Flo was delighted to see Rose and Alice, working together to ensure things backstage were running smoothly.

'Everything all right?' she asked, seeing Alice on her knees with a handful of pins as she made a few adjustments to a costume.

'We're getting there,' Rose replied. 'We've had to change a few things around and one person's ill so we're down an act.'

'No!' Flo's hands flew to her mouth. 'Who?'

'Jeanie Michaelson and the dance troupe.'

'But they were going to close the show!' Flo gasped, her mind running amok with thoughts of a disappointed audience.

'That's why you and Max are doing it instead,' Alice said.

'What?' Flo's jaw fell to the floor. 'My nerves will never last if I have to wait two hours to perform.'

'Welcome to show business.' Max chuckled, breezing past her in his new Liberty's suit. As everyone gasped a little in his presence, Max smiled and nodded his head at the cluster, before pulling Flo to one side. 'Tell you what, let's go up to the bar and we'll make our wait a little more bearable.'

With Rose and Alice nodding encouragingly at her, Flo followed Max, feeling as if she were a circus performer putting her head into a lion's mouth rather than a pianist waiting to take centre stage.

'Does this happen a lot?' she asked as Max placed a gin and orange in front of her.

Max shrugged and took a sip of his pint of stout. 'Nine performances out of ten something gets changed, but it doesn't matter, does it?'

Flo sipped her drink and enjoyed the feeling of the alcohol gliding down her throat. 'I suppose it doesn't. I just don't like change.'

Max laughed. 'Force of habit with this job.'

'How long have you been with ENSA?' Flo asked politely.

'Oh, since the beginning when Basil and Leslie asked me to come on board,' Max replied. 'And yes, I think perhaps at the beginning we might have deserved the nickname Every Night Something Awful.'

Despite herself, Flo chuckled. The nickname was one that she knew had been hounding the ENSA performers for years now, and it was largely unfair – though she had to confess she and Aggie had seen a couple of dreadful performances some years ago. Flo smiled as she recalled the time that she and Aggie had howled all the way through a particularly painful variety show where the singer was tuneless and the most magical thing about the magician was the way he walked off stage.

'I can't say I'd heard that nickname,' Flo said diplomatically.

'You're a terrible liar, darling.' Max laughed, the grey in his hair shining silver under the bright light of the bar.

'How did you get into singing?' Flo asked, changing the subject.

'My mother sang,' Max replied. 'She used to earn extra money for the household by singing at posh parties for the landed gentry.'

Flo gasped. 'So did my aunt.'

Max looked at Flo in surprise. 'Well, fancy, it's a small world, isn't it?'

'I suppose it is.' Flo grinned. 'My aunt was such a talent. She said singing was so much a part of her she couldn't stop even if she wanted to.'

'My mother was the same, and I suppose I am too,' Max admitted. 'That feeling when you open your mouth and allow the power of the words and the lilt of the music transport you to a place far, far away.'

Flo nodded. She knew exactly what he meant. 'Did you ever consider doing anything else?' she asked.

Max scratched his chin and regarded Flo thoughtfully. 'No, I didn't. I was in the army in the last war and I used to sing all the time then for my comrades. I must admit it probably did me as much good as it did them. We saw such atrocities, it was a way of boosting our spirits and better than any medicine.'

'I've always felt that way myself. Singing brings people together, lifts them up; it's a real tonic,' Flo replied.

'It is' – Max nodded –'so the question is, when are you going to make the most of your tonic? I hear you're an incredible singer as well as a wonderful pianist.'

Flo gaped at him in surprise. She was just about to reply when the gong sounded, calling them to the stage.

'Ooh, that's us already.' Max grinned, slamming his empty glass on the table and getting to his feet. 'I told you the time would pass quicker than you thought.'

As Max walked confidently down the halls towards the stage, Flo struggled to keep pace, the nerves building all the while inside her. By the time she reached the wings Flo felt so dizzy and sick she thought she would pass out as the audience clapped and cheered the penultimate act before they walked off stage.

The only thing that grounded her was the sight of the baby grand piano Max had specifically requested sitting in the middle of the stage. Flo had never played on such a beautiful-looking instrument and she ran her eyes eagerly across the instrument's shiny black lid and matching glossy stool. In that moment, Flo thought of Aggie, and how much she would have loved to be on this stage. Taking a seat at the piano, Flo gazed out at the sea of faces and smiled. She wasn't just doing this for Liberty's; she was doing it for her aunt too.

Chapter Twenty-Nine

The theatre was packed and Flo turned to look at Max as he greeted the crowd.

'Hello, everyone,' Max boomed above the audience's cheers. 'It's a pleasure to be here tonight.'

At that everyone broke into another round of applause that was so deafening Flo wondered how he didn't have hearing damage if this was what he had to put up with every night. But one glance at the star told her he didn't seem at all bothered; in fact he was positively thriving.

'We're going to entertain you with a few very special songs. However, before we begin let me introduce you to a friend of mine who will be accompanying me on the piano tonight – Mrs Florence Canning.'

At the sound of her name, the crowd applauded again and Flo felt a sudden rush to her heart as she realised they were all clapping for her. As the noise died down, Max nodded and she hovered her fingers over the keys aware of just how shiny and pristine they seemed. Pressing the tips of her fingers against the keys she tentatively began playing the opening number they had agreed upon, 'Show Me The Way'. It didn't take long for Flo to find the rhythm of the music and allow it to transport her far from London.

Throughout their set, Flo played hit after hit, but it was when they performed 'You're My World' at the end of the show that the audience went wild with appreciation. Flo found herself remembering how she and Aggie had once belted this song out at the pub one night, a rare evening when they had performed together. As Flo played the notes she remembered how happy she had been. Neil had been in the audience, looking proud as punch, while Aggie stood on a makeshift stage telling the audience that he was engaged to be married to the best singer in the world.

She would give anything to go back to that place again. Before she knew what she was doing, Flo found herself singing along with Max. Her voice sounded clear and true and she hit every note with precision, providing the perfect accompaniment to Max's deeper tones. As the song finished, Flo suddenly came to and realised with horror what she had done. But there was no time for recriminations as Max addressed the crowd.

'Well, how about that, ladies and gentleman. Please put your hands together and show your appreciation for Mrs Florence Canning.'

At that the audience exploded and Flo got to her feet to curtsey. As the roars continued, she could hardly believe the sound was for her, but as the house lights went up she could see everyone smiling at her, cheering her on for all she was worth. In that moment, the permanent state of grief she had felt at losing her aunt and husband lifted. She felt light and carefree – a feeling she wanted to hold on to for all eternity.

With that the rest of the cast and the stagehands, including Rose, Alice, Dot and Mary, burst on to the stage and took their bow to the rapturous appreciation of the audience. As Flo stood between Dot and Max, she realised she had never felt so alive. It was all down to Max, encouraging her to be brave and follow her heart.

As they walked off the stage, the sound of applause ringing in her ears, Flo was just wondering how she could hold on to this feeling when she felt Max tug gently at her arm. A surge of worry engulfed her. She knew she had behaved badly.

'Listen, Mr Monroe, sir, I am sorry I started singing and ruined your performance,' Flo began. 'I just found myself getting so carried away with the music – and it was a song I used to sing with my aunt . . .'

Her voice trailed off and she became aware of Max beaming at her. 'You did absolutely nothing wrong at all. You're a talent, a raw, natural talent. I'm here to beg a favour. Please, Flo, you shouldn't be working in Liberty's – you should be on the stage. You should be in ENSA.'

The excitement on the shop floor the following morning could be felt everywhere. Flo had started later that morning thanks to the events of the previous night, for Henry had very generously offered to let her sleep in.

She needed the rest. She had spent most of the night tossing and turning over what had happened at the concert, furious with herself that she had interrupted and ruined Max Monroe's performance. The man had really been too kind, congratulating her like that and telling her she ought to join ENSA, when really she should be reported to the board and reprimanded for bringing the reputation of Liberty's into disrepute. Still, a little part of her had fantasised about what it would be like to join the famed entertainment troupe. She pictured crowds from all over the world applauding her as she stepped on to the stage.

'Here she is!' Henry beamed from his position behind the till. 'The new star of Liberty's, Mrs Flo Canning.'

At that he gave a small round of applause, causing Flo to flush with embarrassment; she was grateful there were no customers on the floor and only Alice and Dot in the corner, too far away to hear.

179

'Stop that!' she groaned, walking around to her place behind the till to take over. 'I'm cross enough with myself as it is.'

'Why? You were brilliant.'

'Because I showed Liberty's, Mr Monroe and myself up. I was a fool.'

Henry's face creased with concern. 'You can't seriously think that, Flo. You were wonderful. I knew you could sing, your friends kept telling me, but I had no idea you were that good. The audience loved you too, they were all applauding – you must have heard that?'

Flo's cheeks were now burning with mortification. 'You're too kind, but honestly I must apologise to Mr Monroe again. I shouldn't have done what I did, and he must have felt terrible for me to have made me the offer that he did afterwards.'

'What offer?'

'He asked me to join ENSA. I know he wasn't serious – he must have been so embarrassed for me that he said the first thing that came into his head to try and make me feel better.'

Henry shook his head in despair. 'Max Monroe offered you a job singing with ENSA? Flo, that's incredible. Are you going to take it?'

'Of course not!' Flo snapped, feeling more irritable than usual thanks to lack of sleep. 'He wasn't serious, and even on the off-chance that he was I wouldn't be interested; my life is here at Liberty's.'

The deputy store manager said nothing, merely raised an eyebrow and closed the sales book he had been examining.

'How was the rest of the evening?' Flo asked, keen to change the subject. 'Was it a success?'

'It was a huge success. We raised almost a thousand pounds.'

Flo's jaw dropped open. 'How on earth did we raise so much?'

'Because we had some very nice donations from Betty Fawcett and Princess Valentina. We also sold every ticket and even had some extra donations this morning.'

'Almost a thousand pounds. Imagine what that money will do.' Flo murmured.

'Well, that's it, isn't it? The war effort should hopefully be well aided with that kind of money. So we'll be making a presentation to the war office at the New Year dinner.'

'Where's Evie?' she asked, changing the subject again. 'I thought she was supposed to be covering for me this morning. I didn't see her last night either.'

'She's out sick. She let the superintendent know that she's caught a dreadful stomach bug so you've got me instead.'

'I can live with that' – Flo smiled – 'as long as you stop teasing me about singing.'

'I won't say a word.'

'Has everything been all right here?' she asked, taking the sales book from Henry's hands.

'No problems. We haven't been busy but then everyone is hanging on for the New Year sale.'

'Is that what Alice and Dot are doing?'

'Yes. I asked them to sort through the stockroom and start discounting the fabric rolls that have been selected for the sale.'

'Good.' Flo nodded, shutting the book with a snap as she turned to face the deputy. 'So who's really going to be making the presentation to the war office then?'

'We're hoping Princess Valentina might do it, otherwise Mr Button will step into the breach.'

'Will he have the time?' Flo asked. 'He's been so busy.'

'We hope so. It's been a difficult time for all of us with Edwin away from the shop floor so much, but his work with the Board of Trade should ease off a little next year. Utility fashion and fabric are all in place so everything should be back to normal.'

With that Henry broke away to serve a customer. As Flo watched him smile and laugh, she thought about what he'd said about life returning to normal and realised she wasn't at all sure that was what she wanted.

Chapter Thirty

Exactly a week after the fundraising evening, the day Flo had been dreading arrived. Waking early on Christmas morning Flo closed her eyes and buried her face in the pillow, wanting nothing more than to stay in bed all day and pretend Christmas had been cancelled. She had successfully managed to avoid the festivities at work, all but ignoring the carols, decorations and excited shoppers. Instead she had tried to pretend this was just another Friday, but now it was here, Flo knew it was anything but. This was the first Christmas she had faced without Aggie and Neil. The pain of it blindsided her for a second, and she felt so sick with grief she didn't think she could face the day. Just how was she supposed to keep going like this?

Flo wasn't sure. But then, hearing Arthur downstairs gurgling in delight, Flo knew she couldn't put off facing the day any longer. She would simply have to make the best of it and at least she would be doing it in good company. Dot had invited Mr Button, Mary, Rose, her dad Malcolm and Tommy, who was back on leave, to join them for dinner as well as Jean and Bess. They were going to be collected by Mr Button in his motor car. He had been saving up his fuel for the job, Dot had told her proudly. Alice had invited Jack, and Flo had invited Celia, Henry and Stan, so she was sure there would be at least enough of a distraction if she found the day proved a bit too much.

And so Flo had dragged herself out of bed, wished Dot, Alice and Arthur a merry Christmas and made the tea.

Then she had dutifully helped peel the potatoes and organise the chairs ready for a lunch she was secretly dreading.

Now as the assembled group crowded around Dot's kitchen table, ready to eat, she felt as if she might crumble. The grief she had successfully managed to avoid all morning was somehow finding its way back into her heart. Lifting her chin, she looked across the table and found Henry looking at her sympathetically. She smiled in gratitude, grateful for the support, and turned her attentions back to the table.

'So, Tommy,' she said, turning to the soldier seated on her right. 'When did you get back?'

'Last night. I go back tomorrow. But it's worth it to spend Christmas with my Rose.'

Flo nodded. She couldn't miss the look of love plastered on Tommy's face. He had barely taken his eyes off Rose and Rose too appeared overjoyed, the smile on her face seemingly permanent. Rose deserved a bit of happiness, and it was nice to see, especially with Mary wearing a face like a broken clock. She was still devastated at Mrs Matravers' decision and Flo was furious on her behalf. Turning her gaze towards her friend she could see that, like her, Mary was doing her best to put a brave face on things but her smile didn't quite reach her eyes.

'Well, you picked a good weekend for it.' Celia beamed as Dot placed a turkey on the centre of the table.

Tommy raised an eyebrow. His wide-open face was full of awe at the spread in front of him. Not only was there a turkey but there were bowlfuls of veg and a mound of potatoes that Flo thought would feed not just Tommy but his entire platoon.

'Dare I ask you where you got this, Mrs H.?'

184

Dot sat down and winked at Tommy. 'You can ask, dar-lin', but rest assured I won't be telling. And if you want to eat better food than you've been eating in the army these last few months you won't ask no more neither.'

'Fair enough.' Tommy shrugged, before carefully piling Rose's plate high with turkey and then his own.

'Want me to put you some on a plate, Bess?' Dot asked.

Bess smiled and held out her plate with her left hand. 'Could you do me some small bits please, Dot love? If you give me anything I have to cut up we could be here until next Christmas.'

At that Rose laughed, while the rest of the table stayed silent. Bess looked at everyone, her eyes crinkled with mirth. 'You can laugh, you know. In my experience you have to laugh about things in life, because it's flamin' mis-erable if you don't.'

Rose nodded in agreement. 'I make you right there, Bess. Someone shouted "four eyes" at me down the Lane the other day. I had to correct them and say on a good day it's barely two.'

At that Flo couldn't help but smile. Laughter really was the best medicine, and she felt proud in that moment of these two wonderful women: their bravery was inspiring.

'How's your mum getting on this Christmas, Rose? She still with the ATS lot in Camberley?' Jean asked, helping herself to gravy and pouring a little on to Bess's plate.

Malcolm nodded. 'According to her last letter, yes, she will be spending Christmas perfecting square bashing,'

Mary laughed; she remembered it well from her own ATS days. 'At least she'll get slightly better food today. They did pull out the stops around the festivities.'

'They'd have to do summat to cheer the poor buggers up, wouldn't they?' Dot put in.

'Oh come on now, Dot, the food's not that bad in the army,' Mr Button pointed out as Tommy passed the carving knife to him.

'Quite right,' Malcolm agreed, helping himself to some of the no doubt illegally obtained bird.

'Absolutely,' Henry agreed, piling Stan's plate with potatoes. 'We had quite a good cook in our regiment. Won't have a word said against him.'

Dot rolled her eyes. 'That's not what my George used to say. I told him he'd get used to it. He told me you could get used to prison if you tried hard enough.'

At that the table broke into fits of laughter and Flo found herself joining in. Perhaps the day wouldn't be so bad. After all, she was in good company and the food smelled delicious.

'I gotta say this looks even better than the food we have at Rainbow Corner,' Jack put in.

At the mention of the American Red Cross club, where food shortages were unheard of and hamburgers, doughnuts and drinks were readily available, the table groaned.

'Don't you mention that place here,' Dot scolded as she lifted her knife and waved it in the GI's direction. 'Poor Tommy don't want to hear about your bloody Cocoa Lola that you can drink 'til you're blue in the face after you've done a hard day's graft doing nothing but line your bellies.'

'Come on now, Dot, that's enough,' Alice said, her face furrowed with annoyance as she speared a carrot. 'We're celebrating today, not knocking seven bells out of each other, and anyway it's Coca-Cola.'

Dot rolled her eyes. 'Whatever. And you should know by now I'm only teasing.'

'And I should like to say how kind it is of you to have me in your home, Dorothy,' Celia said, lifting her glass of beer aloft. 'I usually spend Christmas just with Henry and Stan so this year has made a very nice change.'

'And we're thrilled to have you,' Dot said, her eyes twinkling with kindness. 'In fact, it's a pleasure to have you all here, safe and well at this table.'

At that Arthur gurgled, seemingly in agreement, and Jack smiled affectionately at the matriarch. 'And I too would like to thank you. But, Dot, let me say this, I'm not gonna be pounding the streets of London long. I'm going to be moved sometime in the early part of next year.'

Flo felt a flash of surprise. 'Goodness. Where?'

'Bristol,' Alice replied before he could say anything. 'So you won't be seeing quite as much of him.'

Flo looked at her friend and saw that familiar steely gaze she often wore when she was trying to disguise her hurt.

'Better Bristol than thousands of miles away,' Rose countered.

'It's not for ever, my love,' Tommy said as he squeezed Rose's hand and gently kissed her fingers.

At the gesture Flo's heart swelled with love for them both. She was so glad Rose had relented and allowed Tommy to take compassionate leave this Christmas. She could see already it had buoyed up her spirits in a way neither the girls nor Malcolm had been able to manage since the girl had lost most of her sight.

'Precisely, Tommy.' Alice grinned in his direction. 'There's a war on; we all have to go without the niceties in life. I shall get used to being with my fella when I can just like almost every other woman in this country.'

'And no doubt you'll appreciate it all the more when you are together,' said Rose, turning to Tommy as if they were the only two people in the room.

With that everyone beamed fondly at Rose and Tommy just as Dot started to speak.

'What about you, Henry love? Has there never been anyone special in your life for you to share Christmas lunch with?'

At the question, Henry looked so surprised, Flo felt sorry for him.

'Dot, don't be so personal!' she exclaimed, before turning to Henry. 'Please don't answer that.'

Henry, who had now regained his composure, waved Flo's concerns away. 'It's all right. But no, Dot, to answer your question, there has never been anyone special.'

'That's a bit odd.' Dot frowned. 'You never had a sweetheart at all?'

'Dot!' Flo hissed as the table broke into stunned laughter at the matriarch's impertinence.

'Really, Flo, it's fine.' Henry grinned, turning to Dot. 'You might find it odd, but I never have. I've always been busy with work or service. Now Stan is my priority.'

'We always said the right girl would come along eventually,' Celia said in a tone that indicated the conversation was closed.

'Now that's something I agree with,' Jack said, reaching for Alice's hand and squeezing it tenderly.

By the time the last mouthful of plum pudding (somehow obtained by Dot) had been devoured, the party retired to her good front room. There they nestled into the floor or sank back into her armchairs complete with pristine white antimacassars, sure they would never need to eat again.

'There is just one thing I wanted to say to you,' Flo heard Jack say as he nestled alongside Alice and held out a letter.

Curious, she took it from him and began to read. Flo watched her friend's face change from scared to overjoyed in just under two minutes.

'What is it?' Flo begged, seeing Alice's face crumple in delight as she smiled weakly at Jack.

'It's from Jack's sister Gracie,' she said, thrusting the letter towards Flo.

Gingerly Flo took it and began to read.

10ᵗʰ December 1942

Dear Jack,

How are you, little brother? You still enjoying that cold British weather and miserable damp rain? Life here at the farm is good. We're preparing ourselves for one of those harsh Montana Christmases where it does nothing but snow – Jack Junior can't wait, of course.

You may not know this, but I received a letter from your special friend, Alice, recently. She didn't say I couldn't talk to you about it so I wanted to send a letter to you first before I write Alice. She's quite a girl. I haven't met her, but from her letter I can tell she's feisty, responsible, and full of love for you, dear brother.

I was surprised to hear from her. Angry, too, in a way. I know I'm way too protective of you, and have only gotten worse since Marilyn died, but Alice made me see there's a man inside of you I don't know. She spoke of a fearless, brave, trusting, loving man, and I realised I only know a part of that about you. For so long now I've put you into this box of grief-stricken widower. Alice has made me realise that I may not like what's going on between the two of you but that won't stop her loving you, supporting you and encouraging you to be the best man you can be. She also told me that with a war on, there are no perfect circumstances, that lives are being wiped out every second and when you find someone or something special, you hold on to it because it's so precious.

I can't pretend to understand what's going on over there or why. I'm a simple girl from a simple farm, Jack, but what I do know about is love. I know I treasure every letter I get

*from my Eric because it means he's still with me. I know you
well enough to know you never make poor decisions, and if
this Alice cares enough about you to lay her heart on the line
and write to me, your older sister, and plead for understanding about your relationship I guess I can take a chance. Tell
Alice I'm going to stop hounding you about falling in love
with a married woman and let her know that, like the two
of you did, I'm going to take a chance and trust you both
enough to take care of each other.*

*I wish you both a very happy Christmas together, and you
should know that we are all thinking of you back home.*

*Yours, with love,
Gracie*

As Flo finished reading, she held the letter out to Alice, her
eyes by now shining with tears.

'It's beautiful,' she replied.

'Isn't it,' Alice said, squeezing Jack's hand.

'It feels like there's a load off,' Jack said quietly. 'Though
I may have to talk to you about going behind my back to
write my sister like that.'

As Alice and Jack lost themselves in each other for a
moment Flo looked around the little group and smiled.
Everyone seemed to be paired off in some form or another
this Christmas. Dot and Mr Button were reminiscing about
old times beneath a sprig of mistletoe. Henry and Stan were
playing with the new wooden truck he had been given that
day. Jack and Alice were gazing at each other in that soppy
way of theirs, as were Rose and Tommy. Even Jean and
Bess were laughing at some private joke, their voices low.
Lastly, her eyes came to rest on Malcolm and Celia. They
were murmuring to one another as they stared out of the

window, the late afternoon sun casting long shadows on the London brick houses opposite. They were both lonely, Flo realised, but in this moment at least they had each other. Whom did she have? Not a soul. She was truly all alone. Looking around at her friends, each one lost in their own bubble of happiness, Flo couldn't help wondering if she would ever find someone special again.

Chapter Thirty-One

A week later it was chaos at the little terrace in Bell Street as they got ready for the New Year's Dinner at Lyons. So much so that Flo wondered if they would ever leave on time as she watched Arthur throw up all over Alice's only good dress, while Dot decided that now was the perfect time to start cleaning her kitchen cupboards.

'Ladies, we need to leave in five minutes,' Flo wailed, worried that the silk navy dress she had borrowed from Liberty's ready-to-wear would crease before they had even left the house.

'Oh, stop moaning, Flo,' Dot complained. 'We're almost ready.'

'You're not almost ready,' Flo fumed, pacing up and down the kitchen with her coat on. 'Alice still hasn't worked out what she's wearing, Arthur's crying, despite the fact Doris is upstairs trying to settle him, and you're spring cleaning three months early.'

'Cleanliness is next to godliness,' Dot put in wisely, sending a tin of hard-won peaches crashing to the ground.

Flo raised her eyes heavenwards and thought there was a very real chance she might explode when Alice finally came down the stairs looking lovely in an old Liberty print tea dress.

'Will this do?' she asked, anxiety writ large across her features.

'You look wonderful,' Flo soothed. 'Jack will be delighted to have you on his arm.'

At the mention of the handsome GI's name, Alice blushed and Flo chuckled to herself. Alice had never been soppy – as she liked to think of it – until she met Jack. However, the American had softened her and Flo had to admit that she liked this new, considered Alice.

'I'll just check on Doris and Arthur, then we'll get going, shall we?' said Alice.

'I thought Mr Button was collecting us in his car,' replied Flo, fighting feelings of rising panic.

'No, darlin', he might be consulting for the Board of Trade but that don't mean he's entitled to any more motor spirit coupons. He's running out so the car has to be saved for emergencies. We're on the bus.'

'Well then, let's go,' Flo grumbled.

Dot rolled her eyes. 'All right, all right.'

Ripping off her apron to reveal a fetching wool suit Flo had seen her alter and customise with new buttons and a split up each sleeve, Dot was finally ready.

'Alice, come on, Arthur'll stop screaming the moment we leave,' Dot called.

With that Alice ran back down the stairs, shouting apologies up at Doris. 'I'm ready.'

This time Flo didn't even wait for a reply. Instead she threw open the front door and marched out towards the bus stop, not even turning around to see if Dot and Alice were following behind.

The bus arrived within seconds of them arriving at the stop. And as the doors opened they all but threw themselves inside to escape the chilly January wind.

After buying their tickets from the clippie, Flo stared out of the window as the bus roared through the streets and concentrated on the evening ahead. This evening was important to her: as manager of the fabric department it was down to her to ensure Princess Valentina was happy before the presentation of the money they had raised was made. The last thing she wanted was to be late.

It only took fifteen minutes for the bus to reach the heart of the city, and as Flo stepped out on to the pavement and took in the beautiful Lyons Corner House that towered over Shaftesbury Avenue, she smiled at its majesty.

'Come on, Flo. I thought you didn't want to be late,' Dot admonished.

Shaking her head Flo followed her friend inside and took in the decorations. Banners wishing the staff a Happy New Year graced the foyer, and a rich red rug she knew she could sink her feet into if she dared to remove her overly repaired court shoes was placed in the centre of the floor. Elsewhere, elegantly dressed Nippies in traditional black and white uniforms were handing out welcoming glasses of port. To her right she heard the strains of music and, peering up the stairs, she saw Stan singing 'Auld Lang Syne' at the top of his lungs to a little group unable to resist his charms. This annual Liberty's event to thank the staff for all their hard work would be the perfect evening to make the presentation.

Leaving Dot and Alice to find their own way, Flo walked up towards Stan and saw Henry right at the back of the small crowd that had gathered. It was hard to miss the pride etched across his face as he watched his little brother.

'He's singing beautifully,' whispered Flo, sidling next to Henry.

'He's wonderful, isn't he?' Henry replied, his eyes never leaving Stan. 'I hear he's had a very good accompanist.'

Flo chuckled. 'It's all natural. Look at him.'

'And look at you! You look beautiful, Flo,' the deputy store manager exclaimed, turning to face her.

Flo felt her cheeks flush with embarrassment. She wasn't ready for compliments. She was still just going through the motions of what was expected. She didn't want to be noticed for her beauty or style; those gifts were reserved for Neil. However, she appreciated the sentiment behind the words and knew it would be churlish not to thank him, so instead she smiled in gratitude and changed the subject.

'The whole place looks fantastic. You wonder how they do it.'

'The powers that be can always find the money when they want to.'

'Speaking of money, who's doing the presentation?' Flo asked just as a large gong sounded signalling the gathered guests to take their places for dinner.

'Rose and Evie have it all in hand, I believe, and they are just settling Princess Valentina into her seat now.'

Flo followed Henry's gaze across the dining room. In that moment, the notes of the song died away, and Stan stopped singing to rapturous applause.

Henry smiled as he heard the boy ask what he should sing next. 'I think I'll just go and rescue those poor people from any more of Stan's tuneful offerings. You go on ahead into the dining hall, Flo.'

'Are you sure?'

But Henry was no longer listening and was instead weaving his way towards his brother.

The dining hall was every bit as beautiful as the welcoming foyer outside. Circular tables with pots of poinsettia were elegantly arranged around a stage with another large banner behind it that read, in giant purple lettering, 'Liberty's Gala Fundraiser'. The scent of what Flo could have sworn was roast chicken filled her nostrils, while elsewhere swathes of red velvet curtain lined the room to create a warm and almost theatrical atmosphere.

Finding her place on the table planner that stood at the front of the room, Flo wasted no time weaving her way towards the table where she was to sit between Mary and Dot. To her great delight, she saw that not only was Mr Button seated with them this year, but that Jack had also joined them as a very special guest and was seated to the right of Alice.

'What a lovely surprise to find you all here,' she said with a grin as she took her seat.

'I'm as surprised as you are to find Edwin at the table,' Dot murmured, taking a sip of her drink. 'I see that little of him at the moment I've almost forgotten what he looks like.'

Mr Button's face clouded over with worry. 'Come on, Dorothy, don't be like that. I've told you, my work with the Board of Trade will ease off soon. Can't we just enjoy tonight, my love?'

Dot's face broke into a smile. ''Course we can, darlin', I'm pulling your leg.'

'Thank goodness for that!' Mary exclaimed. 'We miss you at the store, sir, it will be wonderful to have you back.'

'Not that Mr Masters isn't doing a fine job,' Flo added.

'We've just got used to you and your little ways by now,' Alice put in.

At that there was a round of laughter.

'I think there's a compliment in there somewhere, sir, I suggest you take it,' said Jack.

Mr Button lifted his glass of wine to Jack. 'I learned that the hard way over the years and you're quite right.'

'And to what do we owe the pleasure of your company this evening, Jack?' Flo enquired.

The American glanced at Alice, a look of sorrow passing briefly across his features before he turned back to face the table. 'I'm going to Bristol soon. Want to make the most of my time with this wonderful woman before I head off so I bribed the boss here into giving me a seat.'

Mr Button coloured at the use of the word 'bribe' and Flo smiled. She felt sad the much-loved GI would be departing so quickly. About to say as much, she caught Alice's eye, and saw her give an imperceptible shake of her head. Flo knew at once her friend didn't want her to say a word. She clearly wanted to focus on enjoying this incredible evening and create a lasting memory to treasure while Jack was away. Flo smiled in understanding. If there was one thing she had come to realise since losing Neil and Aggie, it was the power of a beautiful memory to carry you through dark times.

Chapter Thirty-Two

After the main course of what Flo had guessed correctly would be a delicious roast chicken, there was a lull between courses. Rubbing her stomach, Flo leaned back in her chair and idly played with the stem of her wine glass, grateful for a few minutes to recover. Like everyone else she was used to living on a diet that consisted largely of Woolton Pie and the National Loaf. Consequently, her digestive system was struggling to cope with such rich delights.

Looking around the room, she saw everyone seemed to be enjoying themselves. The musical trio from the gift department, who were expertly playing a harp, piano and violin, entertained the crowds with a range of music from Beethoven's Fifth to more contemporary pieces, including one of Max Monroe's.

Closer to home, at Flo's table, Alice and Jack were so wrapped up in one another they weren't paying anyone else any attention. Mr Button had gone to get ready to make his presentation speech before the dessert course was served. Observing Mary across the table Flo saw she still looked pensive. Her friend had been quiet since the news of her postponed wedding had come to light, and Flo wondered how she was doing.

'Penny for them?' she said, inwardly cursing herself for using such a well-worn phrase.

Mary stopped staring at her hands and turned to Flo, her raven hair catching in the light of the chandelier that glistened overhead. 'I fear my thoughts are barely worth a ha'penny.'

'Come on, things can't be that bad,' Flo chivvied.

'They are,' Dot said, taking another gulp of wine. 'She's had a face on her like a wet weekend in Clacton since Mrs Matravers told her she weren't going to let 'em have baby Emma after all.'

Flo reached out a consoling hand to Mary. 'I must say I'm surprised Mrs Matravers' voice carries any weight. I know she's the child's mother, but she's in prison! You would think she would want what's best for the child, and surely that's her being raised by Mary rather than complete strangers.'

Mary let out a hollow laugh. 'But she hates me. Always has done. Hated the thought of me marrying her brother, and just because we've had to put things on hold, she'd like to make me suffer.'

'You'd think she'd have changed since being incarcerated and becoming a mother. I'm surprised she has time for airs and graces,' Flo muttered.

'Well, that's old Mabel for you,' Dot said, arching an eyebrow. 'She's always been power hungry, see. Comes from being starved of it as a child as well as later in her marriage to Alf. She'll take what little power she can find and think nothing of nobody but herself.'

'It's all true, I'm afraid.' Mary sighed. 'And the one that's suffering the most, of course, is little Emma. She's too young to understand now, but the thought of her being raised by strangers, rather than her own family – well, it's immoral.'

There was a pause then, and Flo couldn't help wondering what might have happened to her had her Aunt Aggie not taken her in. Would she too have been raised by strangers like little Emma?

'I thought you might have invited Celia tonight,' Dot said, interrupting Flo's train of thought.

'It didn't occur to me,' Flo replied, feeling a stab of guilt. 'I just thought of it as a work do. But as Jack's here, do you think I should have done?'

'She's a nice woman,' Dot replied non-committally.

'Yes, but Flo's right, it is a Liberty occasion,' Mary added with a smile, trying to make Flo feel better.

Dot shrugged. 'I just thought you and her were becoming good chums, darlin'.'

'We are, and I've been enjoying playing music for the kids.'

'And singing too, if that concert was anything to go by.' Dot chuckled. 'I bet Max Monroe couldn't believe his luck when you piped up; the two of you were a real team. That's why he invited you to join ENSA, I bet; he knows a good thing when he sees it.'

Flo stared at Dot in disbelief. 'How do you know about that?'

'You should know by now, darlin', I know everything. So are you doing it or what?'

'No!' Flo gasped indignantly. 'My place is here.'

There was a pause for a moment as Dot took another gulp of her wine, then beckoned the waiter over to refill her glass.

'Why?' she asked bluntly.

'Because ...' Flo trailed off, unable in that moment to think of a good enough reason. As if sensing her distress, Mr Button took that moment to take to the stage and clapped his hands together to catch everyone's attention.

'Hello, ladies and gentleman,' he said warmly. 'I'm sorry to interrupt you on this fine evening, especially when I know you are all eager to enjoy the delicious sticky toffee pudding the talented chefs here have dreamed up for us, so

I won't keep you long. However, tonight is rather special because we are not only here to make a presentation but also to celebrate you. Mr Masters and myself joked earlier that if there were another kind of service, it would be the Liberty service, as you have all worked tirelessly and diligently to raise money for the gala evening, sharing our news with customers, helping make costumes, performing, providing refreshments – I could go on, but we would be here all night.'

Raucous laughter filled the room as Mr Button paused. 'I am so proud of you all, which is why it gives me great pleasure to welcome to the stage our very special friend, Princess Valentina, who is graciously going to accept the cheque on our behalf and present it to the war office.'

As Valentina came to the stage, a vision in pink tulle, her long dark hair swept into an elaborate bun, Flo felt a pulse of excitement. She looked around for Henry and Stan, eager to share the moment with them, but although they were supposed to be on the table next to her, she saw they were nowhere to be found. Glancing around, she realised that she hadn't seen them since Stan had been singing in the foyer. With a stab of alarm, Flo wondered if the little boy really had been poorly, and Henry had been forced to take him home.

As her eyes darted furtively across the room, desperately hoping to catch sight of her friend and deputy store manager, she couldn't miss the sight of Evie Allingham now at Mr Button's side. She was chattering away in his ear, the store manager seemingly unable to get a word in edgeways. Flo rolled her eyes, unable to help herself at the sight of the woman so obviously trying to ingratiate herself.

Instead, she turned her attentions back to Valentina, who was just giving her closing remarks. 'And now, Mr

Button, if I could trouble you for the collection please?' the princess said.

With that, Mr Button appeared to reach behind him. Only, as he did so, Flo could see that something was wrong. As the applause continued, she could see her store manager's gaze darting this way and that, but the look of panic on his face was evident as he whispered something in Evie's ear.

Watching her scuttle off to the side, Mr Button smiled apologetically at the audience before turning to Valentina. 'Your highness, I'm afraid I must apologise to you and to our employees. It seems the fundraising money is not where I left it and we're having a bit of trouble locating it. I've suggested to the powers that be that we have a short break while we look for it, so, ladies and gentleman, the good news is that your desserts will be with you sooner than you thought.'

With that, Mr Button stepped down from the podium, and Flo couldn't miss the worried look on her store manager's face. Flo took a sip of her wine and got to her feet. She had a feeling something was wrong and it was time to find out exactly what.

Chapter Thirty-Three

Flo rose and all she could hear were hushed whispers as her friends and colleagues discussed with great excitement the money and where it could have gone. Without telling anyone where she was going, Flo weaved her way through the tables to find the store manager.

It didn't take long. In the corner of the room, out of view of everyone else, Mr Button, Rose and Evie were also talking frantically in hushed tones. Rose looked ashen, her beautiful features contorted into a picture of worry, her tortoiseshell glasses sliding down her nose. Evie, meanwhile, was holding court.

'I'm telling you, I saw him do it. Bold as brass he was! Him and that brother of his.'

'Mrs Allingham, we simply cannot go around accusing people without proof,' Mr Button said in a weary tone.

'The money's gone?' Flo gasped.

'That's right,' Evie said smugly. 'And Henry Masters is the culprit.'

'I don't believe you,' Flo said. 'Why on earth would he take the money?'

'Why does anyone do anything in this day and age?' Evie said with a raised eyebrow. 'Because it was there, because he could, because he's struggling to raise his little brother and make ends meet, who knows?'

At that moment, Flo felt a fury course through her bones. Who did this woman think she was? She was just about to say as much when Rose found her voice.

'At this moment we have no idea who has done what or why. The money could very easily turn up in the blink of an eye, Mrs Allingham, and to go around accusing trusted members of staff is slander.'

Flo felt proud of her friend for standing up for what was right. She knew this must be awful for Rose; after all, she had masterminded this whole operation.

'Have any of the staff at Lyons seen anything?' Flo asked suddenly. 'Perhaps they've put the money somewhere safe.'

Evie let out a hollow laugh. 'Yes, like Henry's trouser pocket.'

'For goodness' sake, that's enough!' Flo said with a stamp of her foot. 'Until you have proof I suggest you keep comments like that to yourself.'

There was a brief pause, and Rose took a breath. Immediately Flo leaned forward and pulled her in for a hug. She couldn't help noticing that Rose's forehead was damp with sweat and her previously neat victory roll was now a dishevelled mess. *Just like this whole evening*, she thought sadly.

Then she rallied. 'Come on, Rose, we'll sort this out. This is a simple misunderstanding. We just need a plan.'

Lifting her head she looked pleadingly at Mr Button, who by now seemed to have aged by ten years.

'Mr Button, sir, perhaps you could ask the staff if they've seen anything. And, Evie, perhaps you could speak to the heads of department; they may know something as well. Rose and I will scour the backstage area and see if we can find the box; it can't have just disappeared,' Flo said authoritatively.

'Good idea, Flo.' Mr Button smiled at her gratefully. 'I'll tackle Miss Ellington, who organised the staffing this evening. And of course someone will need to explain to the staff and to Princess Valentina what's going on.'

'I'll do it,' Flo sighed. 'And I'll check she's all right.'

As she turned to go, Flo couldn't miss the look of spite in Evie's eyes. 'I appreciate your need to play Miss Marple, Mrs Canning, but there really is no need: I know who took the money and so does Mr Button – it was Henry Masters.'

'But you can't *know* that,' Rose said, her eyes filled with tears now.

'I do,' Evie replied forcefully. 'It's common bloody knowledge.'

Her voice was so loud, Flo flinched and as she did so became aware that the noise of the crowd had died down and the four of them had now become the source of entertainment.

'Lower your voice,' she said, her face twisting with rage. 'We don't want to cheapen this mess with idle gossip.'

Evie drew herself up to her full height, her petite frame doing its best to tower over Flo's tall one. 'It is not idle gossip. I *saw* Henry with the box earlier on. He was setting it down on the stage in readiness.'

'And what does that prove?' Rose scoffed.

'It proves he knew where the box was and it would have been easy for him to take it.'

Flo narrowed her eyes. 'Why are you so keen for Mr Masters to be guilty? You've refused to entertain any other possibility.'

'Because there is no other conclusion to draw,' Evie replied. 'Once a common criminal, always a common criminal.'

Evie's words hung in the air like day-old tripe as Flo stared at her in disbelief. 'What did you just say?'

Mr Button laid a hand on Evie's shoulder. 'You've said quite enough, Mrs Allingham. I think that should be the end of it now.'

'No, I want to know what Evie meant,' Flo countered.

'Me too,' Rose added, her voice firm.

There was another pause as Evie brushed a piece of imaginary lint from her jacket and looked Flo squarely in the eye.

'Yes it's true. Henry Masters is a no-good crook who has been imprisoned for his crimes. If you ask me, he should never have been given a job at Liberty's.'

'Mrs Allingham, I will not tell you again—' Mr Button snapped, only for Evie to cut him off.

'What Mr Button has been trying to conceal from everyone is that he vouched for Henry Masters, knowing he was a criminal. He told the board that he would personally ensure the safety of the store, and that if there were any problems he would take full responsibility.'

Flo felt her mind was about to implode. 'Is this true?'

Mr Button nodded, his face ashen. 'I'm afraid it is. Henry made a mistake some years ago but I believe everyone deserves a second chance. Until I hear otherwise I will continue to consider him a man who is thoroughly decent and true.'

'Decent and true!' Evie laughed incredulously. 'Henry Masters took advantage of his mother and embezzled money from the factory where she was employed. How does that make him decent and true, Edwin? The police and the courts didn't seem to think so or they wouldn't have sentenced him to three years for theft.'

'He served three years in prison?' Flo echoed, feeling as if the ground was being swept from under her.

'As I live and breathe,' Evie replied triumphantly. 'Henry Masters is a con man. He did it once and now he's done it again.'

'It's not that simple, Mrs Allingham,' Mr Button said, his face contorted with anger. 'May I remind you that you are a temporary guest of Liberty's and I'll thank you to know your place and stop gossiping immediately.'

'Gossiping? It's common knowledge. Everyone at Botheringtons knows for a start.'

'Only because you told them after I swore you to secrecy,' Mr Button thundered. 'You found that out by eavesdropping on a personal conversation Henry and I had in my office several months ago.'

'If it was private you shouldn't have been talking so loudly.' Evie retorted, her eyes ablaze with self-righteousness.

'My office door was closed. You had no right to listen. I considered you to be a religious, moral woman, Mrs Allingham, but I must say your sense of decency is very misplaced.'

Once again, Evie drew herself up to her full height. 'My sense of decency is entirely where it should be. It was a good job I did eavesdrop, so I was aware of the deputy manager's lack of moral fibre.'

At that Mr Button paused and Flo could see the anger flash in his eyes.

'Whatever you may think, Mrs Allingham, the important thing is that we return to the matter of discovering with certainty who has taken this money.'

'Yes, I agree,' Rose said.

There was another pause as Flo found herself struggling to take all of this information in. How could Henry not have told her? She'd thought they were friends; she'd thought they trusted each other.

'So it is true then? Henry went to prison?' She looked at the store manager for confirmation.

Mr Button looked briefly heavenward before turning back to Flo and Rose. 'Yes it's true, Flo, but I know Henry of old. He is a decent, trustworthy individual.'

'But just because he went to prison, that doesn't mean he took the money now,' Flo said desperately. 'I mean, you said yourself it was a long time ago.'

'And that's what I believe,' Mr Button said firmly. 'Now I suggest we all get on with finding out who really took the money before we sully Henry's good name any further.'

With that the group spun around to find Henry walking towards them. Startled to see him, Flo took a moment to drink in his appearance, then she realised he was holding the dark wooden box they had been looking for.

'I found the money,' he called delightedly. 'It was outside in the street.'

'Convenient,' Evie snapped, taking the box with one hand and the key to open it from Rose in one swift moment. 'Empty,' she snarled, casting it to the floor.

Henry coloured. 'But I didn't take it. Surely you don't think I had anything to do with this? I just found the box! Edwin, please?'

Flo looked from Henry to Mr Button and saw him refusing to meet Henry's gaze. Instead his face was aghast, as though he was finally allowing the very real possibility of his own misjudgement to sink in.

Chapter Thirty-Four

More than a week had passed and the mood in the store was still a sombre one. None of the staff could quite believe that the money they had all worked so hard to raise had been stolen. Equally nobody could quite believe that the much-respected Henry Masters was the one who had cheated them of their efforts and taken it.

Flo found it very difficult to grasp and kept going over events in her mind. After Henry had been caught red-handed he had stood protesting his innocence. Much as she hated to admit it the evidence was clear, he had been holding the box and there was no money inside. And if he had been in prison for theft before then it all added up. Did Henry really expect them to believe he had found the box on the street as he said? It was too much of a coincidence.

Back in Lyons, Mr Button had taken charge of the situation and told Henry to wait while he addressed the staff. He said that it was clear the money had been stolen and that an investigation would be launched to find it. He apologised to Princess Valentina for wasting her time. As ever, she had been more than gracious, simply saying that she would love to return to make the presentation to the war office when the missing money was found.

Flo had been grateful for that. Valentina was always so optimistic. Afterwards Mr Button had escorted Henry from the premises, picking up Stan on the way. Nobody had much of an appetite for dessert or dancing after that, and so everyone had made their way home sad and disappointed at the way their evening had ended.

The only person who looked satisfied was Evie. For some reason she looked overjoyed at the news, and for the life of her Flo couldn't understand why.

Since the night of the dinner, Henry had been suspended pending an investigation but that didn't stop Evie telling everyone else her theory. Walking across the wooden floor, through gifts and beauty, Flo could hear Evie's plummy tones before she saw the woman.

'Of course I knew Masters was bad news the moment Mr Button told me that he had been inside. You can tell just by looking at him that he was untrustworthy.'

'I don't know about that,' came a quieter voice that Flo recognised as Judy Bates from beauty.

'Well, I do,' Evie replied indignantly. 'I bet he took that money to pay for some other crime he'd become mixed up in, gambling or hooch most likely. Or perhaps it's something to do with that brother of his. It's in the genes, immoral behaviour like that.'

As Evie paused for breath Flo halted. She stood rooted to the spot, quaking with anger. No matter whether Henry was guilty or innocent it wasn't on to speculate like that. Stalking across the floor towards Evie, she smiled briefly at Judy before gripping Evie firmly by the elbow.

'Mrs Allingham, a word,' she said, all but dragging the woman across the floor and back towards fabrics.

Flo didn't speak until they reached the stockroom, and once the door was shut firmly behind them, she rounded on Evie, her heart racing. 'How dare you talk about Henry Masters like that. You have no proof of anything!'

Evie let out a droll laugh. 'You really think he did nothing? Come on, Flo, I know you've got a soft spot for him, but really. The man was in prison. It is our duty to shine a light on those who have no moral fibre. They let society down.'

'We don't know he had anything to do with this,' Flo hissed. 'The evidence is hardly damning. And even if he is as guilty as Hitler the least you can do is shut up about it.'

'I beg your pardon?' Evie cried, her face full of indignation.

'You heard me,' Flo fired. 'You've no business going around stirring up rumours and creating more trouble just because you like a good gossip. You looked positively joyful when Mr Masters was suspended.'

'Don't be ridiculous!' Evie fired, hands on hips. 'I was merely pleased to see the culprit had been caught. You forget, Florence dear, I am a good deal older than you and remember when the Liberty name meant something. Having someone like Masters on the payroll does you no good at all.'

'Correct me if I'm wrong, but doesn't the precept "innocent until proven guilty" operate in this country?' Flo replied evenly. 'As for our reputation, I think you'll find it is more than intact. You only have to take a look at the visitors' book to see that. Now, I don't want to hear any more from your lips on the subject of Mr Masters. If anyone is letting Liberty's down it's you, Mrs Allingham, with your caustic tongue and nasty little comments. Any more from you and I shall take great pleasure in recommending to the board you are sacked forthwith.'

With that Flo turned on her heel and walked back up to the shop floor. She had a lot to do before her shift at the school began.

The mood in the school hall was precisely what Flo needed later that Tuesday lunchtime. She stepped inside and the sight of so many delighted, excited and happy children, putting their hearts and souls into singing, was the perfect antidote to the stress of the last few days.

Lifting her eyes from the sheet music for 'Summertime' she sought out Stan among the sea of faces. Locating him in the second row, Flo searched his face for any signs of distress but there were none. He looked just like all the other little boys, happy and carefree, and she hoped it would long continue.

As the song came to an end, so did the class, and the moment Flo shut the lid on the piano and stood up she was surprised when the children let out a cry of disappointment.

'Mrs Canning will be back soon,' Celia called over the din. 'You can all practise your very best singing for her then.'

With that the children filed out of the room, Stan shooting her a small smile as he passed her. Once the last child had gone, Flo made her way to the chairs and helped Celia stack them. The older woman had been very quiet since Flo's arrival, and Flo was unsure what to say.

'I saw Henry this morning.' Celia said, cutting Flo's indecision in two. 'He seems well.'

'Good,' Flo said, and meaning it. 'I don't know what he told you ...'

As her voice trailed off, Celia shot her a sympathetic smile. 'He told me that he had been accused of theft, Flo.'

Flo nodded. There was something in Celia's eyes that made her feel ashamed. 'I don't want to believe it's him.'

'It's not,' Celia said sharply. 'I've come to know Henry very well and I know it's not in his nature to thieve.'

'I heard he has previously been in prison, though, for theft,' Flo stated.

'Not everything is as it seems ...'

Celia sighed and sank down on to one of the hard backed chairs. Patting the one next to it she encouraged Flo to join her.

'I don't know what he's told you about his background, Flo, probably not much, but you're a decent judge of character: you must know a good man when you see one.'

Flo bit her lip. 'I think I do. But what other explanation is there other than Henry took the money?'

'That I don't know. But I know this: when a good man insists he didn't do something, he needs help not a cold shoulder.'

'Is that what you think I'm doing?' Flo cried. 'It's been hard for me, Celia. I don't know what to do or say. I'm conflicted.'

'I know you are.' Celia sighed as she patted Flo's forearm. 'Perhaps that was unkind of me – I'm sorry. But Henry needs someone, Flo. He has nobody else aside from me and Stan.'

Flo hung her head in sorrow. She wanted to believe Henry, but at the moment her head felt just too heavy with it all.

'I simply can't make any sense of this,' she sighed.

'I know. But you Liberty girls are so good at helping each other out when one of you is in need, I rather think Henry might like a bit of your help too. At least hear him out?' Celia ventured.

Flo nodded. It really was the least she could do.

'I'll go and see him,' Flo said with a limp smile.

'Tomorrow?' Celia asked hopefully.

Flo shook her head. 'There's another Liberty girl that needs my help tomorrow.'

Chapter Thirty-Five

The heavy wooden doors of Holloway Prison banged shut ominously behind her and Flo couldn't help jumping at the noise. The uniformed prison guards led her down a dank corridor. She wasn't sure where she was going, or how long this corridor would last; only a little light filtered through the tiny windows at the top of the walls towering above her, making her feel confused. She had a feeling that this was deliberate – a technique designed to confuse the poor inmates who were misfortunate enough to end up here.

Immediately, Flo thought of Henry. Had the prison he had been incarcerated in looked like this? Was there paint flaking from the walls? Was the air filled with an acrid smell of bleach and sweat? Flo hadn't been sure what to expect when she entered the prison. She knew it wouldn't be pretty, that conditions were ugly, but this was worse than she could ever have imagined.

It was the noise that was really getting to her. The hollow laughs of prisoners; the shouts of misery that rang across the jail as her feet pounded against the concrete floor. It was unsettling, and Flo immediately wanted to leave. This wasn't a place in which she belonged; in fact, she wasn't sure if this was a place where anyone belonged.

Before long she was shown into a bare room with just a wooden table and two chairs where she was told to sign a sheaf of forms. The sheer number made Flo's hand ache from scribbling her name so often, but she was here now – she would make this worthwhile.

Once she had completed the required paperwork Flo was led down another corridor, one with a series of doors with locks and gates, where jailers with keys stood guard, idly fumbling with huge brass key rings hanging from their belts.

Just when she thought the corridor was leading nowhere, she saw a larger room up ahead: still cold and dark, but with a handful of battered tables and chairs lining the walls. Flo was told which seat to take and to wait.

Dutifully she did so and felt grateful when she didn't have to wait long, as all too soon, there in all her glory, looking as triumphant and as menacing as the day she had been caught red-handed making hooch, stood Mrs Matravers in an ill-fitting grey skirt and blouse, her wrists bound in handcuffs.

'I wondered when one of you would turn up,' she said, her face smug as she took a seat opposite Flo. 'Never thought it would be you though.'

Flo said nothing, merely looking the former deputy manager up and down and taking in her appearance. Mrs Matravers had aged and lost a lot of weight. She was only in her mid-thirties but her hair was grey, her cheeks hollow and her skin lifeless, just like her eyes.

'Mary's tried to see you many times, and you always turned down her application for a visit.'

Mrs Matravers shrugged. 'I don't want her here. Lording it over me with her airs and graces.'

Flo shook her head in disbelief. 'Have you learned nothing since you've been locked away? Mary's not like that, she's never been like that, it's all in your head.'

'If you say so,' Mrs Matravers replied idly, refusing to look Flo in the eye.

Flo didn't know what to say next. She had planned this visit out in her mind for days, practising what she was going to say and how she was going to say it. She had taken comfort in the fact that Mrs Matravers had never really had a problem with her, and there was a possibility she might even open up to her, given she had gone into business making that revolting hooch with Flo's own father. The thought made Flo uncomfortable. She didn't want to talk about Bill Wilson or even think about him. She was here for one reason only, for Mary, to get Mrs Matravers to see reason and sign her child over to Mary and David when they finally married.

But Mrs Matravers had always been a difficult woman. Even when she was married to Alf and lauded in her position as deputy store manager of Liberty's, Mrs Matravers had always enjoyed making life difficult for others.

'You've never liked me, have you?' Mrs Matravers' voice punctuated Flo's thoughts, making her jump slightly.

'Not much, no,' Flo replied with searing honesty. 'You never knew how to treat people properly. The icing on the cake was when you sent Rose nearly blind with your get-rich-quick scheme.'

Mrs Matravers laughed. 'It was hardly that. We needed money for the baby.'

'Because your vile husband was out of a job again,' Flo countered.

'Don't you talk about my Alf like that,' Mrs Matravers snapped. 'He's a good man.'

This time it was Flo's turn to laugh. 'A hardened criminal, work-shy, prone to theft and violence – I can't believe you're still defending him.'

'He's my husband,'

'And not a very good one,' Flo hissed, leaning forward and meeting Mrs Matravers' eye. 'It's about time you faced reality.'

'Meaning?'

'You must know why I've come.'

'You want me to change my mind about giving my child up to my brother and Mary?' Mrs Matravers asked with a loud sigh.

'Yes.' Flo nodded. 'And I don't understand why you've said you don't want them adopting her any more. You must want what's best for your daughter.'

'I'm not convinced that her uncle and the woman who fell pregnant out of wedlock is the best thing for my daughter,' Mrs Matravers said matter-of-factly.

'So, aside from your ridiculous prejudices about Mary, let me get this straight. You want your daughter to grow up in care? Passed from pillar to post, never knowing a loving home, is that really what you want?' Flo asked, shaking her head in despair.

Mrs Matravers shuffled in her seat and pursed her lips. 'It's not as simple as that.'

'It's just as simple as that,' Flo hissed, banging her fist on the table for emphasis. 'When my mother left me, just think what life would have been like if I hadn't had my Aunt Aggie to turn to. I too could have been brought up who knows where, but I had love and I had a family. Surely you want that for Emma?'

'I don't know,' Mrs Matravers said, her tone softer now. 'I don't know what's best for my little girl. I never expected to be here, Florence, surely you can understand that? All I ever wanted was a baby, a family of my own. It was why I went to the lengths I did to try and make ends meet. I thought if I could just get enough money together for us we would be the perfect family and then Alf would find another job, and everything would be all right. The hooch ring was only ever supposed to be temporary.'

To Flo's surprise, a great big tear rolled down Mrs Matravers' cheek.

'Of course I can't stand the thought of her being brought up in a place where she isn't loved or cherished. But the idea of someone else adopting her, so she will never know me, is unthinkable. It means this mistake I made is permanent,' Mrs Matravers finished.

'But she will know you,' Flo cried. 'You've been through all this with David. He and Mary have assured you that when the time is right and you're free, then you and Emma will be reunited in some form.'

'But what form?' Mrs Matravers cried. 'Mary has already lost one baby; she must be desperate to get her hands on another. What if she doesn't marry my brother and then refuses to give her back to me or even let me see her?'

Flo looked at her in astonishment. The depths of Mrs Matravers' imagination knew no bounds. She was so cynical, so untrusting – but then again, Flo imagined that most people who were imprisoned would end up the same way.

'Mrs Matravers, I can sit here and tell you that Mary is a good person, that she doesn't deserve your damnation, that she only wants what's best for Emma, but we both know that's pointless. What really matters is what *you* want for Emma and how you want her to grow up. Imagine the state decides to give her up for adoption to strangers? Then you'll never have anything to do with her. You may not like the offer on the table, but given you're not going anywhere for quite some time you don't have a great many options, unless of course one of those choices is letting your daughter suffer in just the way you are in here.'

With that Flo got to her feet, feeling weary. The visit had been a mistake. She had hoped that she would be able to reason with her former boss, and to show her that Mary and David, whenever they wed, would be the best choice for Emma, but she could see that was impossible.

'Goodbye, Mrs Matravers, and don't worry, I won't visit again.'

'Wait,' Mrs Matravers called as Flo reached halfway across the room. 'Have you seen her with Emma? Mary, I mean. Have you seen her?'

A broad smile slowly crept across Flo's face as she recalled Mary holding Emma at Arthur's christening in the summer. Everyone had wanted to include the baby in as many events as possible and the orphanage didn't object to Mary taking her out for the day.

'Yes.' Flo nodded. 'She's a natural, Mrs Matravers, and she loves Emma as if she were her own.'

After that Flo didn't wait for a response and simply walked towards the door. The jailer let her out, and Flo left the prison without looking back, wanting to get as far away from the poison that woman trailed in her wake as quickly as possible.

Chapter Thirty-Six

The prison visit the previous day had shaken Flo, and consequently she had woken tired and full of despair. The sight of Mrs Matravers sitting behind that table, still holding on to the power she had wielded so mercilessly when she worked at the store, had haunted her all night long.

Staring into a strong brown cup of tea over her morning break, Flo hoped for a flash of clarity or earth-shattering wisdom. Sadly, nothing came.

'You've got a face like a busted clock,' Dot said as she burst into the room.

Flo lifted her chin and smiled at the matriarch, who as usual wasted no time mincing her words. 'It's been a tough few days, Dot.'

Dot pulled out a chair next to Flo. 'Is everything all right, darlin'? You were ever so quiet last night.'

'Am I supposed to be singing and dancing all the time?' Flo snapped.

As Dot leaned back in surprise Flo felt a flash of guilt. 'Sorry, I don't know what's come over me.'

'You've had a lot on your plate, it seems to me,' Dot said. 'Anything you want to talk about?'

Flo sighed. There was so much she wanted to talk about. Her failed talk with Mrs Matravers, the way she had let Mary down, the death of her husband, the singing she loved and still missed, the fundraising night, and the fact a man she thought was a trusted friend had possibly turned out to be a cheat and liar.

'I'm fine,' Flo said eventually.

Dot pursed her lips. 'We both know that's not true. But if you change your mind, you know where to find me.'

Flo nodded. 'Did you need me for something?'

'Ah, yes.' Dot rolled her eyes, cross with herself. 'Almost forgot. Edwin wants you in his office.'

'Me?' Flo exclaimed. 'What have I done now?'

'I don't necessarily think it's something you've done, darlin'. Henry's here and in the office with Edwin.'

Flo got to her feet, washed her cup in the sink and then made her way through the labyrinth of corridors towards Mr Button's office. Rose looked up and smiled sympathetically at her friend and ushered her straight in.

Walking inside the wood-panelled room, she saw Henry and Mr Button going through various documents, heads bent low.

'You wanted to see me, sir,' she said, breaking the silence.

Mr Button lifted his head. 'Ah, Flo. Yes, indeed. Take a seat, won't you?'

Flo did as instructed and ran her eyes over Henry, sitting beside her. She couldn't fail to notice he looked terrible: his hair was greasy and unkempt; his face was covered with stubble. She offered him a small smile, but he didn't notice; his gaze remained rooted to the floor.

'Henry will be away from the store for a little while as we look into the mess of the fundraising evening,' Mr Button began, his voice even. 'That means I need someone who can help me out a little with running the store, and as you've done it in the past I wondered if you would be willing to do it again, on a temporary basis.'

Flo glanced nervously between the two men. This was the very last thing she wanted. She had found Henry's job came with a lot of problems and was stressful to say the least.

'You won't be in the office full-time again,' Mr Button said, spotting the concern in her eyes. 'I'll just need you to be on hand now and again. I've also told the Board of Trade I may need to curtail my consulting duties for a little while as well.'

Flo nodded. 'All right, sir.'

A flash of relief passed across Mr Button's face. 'Thank you, Flo. Now, I'll let Henry explain to you where he's got to with various things. I've got to get across to the Board of Trade offices.'

With that he swept out of the room, leaving Flo and Henry alone. As Flo looked more closely at the former deputy she could see he seemed broken and she felt overwhelmed with a torrent of emotion. She'd thought they had a connection, she'd thought they had reached an understanding, but he had lied to her about so much, not least the fact he had been in prison. She had so much she wanted to say to him yet she felt strangely lost for words.

'So, shall we go through these papers then?' she said eventually.

Henry lifted his head and nodded. As he reached for the manila folder on the table, Flo laid a hand on his arm. 'How have you been?'

'I've been better.'

At that moment Flo felt a flash of anger. She had been so honest with him, so upfront about her feelings, how could he dismiss her with 'I've been better'?

'You know what? You're not the only one that's suffered. Everyone here put their heart and soul into raising that money, and now it's gone,' Flo snapped.

'That's not my fault,' he said, dropping the folder and spilling its contents across the floor.

'I'm not saying it is,' Flo replied more gently. 'But if we want to find out who was really responsible for taking that money, then you need to start talking. I want to help you.'

Henry turned to gaze at Flo, and for the first time since she had walked into that room, she saw his eyes light up with hope.

'Do you?'

'Of course, but you need to talk to me. Why did Evie say she saw you with the money?'

'She knows why.'

Flo frowned in confusion as she bent down to retrieve the folder and its contents. 'If Evie knows, then why isn't she speaking up?'

'You'll have to ask her.'

'Well, I'm asking you.'

'And I can't tell you any more than that,' Henry said quietly. 'I know it's frustrating; it's frustrating for me as well, I want to clear my name but I'll have to find another way. I can't tell you what I know.'

'But why? If you're innocent, why can't you tell me?'

'I'm sorry,' he said, more quietly this time, 'you'll just have to trust me.'

Flo stared at him in disbelief. 'Trust you? You've lied, you've broken promises, you've been in prison and yet you want me to trust you?'

'I know how it looks, Flo, believe me. And I want to tell you, really I do, but I can't. Just believe me when I tell you I'm innocent.'

'You were caught red-handed with the box that contained the money, you've been to prison for theft, but you want me to trust you on face value. Do you think I was born yesterday?'

'I didn't do it. Either theft. I didn't do either.'

'What do you mean?' Flo asked, setting the paperwork back on the desk and folding her arms.

Henry let out a long sigh and Flo allowed herself to feel a pang of sorrow for the man whom she had once looked up to. 'I mean I've never stolen anything in my life.'

'But you've been to prison,' she blurted.

'I took the blame for someone else,' he muttered.

'What do you mean? Who?'

'I can't tell you,' Henry said in exasperation, rubbing a hand across his face. 'I know you want answers, but I can't give you them. I've said as much as I can.'

'But that's not good enough. If you want to clear your name, if you want to come back to Liberty's, then you'll have to start talking to me – or at least to someone. What about Celia or Mr Button? Does he know any of this?'

'Celia knows everything; she was there. As for Mr Button, he knows I took the blame for someone else and went to prison, and he knows why I can't talk about it. It's why he vouched for me with the board, and it's why he's trusting me now when I say I had nothing to do with it.' His eyes filled with earnestness as he gripped her hand. 'Please believe me, Flo. Please help me.'

Flo's heart went out to him. She could see he was upset, that it had all gone wrong for him somehow. But then she remembered the disappointment on the faces of all her colleagues when the money had gone missing, the way that all their hard work and hopes for the war effort had been blown apart. And here was her former superior, who could help clear up this confusion if he would only start talking to people and telling the truth. She understood that he was keeping his mouth shut to help other people but equally he had to think about those caught up in the affair. What about Stan? What about the staff? What about the war effort? What about her?

'I'm sorry, really I am.' Flo sighed. 'But you have a history with Mr Button and Celia. They know you of old, I don't, and much as I want to believe you, unless you give me more of an explanation I'm afraid I can't help. Please believe me when I say there's nobody more sorry about this than me.'

'I understand.'

'Then I think from now on it would be better if we kept our relationship professional. So, shall we go over those notes so I can ensure everything remains ship-shape?'

With that she opened the folder and pulled it towards them. She knew she was doing the right thing, but if that really was the case then why did she feel so wretched?

Chapter Thirty-Seven

It had been a difficult couple of days since Henry had handed over his workload to Flo. Not only had she struggled to make sense of his notes, but she hadn't stopped worrying about him or the state of Liberty's and she had even gone into work that Sunday to try and make sense of her new duties.

It hadn't even helped that she had woken to the news that the RAF had successfully bombed parts of Berlin, dropping over a thousand tons of incendiaries on the city. As she sat in the Bell Street kitchen on Sunday morning, first light pouring through the windows, Flo gulped down a cup of tea with Dot sitting opposite. They were both hanging on to the newsreader's every word that the British raid had been the largest on the German capital in two months.

'Well, that's us done for then,' Dot said, getting up to wash her cup out.

Flo looked at her in surprise. 'Do you think so?'

Dot nodded. 'Hitler will want payback for this, mark my words.'

'I don't know,' Flo said, sipping the last of her tea. 'Maybe we've got him on the ropes now. Maybe he'll retreat.'

Dot snorted. 'And maybe we'll eat bacon regular again.'

Flo said nothing as she got up and washed her own cup. Then, giving Dot's shoulder a kindly squeeze, she finished getting ready for work. There were days when it felt as if the war would never end. And as Flo made her way to the store she couldn't shake the feeling that Dot was right about the Nazis making Britain pay for this latest attack. It seemed as though it was a never-ending cycle of bombing, with the only true cost being the loss of human life.

For the rest of the day as Flo worked to put Mr Masters' affairs in order she couldn't shift the feeling of misery that engulfed her. Everything seemed so hopeless. She had worked so hard to try and make things right, but there were times when it all seemed futile. The war was still in full swing, the troubles at Liberty's seemed to be on-going, and Flo truly wondered just how much she would have to take before she could find a small corner of happiness.

The thought plagued her all day as she worked in Henry's office which overlooked shelled-out London. When Flo finished and made her way home to Bell Street all she wanted to do was have an early night. Yet the moment she walked into the dark hallway she heard the sounds of music and laughter coming from the kitchen. Curious, Flo shucked off her coat and shoes, then padded barefoot towards the source of the noise.

Inside the kitchen, Flo found Alice holding Arthur in her arms, jiggling him delightedly up and down on the spot, while Dot, Mary, Rose and even Jean and Bess were circling the scrubbed pine table, the wireless blaring from the side of the kitchen. All the women were singing and dancing together, their faces alive with merriment.

'What's this?' she asked over the din, noting the bottles of stout that had been pulled from Dot's emergency stash in the basement.

At the sound of Flo's voice, the laughter stopped as the girls gathered to welcome her.

'There you are!' Alice cried. 'We've been waiting for you. Where have you been?'

Flo shrugged. 'Had to work today. I'm taking on some of Mr Masters' duties while he's out of the office.'

At the mention of the deputy store manager's name, Rose grimaced. 'He's a disgrace. I hope he never comes back to work at Liberty's. I don't know why Mr Button hasn't called the police.'

"Cos things ain't always that straightforward,' Dot said bluntly. 'You should know that better than anyone, Rose Harper, after your pick-pocketing earlier this year.'

Rose coloured at the mention of her previous misdemeanours. 'That was different.'

'Why? Because it was you?' Dot put in.

'Dot's right, Rose,' Jean agreed. 'I know it looks awful, but really we don't know. Best to let the Liberty powers that be get to the bottom of it before we start kicking Mr Masters while he's down. Sometimes things aren't always what they seem.'

Rose stretched out a finger to tickle Arthur's chin. 'I suppose you're right. It's just difficult after we all worked so hard to raise the money for the war effort.'

'Life's not fair sometimes,' Bess muttered. 'We just have to make the best of it.'

'And you look as if you're doing a brilliant job of that,' Alice said. 'How are you coping with your injury now?'

'You mean the loss of my hand,' Bess said in a gruff tone. Flo couldn't miss the way Alice winced in apology, clearly regretting bringing the subject up.

'I didn't mean ...'

'I know you didn't,' Bess replied more gently as Alice's voice trailed off. 'I just think sometimes it pays to call a spade a spade. But thank you, Alice, I'm adapting to life well without it. It's early days yet, the medics tell me, and really I'm just grateful to be out of hospital. I'm going to look at other ways to serve my country.'

'Are you?' Rose cried in surprise.

"Course.' Bess shrugged. 'I thought I'd help you out more with your first-aid evenings for a start. I really enjoyed the last one.'

'That would be wonderful,' Rose enthused.

'Good on you, darlin'.' Dot nodded approvingly. 'That's a nice attitude to have, and one we should all adopt given that we're celebrating.'

'So I gathered,' Flo said, helping herself to one of the bottles of stout on the table and pouring herself a glass. 'What's the occasion then?'

At Flo's question, all eyes turned expectantly to Mary.

'The occasion is I'm going to be a mother!' Mary cried proudly.

Flo looked at her in confusion. 'You're pregnant? But how? David's been away for months. Have you only just found out or something? You don't look pregnant.'

'No, you daft mare.' Dot laughed. 'Come on, Flo, use your head!'

'But I don't see what else it can be?' Flo frowned, until suddenly her face broke into a wide smile: 'Unless ...'

'*Unless* is right.' Mary beamed, throwing her arms around her, sloshing stout down Flo's back in the process. 'Mabel Matravers contacted the authorities and Mrs Rawlins at the council was good enough to call in on me this morning of all days to deliver the good news in person. It seems that Mrs Matravers has had a change of heart and has agreed to let me and David adopt Emma the moment we marry.'

Flo stared at her in disbelief. 'Are you sure?'

'More than sure. Mrs Rawlins says Mrs Matravers has even signed the paperwork in readiness,' Mary said triumphantly.

'Well, that's wonderful news,' Flo cried, feeling her bad mood evaporate and happiness flood through her.

'I just can't believe she's changed her mind. She was so resolute she didn't want us to adopt her,' Mary said in disbelief.

'Well, perhaps Mrs Matravers thought about it a bit,' Flo offered, not wanting details of her good deed to go noticed.

'Who cares why she did what she did?' Alice replied, switching Arthur from one arm to the other. 'Let's be grateful she's changed her mind. If nothing else baby Emma is now set to have a good life.'

'And not only that, you deserve it, darlin',' Dot put in, turning to Mary. 'You're a born mum.'

At the mention of the word 'mum' Dot's face clouded over. The sadness that she experienced at never having become a mother herself wasn't lost on Flo.

'Have you contacted David?' she asked.

Mary shook her head. 'I'll send him an urgent telegram in the morning. I know he'll be thrilled.'

'You deserve it, love.' Flo smiled. 'All you need now is for David to come back and marry you and then you'll be a proper family.'

'I know.' Mary hugged herself happily. 'And not only that, the authorities said I can start to take Emma out again. Get to know her a bit better, that sort of thing, so she'll be more settled when we do finally marry and can bring her home.'

'Well, that's wonderful news,' Dot exclaimed. 'You should have said before. We'll have a big party for her.'

Mary grimaced at the thought. 'I think that might be a bit much, Dot. We don't want to crowd the child.'

'Quite right.' Alice nodded. 'Best to do it gradually. Anyway, if you want to throw anyone a party, you want to toast Flo here.'

Flo coloured. 'Me? Why?'

'Well, darlin', correct me if I'm wrong, but you're the one that went to see old Mabel in the nick,' Dot said, grey eyes twinkling.

'How do you know that?' Flo cried.

'Because Mrs Matravers told Mrs Rawlins,' Mary said with a roll of her eyes. 'Did you think one of us had a second career as Sherlock Holmes?'

'I didn't do anything,' Flo protested. 'I just went to see her, pleaded your case.'

'That's not nothing,' Alice said, looking at her with love in her eyes. 'That's a real act of friendship.'

'Nonsense.' Flo shrugged, feeling embarrassed. 'I just did what anyone else would do.'

Mary stepped forward and took Flo's hand. 'You did a wonderful thing for me. I shall never forget it, ever. Thank you.' With that Mary pulled Flo in for another embrace. 'You've made me the happiest woman in the world.'

From nowhere, Flo felt tears of happiness well from deep inside. 'You're welcome,' she managed to whisper, before wriggling free from her friend's embrace. 'Now then,' she said, lifting up her glass. 'I thought we were here to celebrate.'

With that the girls clinked their glasses together.

'Here's to Mary, David and Emma,' Dot called.

'To Mary, David and Emma,' the girls echoed.

As Flo took a sip of her drink she felt her shoulders loosen and her headache lift. Perhaps life wasn't all doom and gloom. Perhaps there were still moments of joy to be found amongst all this hardship.

Chapter Thirty-Eight

The following Wednesday morning Flo made her way to the school for another piano shift feeling uncertain about the future. She had needed to change her days that week because of a stock take at work. Thankfully the school had been more than happy to accommodate. After the impromptu party on Sunday night where they had toasted Mary's future, Flo's unshakeable feeling that Hitler wanted revenge had been right. Bombs had dropped over East Dulwich way that weekend, and the din of heavy anti-aircraft fire had been audible in the Bell Street terrace four miles away. It had been a very disturbed night and nobody had got much sleep.

Since then they had all enjoyed much better nights; however, the newspapers were full of reports of Sunday's blasts. Flo paused at the newsstand near the bus stop and read the headlines. Shivering, she took in the scene of a row of houses being destroyed, people screaming as they fought for their lives. Just a couple of years ago, reports like this were commonplace, when London was struck by the Nazis almost every night. For the last year and a half Londoners had scarcely heard or seen a bomb. Occasionally, if you turned your back against the shelled buildings and scenes of devastation, it was almost possible to pretend that they were back in peacetime. Until front pages such as these propelled you back to the present.

Flo turned her back on the papers and walked down the road towards the school. Like everyone else, she'd had enough of her life constantly being overshadowed by war but there were times when it seemed impossible to think about anything else. Pushing open the staff door at the back of the school building, Flo knew she had to put her feelings aside. Today would be a busy day. Not only was she helping out with the lunchtime music session – she was a bit early, in fact – but she had to cover her own job and Mr Masters' later.

Celia wanted to put on a big performance at the end of term, something to keep the children's spirits up in the deep midwinter, and Flo had agreed to lend a hand, thinking there was nothing better than music to lift the spirits.

Walking into the large hall, she was pleased to see Celia was already there putting out rows of chairs.

'Flo, love,' she called cheerily. 'How are you?'

'Not bad,' replied Flo. 'How are you?'

Celia shook her head vigorously, causing a lock of hair to fall from her bun and into her eyes. 'Fed up with them bloody Germans! Thanks to them, I'm missing my outdoor privy.'

'Of course!' Flo exclaimed. 'You'd have been just around the corner from where the bombs dropped.'

'It was a nightmare,' Celia sighed, sitting on one of the chairs for a moment. 'The place was chaos. One poor lad fell through the ceiling into the room below. When he came to, he found hisself in the kitchen with a cooker on his chest!'

Flo looked at her wide-eyed. 'Oh my word! Was he all right?'

Celia nodded and pushed the lock of hair behind her ear. 'Miraculously he was unharmed. But enough about the Nazis. They've stolen enough of my weekend; I'm not letting them ruin my week as well.'

'Well said,' Flo replied, doing her best to smile.

Celia frowned and laid a hand on Flo's shoulder. 'What's got into you? Germans didn't bomb you out 'n' all, did they? Dot didn't end up with a kettle on her backside?'

This time Flo managed a half-smile. 'Ignore me. I'm feeling sorry for myself.'

'Well, I think you're allowed, Flo love,' Celia offered. 'You've had a lot to put up with lately. Forgive yourself a bit.'

'I don't know, Celia, I really don't. It's just, well, I feel so overwhelmed. I mean, first I lost Aggie, then Neil, and what with the renewed attack on London, not to mention all my friends that have been hurt through this flamin' war like Rose and Bess, all of it just feels so pointless. I feel that life is one long stretch of misery.'

As Flo finished speaking, there was silence, and she wondered if she had gone too far. Even in her miserable state she knew she sounded riddled with self-pity. She was about to apologise when Celia threw her arms around her and pulled her into her chest.

'Flo, my love, you've every right to feel the way you do,' she whispered. 'You've had to weather more than your fair share, you really have. But I promise you that you will know happiness again. Actually, if you don't mind me being honest, I think it's time for you to face some cold hard facts.'

'How do you mean?' Flo asked.

There was a brief pause as though Celia were weighing up the pros and cons of speaking up before she continued.

'Flo,' she began, her tone firmer now. 'I understand you're grief-stricken, of course you are, but it's as though grief has overtaken you and you've been frightened to live your own life. Refusing to do the things that bring you pleasure won't bring your Neil or Aggie back, you know.'

'I haven't been,' Flo protested. 'I've been playing the piano.'

Celia tutted. 'Half-measures. It's singing that will make you happy. I saw the way you lit up at the Palladium that night.'

At the suggestion Flo shook her head. 'I can't.'

'Why?' Celia snapped. 'And don't give me some nonsense about lies and guilt over some silly letter. Your Neil loved you; if he didn't he never would have been so hurtful. Indifference is the enemy in marriage, sweetheart, not hurt.'

Flo locked eyes with Celia and knew it was time to tell the truth. 'Because I enjoy singing too much; that's the real reason.'

'What on earth does that mean?' Celia demanded.

'I mean, I lose myself when I'm singing; I forget everything and everyone. Nothing else matters. I saw it with Aggie and I see it in you too. I'm the same and that's the problem. Because if I sing then I forget to think about Neil and Aggie, and I can't bear for them to slip from my mind for even a second.'

With that Flo broke down and Celia wrapped her arms around her.

'Enough now, Flo. You've suffered enough,' Celia whispered.

With all her might, Flo clung to her new friend, enjoying the comfort Celia's embrace offered. She wasn't sure how long the two of them stood there, holding each other like that, but Flo did know that when they parted she felt much better than she had done for weeks.

Flo was just about to ask what they were doing that lunchtime when the sound of a siren could be heard in the distance.

'Did you hear that?'

Celia looked up and paused for a moment. 'It's just before half past twelve; it's the lunch bell.'

Flo shrugged, thinking nothing of it, until the wail came again. Louder and more urgent this time.

'That doesn't sound like a lunch bell,' Flo insisted.

Celia's eyes widened in alarm. 'It isn't. It's the air-raid siren. Looks like the bloody Jerries are at it again.' With that Celia grabbed Flo's hand and together they made for the door, the wail becoming louder and more insistent.

'Where's your shelter?' Flo asked immediately.

'Second floor. It's a bricked-up classroom,' Celia said. 'But we need to get the children. They'll be in the dining hall. Some may even be outside.'

Instinctively Flo followed Celia out to the hall. There was no mistaking the sound of the tearing, ear-piercing wail now, and it chilled her to the core.

Releasing her hand from Celia's warm grasp she looked around at the children. The air was ripe with fear as they looked out of the windows at the grey sky. Following their gaze, Flo immediately spotted what had caught their attention. A German plane was flying perilously low, swooping and diving as it circled the school. Flo swallowed the bile rising in her throat; she knew she had to get the children and herself to safety. The single-engine bomber with the ominous black cross of the Luftwaffe was now so close you could see the pilot, who seemed to be waving at the children, and incredibly some were waving back.

Flo felt a surge of fury pulse within her as she made out the pilot's face. How dare he? Didn't he have children? A wife? A family?

'Into the shelter now,' she called out authoritatively.

Immediately the children followed Flo's orders and together they raced through the corridors and up the stairs.

'First door on the left!' one of the children cried.

Locating the door, Flo pushed it open and saw a handful of children had already taken shelter. Closing the door once the last child was inside, she threw herself on to the bench and exhaled, only to realise that she hadn't seen Celia for some time.

'Has anyone seen Mrs Hallam?' she asked urgently.

'She was just going into the playground, miss,' Stan piped up. 'Said she'd be up in a minute.'

'All right.' Flo drummed her fingers against the edge of the wooden bench. The room was dark, and filled with a heady mix of terror and desperation. Rows of white eyes were fixed on her and she could hear some of the children crying, while others didn't seem worried at all as they continued to eat their sandwiches.

Flo didn't know whether to laugh or cry. She was about to get up and comfort those who were distressed when the ear-piercing sound of a whistle made her freeze. As the whistling grew louder Flo's pulse beat faster and she braced herself for what was undoubtedly to come next.

'Everyone down,' she bellowed, throwing herself on top of Stan and another child.

Just then, Celia and another army of children flew into the room and Flo had never been so grateful to see anyone. They were all just in the nick of time as the bomb she'd heard a split second earlier rocketed to the ground. Debris and rubble immediately fell around them, a wooden lintel striking Flo neatly on the back of the neck, and sending clouds of dust into the air that filled her lungs with thick, dry powder. Somehow the lintel had managed to topple down next to her, and as she listened to the sounds of the children choking, she managed to find two hankies in her pocket. Giving one to Stan and another child to breathe through, Flo used the sleeve of her cardigan to filter as much dust as she could.

The children were crying, Flo noticed, but they didn't seem panic-stricken. Instead they were trying to make sense of what had happened. These little ghosts who had looked like normal schoolchildren just seconds earlier now resembled ghouls of the night, they were covered in so much dust. Getting to her feet, along with Celia, Flo smiled reassuringly at them as she tried to recall the training she had received during Rose's first-aid nights. *Stay calm; prioritise the most life-threatening conditions.* Casting an eye across the kids, fear lurched in Flo's heart as she peered through the large smoking hole and down into the lunch hall directly below. The scene made her want to cry out with horror at the cruelty.

Clouds of smoke and fire distorted her view, but she could just make out the tiny forms of lifeless and injured children lying amongst the wreckage. The sound of those little mites crying out for their mothers left Flo feeling furious and desperate to help.

Glancing across at Celia, Flo saw tears were streaming down the older woman's face too, but her chin was high as she gave a sharp nod. Together they would do whatever it took to save as many lives as they possibly could.

Chapter Thirty-Nine

The stench of fire and of charred flesh filled Flo's nostrils. She had to cover her mouth with her hand to keep from gagging as she tried to move, the smell was so pungent.

Through the hole in the floor, she could see some of the older surviving children dusting themselves down and moving cautiously, doing what they could to help others. Shouts of 'What can I do, miss?' echoed through the noise and chaos and Flo was astonished to see these children coming together to help with the rescue effort.

Surely, though, there ought to be more help than these surviving children? Flo looked around, as if expecting an ambulance or fire crew to miraculously turn up, but there was nobody. She turned to Celia. 'Are you all right?'

Celia nodded. 'Are you, sweetheart?'

'I'm fine,' Flo said, doing her best to ignore the thumping headache from where the lintel had struck. 'Where shall we start?'

'Let's clear what we can here,' Celia replied. 'We can try and treat the wounded and drag the others to safety as best we can.'

Flo nodded but, as she did so, pointed at the blood that streamed from Celia's forehead. 'Are you sure you're all right? You're bleeding.'

Celia touched her forehead; her grey hair was plastered to the blood. 'I'm fine. Just a scratch. Come on, it's up to us until the rescue teams get here.'

Flo didn't need to be told twice. Up close the devastation was even worse than she could have predicted. There was rubble everywhere, and bricks and debris continued to fall perilously to the floor. The children who had survived were working marvels. The older ones were pulling the injured to safety, while others were ripping up their own clothes to make bandages or tourniquets to stem bleeding.

Watching Celia help one small girl work herself free from the bricks that were trapping her leg, she frowned with concern. The older woman seemed to be struggling. Even from this distance Flo could tell that her breath was laboured and blood was continuing to stream down her forehead.

By the time help had arrived Flo felt physically and mentally exhausted, and her hands and legs were cut to ribbons. She had seen to cuts, bruises and broken bones, patching up as many children as possible. But it was the bodies of lifeless children, being cleared by others of similar age, that broke her heart. Pausing to take a breath, her nostrils singed with smoke, Flo glanced around. Everywhere was chaos, and even though Celia, herself and the handful of teachers were all working tirelessly it felt as if they were never going to get anywhere. Then Flo saw what resembled an avalanche of rescue workers arrive like a beacon of light. Soldiers home on leave, passing volunteers and fire crews were helping to clear the area and Flo felt relief flood through her.

Getting to her feet to greet the rescue workers, she was astonished to see a familiar face.

'Flo! Are you all right?' Henry said, carefully picking his way through the carnage. 'I came as soon as I heard what had happened.'

At the sight of her old friend, Flo fell into his arms. 'I'm fine. But there's not enough help, and so many of the children are injured.'

Henry nodded, his face contorted into despair as he took in the scenes of devastation. 'I've told Stan to go home and ask our neighbour Mrs Hope to look after him until I get back. He said he was fine after you threw yourself on top of him, but I don't want him taking any chances and this air raid is all anyone in the community can talk about.'

Flo smiled. 'He's been helping the younger ones. Doing his best to cheer them up while they were in pain.'

Henry shot her a sympathetic glance. 'It could have been so different if you hadn't looked after him as you did. I shall never forget it.'

Flo waved his gratitude away. 'I did nothing. Truly, look around you, there's still so many we have to help.'

'Then we'd better get on with it.'

Together, Flo and Henry worked with the rescue teams, never faltering or giving up hope of saving life. As she continued to work into the evening, all thoughts of Liberty's gone from her mind, it seemed to Flo that the whole of South London had descended upon the school to help their community when they needed it most. News had spread fast and the children's loved ones had arrived, digging at the debris with their bare hands, desperately searching for lost ones, ignoring their own safely as the rubble continued to fall.

At some point, Flo became aware that the WVS had arrived and were busy making tea and tending to the sick in the church hall across the road from the school. Someone handed Flo a cup and she gulped at it gratefully. Eventually, when the worst of the debris and rubble was cleared, Flo was led away by one of the rescue workers who told her under no uncertain terms that she had done enough.

Flo was taken to a bench outside the school and handed yet another cup of tea. Hands wrapped around the mug, she suddenly became aware of her aching bones and throbbing head. Looking around she realised the scene looked different now. The fires and smoke had begun to die out and there was a sense of order, if such a thing was possible, to the devastation.

As Flo sipped her tea she saw Henry towering over Celia by one of the ambulances. She was clearly struggling to breathe and she looked even more shattered than Flo felt. Judging by the look on Henry's face it seemed that he was becoming upset about something. Getting to her feet, Flo threaded her way over to them through the volunteers still working. 'What's going on?' she asked.

Henry turned and gave her a sheepish grin. 'Everything's fine. I'm just trying to persuade Celia to go to the hospital. She's tired, the gash on her forehead looks nasty and she won't stop coughing.'

'And I've told you I'm fine,' Celia said firmly, before erupting into a coughing fit.

Flo winced. It sounded awful. 'I think Henry's right. We'll both go, get ourselves looked at. There's no harm.'

'Except it's a waste of time, that's all,' Celia growled as she continued to cough.

At that moment a female first-aider approached them and frowned. 'You, young lady,' she said, pointing to Celia, 'are going to hospital. You want that cough looked at. And as for you two' – she gestured towards Flo and Mr Masters – 'you'll both need to be examined by me before anyone goes anywhere.'

There was something about the woman's tone that brooked no argument. Within a few minutes she and Henry were pronounced fine while Celia was led into the back of a waiting ambulance.

'Where are you taking me?' she demanded.

'Lewisham Hospital,' the female first-aider replied. 'Not far. Your friends can come along and see how you are.'

'We'll be right behind you,' Flo promised.

As the ambulance doors banged shut, Flo turned to Henry. 'We need to find a bus. How long will it take to get to the hospital?'

'Not long.' He frowned. 'But are you sure you want to go charging off there? You need some food? Rest?'

'I need to be with Celia,' Flo insisted. 'She deserves to have someone with her and I want to be that person.'

'All right,' he said, leading the way to the bus stop around the corner.

Within minutes a bus appeared, and as they took a seat and handed the clippie their money, Flo took a moment to gather her thoughts.

'Wait a minute!' she cried in alarm. 'Where's Stan?'

'He's being cared for by Dot. Everyone heard about what happened and wanted to help. Dot appeared on my doorstep offering her services and Alice and Mary helped out the ladies at the WVS making tea. Didn't you see them?'

Flo shook her head. She had been so busy tending to the children she hadn't registered anyone else's presence.

At that moment the bus pulled up outside the hospital and together she and Henry walked towards the entrance. Outside, Flo inhaled great big lungfuls of fresh air, grateful for the change in atmosphere after so much smoke.

'Are you ready?'

Flo nodded and together they walked inside. Unsurprisingly, given the events at the school, the place was a hive of activity as nurses and doctors rushed through corridors coping with the emergency.

Gingerly, Flo made her way towards an officious-looking nurse. 'Can you tell me where Celia Hallam is please? She was brought in by ambulance earlier.'

The nurse looked down at her notes, just as a doctor approached looking stern.

'Are you relatives?' he asked, taking the clipboard from the nurse's hand.

'Yes,' Henry lied. 'This is her cousin, and I'm her husband. We were all together working at the school to try and clear the wreckage and save the children.'

The doctor's expression changed and he looked fondly at the pair. 'You must be exhausted.'

'We're all right,' Flo said with a conviction she did not feel. 'How is Mrs Hallam?'

There was a pause and in that moment Flo felt a sickening sense of dread.

'I'm afraid she has sustained a very serious head injury, but that's not her biggest problem,' the doctor explained, his face grave once more. 'She has inhaled a great deal of smoke, possibly because she was in an area where the smoke was much thicker – it's impossible to know. What I can tell you is her heart is at risk.'

'That sounds serious,' Flo gasped.

'It is.' The doctor nodded. 'But we're doing everything we can. However, I must ask you to prepare yourselves for the worst. The casualties of this dreadful atrocity aren't over yet.'

Chapter Forty

As Flo and Henry were shown into Celia's room, Flo couldn't help but do a double take as she took in the sight of her friend. Celia had gone downhill rapidly since she had seen her less than an hour ago. Her eyes were closed, her skin grey, and her breath was now so laboured that every inhalation looked like a struggle. A large bandage had been wrapped around her head, giving her the appearance of a little girl, rather than a grown woman who deserved a hero's welcome.

'Celia,' Flo said cautiously, approaching the bed. 'It's me and Henry. We've come to see how you are.'

Opening one eye, Celia regarded Flo fondly and smiled. 'Thank you, love. You've always been a good girl.'

'I don't know about that,' Flo said tenderly. 'Like you, I was just doing my job today, doing what had to be done. How are you feeling?'

'Like a great big bus has fallen on me,' she croaked.

Flo looked anxiously at Henry, who mouthed that he would go and get some water.

'Don't try and talk, Celia, just get some rest. Henry's gone to get water; he'll be back in a minute, then we'll leave you to it and come back and see how you are tomorrow.'

At that Celia gripped Flo's arm. 'Don't go. We both know I'm not getting out of here alive.'

'Don't say that,' Flo said furiously, doing her best to swallow back the tears. 'The doctors said you're fine.'

'You're a lovely girl, Flo, but a terrible liar,' Celia croaked again. 'I need to talk to you.'

'About what?'

'About you, about your life.'

Flo sighed. She was exhausted and she knew Celia was too.

'Let's talk tomorrow,' Flo said again. 'We're all tired; we need some rest.'

'No,' Celia said, more forcefully this time. 'You need to hear this and I need to say it.'

Flo eyed her friend cautiously. 'All right.'

'There are some things you don't know,' Celia rasped. 'Things you should know. Things Aggie should have told you before she died and didn't.'

Flo was surprised. 'What does Aggie have to do with anything? Did you know her?'

Just then Henry reappeared with a jug of water. At the sight of him, Flo turned and looked at him with concern. 'Celia wants to talk to me. She says it's important.'

'Oh?' Henry said, placing the jug down beside Celia's bedside and clamping her hand between his. 'Just try and rest, there's plenty of time for all this.'

But Celia was insistent. 'No, it's time, and I need your help.'

Henry said nothing, simply closing his eyes and raising his face heavenwards as if in deep thought.

'All right,' he said eventually. With that he turned to Flo and smiled tenderly. 'What I've got to say isn't going to be easy.'

Alarm pulsed through Flo as she glanced from Henry's face to Celia's. 'What do you mean? Has this got something to do with the missing money?'

Henry shook his head. 'This is about you. You see, I wasn't entirely honest about the reason I wanted you to sing at Stan's school.'

'What do you mean?'

'I wanted you and Celia to meet. After Aggie died, Celia wanted to become more involved in your life and together we thought that getting you to play the piano at the school would be the best way.'

'But why?' Flo asked.

'Because you needed a family,' Henry explained.

Flo shook her head in shock. There had to be some mistake. Celia was obviously delirious and Henry must have taken a blow to the head because none of this made any sense at all. 'What are you talking about?'

'Aggie was my younger sister,' Celia managed.

Flo's jaw fell open in shock. 'You can't possibly mean that. It's been a long day and night and you need to rest,' she said, her mind a whirl.

She got to her feet, ready to plump Celia's pillows, but Celia shook her head, tears in her eyes.

'I don't need to rest,' Celia croaked. 'I need to offload the burden I've been carrying for years and tell you the truth. Aggie was my sister. We grew up together in Islington; we were closer than any two sisters have a right to be.'

'Which, if it's true, means you're my mother,' Flo gasped as she tried to make sense of what she was hearing. 'You're the woman that left me with Aggie when I was five years old ...'

As the realisation took hold, Flo struggled to catch her breath. Trembling now, she stepped away from the bed. Turning to the window she stared blankly at the blackout blind as she did her best to understand. How was this possible? She had dreamed of this moment for so long, the moment of actually finding her mother and bonding with the woman who had carried her, given birth to her, given *life* to her, but now the moment was here, she had no idea what to say, what to think or what to feel.

'No, Flo love,' Celia croaked. 'I'm your aunt, I'm not your mother.'

Flo felt as if she was falling. There was so much to think about, so many things she wanted to know.

'I don't understand. If you're not my mother then who is?'

Celia glanced at Henry, who gave her an encouraging nod. With that one glance, Flo knew her world was about to fall apart. Whatever Celia was about to say, there was no going back.

'Aggie,' Celia croaked. 'Aggie was your mother.'

Chapter Forty-One

Flo could barely take in what Celia had just told her, and her eyes filled with tears. This had to be a mistake – Celia was in a terrible state, after all. Even now, her breathing had become shallower and she appeared to be drifting in and out of consciousness.

Flo watched Henry take a deep breath before bending down to kiss Celia's forehead. 'I'm just going to take Flo outside for a moment,' he whispered. 'I'll explain everything. Don't you worry, this is going to be all right.' With that Henry walked around to the other side of the bed, reached for Flo's elbow, and steered her out of the door and into the stark white hospital corridor.

'What is going on?' she asked, her voice shaking as she spoke. 'Aggie wasn't my mother – she was my aunt. Tell me this isn't true, Henry. None of it makes any sense.'

Henry reached for her hand. 'I'm sorry, Flo, but it is true. Celia is your aunt. She has wanted to tell you for some time now but knew it wasn't her secret to share. She's always kept a careful eye on you, even when you didn't know it. Aggie would write to her in Harrogate and tell her how you were getting on with her and Ray. When Celia moved back to London she would stand outside Liberty's hoping for a glimpse of you. She always wanted to stay in your life. When Aggie passed away, followed by Neil, she felt that the time was right for her to step in and help take care of you. She thought you needed her.'

'How do you know this?' Flo asked, her mind struggling to take it all in.

'Because when Mum died Celia was my rock, and we spent a lot of time talking about love and grief. We came to rely on each other – we still do,' Henry admitted. 'One night, Celia told me that her sister Aggie had given birth to a little girl while she was unmarried and so she raised the child as her own for a little while.'

Flo's head was spinning as she tried to take everything in. Could she really be Aggie's daughter? Something didn't add up.

'Celia can't be Aggie's sister. None of this is true,' she said.

'Why not?'

'Because Aggie always said her sister was Sheila not Celia,' Flo said with a note of triumph in her voice. 'I don't know why you and Celia are making things up but there's proof that this isn't true and it's all a fairy story.'

'Sheila is Celia's real name. She amended it so her husband wouldn't find her. Her last name's not really Hallam either, it's Wilson.' Henry sighed as he gestured to a pair of chairs that had just become vacant.

Flo sat down and gazed at her hands, which were neatly folded in her lap. They were the same as Aggie's, she realised. Long slender fingers, short square nails and wide palms. Looking down at them now, she started to wonder whether Celia and Henry could be telling the truth.

She closed her eyes and, leaning against the cool tiled hospital wall, she brought Aggie's face to mind. Flo missed her more than she had ever thought possible. Lifting her chin she stared at Henry's face, which was so full of hope, and knew that he held the answers to her questions.

'Why did Aggie give me up in the first place?' Flo asked eventually. 'She and Ray always wanted children. Is Ray really my father?'

'Bill Wilson is your father. He was Celia's husband,' Henry replied. 'He worked down the tanner's yard and at weekends was out gambling all his money away. Celia always knew Bill Wilson was a bad sort but I think perhaps she thought she could tame him. For a while she managed it. When he asked her to marry him she was cock-a-hoop and they wed when she was twenty-two in the church just off the Holloway Road.'

'So where did it all go wrong?'

'They had been married a year when Celia fell pregnant. By all accounts Bill had changed his ways by then and was adapting to life as a husband. When he discovered he was going to be a father, he was over the moon. Aggie was excited too, of course, at the thought of becoming an auntie. She would only have been about eighteen and still living up home with their mother. All she could talk about was how she and Celia would take the baby out singing with them when he or she was old enough.'

'Sounds like it would have been nice,' Flo said with a smile.

'It would have been, but when Celia went into labour, things started to go very wrong. Celia's baby boy was still-born. She barely got to hold him and say goodbye.'

Flo struggled to breathe. She'd had no idea such tragedy had befallen her family.

'So what happened after that?'

'Celia wanted another baby but it never happened and I believe Bill returned to old habits as a result. He started womanising again, cheating, gambling – he even got in with a gang for a time. He was so angry at the loss of his boy and he loved the cut and thrust of running around with the mob. After Celia and Aggie's mother died, he started to become violent with Celia, and Aggie too. Celia felt frightened most days,' Henry continued, 'but she knew she had made her bed and had to lie in it, until he started giving Aggie the same treatment, that is.'

'What do you mean?' Flo asked, feeling a sense of dread deep in the pit of her stomach.

Henry grimaced. 'There's no easy way to say this, Flo, but it seems that one night Celia came home after she had been working in the pub and found Aggie weeping on the kitchen floor. Bill had taken advantage of her.'

'He attacked her?' Flo gasped.

'It wasn't quite like that,' Henry said. 'As I understand it Aggie and Celia had a row shortly after their mother died. Aggie had come over to make it up to her but Celia wasn't in and Bill poisoned her mind. Told her that Celia never had a good word to say about her sister, thought she was just a stupid child, whereas he really appreciated her. He took advantage of her, plain and simple.'

Flo's stomach turned at the thought. Aggie would never have betrayed her sister; Flo knew her to be a loyal and loving woman who always put family first. Bill Wilson would have engineered something despicable to have made Aggie lose her way like that when she was at her lowest. Flo could easily imagine what he could have said. She knew her father to be a charmer when he wanted to be; he would have no doubt offered her the love and comfort she needed while she was awash with grief. Not for the first time Flo felt hatred like no other burn deep inside her soul at the thought of this man. Were there no depth he wouldn't stoop too?

'Poor Aggie,' Flo murmured. 'And poor Celia too. Did they ever make amends?'

'They did.' Henry nodded. 'Aggie told her straightaway what she had done, and of course blamed herself. Celia knew better, though, and realised instantly that Bill was at fault. Celia told her to forget all about it, to move on and not let it ruin her future. But before long Aggie discovered she was pregnant and she was terrified of the shame having a baby would bring.'

'So what did they do?'

'The sisters came up with a plan. Aggie went away to an unmarried mothers' home in Kent and when she came home with you she gave you to Celia to raise as her own. It seemed like the best thing for everyone. Aggie could be a treasured aunt, and a part of Celia hoped that bringing a baby into the house would tame Bill again as, sadly, even though Celia had tried to fall pregnant again she had failed.'

'It would have seemed like a good idea, I suppose,' Flo said.

'It was for a while. Celia adored you, and everyone seemed to believe the story about Aggie being your aunt. Aggie found her own happy ending by marrying Ray when you were about one. Ray adored you too in his own quiet way and never knew the truth.'

Flo closed her eyes, a fleeting early memory appearing in her mind's eyes as she remembered how she and Celia used to go to Aggie's house. Together they sat around the piano, and the sisters taught Flo to play and sing. Flo could vividly remember the Yardley's scent her aunt had worn, filling the room as easily as her uncle's rolling laughter as he clapped and giggled in all the right places. She had been so happy then; where had it all gone wrong?

'You got to about five years old before Bill became horribly violent again,' Henry carried on, as if reading Flo's mind. 'He inflicted so much misery on Celia that she couldn't stand it. She was terrified he would hurt you too.'

'So that was why Celia left?'

Henry nodded. 'The sisters had it all planned out. Aggie would raise you as her niece, even though you were her own flesh and blood. Celia took some of the money she had been saving from the pitiful housekeeping Bill had given her, and Aggie gave her some extra from the money she had saved from her singing nights. She told Celia to get away, start a new life somewhere and promised Bill would never hurt you or Celia again.'

'Celia said we were just popping round for tea and that I could play in the park after,' Flo said, the memory of the day rushing back to her. 'Then she had kissed my head and left. I kept begging Aggie to take me to the park, I was desperate to find her and looked for days.'

'She stayed in South London for a while, then went over to Kent and finally up to Harrogate with her new name, Celia Hallam.'

Flo rubbed a hand across her face, her mind working at a rate of knots as she tried to make sense of the story. She suddenly felt very tired but she knew there was so much more to say before this wretched day was over.

'I need to see Celia,' she said, getting to her feet. 'And I think I need to see her alone.'

Henry nodded in understanding. 'I'll be here if you need me.'

Flashing him as grateful a smile as she could muster, Flo walked wearily back into Celia's room and closed the door.

She stood for a moment by the door and observed the woman she now knew to be her aunt lying in the bed. Her breathing was even more laboured now and Flo noticed that her skin had gone a deathly grey. She didn't have much time to atone for the sins of the past, but she wanted to do what she could while she still had the chance.

Stepping cautiously across the floor towards the bed, she took her aunt's hand and squeezed it tenderly. Up close, Flo could see immediately why she'd thought her familiar when they first met at the school all those months ago. Celia had the same face shape as Aggie, the same build, the same sloped nose and high cheekbones. Even the hair, fanned out across the pillow, contained the same rich mahogany. The clues had been there all along.

All Flo wanted in that moment was a chance to start again. She wanted to make everything right, for her, for Aggie and for Celia. But Flo knew that would never happen. She gazed at her; she knew Celia didn't have long and she so wanted to make these final few moments count.

'Celia,' she whispered into her aunt's ear. 'Henry has told me everything.'

There was nothing but silence and for a moment Flo wondered if the worst had happened and Celia had passed before Flo had been able to tell her how she felt.

But then Celia managed to blink her eyes open and gingerly turn her face towards Flo. 'My love,' she croaked. 'I'm so sorry, I never wanted to lie.'

Flo laced her warm fingers through Celia's cool ones. 'You have nothing to be sorry for. You loved me, and you placed me in a loving home, and you've shown me nothing but love since we were reunited. I want to thank you for everything.'

'No,' Celia begged, the smallest of words now clearly almost too much of an effort.

'Yes,' Flo said gently. 'Don't try and speak any more, just listen. You were the one that helped me face my grief and you were the one that helped me live again. You were the friend I needed most when I didn't know how to heal, and you have been there for me all my life. Celia, I will never forget you and I will always love you.'

Celia opened her mouth and closed it and Flo could see that the life force within her aunt was draining away.

'Love …' she managed, the effort now clearly far too much.

'I know,' Flo whispered as she pressed a kiss to her aunt's hand. 'You don't need to say it. I know you love me; you always have.'

With that, Flo watched as Celia's chest sank and a final rattle echoed in the back of her throat. Flo knew she had gone.

Chapter Forty-Two

It was Henry who brought Flo back to Bell Street. After such a long day, with so many truths revealed, Flo had left the hospital feeling shaken and the former store deputy had led her to a chair and tightly held her hands while she told him that Celia had died.

Henry had taken charge and brought Flo home, where he told Dot and Alice everything that had happened, suggesting that she get some rest immediately.

The girls had thanked Henry profusely, and although Flo had no real memory of it she remembered Dot had bundled her upstairs, put her to bed and told her to forget everything else; she would have a word with Mr Button and take care of it all.

It was just as well as Flo slept for thirty-six hours straight, so exhausted was she by everything that had happened. She woke with a start. She reached for her watch and saw it was late morning, and got out of bed, wincing from the bumps and bruises she had sustained during that terrible day.

Just then there was a knock at the door and Dot's head appeared through the crack. 'Made you a cuppa.'

Walking in and sitting next to Flo on the edge of her bed, she held the cup out to Flo who took it gratefully.

'Thought I heard movement. About time you woke – it's Friday! You slept the whole day yesterday.'

'What? I can't believe it! That long?' Flo exclaimed, yawning.

'You needed it,' Dot remarked. 'How are you feeling?'

Flo let out a hollow laugh as she set the cup down on the little wooden table beside her bed. 'I feel like I've been run over by a great big steam train.'

'Understandable, darlin'.'

'I just can't believe it. Aggie was my mum all along, Dot. Did you know?'

Dot shook her head. 'I didn't, darlin'. If I did I'd have told her to tell you. Secrets aren't good for a family, but then again some secrets are best kept.'

Flo nodded. 'I just wonder what our lives would have been like if she'd told me.'

Dot took hold of Flo's hand, the stiff material of her housecoat bristling against Flo's arm. 'I suppose she thought she was doing the right thing, she didn't want to cause you any more upset.'

'But if I'd known, maybe we could have found Celia and we could all have been reunited. We could have lived like a proper family,' Flo moaned, the memory of Celia's final breath all too clear.

'You mustn't think like that, Flo,' Dot said firmly. 'Aggie and Celia acted in your best interests always.'

'I don't know,' Flo said. Tears were rolling down her face now.

'I do,' Dot replied. 'You were the little girl Aggie and Celia made together. They poured that much love into you, and you were Aggie's world.'

'And she was mine,' Flo wept. 'I just think if only she had told me the truth, I would have understood why she was so terrified of Bill coming back. I would have done more to protect her. I've missed out on so much, on knowing who my real mother was, on getting to know my aunt and it's all because of one vile brute of a man ...'

258

As Flo's voice trailed off Dot wrapped an arm around her. 'Listen to me, Florence Canning. I may not have known the truth of your parentage, but I did know Aggie and I got to know Celia. Neither one of them would want you thinking like this. They would only have ever wanted the best for you and would have been destroyed if they thought you were blaming yourself. Those women did everything they could to keep you safe, my girl. It's time to repay them by being happy. Enough is enough now.'

'You sound like Celia.' Flo smiled through her tears.

'What do you mean?'

'Celia said I had grieved enough. That it was time to start living.'

Dot got to her feet and kissed Flo's cheek. 'So we'll add wise to the list of things that was wonderful about Celia too, shall we? You've shed enough tears, darlin'. Don't let guilt eat away at you and rob you of your life. There's been too much death round here lately as it is.'

Despite Dot having a word with Mr Button, Flo knew that she couldn't sit around the house all day musing over her lot. After her chat with the Liberty matriarch Flo had felt a lot better and ready to face the world. The first step was returning to work and seeing how the department was managing without her. She could scarcely imagine what Evie Allingham had been up to in her absence, and could only hope that Alice had taken charge.

Sure enough as Flo stalked across the floor just after four o'clock she saw Alice, resplendent in a Liberty raspberry utility print dress, blonde hair gleaming under the shine of the overhead lights, briskly issuing instructions to Evie, Jean and Mary.

'Looks like it's business as usual then,' she chuckled as Alice, Mary and Jean beamed delightedly at her.

'Are you sure you're well enough to come in?' Alice frowned. 'You should be at home resting.'

'I've just spent the last day and a half resting. I need to get back to normal,' Flo insisted.

'Even so, you should take it easy,' Mary said, her voice rich with concern. 'You're covered in cuts and bruises.'

Flo looked down at her hands as if seeing them for the first time. Mary was right; her hands were battered, and her nails torn to shreds, but that was the least of her worries.

Shrugging, she smiled back at Mary. 'So, how have things been in my absence?'

'Wonderful!' Now Evie was beaming too, walking towards Flo after she had finished serving her customer. 'We've been incredibly busy, and we've taken orders from a couple of new customers too.'

Flo nodded before seeing Alice's worried expression. 'What's wrong?'

'We may have been busy, and we may have taken two new customer orders, but sales are still down,' Alice admitted.

'You obviously didn't walk past Botheringtons earlier on,' Mary said, her voice low.

'Why? Should I have?'

'Well, if you had you would have spotted that Botheringtons are also stocking utility prints,' Alice exclaimed, red blotches of anger blooming across her neck.

'I don't suppose we can expect to be the only ones that stock utility fabric,' Flo pointed out.

'That's just what I said,' Evie put in.

'I know everyone else stocks utility print, but the trouble is they're stocking carbon copies of what we've got for half the price,' Alice fumed.

'And of course the customers are coming in to see what we've got before going up the road and seeing if they can get it elsewhere for a fraction of the price,' Jean explained.

'But how did they know how to replicate it?' Flo asked.

'Oh, heavens above,' Evie put in. 'All they'd need to do was walk past our shop window. I wouldn't worry about it – anyone that's anyone will come to Liberty's for their prints; Botheringtons can't compare.'

Flo wasn't sure Evie was right. Times were hard in the face of war and if sales went down any more then it was likely staff would end up being made redundant again. However, she knew it was better to put a brave face on for the rest of the girls.

'Yes, that's probably true. Well, if you're all right, I shall just pop upstairs and take a look through the deputy store manager paperwork. I'll pop back down before we shut.'

With that she walked back up the stairs and through the labyrinth of corridors into Mr Masters' office.

As she took a seat and caught sight of Henry's familiar handwriting she felt overwhelmed with disappointment and uncertainty. Henry had been such a good friend to Celia, and such a tower of strength that horrible night, she couldn't believe he was responsible for taking the Liberty fundraiser money. Nobody who went to so much trouble to look after so many people in their life would be capable of such a thing.

Rubbing her hands across her face, she tried to make sense of what had happened. Henry had been such a support: she owed it to him to get to the bottom of the mystery. But first she had to turn her attention to his workload.

Going through the papers, she was relieved to find Henry had left comprehensive sales figures for all the departments. Running her finger through every one she didn't know whether to feel pleased or disappointed that all the other departments were down on last year, just like her own.

Although she knew it was temporary, Flo had to admit it felt good to be in charge again. She knew she had the department to look after, but since Neil's death, Flo couldn't help feeling that she had been letting things happen to her, without making any decisions for herself. Dot and Celia had been right, enough was enough, and now, following the revelations about her own family life, Flo felt she needed to take back some of that power. She felt she needed to be closer to the woman who had turned out to be her mother. Dot and Alice had been a wonderful stand-in family over the last few months, but as she pushed the papers away to the edge of her desk instinct told her it was time to stand on her own two feet. It was time to face her future by facing her past.

Chapter Forty-Three

It hadn't taken long to move the few things Flo had brought with her to Bell Street back to her Islington home. In fact it took even less time with Alice, Mary and Dot's help in the back of Edwin's precious Standard.

'I thought you knew how to drive, Mary,' Alice grumbled as Mary took a corner at top speed.

'I do,' Mary fumed, putting her foot on the accelerator again as she headed towards the Holloway Road. 'This is how it's done.'

'It'll be me that's done if you carry on driving like this,' Dot roared from the back seat. 'Take your foot off that sodding accelerator. There's a speed limit in case you hadn't noticed.'

'And I'd rather like to get back home in one piece if it's all the same to you,' Flo said cheerfully as Mary turned to pull into her road.

When Mary brought the car to a screeching halt, Flo held on to her possessions with both hands, grateful the journey was over.

'Thanks for the lift, love,' she said, clambering out of the front seat.

'You're welcome!' Mary beamed, hopping out to open the door for Alice and Dot. 'Have you got everything?'

'I think I left my kneecaps back in the road there, but apart from that I seem to have the lot,' Dot teased.

Mary groaned good-naturedly. 'Come on. Let's get Flo settled in and then we'll drive back.'

'God help us all,' Dot muttered in a stage whisper, as she followed Flo up the path.

Shaking her head with mirth, Flo went inside. She was delighted to see the place was no longer a mess. Instead it looked as if Jean had been keeping her home clean and tidy. The jars were arranged alphabetically, the mantel was free of dust and the sink sparkling clean and clear of mugs. There was even a thoughtfully placed bunch of nasturtiums in the centre of the kitchen table with a note welcoming Flo home.

'Home sweet home.' Alice beamed. 'What a lovely job Jean's done.'

'Hasn't she?' Flo agreed, looking around at the place. It was all so strange, and yet so familiar. Here were all of Aggie's treasured blue and white plates on the dresser, the photo of her with her Uncle Ray on their wedding day, and of course another of her and Neil nestled right beside them. On the chair was Jean's leather work bag. A lovely mix of old and new, Flo thought, realising that it felt good to be back. It had been the right decision.

'Can I get you all a cuppa?' she asked, setting her bags on the kitchen floor.

Dot checked her watch. 'Just a quick one, darlin', Edwin needs his car.'

'That's if Mary gets it back in one piece!' Alice chuckled, before turning to Flo. 'Yes, a quick one for me too. I promised Doris I wouldn't leave Arthur for too long. He's got another tooth coming through and he's a right little sod at the moment.'

'Alice! That's no way to talk about your child,' Mary admonished.

Alice rolled her eyes. 'Trust me, when you've got Emma all to yourself, you'll be saying the same thing.'

'Have you thought any more about taking her out for the day?' Flo called, putting the kettle on and checking the larder for milk. She was thrilled to see that Jean had efficiently stocked up with another pint and pulled it out before getting the tea things ready.

'Yes. I'll be going in next week on my day off. It's all arranged,' Mary said, her voice full of excitement. 'And I thought we could celebrate her birthday, too?'

'How wonderful.' Alice clapped her hands together.

As Flo busied herself making the tea, her eyes strayed to the dresser once more. Suddenly she spotted a letter resting on the top of the dresser in Neil's father John's handwriting. Wordlessly she picked it up and frowned as she ran her fingers over her name on the front of the envelope. What did he want with her? He didn't usually write.

'What have you got there?' Dot called nosily.

'Just some post,' she called, putting the note down. 'Nothing important, I'm sure.' Turning back to the tea, she carried the pot and cups across to the table and then smiled at the girls. 'Thanks for helping me today.'

'You're welcome,' Dot said softly. 'And you know you're welcome back south of the river anytime, don't you?'

Flo nodded. 'I do.'

'And anytime you feel like babysitting Arthur you just have to say the word.' Alice laughed good-naturedly.

Chuckling, Flo leaned back in her chair, sending Jean's bag that had been on the edge crashing to the ground.

'Hells bells!' she groaned, stooping down to retrieve the contents. Only as she did so she saw that amongst the hand cream and gloves was a stack of papers. Frowning, Flo turned them over and saw the papers were marked 'Private and Confidential' with the Liberty letterhead all over them.

'What's that?' Mary asked, peering over her shoulder.

'It looks like some work documents I asked Jean to bring back for me.'

Alice frowned. 'Wouldn't you just do it yourself?'

'Ah, she's got all high and mighty,' Dot teased. 'Now she's back to being a high-up she doesn't like getting her hands dirty!'

Flo swatted Dot's hand with the papers. 'Flamin' cheek. It was just easier to ask Jean, that was all. She was working late with Evie the other night,' Flo lied.

Seemingly mollified, the girls sipped their tea, giving Flo a moment to flick through the papers again. At first glance they looked like confidential sales documents and patterns for the new prints that were going to be released into store next season.

Horror pulsed through her. What was Jean doing with these and how had she got her hands on them? Even Flo had to sign all sorts of forms to see these patterns, for they were highly confidential. More to the point, what did Jean need them for?

Stuffing them back into Jean's bag, Flo hung it on the chair and smiled as she turned to the girls, doing her best to concentrate. But all the while Flo's mind was whirring. She had no idea why Jean had those papers, but she certainly didn't want anyone else to know what was going on until she did. Much as she adored working at Liberty's, and the girls who worked with her, Flo had noticed that gossip, no matter how well intentioned, travelled fast. For the moment, she wanted to keep whatever Jean was doing under wraps.

Chapter Forty-Four

The girls left Flo's about an hour later with promises to come round for supper one night the following week. Flo shut the wooden door behind them, listening to the roar of Mr Button's car as Mary sped down the road, then sank her forehead against the window pane. Here she was then, home sweet home.

It had been a long time since she had been alone and for a moment she felt lost with only silence for company. But equally Flo knew it was where she needed to be. Slipping her shoes off, she found her slippers by the umbrella stand, where she'd always kept them, and pushed her feet into the warm wool. Padding through to the kitchen, she thought about making another cup of tea while she unpacked but then her eyes strayed to Jean's bag hanging innocently from the back of the chair, and couldn't resist one more look.

Reaching for the papers, Flo sat down at the kitchen table, trying to come up with a logical answer as to why Jean would have these patterns in her possession. Could she have taken them mistakenly? Could someone have given them to her in error? Flo doubted it. Jean wasn't a stupid girl, and these papers had 'Private and Confidential' marked all over them. She would have known they weren't meant for her eyes, which begged the question again: why did she have them?

Just then the sound of the front door opening rang through to the kitchen. Flo scrambled to her feet, eager to try and put the papers back where she had found them. But it was too late: Jean walked straight through to the kitchen wearing a welcoming smile only for her face to fall as she took in what was in Flo's hands.

'What are you doing with those?' Jean looked furious.

'I might ask you the same question,' Flo replied, her tone even.

'They're private,' Jean hissed, stepping forward and doing her best to snatch the papers from Flo's hand. But Flo was too tall and too quick and lifted the papers high out of Jean's reach.

'Too right they're private,' Flo exclaimed. 'These are confidential Liberty papers. What are you doing with them?'

'Nothing.' Jean shrugged. 'I must have taken them by accident.'

Flo laughed as she lowered her arm and looked at the papers again. Nobody accidentally took papers like these.

'You took them by accident?' Flo echoed in disbelief. 'Please, Jean. Don't treat me like a fool. Now, I'll ask you again, as your boss and your landlady – and I really want you to tell me the truth this time – what are you doing with these papers?'

As Flo looked at her, Jean remained rooted to the spot, colour creeping up her neck and face as her eyes darted nervously back and forth. Flo wondered just how long Jean was going to stand there trying to come up with something when the sound of the door banging shut behind her caused the atmosphere in the room to shift.

'It was me that took the papers, not Jean,' a voice called from behind Flo.

Whirling around, Flo came face-to-face with Bess. Still in her coat and shoes, she stood there in the kitchen doorway, her face ashen and her eyes stern.

Anger flooded through Flo. First Jean was lying to her and now Bess. How dare they treat her like a fool?

'Really?' Flo said in mock surprise. 'And how would you have access to private papers at Liberty's, Bess?'

'It was when I was at the first-aid night,' Bess said casually. 'I took them then. I just gave them back to Jean to return.'

Flo let out a deep sigh. 'And why would you need these private Liberty papers, Bess? What possible use could they be to you?'

Bess pursed her lips and shook her head. 'I'd rather not say if you don't mind. I appreciate it looks bad but there's no easy way to explain it.'

Flo looked from Jean to Bess and saw that they were both wearing matching stern expressions, and she didn't know what to say or do. Walking back across to the kitchen table, papers still in her hands, she sank into one of the chairs and rested her head in her hands. She thought for a moment. The sisters were inseparable, always had been; Flo knew that. She also knew that attacking them now like this was probably the worst way of handling the situation. More than anything she wanted to get to the bottom of what was going on and she knew she wouldn't do that by trying to fight with the sisters.

'I know that one of you is lying to me,' Flo said, glancing between the two girls. 'I also know that there will be a very good reason that you have those papers in your possession. But you must try and understand it from my point of view. I've seen these papers in your bag, Jean, and I have to go to Mr Button.'

Jean looked anxiously at Bess, who gave a quiet but determined nod.

'If that's what you have to do, Flo, we understand,' Bess said quietly, 'but I'm asking you not to. There's a very good reason that we have those papers.'

'I don't doubt it,' Flo said tiredly. 'Would you like to tell me what that reason is?'

Flo paused, hoping for an answer, but as the girls just looked at their feet, Flo knew she wasn't going to get any more sense out of either one of them. 'In that case I don't have a choice,' she said, pushing the papers back across the table towards Jean. 'I hoped you girls would trust me with whatever's going on, but if you can't that's up to you. I suggest you put those papers back where you got them, Jean, and I'll be talking to Mr Button about this tomorrow.'

As she stood up to walk away from the table, she was surprised when Bess reached out and gripped her hand. 'Please don't do that, Flo,' she said. 'I know this looks bad; we both do. But please trust me. If you'll just give us a bit more time to sort this out we can tell you everything. Then when you've heard us out you can decide whether or not to go to Mr Button. If you go to Mr Button now he'll sack Jean, and with my hand and everything we've lost we can't afford that. Please, Flo, please trust us for just a little bit longer.'

As Flo looked at the earnest expression on Bess's face she felt conflicted. She loved her job, adored the store and knew her loyalties really ought to lie with Liberty's. Yet the store was under so much stress already with Henry's alleged actions and the fact Mr Button was trying to juggle his Board of Trade work. Not only that, there was something in Bess's expression that told Flo it might be best to bide her time. Perhaps she ought to try and find out more about what was happening before she made her move. Flo wasn't sure if she was in fact doing the right thing, but she did know that sometimes doing nothing was better than doing something.

'I'll think about it,' she said, getting to her feet. 'That's all I can promise you for now.'

With that, she went upstairs, her mind reeling. Whether or not she went to Mr Button, she would find out what was going on herself, no matter what Jean or Bess thought.

Chapter Forty-Five

It was the following week and Flo, dressed in her best black dress, hat, coat and gloves, had gathered with the other seven thousand mourners at Hither Green cemetery to say goodbye to Celia. Flo could hardly believe it was happening. Over the past few days, she had done a lot of thinking about the revelations Celia had made as she lay dying.

Flo didn't know whether to feel angry, hurt, sad or glad that Aggie had been her mother. There had been times when she woke in the middle of the night, tangled in sweat-filled sheets, angered at the secrets that had been kept hidden from her for so long. But then came the intense sadness that she had been cheated out of real relationships with the women she had adored.

Her friends had been wonderful and Flo truly felt that she would have been lost without them. As she glanced at them now, these wonderful women who never failed to look out for her or each other, Flo felt blessed. No matter what uncertainties lay ahead in her life, no matter the secrets she still had to uncover, Dot, Alice, Mary and Rose would always be her rock.

The cool wind nipped at her neck as she stood towards the back of the crowd and huddled into her coat to keep out the January chill. Because so many had been killed in the atrocity, the powers that be had decided to hold a mass funeral and Flo had thought it only right and proper that Celia be interred during the service performed by the Bishop of Southwark. Being amongst so many mourners had been a powerful experience. But once again, it was the support of her Liberty girls, who had all somehow managed to take time away from work to attend this very special funeral with her, that had given her the most comfort.

Like many of the mourners she had chosen to walk through the streets of Catford behind the cortèges to the church. It had been moving and emotional as Flo felt the waves of sadness pulsing through the crowd. There were young, old, rich and poor, all united in their grief as they came out to pay their respects to their dead.

As the ceremony came to a close, Flo looked through the sea of faces and saw Henry and Stan. Even from several feet away, Flo could see that Henry was gripping Stan's hand tightly and that both sets of eyes were red and swollen. Suddenly the former deputy store manager's eyes lifted and found Flo's. In that moment it felt as though the two of them were communicating with more than words as each acknowledged shock, sorrow and horror at the atrocity they had been involved in.

'It was a beautiful service,' Alice mumbled as they made their way out of the churchyard and on to the street.

'I think Celia would have been very proud of all that's happened here today,' Dot added.

Flo gave a half-smile. 'I hope so. It felt the right thing to do. If you don't mind, I'll just go and say hello to Stan and Henry.'

Henry and Stan were now talking to one of the teachers; Flo went over, smiled politely and exchanged pleasantries until she was finally left alone with the two of them.

'How are you feeling?' Henry asked.

'About as well as you, I imagine,' Flo replied, feeling suddenly bashful. 'It was a lovely service, or as lovely as these things can ever be.'

Henry nodded in agreement as Stan tried to wrestle his hand free. 'I've been meaning to ask you, Flo,' he began somewhat nervously, 'if you might think about popping over for supper one night. Stan's missed you – haven't you?'

'Yes!' the boy said obediently. 'Please come, Auntie Flo.'

Flo raised an eyebrow. 'Auntie Flo, eh?'

Henry offered a sheepish smile. 'I might have suggested it was polite to call you that.'

Flo was just about to open her mouth to reply when the sight of someone staring at her in the crowd caught her attention. At first she couldn't believe it, thinking her eyes must surely be playing tricks on her. But as she stared back she realised with a sickening sense of dread that just feet away was a man she had hoped she would never have anything to do with again.

Because there, standing by the bus stop, not even pretending to be interested in what the mourner next to him was saying, was her father – Bill Wilson. He was leaning against the stand, grey hair billowing in the wind, and smoking a cigarette as if it were the most casual occasion in the world.

'Excuse me,' she said, so fuelled with anger that she didn't even wait to hear Henry and Stan's reply.

Crossing the road, narrowly missing a passing cyclist, she stalked towards her father, the anger she felt inside increasing the closer she found herself to him.

'What the hell are you doing here?' she hissed.

Bill regarded Flo for a moment; then he threw his cigarette to the ground, not even bothering to stamp out the end.

'Hello, girl. Thought I'd find you here.'

'What do you want?' Flo asked, getting straight to the point.

A look of mock hurt crossed Bill's scar-ridden face, giving Flo time to look at him properly. He'd aged, she thought; his lined face was craggy and worn. He had bulges hanging from under his eyes and his cheeks were red and rosy from too much booze. His hair was thin and the old camel coat that hung from his already slender frame did little to disguise the fact that he'd lost even more weight since she'd seen him last.

'Now, Flo, that's no way to talk to your old man, is it? Where's your respect?'

'Respect has to be earned, Bill, you know that as well as I do,' she sneered. 'I've got more respect for the mud on my shoe.'

Bill looked at her and laughed, the sound radiating pure menace. 'You were never backwards in coming forwards, my girl, I'll give you that.'

At the term 'my girl', Flo shivered. Knowing she was related to this man had always made her flesh crawl; now it made her want to scream with fury.

'You still haven't answered my question. I'd have thought you'd be terrified to show your face, what with you being wanted by the police and all that for your part in the hooch ring that sent innocent people blind.'

At the mention of his crime, Bill looked shiftly around him before turning back to face his daughter.

'Well, like you, Flo love, I'm here to pay my respects to the dearly departed. Oh, and of course I'd read in the papers that my wife Sheila Wilson – or Celia Hallam as she was going around calling herself these days – was dead.' Bill chuckled. 'Seemed only right, as the grieving widower, to say goodbye.'

A flash of fear passed through Flo as she looked at Bill.

'Ah, you thought I didn't know my wife was living in London and had changed her name?' Bill laughed, lighting up another cigarette as he did so. 'Nothing gets past me, Flo love, never has, never will. It suited me to let my missus play her daft games, mind – at least it did for the moment. 'Course, I never forgot that she owed me money. Left me penniless, she did, when she buggered off.'

'My heart bleeds,' Flo spat.

Bill laughed again. 'You've got fire, girl, always have. Still, as you're in a compassionate mood, love, I'm sure you'll want to make sure my loving wife repays her debt. You know, she was your mother.'

At that it was Flo's turn to laugh. 'Come off it, Bill. We both know who my mother really was, and it wasn't Celia.'

'What do you mean? Don't talk daft. I know you two were working together down that school. She'd have told you everything,' he said, blowing clouds of smoke into Flo's face.

'She did tell me everything,' Flo snarled, 'she told me how she lost her baby, how you used to hurt her and perhaps most shockingly of all she told me how you took advantage of her sister when she was at her lowest point after her mother had died, and that Aggie was in fact my real mother.'

At Flo's outburst it took a minute for Bill to recover.

'I don't know what she told you but it weren't like that. Your Aggie was sweet on me, always was—'

'Oh, stop it!' Flo shrieked, unable to listen to any more lies. 'Just stop it, Bill. Aggie wasn't sweet on you, you took advantage of a young innocent girl and I'm the result!'

At that Bill fell silent, as did the crowd around her as, agog, they watched the unfolding scene. But Flo didn't care. She had more to say and she wasn't going to stop now. All the anger and the upset at the betrayals and lies she had endured over the years had to come out and she had her sights trained on Bill.

'Do you know how much I hate you?' Flo continued, her voice low and steely. 'The never-ending lies, the hurt and ruin you spread everywhere you go. I'm ashamed to be related to you. I wish I could go back in time and make it so that I'd never been born. You disgust me. To know you're my father makes my skin crawl. You're the one that should be lying in that grave now, not Celia.'

As she finished, she was suddenly aware of the hushed whispers of the crowd and Henry standing next to her.

'Flo, is everything all right?' he asked.

'Fine,' she replied, her eyes never leaving Bill's.

Her father's face was contorted with anger now, twisted and bulbous. He threw the second cigarette to the ground; the bright amber end continued to glow as he looked first at Henry and then back to Flo.

'This your new fella is it, love? You don't hang about, do you? Your Neil's barely cold in his grave.'

'Lecturing me about morals? That's rich coming from you,' Flo said with a braveness she didn't feel. 'The little you know would barely fill a ration-book stamp.'

'You cheeky little ...' he began, balling his right arm into a fist, ready to strike.

Just as quickly, Henry reached forward and clamped his hand around Bill's arm in a vice-like grip.

'I don't know what you want and I don't know who you are, but I do know that if you hit this woman you're going to have me to deal with and who I am to her is none of your business.'

Bill laughed as he shucked off Henry's hand. 'Got to you, haven't I, pretty boy?'

Henry lunged forwards so he was nose-to-nose with Bill. Pointing to a large bump on his nose, he grinned. 'Pretty boy, eh? Know how I broke my nose? Fighting with an inmate in prison. And see this bump right here?' he continued, pointing to a lump on his ear. 'I lost that bit of flesh when another lag bit my ear in a different fight. You ever been in prison?'

Stunned, Bill leaned back and nervously shook his head.

''Course you haven't.' Henry laughed. 'I've met petty little thugs like you before. Think you're the hard man when you know nothing, and you'd rather beat up defenceless women than face a man head on. Now here's what I do know: you're going to turn around, walk away and leave Mrs Canning here alone. I learned a few things in prison, and one of them was how to almost kill a man while leaving no trace of injury. Don't make me put that into practice, sunshine.'

At that, Flo turned to look at him in astonishment but Bill wasn't leaving before he had the final say.

'You don't scare me, pretty boy, but as you for you, *my girl*,' he snarled, turning to Flo, 'I won't forget about that debt. You owe me.'

Chapter Forty-Six

After Bill stormed off, the interest amongst the crowd died away and Flo found herself alone with her former boss. As she ran her eyes across his lined, weary face, she wasn't sure whether to feel grateful or amazed at the way he had spoken to the man she was unfortunate enough to call her father.

'Are you all right?' he asked gruffly.

'I'm fine, thank you.'

'You're welcome. Look ...' He shifted from foot to foot. 'If you're all right, I'd better be getting back. I left Stan with one of the teachers and promised I'd only be a minute.'

'Yes of course,' Flo said, still feeling slightly breathless at the exchange that had just taken place. 'But, before you go, thank you. You didn't have to stand up for me like that, but, well, I'm ever so glad you did. My father ... he's not the nicest of men, so thank you again for what you did.'

Henry shook his head. 'It was nothing. I didn't know he was your dad, Flo, but he looked like trouble to me. To be honest, I think you've had enough of that in your life of late.'

'You can say that again,' Flo agreed, looking hesitantly at Henry. 'Those things you said, about you getting hurt in prison and fighting. Was that true?'

Flo saw a flicker of pain pass across his face.

'They were true.'

Flo couldn't even begin to imagine the indignities and atrocities he must have witnessed and been subjected to in prison. She thought back to how Celia had defended him. For her aunt's sake as much as her own she wanted to find a way to help him.

'Why won't you tell me what happened with the money? I believe you didn't do it, so why won't you tell me? I want to help you.'

Henry gave her a half-smile. 'I'm fine, Flo, I don't need your help.'

'But I want to,' Flo tried again. 'You should have your job back and we should catch the person who really did this.'

He reaching out a hand and Flo felt him squeeze her shoulder. 'And I'm grateful, truly I am. But you have a lot to deal with. I'll get through all this on my own.'

At those words Flo felt a pang of regret that she had misjudged this wonderful man. As he leaned towards her, she felt the roughness of his cheek brush against hers when he planted a tender kiss against her skin.

'Take care, Flo,' he said as he turned to walk away.

At home later that night, Flo was relieved that the house was empty. Since Jean and Bess had been caught with the confidential Liberty papers, Flo had barely seen them, and tonight, after a trying and difficult day, she had to admit she was grateful.

Draining her second cup of tea of the evening, Flo sat back in the chair at the table and tried to relax. She felt restless after such a busy day, and toyed with the idea of going to the pictures. At only eight o'clock it was too early to go to bed and she didn't feel in the mood for reading or listening to the wireless. Pushing her cup and saucer across the table, Flo resolved to knit for a while, only as her eyes strayed to the dresser she caught sight of the letter Neil's father had posted through her door. She had completely forgotten about it, and her breath caught in her throat. She knew she had to look at whatever was inside. Gingerly she reached for it and, as carefully as if she were exhuming buried treasure, ripped the envelope open. To her surprise another letter, in Neil's handwriting, addressed to his father, came tumbling out. She paused and looked at it for a moment. Why was Neil's dad sending her a letter addressed to him?

Tracing her fingers across the pen strokes, she closed her eyes and brought her husband's face to her mind. In that moment it felt as if Neil was close to her all over again.

Pulling the letter out of the envelope, Flo gasped as she saw it was dated just a few days before Neil's ship had been torpedoed. These would have been his final words.

20ᵗʰ September 1942

Dear Father,

Thanks for your last letter. I received it yesterday and enjoyed reading it during a quiet moment out on the deck with just the clouds and noise of the waves for company.

I thought I'd reply straightaway. It sounds like you and Harry had a good day by the sea the other week. I could just fancy fish, chips and mushy peas myself, all washed down with a cold beer. I hope you had one for me, Dad.

I'm doing all right. I'm sorry if my last letter made you worry. I didn't mean to sound funny with you. Truth be told, I've had some things on my mind, and find life on board this great big ship gives me time for reflection. I suppose I've been a bit down about a letter I sent Flo. We had a row the last time we saw each other and things were said that shouldn't have been. I can hear you now, telling me to think before I speak. I've never done that in my life, have I, Dad? Anyway, it'll be all right. I'll write to her soon, now that I've calmed down since I last wrote to her and got everything off my chest. I'll make things right with her now. I suppose I'm just searching for the right words to say.

That's what's so daft about this flaming war. You can't have a normal row with your wife and make up when you're ready. You're separated for weeks or months, and suddenly things seem so much worse. Flo's my world, Dad, always has been, and I only ever want her to be happy, so I'll write to her soon and tell her and then we'll be back to normal and I won't feel as low as I do on board this floating city.

Anyway, say hello to Harry for me when you see him next and tell him he still owes me for that tip I gave him up Wimbledon Dog Track four years ago.

I'll see you soon.

Your loving son,
Neil

When Flo finished reading the letter, she dropped the paper as if it were a hot potato. Her Neil, her precious Neil, had wanted her to be happy no matter what. Her Neil, the man she had known and adored since they were children, had forgiven her for her lies. This was everything.

Shakily, she got to her feet, still holding the letter to her chest. Tears were streaming down her cheeks as she went over to the dresser and picked up the last photo that had been taken of the two of them – their cherished wedding photo. As she looked into the eyes of the boy she loved with her heart and soul, she kissed the face behind the glass and held the frame to her heart.

'I'm going to follow my dreams, my love, and you will be with me every step of the way.'

Chapter Forty-Seven

The moment Flo read Neil's letter to his father it was as though a beacon of light had illuminated the advice Celia had given her before she died. Flo knew now without doubt that turning her back on singing was not the answer.

She had been so overjoyed to see her husband's handwriting again that she had ended up reading and then rereading the note, losing herself in Neil's words. That he had loved her was the most important thing of all. He had thought they would have time to make up; it wasn't his fault that Hitler had had other ideas.

As she walked along Argyll Street towards Liberty's the following week, flakes of cold February snow landed on her face but Flo didn't care. She felt as if she had a renewed sense of purpose. She wanted to make things right in her world, and she knew just how she was going to do it.

'Rose, are you here?' she called, making her way through the corridors towards her friend's broom cupboard of an office on the top floor.

'I'm in here,' came a tinny voice.

Whirling around Flo saw that her friend was on hands and knees in the stationery cupboard.

'What are you doing?' Flo asked, looking at the trail of pens that lay on the floor.

'Trying to find last year's accounts for Mr B.,' Rose grumbled, standing upright. 'And let me tell you it's not easy when you're partially sighted. It's like the blackout in that cupboard.'

Flo smiled at her friend. 'Here, let me,' she said, gently pushing her towards her desk.

It didn't take long to find them – right at the back sandwiched between a box of envelopes and some headed notepaper. As she handed them to Rose, she felt a pang of guilt. For the past few months, they had all been treating Rose as if everything was back to normal, and her restricted sight was no longer the disability it had once been, but perhaps they had been wrong, perhaps Rose needed more help than she let on.

'Are you all right, Rose? she asked hesitantly. 'I mean, really?'

Rose smiled at Flo. 'I'm fine. It's frustrating to no longer be able to see as I used to, but I've got used to it for the most part. It's when things aren't where they're supposed to be, like these accounts' – she sighed, pushing them across the table – 'and of course not everything is duplicated in Braille, so if I do stumble across some normal paperwork then I've no idea what it is.'

'That's frustrating,'

Rose shrugged. 'It is, but what can I do? I've got to make the best of it, Flo. We none of us are having an easy time of it. So many are coming back from the war now having lost something – whether it's their sight, a limb or even their sanity – but we forget that. We think about the war effort as a whole, which is right of course, but more needs to be done for those people.'

Flo sat on the wooden chair opposite Rose and thought for a moment. As ever, the younger girl was right. More did need to be done for those at home as well as those fighting abroad. Suddenly an idea dawned.

'How do you feel about us doing another fundraising night?'

Rose raised an eyebrow behind her large round glasses. 'We've just done one, Flo, and I'm sure I don't need to remind you how it turned out.'

'I know that. But look, we could do one to recoup the money, only this time we could raise funds for both the war effort and for charities closer to home. Liberty's has always been very philanthropic; maybe it's time to raise money for those here in England.'

'Like charities for the blind,' Rose said, her eyes shining with excitement at the possibility.

'Exactly,' Flo said triumphantly.

'But what can we do?' Rose asked. 'I mean, it was a big draw getting Max Monroe last time – I can't imagine he'll want to perform for us again.'

Flo laughed. 'Maybe not, but I'll see if I can persuade him. If he won't, I'll sing. It won't be the same, but at least you'll have someone there who can hold a tune.'

'Are you sure?' Rose gasped.

'Quite sure.' Flo nodded with a smile. 'Neil's dad gave me a letter that he wrote to him just a few days before he died. To cut a long story short, it turns out he wasn't as angry with me as I thought and all he wanted was for me to be happy – and singing makes me happy so I want to do this, Rose. For you, for me and for Liberty's.'

Sitting back in her chair, Rose looked at Flo in astonishment. 'Well then, how could anyone refuse? There is just one question though: how are you going to persuade Max Monroe?'

Flo got to her feet and tapped the side of her nose. 'Leave him to me.'

*

After work that day Flo turned down the offer of a quick drink in the French Pub with the girls. Much to their surprise and disappointment, she insisted she had somewhere else to be, and after waving them goodbye with promises to have one for her, she had stepped on to the Tube at Oxford Circus and made her way west.

Following her promise to Rose that morning, Flo had spent the day feeling fired up about the idea of singing again. So much so that she had decided to do all she could to make sure this second fundraising evening was a success. Yet, despite her new-found desire to take to the stage again, Flo knew that she wouldn't be that much of a draw. However, Flo wasn't above using her connections. After rifling through Rose's precious filing cabinet she found the information she needed, which was why at just after seven o'clock that evening she found herself standing outside a pretty little mews house in the heart of Chelsea.

For a split second Flo had second thoughts about coming. Had it been too presumptuous an idea? Should she turn back now before anyone saw her? But in that moment, the heavens opened, and Flo had a feeling that someone had made her mind up for her.

Quickly she dashed to the front door and rapped her knuckles on the solid wood. Turning up the collar of her grey wool coat for protection, she heard the sound of footsteps and then the door swung wide open, revealing a warm and inviting living room with a blazing fire roaring in the grate.

'I hope you don't mind that I'm here,' Flo began nervously.

'Mind?' Max smiled, his white teeth piercing the darkness of the street. 'It's a pleasure. Come on in out of the wet.'

Flo didn't need to be asked twice and eagerly crossed the threshold into the warmth of the house.

'I wasn't sure whether you would be here,' she began, shucking off her coat and handing it to Max.

'A rare bit of time off before we start a new tour,' Max said. 'Can I get you a drink?'

'I'm fine,' Flo said, shaking her head, as she approached the fire. 'I won't take up much of your time.'

Max turned away from her and filled up a glass tumbler with what looked suspiciously like Scotch. 'I'm having one, and I insist you do too. Medicinal and all that.'

As she took the glass, she saw his eyes were crinkled with kindness and she took a sip, immediately enjoying the burning sensation of the liquid trickling down her throat.

'So what brings you here on this chilly night?' Max asked, gesturing her to sit down.

'Well, it's a bit awkward,' Flo began nervously. 'But you know about the money for our last fundraiser?'

Max gave a small nod of his head. 'Terrible business, that. Are they any closer to finding out who took the money?'

'No,' Flo said quietly. 'There's an investigation now though.'

'I see,' Max said gravely. 'So what does this have to do with me?'

Flo shuffled forwards to the edge of her seat, her hands clutching the tumbler of whisky. 'I've had an idea, and I was rather hoping you would help me.'

'Go on,' Max encouraged.

'I want to hold another fundraising evening, to try and recoup the money lost.'

Max raised an eyebrow. 'I rather thought it had been stolen.'

Flo said nothing. 'It would be good for staff morale, and good for the war effort, but this time I thought that we could also raise money for causes closer to home, such as those who are blind or partially sighted.'

'Like your friend Rose.' Max said.

'Exactly like my friend Rose,' Flo echoed. 'I want to do something constructive. I realise I've got a talent and I should be putting it to good use.'

Max took a sip of his whisky before looking at Flo in surprise. 'Does that mean you'll be doing more than playing the piano?'

'I've already told Rose I'll sing,' Flo said shyly, 'and she's taken me up on it.'

'Well, good for you.' Max grinned. 'I must say it's about time. That church mouse act you were peddling was doing nothing for anyone. So what changed your mind?'

'Let's just say I realised that it was important I follow my dreams. I'm going to do that now.'

Max nodded. 'And you want my help?'

'If you feel you could spare it,' Flo said nervously. 'I know it's a lot to ask, when you've already been so generous with your time for one fundraising evening as it is.'

Draining his whisky, Max set his glass on the table and eyed her carefully. 'I will help you, but I want you to be prepared,' he said. 'Your performance was good when you joined in with me that night – you've got raw natural talent, anyone can see that. But you're out of practice, my girl, and if you really want to get serious about singing you'll have to give it your heart and soul. You need more practice, more variety, and to experience different audiences.'

Flo swallowed nervously. 'So does that mean you will sing?'

Max laughed. 'If you can get it organised for a month's time and get yourself some singing practice then yes I will sing again. I ship out with ENSA to Egypt and beyond at the beginning of April and I'm not sure when I'll be back.'

'Oh.'

'Trust me, it's all very fixable.' Max beamed, getting to his feet. Fishing out his wallet from his trouser pocket, he reached inside and pulled out a business card. 'Here you go,' he said, handing it to Flo. 'Pop down to this address next Tuesday night and tell them Max Monroe sent you. Ask for Eddie.'

Flo ran her eyes across the card: 'The Kitty Cat Club, Chelsea'. She'd never heard of it, but looking back up at Max and seeing the encouragement in his eyes, she realised that was perhaps the point.

Chapter Forty-Eight

The following Tuesday night, Flo found herself in the heart of Chelsea walking down a dank, dark alleyway. The pitch black of the night was doing nothing to fill her with confidence.

Following Max's advice, Flo had promised herself that she would sing at the club he had picked out for her. And so after work, she had taken the Tube and then a bus to Chelsea, expecting to find a glittering club in a well-heeled part of town. The address Max had given her couldn't be further from her expectations: run-down, dingy, surrounded by boarded-up shops and litter piled high in the street; Flo looked around her and quickened her pace. She felt as if she were about to be mugged – or worse – any second.

Wondering if she had the right address, Flo stole a quick glance at the card in the half-light of the moon: '101B Piccadilly Mansions'. Flo raised an eyebrow; she was definitely in the right place, and if she squinted her eyes she could just about make out number 101B two doors up. Hurrying towards the dark wooden door, she tried to push it open and was surprised to find it locked shut.

'*Oh, for heaven's sakes,*' she muttered angrily, cursing Max under her breath. What was he thinking of sending her here?

Even though she wanted to walk away, she knew she had to give it one last try. And so instead she rapped loudly on the door with her fist. 'Hello, anyone there?' she called. 'I'm looking for Eddie.'

Immediately the door swung open and Flo came face-to-face with an older woman. She was beautiful, Flo thought, tall and dressed in a man's suit with her hair fashioned into a shiny black bob that hung just past her earlobes.

'Who sent you?' the woman barked.

'Er, Max Monroe,' Flo tried again. 'He told me to come and sing here tonight, to ask for Eddie and tell him that Max sent me.'

At the mention of Max's name, the woman's face broke into a wide smile. 'Then you must be Flo.' She beamed, beckoning her inside and slamming the door behind her. 'Yes, Maxie told me you were coming. Can I take your coat?'

Flo smiled as she handed it to the woman. 'Thank you. So this Eddie, is he around?'

The woman laughed, and offered her hand to Flo. 'I am Eddie. Actually it's Edwina, but I much prefer Eddie.'

'Oh, I'm sorry,' Flo said, feeling her cheeks flush with embarrassment at the mistake she had made.

Eddie waved her concerns away. 'It happens all the time. Now why don't you come with me? You'll sing in about half an hour, if that's all right?'

Nodding, Flo trailed behind Eddie. She allowed herself to be led down a steep flight of stone steps. As they reached the basement Flo heard the thrum of the music mixed with the sounds of people laughing and talking.

Eddie pulled open the door and Flo could see a throng of people surrounding a stage area, all laughing and dancing to a jive band playing on the small central stage. Despite the unassuming entrance, the club itself was beautiful. A large chandelier hung from the vaulted ceiling, and rich red and black velvet drapes lined the bar area, with exotic and colourful-looking bottles Flo had never come across before lining the glass shelves. Amongst it all Flo could see women dressed outlandishly. Some of the ladies were dressed like Eddie in men's suits and monocles, while others were dressed in exquisite ballgowns and made up to the nines, seemingly only dancing with one another.

Flo was only wearing a simple teal dress in a Liberty print. Max hadn't told her to dress up and she'd assumed it would just be an ordinary singing event like the ones she used to perform at in the Lamb and Flag. She felt wrong-footed as she looked around. Where were the men? She spotted a handful gathered in the corner by the stage. One, sporting a hat with a feather, was drinking what looked like a purple drink, while another wore an elaborate crimson smoking jacket, the likes of which she hadn't seen since before the war.

She turned to Eddie. 'I'm sorry, is this some sort of fancy-dress event? If so, Max didn't tell me.'

Eddie laughed. 'It seems Maxie didn't tell you much.'

'Like what?' Flo frowned.

Eddie shook her head. 'I'll fix you a gimlet and let Max tell you himself.'

Without waiting for Flo to ask her what a gimlet was, Eddie pushed her towards the bar, then disappeared behind a red curtain. There, just beyond two women laughing over a drink was Max, sitting alone at the bar and enjoying the music.

'Flo,' he exclaimed, kissing her on both cheeks as the mysterious gimlet was suddenly placed in front of her. 'You found it then.' He smiled, gesturing for her to sit at the bar stool next to his.

'I did,' Flo replied, gazing around her and absorbing the atmosphere. 'It's not what I expected.'

'What did you expect?'

Flo shrugged and reached for her drink. 'I don't know. I don't think I've been anywhere like this before. Everyone seems quite eccentric, I suppose, in all their outfits.'

Max threw his head back and laughed so hard she could see the back of his teeth. 'Oh Flo! Do you know, you should be on stage as a comic not a singer.'

She frowned as she took a sip. She still wasn't sure what it was, but this gimlet was gorgeous.

'I don't see why that's funny. Is this some sort of private members' club? Do you come here a lot?'

It was then Max looked at her with a hint of pity in his eyes as he leaned forward and whispered in her ear, 'Flo, this is a club for homosexuals and lesbians, and yes, let's say I do come here rather a lot.'

It was all Flo could do to hold on to her drink as she looked around the room in shock. She had heard of homosexuality and knew that it was illegal. But equally Flo wasn't green enough to think it didn't exist. She knew what went on behind closed doors, and she knew there were clubs like this one. At the store, they had welcomed enough customers that batted for the other side, as Mrs Matravers had always skilfully called it, but equally Flo didn't think it was any of her business what people got up to in their private lives. She'd had an elderly uncle who Aggie had told her liked male company more than a lady's.

Across the room she saw two people locked in a passionate embrace and realised that although they looked like a man and a woman, they were in fact two women. As she turned away she was surprised at the emotions surging through her body. She felt curious, surprised, confused and, if she was honest, a tiny bit appalled. It was shocking to see something that was deemed so wrong by society played out so publicly and Flo wasn't sure how she felt or indeed how she should feel.

She turned back to Max and regarded him coolly. 'So why did you want me to sing here? To shock me? Did you think I was too green, too stupid?'

At Flo's outburst, Max looked taken aback. 'No, that wasn't it at all. I just wanted you to think about playing in different venues, for different people. If you join ENSA—'

'I'm not joining ENSA,' Flo said firmly.

'But you said you were going to take your singing seriously now,' Max replied, a small smile playing on his lips.

'That doesn't mean I'm joining ENSA,' Flo protested. 'I have a job, a life here in London.'

Max merely shrugged and took a sip of his drink. 'All I'm saying is, and this applies whether you join ENSA or not, if you're going to take your singing seriously you'll be a better performer if you get used to entertaining a wide variety of people. I thought that getting you to sing in The Kitty Cat Club would give you a new experience, shall we say.'

Flo nodded and took another sip of her drink. She knew Max was right; if she wanted to get serious about her singing career then she couldn't always be in the Lamb and Flag. Even so, she wished he had been more honest with her about his motives when she had called on him last night.

She was about to open her mouth and say as much, when it hit her. Was this Max's way of telling her that he liked men more than he liked women? Was he trusting her with his secret? She looked into his eyes, searching for some sort of confirmation, but there was none as he sipped his gimlet and gave her a mysterious smile. With a sigh, she was about to ask another question about the club when she felt someone tap her on the shoulder. Turning round she saw Eddie smiling at her.

'You're on next, love,' she said, gesturing to the stage.

'Break a leg, my dear,' Max said, raising his glass towards her.

Walking through the throngs of people, Flo tried to calm her racing pulse. She had sung so many times before she wasn't sure why she felt nervous. And then she realised this wasn't just about impressing the audience, she wanted to impress Max.

Stepping on to the stage, she glanced at the faces gazing up at her and then turned towards the pianist. 'How about "I Don't know Why I Love You",' she mouthed, and the pianist nodded.

As the first note sounded, Flo felt herself relax. Staring out into the crowd, feeling all eyes on her, she began to sing, losing herself in the music and the song. As a performer she knew not to try too hard to read the crowd but as she glanced across at Max she couldn't miss the big grin on his face.

Feeling the butterflies in her stomach start to shift, she turned back to the crowd and was delighted to see they all looked to be enjoying themselves. Most were dancing; some were mouthing the words others looked as if they were happy just to be amongst friends and loved ones. All except one couple who were sitting in the corner by the bar, locked in a loving embrace, each lost in the arms of the other.

As the song came to a close and the audience broke into polite applause, Flo smiled and mouthed '"Wake Me Up, Cookie", ' to the pianist. As he flicked deftly through his sheet music, Flo noticed the couple break apart and for the first time that night her jaw dropped. The couple weren't the strangers she believed them to be. In fact the pair who had eyes only for each other were none other than her friends and lodgers, Bess and Jean.

Chapter Forty-Nine

It was a testament to her professionalism, Flo thought as the pianist played the opening chords to the next song, that she was able to carry on in the face of such a surprise. What Flo had really wanted to do as Bess and Jean stared up at her in horror was to walk straight down into the crowd, pull them aside and ask them what was going on.

They were sisters, weren't they? Yet in all Flo's twenty-seven years she had never seen two sisters kiss each other like that. But if they weren't sisters, that meant they had been lying to her. Flo wasn't sure what she was more upset about: the discovery that Bess and Jean weren't who she thought they were, or the fact that she had been made to feel like such a fool.

But right now she had a job to do, and that job was to sing to the best of her ability and convince Max Monroe that another Liberty's fundraiser was worthy of his time. And so Flo ignored Bess and Jean, breathed in the smoky air and finished her song, following it with another two just like it, imagining she was giving a performance to a packed Royal Albert Hall.

It was worth it. By the time she had finished the crowd were cheering in delight, and crying out for more. When she left the stage she was elated as people clapped her on the back and congratulated her. She made her way towards Max, overjoyed to see him give her a big thumbs up.

'You did well,' he told her, pushing another gimlet into her hands.

'Thanks.' Flo slugged the drink back in one. 'Can I have another please?'

Max laughed and gestured to the barman for another. 'I didn't think it was *that* terrifying.'

'It wasn't.' Flo smiled, this time merely sipping the drink the barman pushed her way. 'I was just a bit rattled, that's all.'

She could see Max was about to ask why when she saw Bess and Jean, hovering beside the legendary singer.

'Could we have a word, Flo?' Bess asked, her tone flat.

Flo took in her appearance. Bess was dressed like Eddie in a dark grey lounge suit with paisley-patterned tie. Jean, on the other hand, was wearing the utility dress from Liberty's Flo had helped her run up only the other day. Their faces, however, had drained of all colour and for a moment Flo felt sorry for them.

'Of course.' Flo turned to Max. 'Excuse me for just a moment.'

Following Jean and Bess towards a dark corner of the club, she stared at them, arms folded.

'We've always wanted to tell you, we never wanted to keep secrets from you, but I'm sure you can understand why we didn't,' Bess said.

'We wanted to tell you, but we couldn't,' Jean added, her eyes filled with earnestness and sorrow.

'I take it you two aren't sisters then?'

Bess shook her head and locked eyes with Flo as if daring her to challenge them. 'No, we're lovers, have been for almost four years now.'

Now Flo felt the colour drain from her own face. What was she supposed to say? 'Four years?'

'That's right,' Jean said, lifting her chin a little higher in defiance. 'I love Bess, and Bess feels the same.'

'Does that shock you, Flo?' Bess said in a mocking tone.

'No,' Flo snapped, refusing to look away from the girls. 'What shocks me is the fact you were living under my roof all that time, and you weren't honest with me. What shocks me is the way you lied to me. I can imagine you both now having a good old laugh at me upstairs in your bedroom. You were sharing a bedroom! All this time I thought you were being kind and considerate with each other. I thought you were close, when in fact you were up to, well, I can't even imagine what you were doing.'

Flo broke off; her voice was now dangerously low and she could tell that her cheeks were red hot with rage. With a start she wondered if this was how Neil had felt when he had discovered she had gone behind his back in the way she had. Did he feel as betrayed as this?

'I'm sorry,' Bess said, her voice lower now. 'We never wanted to lie to you, truly we didn't. We had no choice.'

'Can you imagine what people would have said if they'd discovered the fact Bess and I were lovers? People would be disgusted,' Jean threw in.

'We've seen it first hand,' Bess continued. 'It's why we left Cornwall. Because all we faced was bigotry and hatred.'

'Our secret was discovered,' Jean said miserably. 'My brother found out and said he would kill me if I didn't stop seeing Bess. He said I was bringing shame on the family, that I was a dyke. He said he'd wash me in bleach to make me clean again.'

Flo's mouth dropped open in shock. That really was disgusting.

'Surely he was just upset,' she tried. 'People say all sorts of things they don't mean.'

'Oh, he meant it all right,' Jean replied, lifting her hair back to reveal a massive scar at the tip of her forehead.

'That was where he tried to shave my head. Said that I was behaving like a man so that's what I should look like. When I got away, he beat me, told me to stand up and fight him like a man, when all the time he was holding me down and I couldn't fight back.'

'He broke her nose and her arm in two places,' Bess continued, linking her arm through Jean's. 'We left as soon as Jean was well enough. We knew, after he tried to harm Jean like that, that even if she promised to stop seeing me, he'd have come for her again.'

'So we took the first train out of Penzance and ended up in London,' Jean added.

'Found a grotty little room in Peckham first.' Bess half smiled at the memory. 'The landlady told us she only had one room, and that was when we struck on the idea of being sisters.'

'That way we could share a room without question,' Jean finished. 'It all seemed to work out all right. I got a job at Liberty's, Bess got a job at a café in East London and then we moved across to a flat in Queens Park. The sisters' line seemed to work out, and we were happy.'

Bess reached out and squeezed Jean's hand. 'We still are happy, my love. No matter what happens, we've got each other and always will.'

As Flo watched Jean and Bess share a secret smile, she felt a pang of sorrow and love for the couple before her. They belonged together, she could see that, no matter what society thought.

'So what happened after that?' Flo said, interrupting the couple. 'You said you were happy – what changed?'

'My brother Fred found us.' Jean sighed. 'About two years after we left Cornwall he tracked us down and said I had to come home. He said he was sickened to discover I was still in this dirty little relationship, as he called it. He told me that if I didn't come back with him immediately he'd teach me a lesson.'

'I came home to find Fred had pinned Jean down on the floor again. This time he was holding a knife.'

Horror flooded through Flo as she took in the full implications of what Bess was saying. 'You're telling me your own brother tried to *hurt* you.'

Jean nodded miserably. 'He kept saying I needed to be taught a lesson, that I was unnatural, that I was going to hell and he would make me forget about Bess, that it was his duty as a brother.'

'How was doing gawd knows what to you with a knife going to make you forget about Bess?' Flo begged. 'It makes no sense.'

'It never does with Fred,' Bess growled. 'He's not right in the head. I tell you Flo, I have never been so angry. In that moment, when I saw him, well, I didn't think about what I was doing, I just pulled him straight off Jean and then smacked him right in the eye. He was so surprised and I was so angry I didn't stop.'

'He was furious,' Jean continued. 'He flew at Bess and started beating her. He kept saying how we weren't women, we were animals. Then I started hitting him, and he rounded on me. We ended up fighting, the three of us, and I think that's when it dawned on him he'd need extra help if he was going to get me to come home.'

'Your shiner,' Flo said suddenly, remembering the black eye Jean had come into work with last year. 'It wasn't Bess's wayward boyfriend, it was your brother.'

'I'm so sorry, Flo,' Jean murmured.

'And that story about your mum being too busy on the Isle of Wight?' Flo asked. 'And about you being married before? And why you were called Green?'

'Green is my real name. But the Mrs part was made up. We made up lots of stories,' Bess explained. 'To keep people off the scent, or more specifically Fred.'

'My brother was why we moved in with you,' Jean put in. 'We had to leave our flat quickly.'

'And he's still looking for us,' Bess added. 'It's why I moved from the café, because I came home in my uniform that day and he worked it out, but he never found out Jean was at Liberty's.'

'We couldn't take the risk though. I moved jobs and we moved house but since I've been at the convalescent home I haven't been able to look out for Jean in the way I normally would. The few days I can come home while I rebuild my strength are precious but it's not enough. I need to be home. I need to be with Jean.'

With that Jean kissed Bess tenderly on the cheek and Flo could see the love that radiated between them.

'We never meant to cause any trouble for you Flo,' Jean put in, her eyes brimming with earnestness. 'You've been so good to us; we don't want you to think badly of us.'

Flo looked at the girls before her, so broken and bruised. They had dealt with too much hardship; who was she to cause them any more? Her heart went out to them. She knew she was supposed to feel disgusted at their relationship, but Flo couldn't bring herself to think that way. Instead she remembered the sadness her uncle had faced day after day simply for choosing to love someone of the same sex. She might find it odd, but was it really so wrong? Was it really so awful? Surely love was love, wasn't it?

'Girls, you don't need to apologise to me for being who you are,' Flo sighed. 'I wish you hadn't lied to me, but I understand why you did. I want to help you – you two shouldn't have to live like this. What can I do?'

The girls looked at each other, their eyes shining with happiness.

'You've already done it,' Bess whispered. 'You've just given us the greatest gift of all.'

Flo frowned. 'But I haven't done anything.'

'You've done more than you know.' Jean smiled. 'You've given us acceptance and you've made us proud.'

'You've said that we're as good as you, and that means more than you will *ever* know,' Bess finished.

Chapter Fifty

'You sang where?' Dot echoed in disbelief. 'The Kitty Witty Club?'

Flo choked back her laughter as she handed Dot a stack of orders to sign. 'The Kitty Cat Club. In Chelsea.'

Dot shook her head as she signed her name, then passed the papers back. 'Never heard of it, darlin'. Daft name though, isn't it? What's that all about? Do they provide a home for all the waifs and strays of London?'

'I suppose in a funny way they do.' Flo smiled, thinking of how Jean and Bess had seemed very at home there. 'The point is, though, that it went well and Max has agreed to sing at another fundraiser, as long as I do three duets with him.'

Dot raised an eyebrow. 'Three? Blimey. He thinks a lot of you.'

'And I think a lot of him,' Flo replied.

'I'm only teasing, darlin',' Dot replied, stifling a yawn. 'Ignore me, you're not the only one that had a late night last night. I'm not myself today. Bit tired.'

'Any reason?' Flo asked, sweeping her finger across the cash register to check for dust.

'Only Edwin, going on about Henry again, right up until the small hours he was.'

'What do you mean?' Flo asked, eyes narrowed.

'He's got a bee in his bonnet that the man's innocent.'

'I must say I agree with him,' Flo replied.

'Oh, not you 'n' all.' Dot rolled her eyes. 'I'm all for innocent until proven guilty and Henry was good to you and

Celia of course. But he's hardly laid all his cards on the table. I mean, he went to prison, for crying out loud. For theft, and he refuses now to tell us what's going on with the money. If he's innocent of this crime he must see how this will look to everyone else.'

'And I must say that for once I agree with Dot,' Evie cried, scuttling across the parquet floor towards the cash register.

'Oh Christ, I will change my mind if she starts agreeing with me,' Dot muttered under her breath.

'Well, I'm sorry you both think that,' Flo said. 'Because I completely disagree and as a result have asked Henry to come into the office later this morning. Mr Button and I are going to see if we can shed any light on who else might have taken the money.'

Evie let out a long sigh and folded her arms against her rayon polka-dot blouse. 'What a waste of time. Henry Masters was caught red-handed, he is not of good moral character, he should not be working at this store. What else do you need to know?'

'I need more evidence,' Flo said with an air of finality. 'And so do the board.'

Now it was Evie's turn to look surprised. 'Really? I thought they were ready to sack him? When I spoke to Mr Button last week he suggested that the board were far from impressed by Henry's behaviour.'

'You thought wrong,' Flo replied curtly.

Ignoring Evie's irritated glare, she checked her wristwatch and saw there were just two minutes to go until opening time. Jean was due in to work this morning. She knew they had both endured a late night the previous evening but Flo was here bright and early and Jean ought to be as well.

Right on cue, the sound of heels tip-tapping across the floor made Flo look up. At the sight of Jean, immaculately dressed in her Liberty floral print skirt and blouse, she smiled warmly, wanting to let the younger girl know she needn't worry about the night before.

'Morning, Jean darlin',' said Dot. 'You look as tired as the rest of us. Don't tell me you were out 'til all hours singing at the Kitty Nitty Club as well.'

'Kitty Cat Club,' Flo said crossly. Turning to Jean she couldn't miss the look of alarm spreading across her face. 'No, it was just me,' Flo added quickly, sensing that Jean didn't want that particular bit of information broadcast across the shop floor.

'The Kitty Cat Club?' Evie exclaimed in disgust. 'My goodness me. Mrs Canning, please tell me you weren't at that den of iniquity. You know that it's a place for' – at this point Evie lowered her voice as she looked furtively around her – '*dykes and nancy boys*, don't you?'

Flo rolled her eyes at the stupidity of Evie's words. 'Yes, Evie, I am well aware of the kind of club it is.'

'And you went there knowing it was full of poofs! Whatever is the matter with you? You'll be bringing your own good name and the reputation of Liberty's into disrepute,' Evie snapped. 'There's no place for people like that in society, it's sick.'

Drawing herself up to her full height so she towered over Evie, Flo found herself glowering at her. 'No, Mrs Allingham, the people that are sick are people like you, who find something so very wrong in people living their lives. I don't wish to hear any more of that sort of talk in my department. Is that understood?'

'Mrs Canning, I was merely pointing out that this kind of moral depravity is precisely what is wrong with the world today. You going to places like that will do nothing for Liberty's reputation or your own. I am only trying to help,' Evie pointed out.

'So am I, and that is all I have to say on the matter. I don't want to hear another word about it,' Flo said firmly.

About to walk away, Flo saw Evie round on Jean, clearly still keen to speak her mind. 'And what do you think? Don't you think these men and women, these horrible people up to no good with their disgusting behaviour should be stopped, eh, Jean?'

Flo saw Jean's cheeks flush with colour.

'I … I don't know, Mrs Allingham,' the younger girl said.

'Don't you?' Evie chuckled, looming over her. 'I would have thought you would have had an opinion on these disgusting dykes.'

'She just said she doesn't,' Dot fired. 'Now stop using such filthy language and leave the poor girl alone. Go and spread your hate somewhere else, will you?'

Smiling in satisfaction, Evie turned away and walked over to the new range of fabrics that had come in yesterday morning. As she tidied them, Flo looked at Jean in concern. She seemed thoroughly rattled at Evie's outburst.

'You all right?' she asked in a low voice.

But Jean barely looked up from the packets of zips she was sorting through. 'Fine. Although, would you mind if I just nipped to the bathroom? I'm not feeling very well.'

'Of course.'

As she watched the younger girl disappear, she checked her watch again. Henry would be here any moment and she wanted to catch him before they went into Mr Button's office and see if she could try one last time to persuade him to tell her the truth.

'Just nipping upstairs, Dot,' she said. 'You and Evie will be all right for a few minutes, won't you?'

Dot rolled her eyes. 'She's disappeared somewhere, but frankly I'm glad to see the back of her.'

Flo frowned as she scanned the floor. Where had Evie got to? 'Well, Jean won't be long. Any problems, just call up to the office.'

'Righto,' Dot said cheerfully.

As Flo quickly made her way upstairs she tried to prepare herself for the difficult conversations that no doubt lay ahead. If she was honest, there was a small part of her that still felt annoyed with Henry. When she had given up the job of deputy store manager last year she had done so in the knowledge that she was better off back in her beloved fabric department. She wasn't a natural manager, and hated dealing with staffing issues such as these. To have Henry dragging her back into it, when according to him there was a simple explanation for the missing money that wouldn't cost him his job, made her want to explode with anger.

Swallowing back her feelings, she walked past Mr Button's office and saw the wooden door was ajar. There were still a few moments before they were all due to meet, and perhaps he could do with a cup of tea before they began. Peering around the door, she was just about to ask as much, when the sight of two people standing on the rich red Persian carpet bent over his desk, rifling through papers, made her jaw drop.

'What are you two playing at?'

'It's not what it looks like,' Henry said.

'Really, it's not, Flo,' Jean added nervously.

Flo walked towards the pair of them, and saw a sheaf of papers marked 'Private and Confidential' in Jean's trembling hands.

'These ...' she said, plucking them from Jean's hands, 'belong in Liberty's. And as for you,' she said, rounding on her former boss, 'I should have known you'd be involved in all of this somehow.'

Henry laid a hand on Flo's arm. 'Trust me, I know this looks bad, we both do, but there is a reasonable explanation.'

'Well, fire away,' Flo spat, shaking his grasp off her arm. 'I'm all ears.'

'The thing is, Flo, it's not easy to put into words,' Jean began.

'Well, let me put it another way,' Flo said, feeling the anger building deep within. 'I'm sick and tired of hearing how there's a reasonable explanation. If it's so reasonable then spit it out now or I'm going to the board.'

'If that's what you think is best,' Henry said with an air of petulance as he drew himself up to his full height.

Flo wasn't intimidated and scowled at him.

'No,' Jean said suddenly. 'No, Henry, you've done enough for me and Bess as it is, it's time Flo knew the rest. There have been enough lies. Besides, she saw us together at The Kitty Cat Club last night; maybe she can help.'

Henry's face softened as he glanced first at Flo and then back at Jean. 'She saw you both?'

Jean nodded. 'And she was wonderful about it. We need to tell her. It's time.'

'All right,' he sighed, taking a deep breath before turning back to Flo. 'Jean and I are being blackmailed.'

'Blackmailed?' Flo frowned. 'By who?'

'Evie,' they whispered in unison.

Chapter Fifty-One

Flo's jaw dropped in shock for the second time that morning. As she took in Henry and Jean's faces she could see the look of relief and despair written across both of them. Instinctively she knew that they were telling the truth.

She wasn't surprised that Evie had this in her. Flo had never liked the woman, but Mr Button had always trusted her and considered her to be a reputable expert; even the Board of Trade had agreed. Walking across to the window, Flo leaned against the draughty pane, the fresh air helping to cool her hot, angry face. 'So tell me, why on earth is Evie blackmailing you?'

'She's still on the board at Botheringtons,' Henry said.

'I had a feeling that she was. Even though she insisted that she wasn't. Mr Button doesn't know though, I don't think. You know how he always likes to see the good in people,' Flo said pointedly.

'She's also still working there,' Henry said in a low voice.

'She's working there?' Flo echoed. 'How?'

'She's managing fabrics. Executive departmental manager is her official title,' Jean explained.

Flo pinched the bridge of her nose. 'That I didn't know. Why did she want to work here if she had a job already?'

'She's been trying to replicate Liberty's success with the utility prints we've been introducing,' Henry said. 'When Mr Button asked her to become involved in the Board of Trade, and then when Jean could only work part-time, everything fell into her lap.'

Flo shook her head in disgust. She had always known the woman was trouble; why couldn't Mr Button see it too? Then she frowned. 'That still doesn't explain why she was blackmailing you two.'

'As you know, Botheringtons is a religious store,' Henry explained.

Flo nodded. Everyone knew that the Church came before business at the shop. It was part of their success; people looked to them for direction, especially now during these troubled times.

'And as a result of her position on the board of Botheringtons she is also a member of the Public Morality Council,' Jean continued.

'No,' Flo gasped. 'What is she doing mixed up with that trumped-up group of fascists? And if she's part of the Public Morality Council what's she doing going round blackmailing people? That doesn't sound very moral to me.'

'She wants Liberty's out of business,' Henry sighed. 'Starting with the fabric department. She let Dot think she had designs on Mr Button, all so Dot wouldn't focus on what she was really up to, which was finding out about Liberty's and ruining us. Botheringtons is a nice store, tied to the Church, part of a decent and upstanding community. Liberty's is the devil as far as she's concerned. All the passion we have for the arts, for creativity, for bohemian life and the loose morals and alternative lifestyles that apparently accompany that. She and her brother aren't estranged; they have been plotting for a long time to drive customers to Botheringtons, and so she thought she would steal our utility fabric prints and hurt Liberty's that way.'

It was all so much to take in. Flo looked out of the window again, and only the shouts and jostles of the men who worked in the loading area directly below Mr Button's office interrupted her thoughts.

'There's still something I don't understand,' Flo said at last. 'And that's how Evie managed to blackmail either of you. I mean, what did she have on you?'

'Evie caught Bess and me holding hands at the first-aid night,' Jean said in a low voice. 'She said people like us had no place in society, that we were ill, a disgrace, and we ought to be hanged for crimes against nature.'

Flo's eyes widened in shock as she started piecing it all together. That must have been why the girls had been arguing with Evie during the first-aid night.

'She put two and two together and told me that unless I stole the money from the fundraising night then she would tell everyone about me and Bess.'

Flo gasped. 'What a wicked thing to do.'

'It was evil. Jean and Bess have dealt with bigotry their entire lives. To find it here at Liberty's has been a disgrace,' Henry growled in Jean's defence. 'Flo, Jean had no choice.'

'But why did she need you to steal the money?' Flo asked. 'I can understand her wanting the patterns and details of the utility fabrics to try and destroy us, but why the money?'

'Botheringtons is in a lot of trouble financially,' Henry replied grimly. 'She saw an opportunity to boost their coffers.'

'And Botheringtons knew about this?' Flo asked, aghast.

'Us department store managers talk, and the Botheringtons lot have never liked Liberty's, we're too artsy.' Henry smiled grimly. 'I understand that unofficially they knew about the patterns but they had no idea about the money. I think Evie told them a beneficiary had given it to them.'

'I can't believe what I'm hearing,' Flo gasped. 'And, Jean, you were the one that stole the money?'

Jean hung her head in shame. 'I'm sorry.'

'And that's also why you had those papers marked 'Private and Confidential' in your bag,' Flo said in realisation. 'You were going to give them to Evie.'

Nodding her head again, Jean remained silent.

'So what I don't understand is how you got to be involved in all of this?' Flo frowned as she turned to Henry.

'It was the night of the fundraiser,' Henry said with a sigh. 'I caught Bess helping Jean steal the money and took it from them to put back. I asked them then what was going on but they wouldn't tell me anything.'

'Though Bess told you if you wanted answers you'd better go to Evie,' Jean said miserably.

'That's right, though I had a hunch,' Henry explained. 'I knew Evie was on the Public Morality Council. The father of one of Stan's friends is on it and I saw him talking to Evie about it near Liberty's. The chap told me that Evie joined after her husband died. It wasn't all down to a bad business deal, though that was the official line. Apparently he had been seeing prostitutes behind her back, and when she found out she decided to take a stand against immoral behaviour.'

Flo shook her head in horror as Henry continued: 'I did express my reservations about her when Mr Button took her on but he thought that she had done such a good job at the Board of Trade that there would be no harm having her here in Liberty's. So that night, I went to Evie and asked her to tell me why she was getting Jean and Bess to steal money. She started laughing, and said Liberty's was immoral. Not only did it employ lesbians, but criminals like me. Liberty's didn't deserve to keep its doors open, she said; she was acting in the best interests of the community by doing her damnedest to get rid of our immoral store.'

'What a wicked, spiteful cow,' Flo murmured with vehemence in her voice.

'It doesn't stop there. She told me that she knew I had been to prison, and that if I said anything then she would go straight to the authorities and let them know an ex-convict was taking care of a little boy. She said it wasn't right that I was taking care of a child, but he should be placed in the care of the state.'

'The new adoption act,' Flo muttered miserably. The very same act that had made life difficult for Mary and David. She could only imagine how difficult it would have made life for Henry and Stan.

'So what then?'

'I'm afraid I was weak, Flo,' Henry admitted, running a hand through his hair. 'I didn't want Jean and Bess's secret to come out, not after they had been through so much, and I didn't want to lose Stan, so I told her I would take the blame for the missing money and said she could have it.'

'And is that why you walked towards us, clutching the box like that?' Flo asked, everything becoming clear. 'To make us think that you had stolen it?'

Sheepishly Henry nodded. 'I thought it was for the best.'

Flo let out a loud sigh. How could all this have been going on right under her nose without her noticing? Her heart went out to Jean, to Bess, and to Henry and Stan. She thought about Celia, and how she had urged her to listen to Henry and find a way to help him.

'Did Celia know about this?' she asked.

'I needed someone to talk to,' Henry admitted. 'Celia was there for me.'

313

'He's a good man, Flo,' Jean ventured. 'You know he didn't do any of this, he only had my and Bess's interests at heart.'

Flo's mind was reeling. This was such a mess.

'You said you were innocent,' she said, her tone abrupt. 'When you went to prison, I mean. What really happened? I need to know everything if I'm to help.'

Henry took a deep breath. 'You have to understand, Flo, this is a secret I don't share. I made my mind up for Stan's sake that I would take the blame for this and I meant it.'

'I will only use this information to help you,' she promised. 'You've got to trust me.'

'It wasn't me that stole from the factory I was working at; it was my mother. She was hard up after my dad was killed and that new husband of hers never had any money so she started nicking money from the safe at the factory where we worked. Just little bits at first, but then the amounts got larger and larger. I caught her in the office one day and took the money right out of her hands.'

'A bit like at the fundraiser,' Flo murmured.

'I was trying to convince her to put it back but she wouldn't listen,' Henry continued. 'We were arguing so loudly that the boss walked in to see what was going on. He saw me with the money and before Mum could stop me I confessed.'

Flo clasped her hands to her mouth. Surely his mother would have stopped this?

'Mum tried to say it was her fault, of course, and so he called the police to sort it out. While we were waiting I told Mum not to be so daft, that she had Stan, who was just a baby at the time, to think about, that it would be no use to him if she got in trouble. So I told her to let me go to prison for her; it was my way of making up for what happened with Dad.'

314

'Oh Henry,' Flo said, shaking her head in disbelief. 'And Stan doesn't know?'

'He must never know. I only want him to think well of his mother. Better he thinks I'm a thug.'

'But your reputation?' Flo broke off.

'Celia knew, of course. She was the one that came to see me in prison, and it was how we became such good friends. Mr Button knew me of old and I told him. We had worked late one night years ago at Bourne and Hollingsworth, shared a pint and the truth came out. When a job came up here, he personally vouched for me; he was the one that really put his reputation on the line.'

'But we have to tell him everything now,' Flo gasped. 'I mean, if we tell him the truth he will be able to stop Evie.'

A look of panic flashed across Jean's face. 'You can't tell anyone, Flo, you promised!'

'I know and I mean it,' Flo insisted. 'But, Jean, you must see this is the only way. You can't let her get away with this.'

'It's not that simple, Flo,' Henry said, his tone filled with sadness. 'If we confront her she'll go to the authorities and tell them that I, a convicted criminal, am guardian to a little boy. She'll have Stan taken away from me and then she will destroy Jean and Bess just by opening her mouth and telling the world about their love.'

'You saw what she was like this morning, Flo, when you mentioned The Kitty Cat Club,' Jean pleaded. 'The hate and venom that spouted from her mouth. You and Mr Masters are in the minority; most of society thinks people like me and Bess are sick and should be locked up. What if Mr Button thinks like her? What if word gets out? We can't take the risk. We will be destroyed. Bess is only just coming to terms with the loss of her hand; if my brother found us again I don't think she could take it. She's not as strong as she looks.'

'There has to be another way, Flo,' Henry insisted.

Flo took a deep breath and regarded the pair of them. They looked broken, she realised. Their faces were lined with pain, and their bodies hunched over as if they had given up. She couldn't burden them with anything else.

'We'll find another way,' she promised them. 'I won't breathe a word.'

As the relief passed across their faces, Flo knew she had done the right thing. The bigger question was how was she going to unpick this mess?

Chapter Fifty-Two

The following Sunday afternoon was unusually warm for February. At home in Islington, Flo had just finished putting the final touches to the birthday party display on the kitchen table when the sound of the door knocker echoed through the house.

'I'll go,' she called to Jean, hurrying to the door dressed in her best lemon tea dress.

Glancing in the mirror that hung in the hallway, she briefly checked her appearance. Satisfied, she flung open the door and welcomed in the last of the guests to the little birthday party she had arranged.

'Emma!' Flo beamed at the little blonde girl balancing on Mary's hip.

'Look!' Mary smiled. 'It's Auntie Flo.'

Flo couldn't help but get swept up in her friend's excitement and wrapped her hand around Emma's tiny one.

'It's very nice to see you, Emma.'

The little girl giggled at the grown-up gesture, before promptly burying her face in Mary's chest.

'I think she's over-excited,' said Mary as she followed Flo inside and walked down the corridor towards the kitchen.

'I don't think she's the only one.' Flo laughed. 'Come on through. Everyone else is already here.'

As she followed Mary along the corridor, towards the kitchen, she smiled at the decorations that festooned the little house. Newspaper chains had been strung from lampshades and picture rails while homemade cards lined the mantel.

'Blimey, this looks fantastic,' Mary marvelled.

'Jean and I did it all,' Flo said, a hint of pride in her voice. 'You should see the kitchen.'

Right on cue Mary followed Flo into the kitchen and gasped in delight. There were Alice, Arthur, Jack, Rose, Malcolm, Dot and Jean standing proudly around the scrubbed pine kitchen table. Holding glasses of port and lemon they raised them in greeting towards Mary and the guest of honour.

Flo stood back to watch Mary's delighted face and couldn't stop smiling as she saw her friend drinking it all in. Following her gaze, she had to admit she, Jean and Bess had done well. On the table stood two bottles of bright red fizzy pop, and a yellow blancmange, wobbling dangerously next to a tray of paste sandwiches.

Yet the real star of the show, arranged on a homemade doily cut from newspaper, was a bright pink cake filled with mock cream and decorated with pink and white icing, complete with matching candle in the centre.

'Ta da!' Flo cried, gesturing to the cake with one hand, and stroking Emma's cheek with the other.

'It looks beautiful, Flo,' Mary said, tears of joy filling her eyes. 'However did you get the rations for all this?'

Flo smiled. 'I didn't, Dot did.'

Dot tapped the side of her nose as Mary looked enquiringly at her.

Rose giggled. 'I think we all know it's best not to ask.'

'Cheek!' Dot laughed.

Just then, Arthur, who had been sleeping in Alice's arms, woke up. He blinked his eyes open, and Flo laughed as she saw him and Emma reach for each other.

'Perhaps we should let them have a play before the party gets really started,' Alice suggested.

'Good idea,' Mary exclaimed. 'Shall we take them through to the front room?'

'Let me,' said Jean, who was desperate for a rest after hurrying back from visiting Bess in the convalescent home to make it in time for the party.

'Go on, love.' Dot smiled. 'Careful though, darlin', don't want you getting broody.'

Jean said nothing as she scuttled out of the kitchen clutching Emma and Arthur, leaving Flo feeling uncomfortable.

'So how long do you have Emma for?' Flo asked Mary, keen to change the subject.

'Until six tonight.' Mary sighed. 'Then I have to take her back to the orphanage.'

'That's a shame.' Alice frowned. 'It would be much easier for you to have her overnight.'

Mary shrugged. 'What can I do? I'm just grateful Mrs Matravers has agreed to let us adopt Emma. I'm hardly going to rock the boat now.'

'Fair enough,' Alice replied, taking a sip of her own drink. 'But it was a lovely idea to have a first birthday party for her.'

'I know. And I know she's not quite one yet, but I thought that as we're going to be family, we should mark these important occasions and I'm so grateful to you Flo for organising it,' Mary said, her face a picture of delight.

'It was my pleasure. Has Mrs Matravers sent Emma anything yet?'

Mary shook her head. 'I don't expect her to, if I'm honest.'

'It must be hard for her being inside and knowing that her daughter is being adopted,' Flo put in, reaching for a paste sandwich.

'I know,' Mary sighed, taking a seat at the table next to Dot. 'I remember when we were almost bombed in

Whitstable that time and she was so terrified of losing her baby. All she ever wanted was to be a mother.'

'But that's in the past,' Alice offered. 'What we have to think about now is the future, yours and Emma's.'

'Seriously, you can't think like that, Mary,' Jack chimed in through a mouth full of sandwich. 'I miss Jack Junior every day of my life, and I know that when me and Alice have kids they'll get under my skin in just the same way. But you'll always want what's best for them, and this Mrs Matravers will want that too.'

There was a small pause before Alice turned to Jack and squealed with delight. 'We're having kids, are we?'

Jack wrapped an arm around Alice and pulled her to him. 'We're having dozens, lots of brothers and sisters for Arthur and Jack Junior, so you'd best get used to being a truly great mom.'

'Mum,' Dot scolded Jack affectionately. 'You bloody Yanks don't know the King's English!'

Jack rolled his eyes; he had become more than used to Dot's gentle teasing by now.

'Well, I think we deserve a toast.' Dot grinned, getting to her feet and refilling everyone's glasses. 'To celebrating the small victories in life, like Emma's first birthday.'

'I'll drink to that.' Mary smiled, raising her glass.

As the girls clinked their glasses against each other the sound of the door knocker echoed through the kitchen.

'I'll get that,' Dot said, rising to her feet. 'It's probably Edwin. He said he'd pop round.'

Sure enough, Mr Button followed Dot into the kitchen.

'Hello, everyone,' he said, a smile on his face as he took in the table full of food. 'Sorry I'm late. Board of Trade business.'

'It never stops, does it,' Jack marvelled, standing up to shake Mr Button's hand. 'Even working on a Sunday.'

Dot rolled her eyes. 'There'll come a time when I'm top of your list of priorities, Edwin Button. But I've a feeling hell will freeze over first.'

As Mr Button opened his mouth to protest, Flo laid a hand on his arm. 'She's teasing,'

'I know,' Mr Button replied, taking a seat by the door. Loosening the navy tie that complemented his Liberty pinstripe suit he gulped gratefully at the beer Jack offered him. 'Must say, I needed that.'

'Long day then?' Flo asked.

'You could say that.' He sighed. 'I am sorry I was so late. I didn't mean to be the last.'

'Stop apologising, Mr B.,' Alice soothed. 'We're all here, that's what matters.'

Mr Button looked around. 'Oh good. Only I wasn't sure if the chap outside was one of your guests.'

Flo frowned. 'What chap?'

'Some chap with dark hair. Short. Looked a little surly, if I'm honest. He was leaning against the lamppost, staring directly into the house.'

'Well, who the hell's that?' Dot thundered. 'It better not be a burglar. I'll be ready for him with one of your Aggie's good saucepans, Flo. One crack to the back of his head and he'll be down before he's even had a chance to peek at your silver.'

Despite the situation, everyone chuckled at Dot's dramatics.

'I'm sure it's just a misunderstanding but I'll ask Jean if she knows anyone that looks like that,' Flo said, getting to her feet. 'Might be a friend of Bess's or something, hoping to wish her well.'

With that Flo crept down the corridor and peered into the front room. There was Jean, sitting on the settee, a baby under each arm and a book on her lap. She was reading to them. All three looked so peaceful.

'Everything all right?' she asked softly.

Jean looked up from the story book and smiled. 'Yes, fine.'

Flo took a seat beside her friend and saw that she looked tired. 'You seem worried about something.'

Jean shrugged. The babies were pointing at the book now, seemingly clamouring for Jean to keep reading. 'Nothing's wrong apart from the usual.'

'I see.' Flo smoothed back a kink in Arthur's hair before asking, 'Mr Button says there's a young lad hanging about outside. Dark hair, short, bit surly. Sound like anyone you know?'

There was a pause as Jean pursed her lips, then bent down to give Emma and Arthur a kiss each on the forehead.

'It sounds like my brother, Fred,' she admitted. 'I think he's found us.'

Flo nodded; she'd had a feeling that might be the case. 'Have you seen him before?'

'Bess thought she saw him loitering outside the other day,' Jean said in hushed tones. 'I told Bess we should run but she won't have it.'

'Quite right,' Flo agreed. 'Bess is still recuperating, and your Fred's a bully. There must be a way to deal with him.'

'Well, if there is, I don't know what it would be.'

The sound of laughter could be heard from the kitchen as Flo reached out and squeezed Jean's hand.

'There you both are! We thought we'd cut the cake now everyone's here. Mr B. has to rush off soon and take care of his neighbour's leaking pipe apparently,' Mary interrupted, her head appearing around the door.

'That man is too good to be true,' Flo sighed, getting to her feet.

Mary made a face. 'I know. Much as I adore Mr B., this quality he has of always being helpful gets right on my pip sometimes.'

Flo laughed. 'I think Dot feels the same. It's just the way he is, I suppose. He can't help himself.'

'It isn't half annoying. I mean, I don't think I've ever heard him say a bad word about anyone. He always gives people a chance.'

'Even when they don't deserve it,' Jean said morosely. 'But then, I suppose that's a lovely quality, isn't it, to always think the best of someone?'

'I wish I could be half the man he is,' Mary mused, and then chuckled, realising what she'd said as she bent down to scoop Emma into her arms. 'You know what I mean.'

Flo nodded. 'I do. You want to show Emma that you can also be a good person, someone who always tries to see the good in everyone no matter what.'

'Oh, and to always be there to soothe troubled waters,' Mary added. 'He only ever raises his voice when provoked.'

Flo thought for a moment. It was little wonder she had asked him to give her away at her wedding. He was the father she had always wanted, the man she had always trusted for advice and instinctively she knew he was the man to help her with this Evie Allingham situation. There had to be a way to get Mr Button to see what was going on without breaking anyone's trust. Not for the first time she found herself wishing that Aggie were here. The mother she now knew her to be would have the answer, of that she was sure.

But that was the problem, Flo thought sadly: all her family were gone. All she had left now were her Liberty girls, and though she couldn't confide in them, they could help her see the way. As she looked at Mary, she felt a flutter of relief and gratitude in her heart that one of her Liberty sisters had stepped in to show her what had to be done.

Chapter Fifty-Three

It had been over a fortnight since Emma's birthday party and although Flo had got a little closer to a plan that would help her friends, she hadn't been able to put anything into action yet. She had thought that after chatting to Mary she would come up with a way of casually letting Mr Button know that there was a problem with Evie. Then she would explain, with just enough detail, that the woman was bad news without betraying the secrets entrusted to her.

Yet despite her best efforts she had barely seen the store manager. As usual he had been busy with the Board of Trade, the only upside to that being that Evie had also been with him and therefore out of their hair.

Still, with every day that passed, the sales figures seemed to get worse and worse. Flo had been diligent with her paperwork each day, looking for signs progress was being made within the department, but she could see how sales were slipping. With more of the new prints due any day now, Flo needed to resolve this situation before Evie could cause any further damage.

But before that she had to turn her attentions to the second fundraising evening, which was due to take place at the end of the week. Flo and Rose now found themselves tucked away in the pleating room for one final check.

Unlike the first fundraising evening, they were unable to host it anywhere as grand as the Palladium. After much cajoling, the board had agreed to let a smaller, but just as glamorous, event be held in the Liberty crypt and afterwards Mr Button would make the presentation. Thankfully ticket sales had been high, with almost all the staff purchasing at least two, and many of the store's customers had been only too delighted to help fund a second evening.

'So shall we open with the girls from carpets doing their poetry recital, and then move on to your songs?' Rose asked as she chewed the end of her pen.

'Good idea,' Flo said in approval. 'Hopefully I'll cheer them up after all that reading.'

Rose shot her a sideways glance. 'Come on, we have to try to make the evening a bit different to the last one. Are we still going to have Max close the show?'

'I think so.' Flo nodded as she checked her watch. It was almost two in the afternoon. 'Look, I'm sorry, Rose, I'm going to have to get back to the floor so that Mary can get off for lunch. Alice is over in Merton overseeing the new print samples, Jean's off with Bess, and Dot's looking after Arthur so I'm short on the floor with Evie out as well.'

Rose frowned. 'But Evie's here. She came in to see the latest designs.'

Alarm pulsed through Flo. 'She's done what?'

'I thought you knew,' Rose said, tucking her pen behind her ear. 'Something to do with needing to show the Board of Trade how they're keeping the public happy or something. I didn't quite understand if I'm honest.'

Flo didn't hang around to hear anything else Rose had to say; instead she raced up to the shop floor. As she crossed the parquet, weaving her way through customers delighting in the wares on offer in jewellery and gifts, her mind was in overdrive. This woman seemed hell-bent on destruction and Flo was damned if she was going to let it happen any more.

Reaching the entrance to fabrics, Flo paused for a moment and took a deep breath. She knew it wouldn't do her any good to arrive angry. A few seconds later, once she had composed herself, she walked across the floor. Yet the sight of Evie and Alice poring over the new pattern samples was almost too much to bear.

'Evie, what a pleasure. I didn't realise you were with us today,' Flo said through gritted teeth.

Evie looked up and smiled pleasantly at Flo. 'Yes. I knew Alice was coming back from Merton and I thought it would be wonderful to take a look at the new spring samples. They are marvellous. I've made a few notes so I know just how to tempt our customers.'

'*I bet you have,*' Flo muttered under her breath before turning to Alice. 'I know Mary's going to lunch now, but could you mind the floor for a few minutes while Mrs Allingham and I have a word in Mr Masters' office?'

'Mr Masters' office?' Evie chuckled. 'Not for much longer.'

Ignoring Evie, Flo looked at Alice, who nodded her assent. 'One of the boys got me a sandwich at Merton so I've eaten. Take as long as you need.'

'Thank you,' Flo said quietly, before glancing at Evie. 'Shall we?'

Without waiting for an answer Flo made her way back across the shop floor and up the stairs towards the deputy store manager's office, Evie's heels clattering loudly behind her.

Pushing open the door, Flo steeled herself as she sat behind Henry's desk and gestured for Evie to sit opposite.

Without bothering to shut the door, Evie waltzed straight in and sat down, an amused expression on her face.

'What is all this, Mrs Canning? Playing at being the boss while Mr Button's away? I do hope you don't have designs on his chair as well as Mr Masters.'

Flo ignored Evie's petty claims and looked at the woman with contempt. 'I wanted to ask why you're here at Liberty's.'

'Because dear Edwin invited me to help the department,' she said mockingly. 'And I believe I have done a sterling job.'

'Indeed you have,' Flo agreed. 'But I think the sterling job has been for Botheringtons, not us.'

Evie's smile slipped. 'I don't know what you mean.'

'I think you know exactly what I mean,' Flo said, a hint of grit to her voice as she leaned forward and locked eyes with Evie. 'You know perfectly well that I'm on to you.'

'What rot.' Evie laughed, shaking her head in disbelief. 'On to me about what? About the fact I'm more knowledgeable about your own department than you are?'

Flo didn't miss a beat. 'No, about the fact you're still working for Botheringtons and sitting on their board. About the fact you're stealing Liberty's print lines so Botheringtons can make cheap knock-offs; about the fact that Botheringtons is so broke you gifted them a donation to boost their coffers, courtesy of our fundraising night; and finally about the fact you're a member of the Public Morality Council and want to ruin Liberty's because you believe it's a place of impropriety. In short, Evie Allingham, you're nothing but a thief and a liar and I shall be letting the Public Morality Council know what you've been up to immediately.'

For a split second Evie looked panicked; then she composed herself. 'How dare you! After all I've done for you, for this company, for my country even, this is how you talk to me. Who do you think you are? You're a jumped-up little trollop who, rather than respectfully mourning her dead husband the way any decent wife should, is in the throes of passion with another man already. That's what all this is about. You're in love with Henry Masters, a no-good criminal. You should be ashamed of yourself. Where are your morals?'

'I see you don't bother to deny it though,' Flo said, ignoring Evie's insults. 'You're too busy hurling accusations at everyone else to refute what's being laid at your own door.'

'I don't need to deny it. Anyone worth their salt would see that isn't true,' Evie fired.

Flo said nothing. Getting up from her chair, she walked around the desk and leaned against it, arms folded as she gazed down at Evie, who sat ramrod straight.

'Let me tell you what I know, shall I?' she said in a low voice. 'I know that you're a vile little individual who has been blackmailing some of my most trusted members of staff. I know you have been getting Jean and Bess to do your dirty work for you because you think you've got something on them. I also know that you've been blackmailing Mr Masters to take the fall for stealing the money so you could give it to Botheringtons.'

Evie laughed. 'Stuff and nonsense.'

'But we both know that it's not,' Flo said, doing her best to keep her voice even. 'We both know that you told Jean and Bess you would reveal them to be lesbians to the entire world and make their lives a misery if they didn't do what you said. And we both know you told Mr Masters that, unless he took the blame for the missing money, you would go to the authorities and have his brother taken away from him because of his police record.'

Evie laughed again. 'All right, so it's true. But where's your proof?'

Flo faltered. Proof was the one thing she didn't have. 'I'll go to the board, tell them what you've been up to.'

'Like hell you will,' Evie snorted. 'You won't go any-where because, if you do, you'll have to start telling folk that Bess and Jean are a couple of dykes, and you'll see what that does for Liberty's popularity.'

Flo winced. 'You're a disgrace, Evie, I don't know how you can sleep at night.'

'Probably not as well as you,' Evie conceded, 'but then I'm not a jumped-up chorus girl with a man like Henry Masters to keep me warm in bed.'

Fury raged through Flo like nothing she had felt before. Before she knew what she was doing she'd slapped Evie hard across the face, enjoying the stinging sensation in her fingers and the sound of the blow reverberating across the room. The time for manners was over.

'You cheeky cow,' she growled. 'You're nothing but a troublemaker and Liberty's deserves better than you.'

Just then a noise at the doorway caused both women to look up. There, with a face like thunder and his arms folded, was Mr Button.

Chapter Fifty-Four

Evie jumped to her feet. 'Mr Button, thank God you're here. I thought you were with the Board of Trade all day. Mrs Canning just struck me with her bare hand.'

'So I gather,' Mr Button said gravely, his eyes darting from Flo to Evie.

Flo felt a stirring of regret. She knew her anger was justified, but she was a senior staff member, she shouldn't have lost her temper like that.

'I want to make a formal complaint,' Evie continued. 'And I'll go to the police. Look – she's left a mark.'

As Evie offered her cheek up for inspection, Flo grimaced as she saw her handprint. Mr Button cursorily examined it, and then glanced at Flo. She shivered, despite the warmth of the room. Mr Button's glare chilled her to her very core.

'Yes, that must have hurt,' Mr Button said, 'and from what I can understand, Mrs Allingham, it was very well deserved.'

'I beg your pardon!' Evie exclaimed.

Mr Button turned around, slammed the door shut and faced the women, his face now puce with rage.

'I heard every word.'

'What do you mean?' Flo gasped, thinking of the secrets she had unleashed.

'I mean I heard everything,' he clarified.

'Then you'll have heard that as well as employing a low-down crook, Liberty's have employed a dirty lesbian,'

Evie exclaimed. 'The whole thing is abhorrent. She must be sacked forthwith. She's bringing the good name of Liberty's into disrepute. What on earth would people say if they knew? And as for that disgraceful *friend* of hers, well, perhaps losing her hand was God's punishment for whatever depraved things they get up to.'

Flo took a step forward, ready to unleash the full extent of her fury, only to find Mr Button had already beaten her to it.

'No, Mrs Allingham, what's abhorrent is you,' he said, his voice taking on a steely tone. 'What's abhorrent is that you thought you could use people's biggest secrets to feather your own nest. You disgust me. I recommended you to the Board of Trade, I valued your expertise, defended you to Mrs Hanson when she tried to tell me how dreadful you were. I disregarded it all out of professional respect. But now I see what everyone else sees: a disgusting and bitter individual who is so obsessed with the morality of those around her she cannot see the immoral behaviour she is indulging in herself. You have no place on the Public Morality Council, and you have no place here at Liberty's or the Board of Trade either. I want you out of my shop immediately.'

'Edwin, please,' Evie began, 'I can explain.'

Now it was Mr Button's turn to roar with laughter. 'Can you really? What will it be, I wonder. Botheringtons made you do it? Your brother? Whom I very much doubt you are estranged from after all, but who made a nice little story for you about your loyalties truly lying here. Please, Mrs Allingham, don't insult my intelligence any further. It's a shame I didn't see it sooner. I let myself down, I let the store down and, worst of all, I let my very valued employees down.'

Evie said nothing. She glared defiantly out of the window, the morning sun burning through the glass.

'What are you going to do?' Flo asked.

'I'm going to sack Mrs Allingham here with immediate effect,' Mr Button said. 'Then I'm going to demand all the notes, drawings, private papers and anything else to do with Liberty's that she's taken are returned. And, perhaps most importantly, I'm going to insist that the money she stole from the fundraiser is returned straightaway.'

'That's impossible,' she cried, 'I don't have it.'

'Then you'd better bloody find it,' he snarled. 'Because if you don't I shall not only sully your reputation over at Botheringtons, but I shall tell everyone at the Board of Trade what you've done. You'll be finished, Evie. Even if you deny it to the hills we all know mud sticks and I shall ensure that every filthy piece of dirt I can lay my hands on sticks to every inch of you.'

Evie opened and closed her mouth, clearly unsure what to say.

'There's nothing else for you here, Evie,' Mr Button thundered. 'Now get out of my sight before I ask Mrs Canning here to slap the other side of your face so you've a set of matching prints on each cheek.'

Evie didn't need telling twice, and scuttled out of the room.

Once she was gone, Flo looked gratefully at the store manager. 'I'm sorry for all of this. Truly. I wanted to come to you the moment I found out, but ...'

'But you didn't want to break any confidences,' Mr Button said gravely.

Flo nodded. 'I've been trying to find a way to tell you. I knew that I could trust you; I just didn't want to betray anyone.'

'Quite understandable,' Mr Button said. 'What we have to do is go about setting things back in order.'

'That doesn't mean you're going to sack Jean, does it, sir?' Flo begged.

Mr Button looked confused. 'Why on earth would I sack Jean? She's one of the best sales girls we have on the shop floor.'

'Some people might feel differently.'

'Well, I'm not some people.' Mr Button shrugged. 'And I couldn't give a monkey's whether any staff of mine decide to fall in love with a man, woman or nobody at all. When I was in the army there were a lot of fairies about. I never understood the problem myself. They were there serving our country just like the rest of us and that was all that truly mattered to me – and to most people, to be honest. Jean's business is nothing but her own, and I'm certainly not going to sack her because of her relationship with Bess.'

Flo felt a surge of warmth grow inside her. She knew Mr Button would do the right thing. He was the pinnacle of decency and with him at the helm of Liberty's she knew the ship would continue to forge ahead.

'And what about Mr Masters?' she asked.

'We'll reinstate him with immediate effect and the board will pay him for all the days off he was forced to take by way of compensation.'

'Really?' Flo gasped in delight. 'That's wonderful.'

'Not as wonderful as not having accused him in the first place,' Mr Button said. 'Now, Flo, I think perhaps the only one that's going to lose out here is you.'

'Me?' Flo looked confused. 'Why me, sir?'

'Well, Mr Masters' reinstatement means I have no further need for your services as deputy store manager.'

Flo felt a flash of relief. 'That's fine, sir. I'm happiest in fabrics.'

Mr Button regarded her fondly. 'Is that true?'

'Sir?' She looked at him again quizzically.

'Is fabrics really where you're happiest or do you think there might be somewhere else you'd prefer to be? The stage, perhaps?'

'Sir, I have no idea what you mean,' she gasped. 'My place is at Liberty's, always has been and always will be.'

Mr Button stepped forward and clamped a hand over Flo's. 'My dear, you will always have a home here at Liberty's whenever you want it. But I wonder if perhaps it's time to really think about what does make you happy? You're no longer the child that came to work here as a Saturday girl in the stores all those years ago. You're a woman now, with a bright future ahead of you if you want it. I wonder if it's time to make those dreams come true.'

Chapter Fifty-Five

Usually the basement crypt was a functional canteen used solely by those on fire-watching duties. Tonight it had been transformed into a glamorous stage that would easily rival any West End theatre.

A rich red rug had been borrowed from the carpet department to create a lush walkway between the row of chairs that had been decorated with silk ties lent by the fabric department. At the front, all the tables had been embellished with heavy white tablecloths and candles, giving the place the air of a very elegant nightclub.

'What do you think?' Alice called as Flo walked in and marvelled at the scene around her.

'It looks gorgeous,' Flo exclaimed.

The area beyond the tables had been turned into a stage courtesy of a large cutting table from the pleating room. The cutting table, along with a pair of red velvet curtains that Flo knew had once lined the old beading room, created the perfect theatrical effect.

'Who did all this?'

'Who d'you think?' Dot chuckled, appearing from behind the curtain. 'The fairy godmother?'

Flo rolled her eyes as Dot swept her up in a hug. 'Ignore me, I'm teasing, but I hear we all owe you a thank you.'

Flo stepped away from Dot's embrace and looked at her in surprise. 'What do you mean?'

'I mean that it's thanks to you we've got rid of Evie bloody Allingham,' Dot cried, her eyes shining with relief.

'And got me my job back,' Henry boomed from behind her.

Whirling around she was delighted to see he was flanked by both Bess and Jean, who were smiling broadly.

'We don't know what you did or said,' Jean said, her voice thick with gratitude. 'But Mr Button said that you had discovered Mrs Allingham was the thief and therefore she had to go.'

'To Flo,' Mary cheered.

'To Flo!' everyone chorused.

Looking at her friends' faces, each filled with delighted merriment, Flo felt herself blushing. She had only done what anyone else would have, of that she was sure.

'There's nothing to thank me for,' she said earnestly. 'The truth would have come out in the end.'

'And I'll flamin' knock her block off if I see her again,' Dot fumed.

Sensing Dot was about to launch into one of her lectures, Flo started to walk towards the area that she could see had been earmarked as backstage.

'I think I'd better get ready. Max will be here soon and I want to have a quick run through of the duets we're doing.'

Alice and Mary looked sheepishly at one another. 'Er, there's something we need to tell you.'

'What?' Flo demanded.

'Max isn't coming,' Rose said flatly. 'He's not well. He suggests you do all the numbers he performed. He says you sing them better than he does anyway.'

'And you do,' Dot said loyally.

Panic flooded through Flo and she leaned on one of the nearby tables for support. 'What do you mean he isn't coming? He has to come! He's the star of the show! His name and face is on all the posters.'

'Well, his name and yours,' Mary said matter-of-factly. 'The show must go on, as they say in show business, so you'd better get on with it.'

'But I can't,' she gasped.

'Flo, sweetheart,' Henry said in a tone she recognised as one he'd used on Stan when he was about to throw a tantrum. 'You were born ready. You're going to bring the house down. Now go and get yourself set up and enjoy this.'

'And you deserve it.' Alice smiled. 'Come on, knock 'em dead!'

With that Alice gave Flo a little push towards the backstage area, and Flo, knowing she was beaten, meekly walked away.

Finding a spot to change next to the violinist from ready-to-wear and the ballet dancer from gifts, Flo started to get ready. For tonight's performance she had chosen to wear Aggie's old red dress. Floor-length and made from taffeta it was every bit as glamorous as her mother had been, and Flo hoped it would imbue her with confidence, ignoring the fact she felt very much like an inmate about to face the hangman. Instead she remembered what Aggie used to say: *If you feel like a star, then you are a star.*

With that Flo waited nervously in the wings as the dance troupe finished. Then she heard Princess Valentina, who had been made master of ceremonies for the entire event, announce her name.

'Please welcome to the stage our very talented mistress of music, all the way from fabrics, Mrs Florence Canning.'

Stepping out in front of the audience, Flo looked down at the sea of people who were all beaming at her and clapping furiously. This time there were only about two hundred, half the number in the Palladium, yet this felt more special and intimate.

'Good evening, everyone,' she said as the applause died down. 'Thank you all so much for letting me be here tonight. Our good friend Max Monroe is sadly unable to make it. I know I'm a very poor substitute but I promise we're all going to have a good time. I thought tonight I would start things off with a song that meant a very great deal to me and my late husband, "This Heart Was Made for Loving You".'

As the pianist began to play, Flo looked out into the audience, felt her nerves disappear and sang. Then an incredible thing started to happen. All the joy and power that she used to feel when she sang for an audience returned. She was alive, exhilarated, and she could do anything. The only thing that mattered in that moment was her and the song.

For the next half an hour that was all Flo could think about, until she reached the final number of the evening. As the pianist rested his fingers on the keys and began to play the introduction to 'Love Is Everywhere', her thoughts turned to Aggie. Was this how she had felt when she performed on stage? Then Flo's thoughts turned to the children she had played piano for. Had they felt a fraction of this power when they had stood as a group and sung their hearts out? She knew that the surviving children had gone on to nearby schools and she hoped that those who had adored singing, just as she did, would continue to do so.

Opening her mouth to start her final song, the audience got to their feet in appreciation as the lyrics flowed from her. As her lips glided over the words, the sentiments of love and loss weren't lost on her. Closing her eyes, an image of Neil, of his handsome face on their wedding day, came to mind. It was so clear, so real, as she took in the love shining from his face and the joy, the sweet, sweet joy, in his eyes as she promised to love him forever. Reaching the end of the song, Flo came to as the audience stamped their feet to show their appreciation. For a moment she felt a flash of sadness that the memory of that beautiful day was just that, a memory. But oh what a memory it was, and what love she had felt. And now, in the present, what love the crowd were showing her as they cheered and applauded.

Glancing out at the sea of faces she saw her loved ones beaming back at her. Mr Button and Dot were clapping furiously, Alice had two fingers in her mouth, wolf-whistling in a most unladylike manner, while Mary and Rose were standing on their chairs whooping with pride.

Once again she felt herself blush. She had been so worried that she wouldn't be up to the job of standing in for Max Monroe, but judging by the affection for her in the room, she had more than surpassed their expectations. Her eyes roamed the audience for Henry, Stan, Bess and Jean but to her surprise she couldn't find them.

'Thank you, everyone,' she said sincerely as the applause died down. 'That's it from all of us tonight. However, the evening isn't over, so if you'd like to refill those glasses before our presentation, which I am pleased to tell you is for even more money than we raised before, now is the perfect time.'

With that she stepped off the stage and made her way to the backstage area, which was empty. Sitting on one of the tables that had also doubled as a make-up table she took a deep breath and allowed herself a moment to revel in the success of the night.

'Well, you were brilliant,' Henry said softly.

Turning around, she saw him hovering in the so-called wings. 'Thank you,' she said, beckoning him to come closer.

'I brought you these,' he said, pulling out a posy of pale pink chrysanthemums from behind his back.

Flo gasped in delight at the gesture and took them from him. 'Thank you. Whatever are they for?'

'To congratulate you on following your dreams. You were amazing up there tonight. A star,' Henry said, his tone still gentle as he took a step towards Flo. 'And to thank you for working so hard to clear my name – and Bess and Jean's too.'

'Oh, no.' Flo shook her head firmly. 'Mr Button did it all.'

'I think we both know that's not true. You've become a very dear friend to me, Flo, over these past months, and I want you to know that if you ever need anything, big or small, I'm here for you.'

With that he bent down and planted a soft kiss on her lips. At his touch, Flo wanted to weep. It had been so long since she had been held and she couldn't deny that it felt wonderful to feel the touch of someone else's lips against hers. Instinctively she kissed him back, lost in the moment, but then reality hit and she pulled away. This wasn't her husband, the man she had loved and adored her entire life. This was Henry Masters, her friend, her very dear friend.

'I'm sorry,' she whispered, her forehead resting against his. 'I'm sorry, Henry, we shouldn't have done that.'

She lifted her head, looked past his shoulder, through the crack in the curtain and out into the audience. Had anyone seen the kiss? She scanned the audience, searching for someone with a disapproving gaze, but she could see nobody.

But then, just a couple of rows away she caught sight of a face that made her feel sick to her stomach. Because there, mere feet away from her, drinking a pint of beer and smiling at her as if it were the most normal thing in the world was her father – Bill Wilson.

Chapter Fifty-Six

A wave of horror passed over Flo as her father winked. What was he doing? Surely he wasn't going to cause trouble again? Not tonight of all nights. But of course he would be here to cause trouble; he never did anything else.

Anxiously she turned to Henry. 'My father's here.'

Henry followed her gaze out into the crowd, and nodded grimly. 'What do you want me to do?'

Flo shook her head. This man had been tormenting her for too long. It was time she took control. 'I'm going to the office briefly. Perhaps you could keep an eye on him? I won't be long.'

'Let me come with you?'

'No, it's best if you stay here. When things get ugly, I don't want anyone getting the blame apart from me.'

With that she turned on her heel, slipped out of the wings and rushed towards the stairs. Fuelled with adrenaline she took the stairs two at a time until she reached Mr Button's office. Pushing the door open, she switched on the light and walked over to her manager's desk. Without a moment's hesitation she lifted the receiver and addressed the operator.

'Police please.'

Within seconds she was connected.

'Hello, my name is Florence Canning and I am fabric manager at Liberty's. I would like to report the fact my father, Bill Wilson, a wanted criminal who has been on the run for over a year, is here at the store and I believe he intends to do me harm.'

'We'll be there as soon as we can, miss,' the officer said quietly.

As Flo put the phone down, she felt a sense of relief wash over her. She could finally put right one of the very many wrongs her father had committed over the years.

Snapping off the light, she walked out of the office and made her way down the stairs. She didn't want to cause alarm or suspicion – best to behave normally until the police arrived and let them deal with it.

Returning the wings of the stage, she took a deep breath and peered out through the curtains. To her dismay her father was nowhere to be found. Had he fled already before the police had even arrived?

'Looking for me, are you, love?' Bill's voice boomed through the shadows.

Flo's shoulders sank. She should have known Bill would find her if he wanted to. He always did.

'What do you want?' she said, turning round to find him leaning incongruously against the table, glass in one hand, only the dregs now remaining.

'To see my darling daughter on the stage,' he said, lifting what was left of his drink towards her. 'You'll be a household name, love, and what father wouldn't want to honour a household name?'

'What do you really want?' Flo challenged.

A look of mock hurt passed across his face. 'Flo, how could you possibly think I would want anything else?'

'Because I know you too well,' she said, her patience wearing thinner than her oldest rayon skirt.

Bill chuckled. 'For years I thought you were too soft and pathetic like your mother, but I saw a bit of fire in you tonight. Perhaps you're more like me than I thought.'

'I am nothing like you,' Flo snarled. 'If I thought I was even a fraction like you I'd kill myself.'

'Bit strong that, love.' Bill chuckled, resting his glass on the table next to him and taking a step towards her.

Instinctively she shrank back, and hated herself for it. He had always had the ability to terrify her, and she was furious he still had that effect.

'Why are you running away from me, love?' he asked. 'I'm only here to collect my dues. Once you've paid up I'll be gone.'

'I'm not paying you a penny,' Flo growled, reaching the end of the wings. 'You can go to hell.'

'There she is, a chip off the old block.' He laughed again. 'But I think we all know that I'm going nowhere until I get my money. That wife of mine was a wicked cow taking all my hard-earned money – surely you wouldn't want to see me go without what's rightfully mine? Now, Flo, I won't ask again, where's my money?'

'In hell, which will freeze over before I give you anything,' Flo thundered, her fear giving way to the anger that burnt deep inside. 'I told you when you had the gall to turn up to Celia's funeral that you could whistle for it, and I'll tell you again. You're nothing but a crook and a parasite the way you prey on other people. You deserve to rot in hell, penniless.'

'Why, you little bitch.' Bill's jaw throbbed with anger as he lifted his arm and went to strike Flo, but she was too quick for him and moved out of the way, sending him off balance.

'That's what you do, isn't it, Bill?' she taunted, whirling around to face him from the other side of the room. 'The only language you understand is hitting women until you get what you want. But not me. I don't care: you can do what you like to me but you'll never get what you want.'

'Don't you talk to me like that,' Bill bellowed, attempting to strike Flo again. 'You should show me more respect. I'm your father, d'you hear me?'

Flo couldn't help herself and laughed. It was just too funny, the idea of showing her father respect after all he had done to her. But the laugh cost Flo the upper hand as, immediately, Bill shoved her roughly to the ground. Looming over her, a sick smile on his face, he kicked her deftly in the ribs, and then again.

'I'll make you respect me, girl, you mark my words.'

But although Flo wanted to cry out in pain, she refused to give Bill the satisfaction.

'That what you said to Aggie when you hit her, is it, Bill? That what you told Celia when you beat her to within an inch of her life? You can beat and kick me as much as you like but it won't change the monster you are. You're scum, Bill.' With that Flo hauled herself up to a sitting position in between blows, and spat on his shoes.

At the gesture, Bill's face contorted with wild rage and she watched him draw his leg back, ready to kick her with greater force. Shutting her eyes, she braced herself for the blow, telling herself it was all worth it to get under his skin in the way she had.

But then the sound of footsteps surrounded her, and she felt herself being helped to her feet. Opening her eyes, she saw Henry looking at her with concern, while a team of police officers wrestled with her father.

'Bill Wilson, you're under arrest,' one of the officers said, while another slapped a set of handcuffs on him. 'You've been a wanted man for a long time.'

'How did you find me?' Bill snarled, before turning to Flo, his eyes wide with disbelief. 'Did you do this? Did you grass me up? My own flesh and blood?'

Flo leaned on Henry for support, her eyes shining with triumph. 'I did, yes. I told you I wanted to see you rot in hell for all you've done. Prison will have to be the next best thing.'

Bill screwed his face up in fury. 'You'll pay for this, girl, you'll see. I know people.

But much to Bill's surprise, Flo laughed again. 'Keep telling yourself that, *Dad*! Your reign of terror's over; nobody's afraid of you any more. Remember that.'

Chapter Fifty-Seven

It was a shock as Flo got ready for work the next day and peered down at her stomach. She could already see the area was black and blue and she winced at the memory of the attack her father had dished out.

It ought to have been her moment of triumph, she thought sadly as she reached for the Liberty print tea dress she knew was most comfortable. Slipping it over her head she did her best not to cry out in pain.

'Flo, let us help you do that,' Bess's voice boomed through the crack in the door, her hand bearing a cup of tea.

Flo turned to smile at the girl. 'I can manage.'

'But you don't need to,' Bess protested, edging her way into the room. 'You've helped us so much; let us help you. That's what friends are for.'

Smiling, Flo took the tea and regarded Bess fondly. They had all come such a long way in the past few months. Jean had become more relaxed and open and Bess had knocked some of the sharpness from her edges. As for herself, Flo thought, her eyes straying to the photo of Neil she kept on her bedside table, she had become more independent and less afraid to strike out on her own.

After Bill had been arrested and taken down to the cells Dot had suggested she come and stay in Bell Street until she felt better. But Flo had refused; she wanted to stand on her own two feet now. After much discussion, Dot had relented, but not before promising that she, Alice, Arthur,

Rose and Mary would come up to Islington the next morning to check on her.

'It took some doing, that,' Bess marvelled, as if reading her thoughts. 'Standing up to your father like that can't have been easy.'

'It wasn't,' Flo admitted. 'But things change. Before, I'd have let him run rings around me, but not any more. Justice needed to be done. For me, for my mother, for Celia and for Rose too and the part he played in sending her almost blind.'

'Even so ...' Bess sighed. 'Me and Jean, we'll have to find a way of dealing with Fred, but for us it won't be as simple as going to the police.'

'I take it Jean told you he's been seen outside the house then,' Flo said quietly.

Bess nodded, her face grave. 'I keep wondering if we need to run again, go somewhere new. But it's not fair to Jean, all this is too much for her.'

'Jean's stronger than you think,' Flo mused. 'You need to stop babying her, Bess. She can cope with more if you let her. She's been a tower of strength since your accident.'

'I know,' Bess admitted. 'I told her to leave me in the early days. Said it was difficult enough us being together, without her being with a cripple.'

Flo winced. 'Don't talk about yourself like that, Bess.'

'It's true. I told her I was neither use nor ornament.'

'But you don't feel like that any more, do you?' Flo asked cautiously.

'Doesn't matter if I do or I don't.' Bess chuckled. 'Jean wouldn't let me go anywhere. She told me she loved me and always would. Seems we're stuck with each other – in your house, if you'll have us.'

'I'll have you,' Flo said softly.

Bess smiled gratefully at Flo, her eyes saying more than words ever could.

'She's loyal, your Jean,' Flo offered, breaking the silence as her eyes strayed to Neil's photograph. 'That means a lot.'

'It does,' Bess agreed, her eyes following Flo's gaze. 'But it's not everything. You have to be loyal to yourself as well as others.'

Flo was just about to speak when the sound of someone banging on the door echoed throughout the house.

'Blimey, is that Dot already?' she gasped, looking at her watch and seeing it was almost eleven. 'And is that the time? You should have woken me.'

'You'd had a rotten night.' Bess grinned. 'You needed to sleep.'

But Flo wasn't listening as she hurried down the stairs to greet her friends. Only, reaching the bottom step, she was surprised to find it wasn't Dot at all but Max Monroe standing in her parlour.

'Surprised to see me?' He grinned, bending forward to kiss her cheek.

'You could say that,' Flo replied. 'I thought you were unwell.'

Max coughed. 'Little white lie, dear. I wanted to see how you did on your own.'

'What? I don't understand.'

'I think he means he was setting you a challenge.' Jean grinned, returning from the kitchen with a tray teeming with cups, saucers and a large pot of tea.

Gesturing for him to sit down, Flo looked at him in surprise. 'Why would you set me a challenge? I already sang at The Kitty Cat Club.'

'And you were a sensation.' Max beamed, taking the tea from Jean's outstretched hand. 'But last night you were a star.'

'You saw me?' Flo coloured.

'I did. I also heard about your father being dragged off by the police.'

'Yes,' Flo murmured. 'It did rather spoil things.'

'Nonsense. Only added to the drama.' Max rubbed his hands with glee. 'Besides, that's show business. And that's what I'm here for, to make one last impassioned plea.'

'An impassioned plea?' Flo muttered. 'What are you on about?'

Just as Max was about to answer the door knocker went again and Flo got up to answer it. This time it was Dot, surrounded by Alice, Arthur, Mary, Rose and Henry too.

'How are you, darlin'?' Dot asked as Flo welcomed her inside. 'I bet you're a bit tender this morning, ain't you?'

'You could say that,' Flo admitted.

'Are you all right, Flo?' Rose asked, her voice filled with concern. 'Can we get you anything?'

'I'm fine thanks, Rose,' Flo replied warmly.

'Best thing you could have done was call the Old Bill,' Alice said fervently. 'I wish I'd done it to my old man. Maybe I'd have saved myself a lifetime of bother if I had.'

Flo exchanged a tender look with Alice as she shut the door behind everyone. If anyone knew what it was like to live with a criminal father it was Alice.

'Thank you,' she whispered.

'Even so, I'd like to knock him into the middle of next week for what he did to you,' Henry growled.

Flo felt butterflies in her stomach as she looked up at him. The kiss they had shared last night was so tender, and she knew they had feelings for one another that went deeper than friendship.

Meanwhile, Dot was making herself at home, walking straight towards the parlour.

'Oh, hello! What are you doing here?' she said, sitting next to Max as if they were best friends.

'Yes, I was trying to find that out myself,' Flo said, edging her way into the room. 'Max was just about to tell me when you all turned up.'

'Well, don't let us stop you,' said Mary brightly. 'We're all friends here.'

Looking mildly uneasy just for a second, Max glanced up at Flo. 'At the beginning of next month, myself and another team from ENSA will be shipping out to Egypt to entertain the troops. I want you to come with me, Flo. I've cleared it with the relevant authorities, this would be war service.'

For a split second there was nothing but silence as she took in Max's words.

'You've told me you're serious about singing, and, Flo Canning, my word, you are a singer, you really are. You should be on a stage every night. What do you say? I promise that if you turn me down now I shall be broken-hearted but I won't ever ask you again.'

Flo felt breathless; this was all happening so fast. 'But my job, my home ...'

'Will all be waiting for you when you get back,' Dot cut in. 'Edwin and I talked about this only the other day. He will get a temporary manager to cover you. When you come back, after we've won this war, your job will still be here – if you want it, of course, assuming you haven't toppled Vera Lynn off her perch.'

Flo's heart was roaring in her ears as she took in this new information. She could have a chance at making her dreams come true and still return to her old life, with her old friends. It seemed too good to be true.

'So you think I should go?' she said eventually.

'Why wouldn't you?' Rose beamed. 'This is a new start, a chance to make something of your life. Do it for your country.'

'And do it for you,' Mary put in wisely.

'We're not going anywhere, love.' Alice smiled. 'You've got us for life.'

Henry looked at her. 'Mind if I have a quick word in private?'

'Just excuse me,' she replied, scurrying out to the hallway to join Henry.

'Is everything all right?' she asked.

Henry clasped Flo's hands and held her gaze. 'The kiss we shared last night meant the world to me. I'm falling in love with you, but I heard what Max Monroe said to you in there. About joining ENSA.'

Flo's face fell. 'Oh, yes. I mean, I'm not going.'

'You *should* go,' Henry urged as he squeezed her hands tightly. 'You should follow your dreams. I love you enough to know I've got to let you go, Flo. If there's anything more than friendship between us, I know you'll come back and we'll see where we end up. For now, as your friend, I think you have to follow your heart.'

Smiling tenderly up at him, Flo leaned forwards and kissed Henry's cheek. He smelled like home.

Pulling away, she looked up at him, bright-eyed, her heart filled with hope and her senses alive with anticipation. She didn't know what was in their future, she didn't know if she would ever be able to love anyone but Neil, but she knew Henry would always be a part of it.

Turning back to the parlour, she drank in the sight of her friends, sitting together drinking tea with a singing legend. For years now, this collection of women had been a constant in her life. They had been there for each other through some of the worst moments of their lives, and also for some of the happiest.

Her eyes strayed to the mantel and she saw the picture of her, Neil and the girls surrounding them on their wedding day. On that day she had been so sure of who she was and what her future looked like. Those dreams lay in tatters, and now she was ready to replace them with new ones.

She turned away from Henry and walked back into the parlour. 'I'll do it, I'll join ENSA,' she said, addressing Max, who clapped his hands in delight.

At that the girls got to their feet and pulled her into their arms. As she felt their warmth and love surrounding her, Flo knew that she could travel to the other side of the world and these girls, these friends for life, would still be there for her, come what may. With her precious Liberty girls in her heart, Flo knew without doubt that her happy ending was just waiting to be discovered.

Welcome to

Penny Street

where your favourite authors and stories live.

Meet casts of characters you'll never forget,
create memories you'll treasure forever,
and discover places that will stay with
you long after the last page.

Turn the page to step into the home of

Fiona Ford

and discover more about

The Liberty Girls...

changes in society, even if not all of them are good. I think one thing we can all be thankful for is that in this country, at least for now, we are free to live our lives and be who we want, deserve and ought to be.

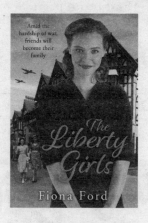